Bonehead

Also by Mo Hayder

Jack Caffery Series
Birdman
The Treatment
Ritual
Skin
Gone
Poppet
Wolf

Standalone Novels
Tokyo
Pig Island
Hanging Hill

MO HAYDER

Bonehead

HODDER &
STOUGHTON

First published in Great Britain in 2024 by Hodder & Stoughton Limited
An Hachette UK company

1

Copyright © The Literary Estate of Mo Hayder 2024

A CIP catalogue record for this title is available from the British Library

Hardback ISBN 978 1 399 73046 4
Trade Paperback ISBN 978 1 399 73047 1
ebook ISBN 978 1 399 73049 5

Typeset in Plantin Light by Manipal Technologies Limited

Printed and bound in Great Britain by Clays Ltd, Elcograf S.p.A.

Hodder & Stoughton policy is to use papers that are natural, renewable and recyclable products and made from wood grown in sustainable forests. The logging and manufacturing processes are expected to conform to the environmental regulations of the country of origin.

Hodder & Stoughton Ltd
Carmelite House
50 Victoria Embankment
London EC4Y 0DZ

www.hodder.co.uk

Foreword
by Karin Slaughter

I clearly remember the first time I read Mo Hayder. *Birdman* was published in 2000, a year before my own first novel was published, and I felt a sort of intense envy grow with every finely crafted sentence. The plotting was fantastic. The characters were not just believable but also brought out an array of emotions from lust to disappointment to love to abject fear. The tension pulled tight like a knot with every turn of the page. I had never read anything quite like it – at least not anything written by a woman. We are supposed to be sugar and spice, the docile victims of these sorts of stories, not the ones who gain control and agency by writing about them with an unblinking eye. That Mo was able to accomplish this, that she broke ground for those who came behind her, will always be an enduring part of her legacy. The women who were able to follow, from Gillian Flynn to Ivy Pachoda to Oyinkan Braithwaite, owe a tremendous debt to Mo for helping carve out space for us in a genre that often celebrates women on the page, but seldom the same way in real life.

In *Birdman*, Jack Caffery is a young, driven, seemingly unshockable detective who is faced with the daunting task of hunting down a serial killer who's leaving behind a trail of horrific crimes – but it's more than that. Caffery is a character who grabs you by your bones and shakes you into seeing all the darkness in the world. He has messy relationships. He screws up quite a lot. But in the end, you're rooting for him – not just because you want the crime solved but because you want something, anything, to finally go right in his life. Readers often take it for granted that they will care about a character, but making them care about a character who does unlikable things is the difference between a writer and a master storyteller.

Mo certainly deserves that title.

Birdman received rave reviews, my favourite being the *Daily Telegraph*'s comment: 'the detail, if you can stomach it, is fascinating . . .' I'm not sure what 'stomach it' means (you don't often read that phrase regarding books written by men), but Mo's readers came in droves. *Birdman* became a well-deserved international bestseller. Her follow-up, *The Treatment*, hit the *Sunday Times* list and put Mo firmly on the map as a name to watch. The awards began to stack up – the WHS Thumping Good Read Award, nominations for the Barry Awards and the Crime Writing Association Daggers. Her 2011 novel, *Gone*, received the Edgar Award for Best Novel, and her *Walking Man* series remains hugely popular today amongst readers and reviewers alike.

Her novels are dark, visceral, bold and brilliant, and she leaves behind a lasting legacy. When she passed away in 2021, the crime writing world was devastated – tributes poured in and readers found solace in her novels, the incredible, brave, important stories she leaves behind. Mo was always a writer – and a person – who lived life to the fullest, as shown by her varied career path. Not one to simply sit down to write in a vacuum, she made sure she had a wealth of life experience under her belt; she worked as a barmaid, security guard, film-maker, hostess in a Tokyo club, educational administrator and a teacher of English as a foreign language, to name but a few. Mo also held an MA in film from The American University in Washington DC and an MA in Creative Writing from Bath

Spa University. Writing was her love and her craft, and she took it very seriously. The legacy she leaves behind is not only that of a thriller writer, but also of a generous, smart, passionate author and champion of other authors. I remember her as someone who squeezed every ounce out of life and did us all the great kindness of pouring some of that energy into her novels.

Over her many years as a writer, Mo, whose real name is Clare Dunkel, and detective Jack Caffery earned a legion of loyal fans, with Mo's compulsive stories becoming staples of every crime reader's bookshelf up and down the country – and indeed, across the globe. The series went from strength to strength, and Mo's unique writing style and her refusal to shy away from the darker side of life became more and more apparent, setting her apart from other thriller writers and making it impossible for anyone to replicate her. I am to this day still in awe of her tremendous talent, and deeply saddened that she is gone.

The publication of *Bonehead*, her final novel, is something to be truly celebrated, and my hope is that readers will adore this in the way they have her previous books. It tells the fascinating, gripping story of the aftermath of a coach crash, and one woman's struggle with her own sanity when she begins to see visions of the mysterious woman known locally as Bonehead. It has all the hallmarks of Mo's writing – speculative, clever, pacy and thought provoking – and it's a story that will grab you by the throat and not let you go until the blistering end.

The novel begins with a definition of 'urban legend' – a modern story of obscure origin and with little or no supporting evidence that spreads spontaneously in varying forms and often has elements of humour, moralising or horror. Mo delivers this in spades. From the moment we are first treated to a description of the terrifying Bonehead, 'A dead woman, body half-decayed, who walked the local parkland, luring people to their deaths,' we are hooked. As the novel progresses, Mo manages to weave her trademark sense of unease throughout the storyline. I loved Alex as a main character – a policewoman who, by her own account, is 'not certifiable'. The final few sentences sent genuine chills down my spine . . . There has always been a sparsity and deftness to Mo's writing that makes every word count and, no matter how intricate the plotting becomes, she manages to keep you as the reader there with her every step of the way. In *Bonehead*, she introduces a cast of characters that will stay with you long after you turn the final page – Maryam, Arran and Minty have glued themselves to my brain – and she paints an eerie, haunting description of a small town torn apart by tragedy extremely well. There's a gothic sense of threat throughout, and Eastonbirt and the nearby lake feel alarmingly real.

This final manuscript embodies Mo's legacy – a richly drawn tale of paranoia, loss, community and secrets – and my hope is that this publication rightly reaches new readers who will go on to explore the treasure trove that is Mo's backlist. It's also a wonderful gift to those of us who have known and loved Mo's writing for the last few decades. Her novel *Wolf* was recently adapted for television, and the idea of new generations discovering Mo and her genius stories fills me with joy. I'm so glad her daughter, Lotte, has given her blessing for this last book to hit the shelves, and I can't wait to see the reviews pour in. Mine is six out of five stars, because she really should have her own category that reflects her level of excellence. Mo was a writer who changed crime fiction forever, and her legacy will never be forgotten – not if *Bonehead* has anything to do with it . . . And, trust me, you don't want to get on the wrong side of Bonehead.

URBAN LEGEND

noun

1.
  a modern story of obscure origin and with little or no supporting evidence that spreads spontaneously in varying forms and often has elements of humour, moralising, or horror

Alex

Every place has its urban legend, right? Every person in every town, village, city, can think of a weird local ghost story. Eastonbirt, the place I grew up in, was no different.

Our legend was the bonehead. A dead woman, body half-decayed, who walked the local parkland, luring people to their deaths. The bonehead wasn't well known enough outside the area to have legend-trippers visiting the village, and anyway Eastonbirt was more famous for the coach accident that happened two years and eight months ago. So the bonehead didn't get talked about that much. I was the only one who took it half-seriously.

Because I'd seen it. Once. I'm not certifiable and of course I knew it was an impossibility, to see a ghost. I knew what I'd actually seen was some form of hallucination. Or a waking nightmare. Something. I was a cop, I was level-headed, so I rationalised it to myself and resolved to forget all about it.

And perhaps that's how it would have stayed. If it hadn't been for the photo of her that arrived at our house one day.

It was a hot July evening. I hadn't been back in the village long. Mum and I had eaten steaks for supper, with salad and wine. We'd cleared away the dishes and I'd decided to replace a tiny cantilever in one of the windows of the conservatory. I was always doing little tasks for her and this wasn't complicated, just removing the mechanism and replacing a stripped screw, but jobs like that had become difficult for me. My bad hand would ache if it was in the wrong position for too long and I was already tired from a day at work, still in my uniform – hadn't had a chance to shower. I took a break from fixing the window and wandered over to the fridge for a can of Coke.

Idly drinking the Coke, I glanced through the pile of Mum's mail on the breakfast counter – the circulars and the communications about her charity work. All the begging letters she got.

That was when I saw it.

At first glance it appeared to be a simple photograph of our house, taken from a low angle, therefore from somewhere inside the park. From that perspective the house – already hopelessly out of place here in the Cotswolds, among the golden stone cottages – looked even bigger than usual. A giant with modern sweeps of glass and aluminium, white walls and balconies.

The photo was on cheap printer paper with no text, nothing to indicate who had sent it. I turned it over, looked at the back – nothing. I turned it again and was about to discard it.

Then the lower-floor window caught my eye.

I sat down at the breakfast bar and angled the sheet under Mum's huge, expensive downlighters so I could see it more clearly. The photograph had been taken, I guessed, at midday, with the sun in the south shining full on the rear elevation of our house. Maybe it was just a trick of that extreme sunshine, but there appeared to be someone in one of the lower-level windows. A blurred, bonelike face peering out.

Sweat pricked under my arms. I couldn't be seeing this. I just couldn't. I glanced sideways, towards the windows, my face hot. It had to be a trick. Was someone watching me, someone who knew? Of course not. I put the paper down, closed my eyes, tried to get myself back on track, then opened my eyes and turned the paper back over. A white, smeared face. Empty black eyes. It was still there.

I carried the paper to the huge plate-glass window where Mum was standing outside on the deck, her hand on the railings, gazing out into the forest that spread out from the bottom of our garden.

'Oh, Alex,' she said. 'Bamber is behaving like a lunatic. He's in the woods again.' She came to the door and tugged off her smart camel suede sandals. Behind her, insects circled, attracted by the bright lights. 'Would you have a look for him? You're still in uniform.'

'Do you know where this came from?'

She squinted at the photo I was holding. 'No idea. Estate agents probably. A new marketing ploy – they're always telling me buyers are waiting.'

'Which estate agents?'

'Not a clue.'

'You don't think it's creepy? That they've taken a photo of our house?'

'No.'

'Does this look like anything to you? Here. This window?'

'Not really, not without my glasses. Alex, please will you find Bamber? He's been gone too long.'

I eyed the stairs that led downstairs to the room where the face had been photographed. But Mum wouldn't be shifted without a good explanation. I couldn't look her in the eye and tell her about the bonehead – my paranoia. Not because she'd laugh, but because she'd be confused. Worried about my mental health. So I placed the paper face-down on the table, shoved my feet into my boots and went out on to the deck.

'Bamber?' I trotted down the steps to the lawn. In the late evening the sun deserted this side of the valley, and our garden was already dark, the paler grey of the lawn blending after a hundred yards or so into the trees that marked the edge of

Eastonbirt Park. The window the face had been in was to my right so I steered sideways until I was close to it. It was Mum's gym, on the lower ground floor. The curtains were closed and there was nothing odd that I could see. The glass pane was clean and shiny – like everything in that house. Did Mum always keep the curtains closed? Perhaps she did.

I turned away and continued down the garden towards the treeline. 'Bamber? Where are you?'

Dad died when I was still a baby and left Mum minted (*I hate that word, Alex. I'm 'very comfortable'. Not 'minted', please*). For as long as I could remember, she and I had lived here in this swag palace of a home, set on the slopes of the village of Eastonbirt. As a little girl I'd thought all people had a panoramic view of fields and valleys, hills and forests. It was a shock to discover they didn't. And then I'd joined the police, done my training, completed two years in the Met on the council estates of Hammersmith, west London, and suddenly I'd seen how extraordinary it was. A house on the slopes of a valley in the Cotswolds? An acre of lawn around it opening directly on to three thousand acres of National Trust parkland? How many people lived like that?

Bamber was crazy about the park. It was full of badgers and rabbits and foxes. He was forever chasing them. I'd never thought it was a problem, I enjoyed seeing him racing around in there. But one evening a few weeks ago our friends' dog had run out into the same park and hadn't been seen since, and that had scared us enough to put Bamber on a short lead. Especially now it was getting dark.

I trudged down to the end of the garden and into the trees where it was dusky and grey, already getting a little cool though we were several hours from sunset. My Force-issue boots were good on the unsteady terrain.

'Bamber? I swear I'll kill you.'

I was just at the point of getting properly scared when he came bounding happily out of the gloom, an orange tennis ball in his mouth. He dropped it and did that thing of his – wagging his tail, waiting for me to pick up the ball. Nudging it with his nose until I gave in.

'Right. You haven't changed.'

I picked up the ball and surveyed the woods – so different from evening in London. No lights, no buildings. When you looked up, just trees and the sky. The sense of night-time creeping in from knee-level, swirling around your feet and silently running up your legs, until it had the whole of you.

'I'll throw it *once*. Over there.' I held up a finger to Bamber. 'But don't you dare go far.'

I sent the ball soaring into the woods. He tore after it, his little grey hindquarters churning up the ground.

He was just a half-mast kind of dog – Schnauzer mixed with, as far as I could tell, mountain bear. A scruffy face and a beard that always managed to get trailed in the dirtiest part of the ground. While he was ferreting around in the woods I walked further into the trees. I didn't often come down here; I'd never thought to.

I stopped and turned to look up at the house, trying to find the spot where the photograph had been taken. The house was huge, imposing. All glazed windows and aluminium balconies. The further back I got, the taller and more impressive it seemed. Had I really grown up there?

Eventually I stopped about twenty yards into the park. I must be in roughly the right place.

The ground-floor window was visible through the trees, like in the photo. But it had fallen into darkness. I couldn't see anything reflected in the glass.

A touch on my calf and I turned. Bamber was there. I hadn't heard him come back – he must have been stealthy. He was sitting close to my ankles, facing away from me, staring back into the woods he'd just come out of. When I reached down and touched him on his haunches I found his fur standing up in bristles.

'Hey, gorgeous boy.' I squatted down next to him. 'You OK? Where's your ball?'

He growled. Low and prolonged. I could feel his ribs vibrating under my fingertips.

I stared into the trees. I couldn't hear anything – no movement, nothing out of the ordinary. This was the park I'd grown up in, the place where I'd run wild as a kid, but abruptly I knew something was different and we shouldn't be there.

'Come on.' I grabbed Bamber's collar and began to pull him away, not taking my eyes off the trees. 'Come on, boy. Let's go home.'

Maryam

They looked for him again, knowing that if they did find him he'd be dead. After all this time he had to be dead. Six weeks he'd been gone.

Maryam walked behind Rhory, her cardigan pulled tight around her, the brambles catching at her bare calves. Her clothes were all wrong for searching in the half-darkness. An old, corded, patchwork skirt. Sandals with a thin sole to them. Her feet kept slipping. She ducked under a low-hanging branch and tried to catch up with Rhory, but he was going fast, his head lowered, crashing through the trees. He was still tall and broad; even now, as he entered his late forties, his breadth was the thing people first noticed. He was carrying a rucksack which contained a torch, a Leatherman tool knife, rubber gloves and a bin bag.

The kit, the bin bag – they said the words Rhory hadn't. He was expecting to take home a corpse.

'Where are we now?'

He stopped and turned to her. 'What?'

'I said . . . ' Her voice was bloodless and tiny. 'I said, where are we? I'm lost. I don't recognise this.'

'It's the driveway to the old mansion. It used to run down through that side valley. There are places around here he might have . . . '

Rhory finished the sentence with a hand gesture that was meant to fill in the words: *places he might have fallen.*

Maryam turned and scanned the thick woods. There might once have been a driveway here, but she couldn't see it any more. Rhory knew all of the forests: the faded, overgrown parts of the once-grand park; the alleys, the towering trees, the fences. The skies that came in on summer nights and clenched the park hard, keeping it pressed against the loamy earth. The way it went on forever and ever, thousands of acres of tangled wilderness trailing up the sides of the valley like a giant hand – long, ponderous fingers spanning the vast escarpment. She'd lived here for almost twenty-three years, but she'd never properly taken this place inside her. It didn't belong in her the way it did in him. It was her husband's secret birthright.

Rhory took a left and plunged into the thicket. She followed. The woods weren't silent. It was late but not quite dark. The time of evening when wildlife changed shifts, rustling the undergrowth. Twitching in the shadows. The land began to rise and soon broke into boulders that they had to climb, her flimsy shoes sliding and cracking. Sweat matted her hair; it twined around broken leaves and sticks, making little twirled nests across her scalp.

At last they reached another level where the land was flat. Rhory paused for a moment to get his breath back, then clicked on the torch and began to walk again. Maryam didn't have time to catch her breath, he was too far ahead, so she put her head down and followed.

They were on a long footpath, well trodden and dry underfoot, overhead trees linking fingers to form a high, rough tunnel. Rhory's torch uplit it like the inside of a cave. To her left, hundreds of feet below, the last of the daylight glinted on the pewter necklace of old lakes that snaked their way through the bottom of the park. She didn't look at them, kept her mind on putting one foot in front of the other. She was afraid of the lakes. They were carnivorous. The trees, too – they had a habit of swallowing things.

A noise behind her. She stopped and edged quickly side-ways to the nearest tree, staring back down the path behind them. It wound away into the dusk, dropping at a slight incline. The ground was paler than the surrounding trees. Was there something down there – just at the place the perspective died? A wavering of the atoms and molecules of air? A shape, a flesh-coloured difference in the light, like a human form moving rapidly away?

'Maryam?'

She jumped. Rhory had come to stand behind her.

'What is it? What are we looking at?'

'Nothing.'

He frowned. 'You're nervous.'

'No. I'm afraid of what we're going to find, that's all.' She ran her hands down her arms. With a deep breath she turned her back on the path and faced the way they'd been walking. She ignored the prickling sensation at the back of her head telling her she was being watched from behind. 'I'm scared of seeing him. If he's not the . . . the same as he was I don't know what I'll do.'

'You need to be prepared.'

'I know.'

They walked on. The daylight left the lakes in the valley below and before long the only light was the torch beam. Maryam lifted her feet to avoid the roots and the creepers, walking with her shoulders thrust forward, her head turned very slightly so her ear could catch anything moving behind them. Whatever harm this park meant her, soon it would have its way. It might be weeks, it might be months, but one day it would swallow her whole. It would consume her thoughts, her body, her memories.

Ahead Rhory stopped. She halted. 'What? Can you see something?'

He didn't answer. He crouched and angled the light into a crevice at his feet. He pulled aside some bracken and dislodged a stone, threw it out far into the valley then shone the torch down again. He was so good with his hands, so practical. His fingers were pure bone and muscle, could pull a nail from a plank in seconds.

'Hold this.'

He handed her the torch, sat on his butt and shuffled himself nearer the edge. She approached the edge, tentatively shining the beam into the crevice. It wavered and threw shadows across the faded flanks of the rocks.

'The smell?'

'Yes.' He manoeuvred himself off the lip of the pathway, dropping about two feet to a smaller ledge. He clapped his hands together to get the dirt off and took a step along the ledge.

'Rhory? What's the smell?'

'Give me the torch.'

She knelt on the path and leaned over, passing him the torch. Her hands were shaking so badly the beam stuttered and jumped.

Rhory braced one hand against the rock and leaned his face into the gap, shining the torch from one side to the other.

'Is it him? Can you see him?'

He clicked off the torch, took a step back and looked up at her. In the dying light his face was drawn and sad.

'Rhory?'

Alex

Back in the kitchen, the photo of the house had disappeared from the countertop.

'Mum?' I pulled off my boots and padded barefoot around the gleaming rooms. 'Mum?'

I found her in the formal dining area eyeing up four small brass sculptures she had placed on the windowsill. Tipping her head on one side and considering the effect of turning one piece through eight or nine degrees.

'Mum. What did you do with that photo?'

'Which photo?'

'The one from the estate agents? I just showed it to you.'

'I don't know – I shredded everything. I cleaned up. Why?'

I sighed. I'd been away too long. I'd got used to a more ramshackle way of living in London and I'd forgotten that back home things happened on schedule, in a clean and orderly fashion. Mum was a neat freak; you put something down and within seconds it would be whisked away and cleaned, ironed, sanitised or binned.

'I was interested in it. How did you know it was from an estate agent?'

'Who else would send something like that? It's a gimmick.'

'Which estate agent? Did it have a logo on it?'

She put her head on one side and frowned. 'No. Why? What was wrong with it?'

'Nothing. I just . . . nothing.'

I waited for her to go to bed. Then I went downstairs to the gym on the lower ground floor, clicking on the lights as I went. Bamber came after me, holding Hat. 'Hat' was a ridiculous Mexican thing he adored. Every other toy would be macerated to within an inch of its life, but Hat would be carried around the place with utter delicacy.

The room was silent in the halogen glow; all Mum's weight machines and treadmills glinted back at me. A faint smell of window-cleaning spray and new carpet. I went to the window and pulled back the curtains, inching my nose close to the place I thought I'd seen the face. I ran my hand around the frame but there was nothing odd about the window. Not even cobwebs or dead flies. Outside it was almost dark; my reflection floated in the glass. Beyond it was the lawn and the dark-leafed trees fifty yards away where the park started.

Though I couldn't see all of the park from here on the fringes, I had a clear image in my head of how it was arranged. Originally it had belonged to a Victorian guano millionaire who'd had great plans but had run out of money at the wrong time. At the centre was the Gothic mansion he'd been building, now decaying. It was a time capsule because mid-construction the workers had simply downed tools and left the place half-finished. Below it was a string of ornamental lakes. Around the lakes, abandoned grounds spiralled out into thousand of acres, encompassing a forgotten arboretum, a lumber forest, and the tiny village of Eastonbirt. The place where I lived.

'Come on, Bamber. Come upstairs with your crazy owner.'

We trudged back up to the kitchen. I finished screwing the cantilever in and tested the window a couple of times, opening and closing it until I was satisfied. At school they always teased me for being the one who wanted to know how things worked – I was always put on the boys' table. It used to upset me until I worked out that was just me. The way I worked. Anyway – that night I liked having the window secure.

I peered out of the window at the parkland. Then I locked the rest of the doors along the back and closed the curtains.

As early teenagers at weekends we would pile up our rucksacks and head into the park for cookouts. Our squad in those days was me, Minnie, Jessop, Ozone and Arran Black. Sometimes Sophie May Hansel would tag along if she knew Arran was going, but Michaela Lewis always refused to come. The park was limitless – you could live there a million years and never visit all the groves and grottoes and endless abandoned woodland. It was ripe for getting lost and telling ghost stories and Hallowe'en pranking, and invariably we'd end up in a lamplit huddle in the woods scaring ourselves shitless telling stories. The clown with the hatchet that chased cars, the dwarf that lived in the basement of the ruined mansion in the centre of the park. More often than not, it would be the dead woman who watched everyone from the trees. The bonehead.

The woman, went the story, had been a prostitute, a gypsy, who at some point in the past century had been murdered in the park by a john and thrown into a ravine. Her face had been eaten back to the bone by rats and foxes, but her body remained, miraculously mummified, so her killer went back time and again to have sex with the faceless corpse. The body, it was said, had never been found. It still lay out there somewhere. Hidden for all these years. But her restless spirit haunted the wood, luring people into the subterranean hole where her body rested. She wore a white dress and her limbs were shrivelled to nothing. According to legend there were scores of missing people who'd disappeared in the park, chased by her until they'd fallen into the dangerous crevices between the rocks.

The boys would hold torches under their chins, or sneak away from the group and come crashing back through the wilderness to make us all scream. We would giggle and sweat and use the opportunity to cling on to the boys. One night it got so real that Minnie started to cry silently. 'I heard something,' she whispered, jabbing a finger out into the dark. 'Something's out there. I mean seriously.'

One or two of us tried to keep the laughter going, but her face was so proper scared – torch-lit and snotty like the Heather character in *Blair Witch* – that one by one we went silent. We all switched off our phone lights and huddled together, barely breathing, listening to the pulse of the woods around us. She was right. Far away in the trees, over near the lake, was the staccato crump of dry undergrowth: someone moving stealthily through the tangled woods.

'It's a deer,' the boys said, unconvincingly. 'It's nothing.'

We must have been about fourteen then. It was the last time we did freak-out nights and the last time any of us had mentioned the bone-faced woman in the park. So when I saw her, years later, I knew it had to be my imagination.

Bamber and I went into the little area off the kitchen where Mum did all her admin. Like everywhere else, it was super-clean and tidy. I switched on the halogen light. Mum spent her life on committees and trustee boards and she was in constant negotiation with various fundraisers and marketing directors. I'd come out of the accident with a damaged left hand – not really a big deal, I'd still passed the police medical – but not everyone in the accident had been so lucky. Seven had died; three would never lead a normal life again. Not long after the crash Mum had founded a charity for children and teenagers with acquired injuries. The office was piled high with her paperwork.

I uncoupled the shredder bin from the cross-cutter and sifted through the contents. The shredded strands of the photo were fairly easy to find – it made me think how useless shredders were in the face of the seriously committed. It took me twenty minutes but eventually I got all the pieces lined up and sellotaped back together.

I pulled it back under the light and peered at the photo of the downstairs window. The blade had sliced directly through the pane, bisecting the floury image. Cobbled back together like this, it no longer made any sense. The face, if it had been there at all, was distorted and now just looked like nothing. A trick of the light, or of my imagination.

Maryam

All along, her biggest fear had been that he'd died slowly. She'd hoped they'd find him on the roadway, like the foxes and pheasants you often saw. Compressed, purpling mounds. Eyes blank or popped, fur greyed out to the colour of the tarmac. Easier to think of your dog killed instantly than trapped here in a crevice to starve.

The last of the daylight left the far side of the valley, sweeping up like a curtain being drawn. The lights in the little front rooms of Eastonbirt slowly pricked up through the darkness; the orange streetlamps clicked on like a glowing necklace. Maryam sat with her back to a tree trunk, knees pulled up to her chin. Shivering with fear. The park was haunted. Now she knew it for sure. The darkness was coming for her.

A clatter of rock a few feet below. Rhory swearing. She rolled on to her knees, crawled to the edge of the path and peered down. His pulled himself backwards out of the crevice. A patter of pebbles dislodged and fell. He was still holding the torch but otherwise his hands were empty.

'What?' she hissed.

He wiped his forehead with the back of his arm. The place his hair was cut short around the back of his neck glistened with sweat. He turned and spat into the void of the valley. 'It's not him. It's a badger.'

Once she'd had time to recover her equanimity, she climbed down to the ledge. She couldn't leave without seeing the animal; she had to be sure there wasn't a mistake. That this wasn't Tumble, their three-year-old mongrel, missing for the past six weeks. That it really was a dead badger.

Rhory was patient. He held the torch beam steady for her so she could push her shoulders into the crevice. There it was, just as Rhory had said, draped over a rock, maybe where it had fallen: the thinning, mummified remains of a badger. The smell.

She winced. Pulled herself out again and turned to the valley. The moon now, coming up above the trees. Cold slice of light. She leaned back against the rock and stared at it, breathing in and out slowly through her nose, the way she'd learned in a meditation book.

Tears were in her eyes. Rare for her to cry.

'Maryam?'

'You don't understand. It's my fault. It's all my fault.'

'It's no one's fault. He ran away; that's no one's fault.'

But Rhory was wrong. This was her doing. All her doing. No untangling it now.

Alex

I woke up early the next day, my head tight. I shuffled upright and pulled the taped-together photograph from my bedside table and studied it again, trying to conjure up what I'd seen yesterday. A face in the downstairs window.

I couldn't do it. Couldn't make it reappear.

Two hours before my shift started. I could sit and stare at this photo or read a book or play on my phone. Instead I pulled on my black police polo shirt and trousers, and went out for a drive.

It was still early but already hot and overcast, the air full of trapped pollen and leaf dust so that the woods seemed to have a shimmer above them. Most of the houses on the lower side of Eastonbirt had gardens like Mum's that opened directly on to the parkland. With the exception of a twenty-three-storey community housing tower at the edge of the village – there by virtue of some glitch in the local planning department in the '60s – Eastonbirt itself was a fairly typical Cotswold village. A high street, a church – famous for the lead font which the villagers had kept hidden during the dissolution of the monasteries – four pubs, a small supermarket and lots of fancy boutique shops. There were no less than five estate agents in town, and in each one I recognised at least one or two members of staff.

I was an old face. Half-famous because of the accident, and because of Mum.

'How's your hand?' asked one of the receptionists, a girl I'd been at school with. 'Still hurt?'

'Nope.' I flexed it. 'Feels good as new. Passed all my police medicals.'

'What was it like being in London?'

'Tiring, but cool. Well cool.'

She shook her head and smiled, half-awed. 'Makes me wonder why you ever came back.'

All the receptionists had questions for me; they all came out of their offices to look me up and down in my police kit, to ask questions about Mum and the charity, but when I pulled out the photo they all went blank. None of them would admit it was anything to do with them. Maybe not surprising – would they confess to such a ridiculous marketing gimmick? It smacked of intrusiveness.

'Maybe it's from one of those bigger offices in Stroud?' one suggested, frowning. 'Mind you, it's a beautiful house, that. Has your mum thought of selling? There's a huge demand for those slopes at the bottom of the village.'

If not an estate agent, I thought as I left the last one, climbing the little stone steps that had seen centuries of traffic, then who had sent Mum a picture of her house? And why?

I paused at the top of the step and turned to look at the estate agent's window – all the images of beautiful Cotswold cottages suspended in mid-air on their wire mountings. My face, my round freckled face with my thick brown hair, stared back at me. In the wrong light even someone like me could look ghostly, skull-like. Light and glass distorted like nothing else when you were haunted by an image. Once you had a picture in your head, of course, you'd conjure it up everywhere you looked. Still, I couldn't quite bring myself to bin the photo.

When I'd applied for a transfer to Gloucestershire I'd hoped I'd get the Stroud police station, and I'd been lucky. There had been a position to fill and I'd slotted straight in. Stroud was five miles from home, but its jurisdiction was huge and included the little village of Eastonbirt. I enjoyed the drive; it was so linear and smooth compared to driving anywhere in London. So weird to be able to go for over five minutes without hitting a red light.

The police station was in its usual state of flux, with officers and PCSOs coming and going. I was a little early for my shift so I went back to the vast room that served as the incident room, the cafeteria and our office, all rolled into one overheated, shadeless, peeling space where we kept our personal belongings in red crates. I found a place at a desk near the window and logged on. Outside the window another hot day was gearing up, the people going by wearing short-sleeved shirts, or T-shirts and shorts.

Someone at the Traffic unit had given me access to the reports from the coach crash investigation, and while technically I shouldn't be accessing this side of the database I reasoned I wasn't doing any harm, only looking. In addition to the SIO's report, the government had done its own report (another way of enhancing their already huge database of crash causes) and I'd read through it over and over again, trying to fill in the parts I'd forgotten. A coach crash and a three-hour segment of my life had become, for me, not a linear narrative of horrors, but a half-remembered, half-trancelike nightmare. A flat dark stretch of time poked through with pain and lights, voices, the sting of needles and stench of ethanol. Hazy hallucinations I couldn't black out three years later. So many faces peering into mine that night: *Alex? Are you OK?*

I'd sat through all the inquests, I'd given my own testimony, but I still wasn't rid of that gnawing gap in my memory.

I opened the photographs file. Some of them were impossible to look at, especially the post-mortems: crushed limbs, heads. The shots inside the overturned coach weeks after the accident – fish cruising lazily between the upside-down seats, a rucksack floating, the contents spilled out. I scrolled through to the shot that for me was the most mesmerising. Nothing special about it, except that it had been one of the first official police photographs, taken when most of us had already left for the hospital. Blue emergency services lights and car headlights, skid marks on the road, the various discarded aluminium blankets we'd been given by paramedics, a few shoes, bags, latex gloves on the tarmac. The tail-lights of cars turning away from the roadblock, the vague blurred faces of people who'd gathered at the barrier to watch.

I leaned back in the chair and chewed on the cuticle of my bad thumb. Trying to think through the accident.

The only facts I could be sure of were the things that had seemed funny at the time but now seemed so sad. It had been a school reunion for all that summer's leavers. Fancy dress; it was the weekend after Hallowe'en, after all. Fifty of us turned up from all over the area. It was hysterical. I went as a dead bride; Michaela went as Daphne from *Scooby Doo*. Minnie, being Minnie, went as Harley Quinn out of *Suicide Squad* and Sophie May Hansel went as Taylor Swift in the 'Blank Space' video. The boys had been equally random – most of them were totally not into it and reluctantly dressed as Dr Spock, or 'Frankenstein's monster' with a few sheets of loo paper fluttering round a basic black T-shirt and black jeans. Ozone, our token gay dude, was Justin Bieber, and Arran, being Arran – the hottest of the guys and also the only one who never took himself too seriously – had gone as a giant penis. He had got his mum, Maryam, to make the costume out of pink foam, with a hole cut in the middle for his face.

Sophie May Hansel was mortified. We all knew she had the biggest crush on Arran and had expected him to turn up dinner-jacketed as the 'Blank Space' guy, to match her Taylor Swift ballgown. The penis was the worst letdown for her. Personally I thought it was wicked so I made a point of dancing with him. We were friends going back years and years, and besides, was there anything more hysterical than a dead bride and a penis doing the neyney?

The guys had all got drunk. Giacomo Amati from Tetbury had thrown up all over Minnie's Harley Quinn costume and it was lucky he was getting a lift home from his dad, because she was now dressed in a black bin liner tied at the shoulders, her outfit in a carrier bag scrunched under her arm and talking wildly about getting him to pay for the cleaning, making him walk into the fancy dress hire shop with the ruined outfit.

Michaela Lewis's dad, Mike, was driving. He worked at the coach company and had volunteered for this job because his daughter was on board. He'd made several stops coming out of Stroud – Eastonbirt was the last, and by the time he began negotiating the winding road into the park there was just the Eastonbirt squad left in the huge fifty-seven-seater coach. Me, Sophie May, Minnie, Arran, Michaela, Ozone Winters, Jessop Jarvis, the Houghton twins, Kaylee Pocket, Keith Brown, and two giggly girls called Sara and Isabelle.

I was gazing out of the window at the world going past beyond my reflection when I realised I could see Sophie May's face reflected beyond my own. She sat on the other side of the coach in the seat ahead, her strawberry earbuds jammed in, the neon lead snaking across her prom gown and into her bag. She was chewing impatiently, her eyes roving out of the window at the rain lashing against the glass, her fingers digging into her palms. The only child of the Hansels, the local accountants, and used to getting her own way, tonight she was in a full-on strop about the Taylor Swift thing and desperate for Arran's attention. I wasn't sure why Arran wasn't giving it to her – she was the one they called princess while everyone called me a tomboy or a lesbian. I wasn't glamorous. I was short, with short brown chunks of hair and freckles. Sophie May had exactly the things I assumed boys liked: blonde hair and tight clothes.

As I watched her, she turned and looked at Arran, who was sitting in front of me, now in just a T-shirt and jeans, his pink foam outfit lying on the other seat. I couldn't see him but she must have caught his gaze because she smiled, slow and sexy. Her top lip curled up first, the curve translating slowly into her bottom lip. Then she pointed at Arran's crotch, licking her lips slowly. 'Get your cock out,' she mouthed. 'I'll do this.' She opened her mouth and mimed a blowjob, her hands circling an enormous penis going in and out.

Any other time I'd have giggled. Maybe booted him in the back of the seat to encourage him to laugh too. Except lately I wasn't sure any more how I felt about Arran Black. There were new levels of complexity. What if he smiled back at her? Invited her over to his seat – maybe back to his house? I didn't want to see.

I turned away, put my forehead to the window. The coach bumped along, winding further and further down into the valley on the road that crossed the two bigger lakes. I tried to focus my attention outside.

That was when I saw it. A greyish-white shape darting out from the side of the road at the top of the causeway. I sat forward to stare, my hands on the windows. But before

I could focus on the image disappearing into the tree, the coach swerved and skidded on the road.

The world was thrown sideways. Darkness and reflections, glass breaking, someone screaming, maybe me. A deafening slap, the coach hitting the water – then nothing. No more engine noise. Darkness and cold.

The mechanics of what happened were right in front of me in the report. Some of us were thrown free out of windows that smashed on the coach's first impact. Me, Ozone and Minnie Frobisher, who landed on her shoulders, breaking a lumbar vertebra. The engine block in the rear was heaviest so it dragged the coach down backwards, water racing in through the wheel arches and the engine. Somehow Arran and Michaela managed to escape through a window near the front and drag themselves to the shore. Arran was awake, sober and fit enough to return to the coach, to pull anyone out that he could. Jessop Jarvis's legs were caught in twisted metal; Arran freed him (though later he'd lose both legs). Keith Brown, too, owed his life to Arran Black.

Arran went in six times before the coach flipped lazily in the water like a bored whale, and slid another twenty feet down into the lake, putting it beyond his reach. Still on board were Sophie May Hansel, the Houghton twins, Isabelle Bentley, Sara Sharp, Kaylee Pocket, and Mike Lewis, the driver. One detail that was never released to the press or the parents was that the Houghton twins – both good swimmers – must have held their breath and made a good attempt to escape the coach. But both got stuck in the underwater weeds. Arran dived ten times for Ben Houghton, who was nearest the surface, and still couldn't free him.

I didn't remember any of that. In my confusion, in and out of consciousness, I'd crawled off the tarmac and into the trees. Vomiting and bleeding, fainting from the pain in my hand.

That was when I dreamt that the bonehead came and found me. She crouched, put one hand on the ground next to me, then lowered her head to my face and . . . there's no other word for it . . . *sniffed* me. As if she were a hungry animal and I was roadkill.

Now, in the silence of the incident room, I scanned the faces in the case files photograph. People shocked, watching the rescue services. Paramedics and firemen going about their work. I was looking for a half-person – a wisp of light, an illusion.

I am death. I am the bonehead. I am watching you.

I pulled out the crumpled, taped photo of our house and smoothed it out on my desk, placed a finger over the window on the ground floor. Nothing there now. Nothing decipherable.

'Alex?'

I looked up. My sergeant was standing in the doorway. I quickly crumpled the photograph and pushed it into my tac vest.

'Sarge?'

'A moment in my office? Now, please.'

Alex

'You're from Eastonbirt, aren't you?'
Sergeant Johnson looked down her nose at me from behind her monitor. She was a beautiful, elegant Scottish woman with maybe Somalian roots, judging by the long ebony neck and the sloe eyes that looked as if they should always be outlined like Cleopatra's.

'Yeah – why?'

'There's a job on the queue up at Eagle Tower there. Do you know it?'

I knew it. It was the monster of a tower that loomed over all of Eastonbirt. Eagle Tower. Evil Tower, the locals dubbed it. It would be funny if it weren't so tragic, but on the crime maps of Eastonbirt all the red dots hung around the tower. No crimes in the little streets and sleepy cottages surrounding it.

'What about it?'

'Couple of kids with laser pens. The CAA sent it over to Intelligence.'

'Is that all?' I'd been to laser-pen callouts over and over. They were routine, and I was a little surprised she'd asked me into her office for something like this. Usually it would have just come out to me on the incident queue.

'Uh, no – actually I called you in because I had a call from the Traffic unit.' She was looking at the screen in front of her, her chin raised, one hand on the mouse. 'They've offered you a placement.'

'I beg your pardon.'

'Sit down.'

I did. 'They've offered *me* a placement? How come?'

'Alex, you have to take this all in context. You've come back from the Met after two years – you were one of the highest commended in training. You did an advanced driving course . . .'

'I did. I financed it myself. Or rather, my mum did.'

'And you came out of that with top marks.'

'Yeah, well.' I looked at my feet. 'I'm a tomboy – I've always liked driving. It's not that ace.'

'The Traffic department think it is. Also apparently you were the best marksman. You know how the Traffic unit is always looking for extra skills.' She shrugged. 'I don't know – I've never seen anyone who is just off probation get a chance like this. People have to batter down the doors of Traffic to even have an application considered. I guess you must just be rolled in London stardust.'

Maryam

Maryam Black. Look at her, struggling along, heavy, weighed down by her hair and her long breasts. Held close to the earth by a curse of her own making. The curse was invisible to the rest of the world, yet so real to her that some days it could be immense enough to blot out the sunrise and sunset, inflamed enough to steal her breath.

The morning after their search she made griddled eggs and cornbread muffins, the back door open to the morning bird-song. She moved slowly in her Moroccan slippers, each step an effort, her eyes stinging from lack of sleep, the smell of the dead badger still in her nostrils. Beyond the open kitchen door the trees brooded along the bottom of the garden. There had never been a fence or barrier between their garden and the park.

I swallowed your dog. I swallowed him and I won't give him back.

She made to close the door, but hesitated, changed her mind. What if this was the day Tumble found his way back through the woods? What if he wasn't dead; what if he'd somehow survived? What if someone very kind had found him: an old lady who hadn't seen the endless posters and Facebook posts and didn't know that a dog might have a chip in its neck that could be scanned by a vet?

No, said the park. *Not that. You know what's really got him. And it's not a kind old lady.*

Maryam used a spatula to coax the eggs out on to a plate, tore up strips of smoked salmon, and arranged the muffins with wedges of butter. She had a thing about breakfast lately. Now that Arran raced out of the door so fast, leaving a whiff of aftershave and a vague blur of laundered shirt, and came home so late, it seemed to Maryam that making sure he had a good breakfast was worth her getting up early for.

'Morning.'

He came into the kitchen in his shirtsleeves, still gingerly patting his cheeks from shaving. 'I'm red, aren't I?'

She smiled. He was far from red. He was slightly tanned and clear-skinned, beautiful like his father. Tall, with a strong neck and shoulders. Sometimes she had to drag herself away from staring at him.

'Here.' She folded out his collar from his neck and wiped a bit of shaving cream from the shirt. 'You look lovely. Just don't get any coffee on your tie.'

'I'll try.'

He sat at the breakfast table, his elbows jammed on either side of the plate, and began forking up the breakfast. He worked for the police now, dressed nicely, dealt with managers and the public, got up in front of rooms of people to speak. But at home he still ate like a carpenter. A man who worked, a man of the land. He got that from his Dad.

'Anything last night?'

'Nothing. Just a dead badger.'

'He'll turn up. He will eventually.'

She filled up his coffee from the cafetière, imagining herself a waitress in an American diner, a yellow pinafore and a name tag on her breast. *Hi, I'm Maryam, author of my own destruction. Ask me about our early bird offers.*

Arran sipped his coffee gingerly, his hand over his tie. He looked even neater and tidier than usual. His eyes seemed brighter against his skin.

She put the cafetière next to the Aga and filled the milk jug and said, 'Alex has been back – what, three weeks now?'

'Four.'

'Have you seen her?'

'Yes. Around. Work and stuff.'

'How is she?'

He shrugged. Didn't look up. 'I don't know. Ask her.'

Maryam didn't push it. Any minute now Rhory would be down. If Minty was awake he'd bring her too – then the two men would talk about cricket and the new bevel-edged chisels Rhory had bought and maybe what was happening at the local pub. But they'd rarely trade feelings. They wouldn't talk about whether there was a girl in Arran's life.

Arran. Twenty-two years old nearly. Still sitting in the same place at the table his highchair used to be. Twenty-two whole years? How had that happened? Where had all that time slid off to?

Maryam had grown up in Wales. Never a beautiful child. *You are just as God made you, and for that you are beautiful,* said her mother, which everyone knew was another way of agreeing she wasn't pretty – not in the strict sense of button noses, blonde hair and tawny limbs. She was bigger and darker than the other children, nothing like her red-haired, freckled sisters, as if a huge chieftain from a distant land had got into the chicken coop one night. Wide-faced, with a squaw's slanting eyes and dense limbs, some days she pitied her family having to be seen with her.

At fifteen she started running errands in the kitchen of her parents' pub. Her arms grew big from lifting barrels and changing the old hop-smelling pipes in the cold basement. Her edges and hips filled out, upholstered and laid over daily from the habit of picking uneaten chips from the plates that waited to be washed, dipping her fingers into the industrial containers of soft-scoop ice cream marshalled in the industrial freezers.

She was a heathen, not fit for the world, but then wasn't that true of most of them round there? Southeast Wales, which felt like an old, forgotten corner of the United Kingdom that never got spoken of. Sometimes it seemed Monmouthshire was a by-word for inbreeding, lapsed manners and bad taste, a place ignored by the posh English. It must be nice to live on the other side of the border. Over in the Cotswolds, maybe, where the people had etiquette and the houses were made of soft melting stone that looked like vanilla fudge. Over there they all painted their windows the same sludge green and instead of making the villages depressing it just made them even more stylish. Maryam dreamed of living there.

She mooched through life, the forgotten in the land of the forgotten, growing steadily rounder by the day, her breasts pushing out, her bottom waxing wide so that the men at the bar, smoking their pipes and digging out the day's dirt from their fingernails, watched her craftily, thinking that maybe with a girl so ugly they could take the chance and wouldn't she be so grateful for it she'd never tell a soul?

Because Maryam wasn't beautiful herself, she set about making everything around her beautiful – she painted her walls in harlequin hexagons, stuck tiny paste gems all over. She cooked, huge, steaming cakes that the whole family dug spoons into the moment they came out of the oven, when they were still too hot to ice. She sewed, too: clothes and curtains and pillows with drooping fringes that her mother said made the place look as though Muslims lived there, and did she really want the rest of the town to think they were Muslims? Then there was wood-carving in the quiet moments. The village was proud of its timber heritage – every town had a lumber yard and two or three furniture-makers. There was never a shortage of offcuts and pieces the size of your hand, which she could carve into tiny sculptures of tree spirits and then paint.

One day there came to town a young man from the other side of the river. Out east in Gloucestershire where the posh people lived. He was dark-haired and taller than the local slope-faced young men. He wore his jeans low, not belted up high round the waist like the others, and his shirts and sweaters had no hoods, no slogans or brand names. He didn't smoke. He chewed nicotine gum and wore a patch on his bare bicep.

His presence made her think of the cowboy films her dad watched at night. A solitary figure in the high street, curtains twitching. *Who's he? Is he on his own?*

His name was Rhory Black and he had an apprenticeship with a furniture-maker at the end of the high street. The work had refined the muscles in his arms so they were hard and toned and all the girls watched him in silence wondering if, under the jeans, the sinews and bones of his legs were just as good. His face had a fighter's ruined beauty, as if he'd been meant to be handsome but had taken a punch to the face, leaving his nose slightly askew, his mouth permanently swollen. *I'd kiss it better*, said the girls. *I would so.*

But it was Maryam who kissed him first. Big, ugly Maryam with the squaw's hair.

Rhory's lodgings were above the chippie two doors down, so naturally he came to the pub to drink. By then Maryam had turned eighteen and was working the bar, pulling the pints, perfecting the shamrock shape in the head of the Guinness. Rhory drank Thirsty Ferret beer which didn't get ordered often, so sometimes the pipe got a clot in it and she'd have to go downstairs and flush it through. He'd eye her thoughtfully as she worked; he'd watch her behind when she bent down. No one had ever looked at her that openly, though she'd looked at many. She was shy, uncertain, but at that age when a heart and belly could liquefy from wanting another human being, send a person quite crazy and into uncertain alleys. A good thing too, because otherwise teenagers might just sit quite still under their parents' apple tree until middle age came and got them.

One day he put down his beer and said, 'It's time.' As if it was something he'd been waiting to be sure of. As if it hadn't crossed his mind that she might say no. Maryam met him after the shift and he took her up to the flat above the chippie where the walls were glazed brown from the grease and nicotine that had seeped up here. He took her into his room and kissed her.

'I haven't got a condom,' he said. 'Have you?'

She didn't know what she was supposed to say. The teachers with their charts and their handouts in PSHE hadn't dealt with this. So she closed her eyes and pulled his face closer to her, kissing him hard. Licking his mouth, licking his teeth because they were so nicotiney and rough. Probably that was how Rhory got the idea it was OK.

She'd never smelled desire on a man before. Under the beer it was sweet and sharp, salty, mean and red. He'd done it before – he knew the ways around her body, what to pucker, what to suck, what to touch softly and when she needed him to push hard. Things inside her opened up, made her cry. She supposed this was how life and sex and love worked; she'd just never imagined she'd be included in any of it.

The weeks of his apprenticeship passed. The skies over the town were purple by three in the afternoon and the snow came. In the basement of the pub the taps froze and Maryam's father was angry. People turned in on themselves, packing themselves into familiarity – the same seats in the pub every day, a microwave meal from the Co-op at five p.m., because what else was there to do after dark in this place?

Rhory fucked Maryam in the frozen evenings. He fucked her in the watery light of lunchtimes, when they crept away from work to meet in the stinking flat with the ragged curtains. There was one packet of cereal and a few pots of dry noodles in the cupboard, and that absence of food made her feel powerful. She could fix those curtains, she told him; she could make meals for him that filled him up. She believed that if she could make his flat beautiful maybe he wouldn't notice that she was the least beautiful of the girls in town.

Afterwards, alone, she'd cry. She'd think about all the beautiful women he had loved and would love. The woman he would marry would be slim, with a London accent and an education. She'd have a fast car and she'd have travelled to America, Africa. She'd have lived in Europe and she'd be a campaigner of some sort. Championing the rights of a small community that had no voice. They'd grow a family in his home town of Eastonbirt, which was famous for its ranging forest. A forest that wouldn't look out of place on this misshapen side of the river, but out there – where people owned second homes and the buildings were all tidy as soldiers – was a rarity.

It was Christmas Eve when she knew. In the pub kitchen, as she was reaching her hand inside the turkeys and pulling out the giblets, with the slurp and the smell of blood, the nausea brought goosebumps to her arms and neck. She might be shy and awkward and an outsider, but she'd lived long enough in the country, seen enough fat bellies of the cows, talked enough to her giggling friends about the way a woman's body worked, to know.

Alex

From the outside, Eagle Tower was almost majestic: a brooding behemoth, catching all the colours of the sun. Inside, it was a different experience from a tower block in London – no one had pissed or shitted in this one and no one had graffitied it. The lights were working too. It was pretty much how I remembered it from my teenage years.

I expected I'd know most of the people who lived there, from my schooldays, and sure enough I rode up in the elevator with the Joiners. Edward used to be a taxi driver; he was short and wiry, and his hair, which I remembered as a thick thatch of ginger, had thinned noticeably in the two years since I'd been gone. Freckled skin had appeared along the hairline. He wore a vest with the word BILLABONG printed on it in dripping letters, and from under his thin, tattooed arms poked tufts of rusty-coloured hair.

'Alright, Alex?' he said. 'You alright in your new line of work?'

'Yes, thank you, Mr Joiner.' I kept my eye on the red light travelling up the floors. 'I'm very happy.'

'Well,' he said, not taking his eyes off me, 'I suppose it's the sort of job as has to appeal to someone.'

At the seventh floor they got off. His wife, whose name I couldn't remember, was tiny, thin as a rail, and seemed to be dressed as if she was expecting customers all night, with a tight PVC skirt, bare, scarred legs like chicken bones, and huge platform sandals. At first I thought she was drunk, by the way he seemed to be looking out for her, occasionally putting a finger under her elbow to steady her balance, until it dawned on me she wasn't drunk, just blind or short-sighted. I'd never noticed this before. Perhaps I was fine-tuned to these oddities because I'd been away so long.

The old woman who'd made the report was familiar too. She pointed me to No. 8014 where there were two teenage boys in brand new Reeboks with guilty expressions. They let me into a flat that was neat and smelled of plug-in air-fresheners. It had low ceilings and one huge living room, which must have been intended by the architects as a showpiece, judging by its size and the way it was dominated by a huge floor-to-ceiling window. The window opened on to a tiny balcony, netted in to stop the pigeons (or maybe to stop people jumping, who knew), and beyond it whole of Eastonbirt Park was visible.

I'd been to the tower before but never properly appreciated the view of the tree-covered valley and escarpment. From here I could see the chain of lakes glittering. The place the coach had gone down into the water – the causeway that led between the biggest two at the head of the chain, Lake Tarquil and Lake Folly – was obscured by the contours. But I could make out the burred sweep of the road winding down towards it.

The two boys were easy, instantly sheepish, especially when I asked if they wanted to do it by the book, with their parents in attendance and a proper verbal warning on their records. Within seconds they'd produced the offending item – a laser pen.

'Cool,' I said. 'A Quarton Infiniter. One of the best on the market.'

'You were in old Gully's class, weren't you?' one of the boys said. 'I remember you.'

'And you was in the crash too, wasn't yer?' said the other, his eyes lingering on my hand. 'We watched the fire engines from here. Mum woke us up when she heard the sirens.'

I went to the window and stood, hands shoved into my pockets, my radio feed pulled a little out of my ear to relieve the endless chattering. That quiet causeway between the two lakes had become the centre of attention for the entire community, the focus around which all consciousness in Eastonbirt slowly turned. A place for ghouls and legend-tourists to visit. A place to leave flowers that dried out and browned. From up here the accident would have appeared as sirens and blue lights, lines of cars queuing up the valley roads. Several days later maybe you'd have been able to see the cranes that came and hauled the old Volvo fifty-seven-seat coach out of the depths, water and silt draining out of the smashed windows. No one doubted that things had been left behind in the lake. At the inquest the accident investigators admitted they hadn't been able to recover every single scrap of evidence; no matter how hard the team tried, inevitably there'd be stuff that had sunk to the bottom and would never be reclaimed. The council put up huge barriers along the causeway (some whispered about bolting horses and stable doors) and restricted access to the lake. They'd also placed a fishing ban on Lake Tarquil. The signs were everywhere. What might an angler pull up? A phone or a wallet? A scrap of a ghost?

I turned back to the boys. 'Is that a crossbow?' On the floor was a case, black fibreglass with an image of a stag skull emblazoned across it. 'Because it looks like one to me.'

The boys' faces fell. 'Not that too. It's a Hornet.'

'I can see what it is. It's beautiful. And completely illegal to fire.'

'Come on,' they said. 'Please.'

'Please what? Please don't tell your mum you've been trying to down passenger jets? Because that's how it's treated by
the law. And unless you can show me a receipt that says someone over eighteen bought that crossbow, you're in trouble.'

The boys grumbled and scuffed their feet, but eventually
the older one picked the crossbow and offered it to me.

'Good. Bring them both out on the landing.'

We went into the corridor, the two boys exchanging glances
and muttering under their breath. The tower block had been
built in the days when designers believed residents would
respect rubbish chutes and use them for jettisoning bin bags,
and not for vomiting down, throwing unwanted pets down,
and, in one heart-stopping case I'd heard about in training,
dumping the body of the child they'd just raped. I stood with
my finger holding the chute open. The smell coming up from
it was fruity and warm and totally sick-making.

'Come on.' I jerked my head to the chute. 'Let's get it over
with. Then nothing formal, no mums or dads involved. No
memory – we clear your browser history.'

I felt for them, these two boys, giving up the things they
loved the best. I knew it felt like crap. But I was just old enough
to see what they couldn't: that it was better this way than ending up in juvie. I told them this as I left, and they nodded,
but they didn't take it in. That was what it meant to be really
young, moving fast from one easy avenue to the next. Maybe
one day they'd thank me.

I rode down in the lift with another woman I recognised,
but couldn't quite put a name to. In the car park I started the
car – and then I stopped it. I got out and walked around the
side of the tower to the concrete ramp that led into the basement, where a council worker in bright orange overalls was

washing the floor down with a hose. I held up my warrant card and he nodded, continued what he was doing.

The green dumpsters under the chutes were overflowing and I saw the crossbow instantly. I stood on tiptoe and pulled it off the black dustbin liners and inspected it. The carrying case had cracked; two of the red bolts had spilled out of the foam casing. But the crossbow was intact, and it would be a hundred times better than the mini catapult Arran and I had been using for ages.

I wiped it off, restored the bolts to the case, closed it carefully and was about to head back up the ramp with my prize under my arm when the lift doors opened and a very pale woman in flip-flops and a pink tracksuit came sloping out, carrying two carrier bags.

Michaela Lewis, Mike's daughter.

I had hardly seen anything of her since the crash except at the inquest. I loitered on the other side of the car park as she crossed to the huge recycling bins, her head down. She looked very tired and old for her twenty-one years. Her hair was flame-coloured and tied in bunches. She dumped the contents of the bags, the crash of bottles echoing around the undercroft, then she turned and sloped back to the lift, her shoes making a *slap slap* sound on the concrete.

I waited until she was gone and went back to the dumpster, opened it and looked inside. Vodka bottles – maybe five or six. A couple of plastic Coke bottles lolling against them. I lowered the lid and looked at the closed doors of the lift. Michaela's dad had died in the crash and in the whole of the past two and a half years I hadn't contacted her. I just hadn't known what to say.

Maryam

All those years ago, back where Maryam grew up, there had been a grey-haired woman who lived half a mile out of the village in a decrepit council house with a shipping container in her garden. She grew her own vegetables and didn't have electricity and travelled the world with a knapsack. One day she brought home a husband. A handsome Indian man half her age with soft hands and sad eyes. He reminded Maryam of a sea mammal that had been washed up on the wrong shore – baffled by its surroundings, mistrustful of any kindnesses shown.

'He's a magic man, a Swami,' whispered the men in the pub. 'Up to all manner of hoochy-hooch nonsense. And he doesn't love her. She's his shoo-in to the country.'

One wet, chilly day in February Maryam got the bus out to the house. The driver dropped her in a rainstorm on the side of the road and she walked the last half-mile, stopping once to be sick, then continuing on, head back, her mouth open, letting the raindrops dilute away the taste.

'In town people say you're a clairvoyant.'

'Do they?' The Indian man raised an eyebrow, smiling. 'What strange things people say.'

He made her milky tea thick with sugar that she couldn't drink because lately tea, coffee, all the things she was used to, turned her stomach.

The living room was cold, a smell of burning paint coming from the rusting storage heaters. Everywhere there was threadbare furniture, half-finished driftwood carvings, huge tropical plants dying and browning in the wet Welsh weather. She set the mug on the table and pulled the sleeves of her sweater down over her hands, hugging herself.

'It's just that I'm in trouble.'

'Baby trouble?'

'How do you know?'

He smiled. 'Because I am clairvoyant.'

They weren't technically alone. The grey-haired woman was outside, dressed in a raincoat, pottering around, feeding chickens and fixing a drainpipe. She drifted past the dirty windows like a storybook hag, bent and preoccupied. Even so, for Maryam it was unnerving to lie on the sofa on her back. To have the Swami stand next to her while she rolled down the waistband of her trousers, exposing her white stomach to the chilly air.

With all the sickness she'd lost weight, and the baby was pulling what it could from the rest of her body – the mound of her stomach was clear and defined, the skin already stretched although she wasn't even four months gone yet. The nights when Rhory lay, his naked stomach on top of hers, he hadn't noticed the change in her body, from fat to baby.

The Swami closed his eyes and put his hands on her abdomen. They were cool and strange. For a long time said nothing, while she looked at the hairs in his nostrils and listened to the shoo-in wife cluck at the chickens outside the window, the patter of rain on the roof. She imagined the baby, a determined fist of bone and flesh turning inside her. Sucking its thumb. They did suck their thumbs inside you. That was what the books in the library said.

'Good,' he said after a while, opening his eyes. She expected him to wash his hands or something, but he went to the table, pulled out a chair and sat in front of her, serious. 'The baby is healthy; he will be happy and strong. He will be a source of pride for you and his father.'

She should have told him then, that the father didn't know. Didn't know and wouldn't care. And that what she really wanted to know was how to tell him. But the Swami had closed his eyes again.

'My friend, it is a rare thing. A rare treat, to meet someone with a third eye so strong.'

'A third eye?'

He nodded solemnly. 'Use it wisely; never doubt its presence. Trust what happens naturally and trust your own instincts.' He opened his eyes, got up and leaned over her. He placed a finger on her forehead. 'It is here, my friend. Here on your head. And in you it is so, so bright. Like nothing I have seen. Like a fireflower.'

She could smell cooking and cigarettes and detergent on his finger. Something else too that she couldn't identify, like fish. She thought of the woman pottering around outside.

'The father . . . ' she whispered.

'Does not know?'

'No.'

'He will know, and all will be well. The baby will be happy. This is a gift to you – the luck of having a baby.'

Luck? Maryam didn't see a baby as luck. Maybe in India, but here? Here it was what the girls and the boys tried to stop happening.

She sat up and pulled on her sweater, her waterproof. Her clothes were still damp from the rainstorm earlier. 'Do I need to pay you?'

The Swami blinked, taken aback. Then, hurriedly, as if he hadn't thought about this. 'My fee is . . . it is five pounds.'

'Is that all?'

He hesitated. 'No. I meant ten.'

For two weeks the baby grew silently in her tummy, while the idea of a third eye grew in her mind. She'd open the window at the back of the pub and stare into the darkness, hearing, above the racket of cutlery being washed, crates being moved, the hoot of an owl. What purpose did a third eye serve? What was it there for? There was no one to ask.

On the freezing unmade bed above the chip shop Rhory would huddle up between her legs and spend long, long minutes licking her vulva. He was fixated on this, lying on his front, peering up into her, as if between her legs was a place of great wonder, an opening to a god-like space. She let him do it without asking. He knew the way sex was supposed to happen and she didn't.

The day after the Swami, for the first time, Rhory noticed the change.

'Oh,' he said seriously. 'Oh.'

He knelt up between her thighs and rested his hands on her belly. He was silent for a long time. Then he lay down next to her, on his back, staring at the ceiling.

She waited for him to speak, but he didn't, and so she got up and dressed in silence, sitting on the edge of the bed to pull on her knickers, her back to him so he couldn't see her stomach or face. She went back to the pub and carried on pulling pints as normal.

He didn't come to the pub that night. Nor the next day, nor the next. Every night she walked past the fish and chip shop and stared up at the windows of the freezing flat. One night there was the bluish TV light flickering against the closed curtains, but other nights it was in darkness. She eyed the old woman in the shop jealously as she leaned over the hot fat fryers. Did she know where Rhory was? She probably spoke to him every day. Maryam's throat balled up tight and refused to unclench.

She used old bits of fabric her mother was throwing away to cut dresses that would hide what was happening down there, at least for a while until she could decide what to do. It was before the time when everyone had a phone, and, even if she'd had one, what would she say to Rhory? The Swami had been wrong. There was no happy ending.

Soon the days grew longer. The evenings stretched and yawned and the pub filled with middle-class families from other counties, out here to gawp at the scenery and the strange locals. The ones who were rumoured to sleep with their cousins.

'I've been away.' Rhory appeared at the bar one day. Dressed in a new shirt, something formal about his appearance, as if he'd washed extra-hard, or had a doctor straighten his punched face. He sat with a pint in front of him and watched her moving, watched the way her belly brushed the beer taps. 'I had to think.'

'You've had time now.'

'And I can't lie – I can't make it easy. It's going to be diffi-cult, what I have to ask you, and you won't want to do it.'

She stopped and turned to face him. She was scared of him, but only in that she was afraid he'd leave her. Which seemed to have happened already.

'I'm six months gone now. I can't get rid of him.'

'Him?'

'Yes,' she said with confidence. 'Him.' It was what the Swami had said: *he* will be healthy and strong. 'And I won't get rid of him.'

'I'm not asking you to.'

'What, then? What are you asking?'

He stared down at his feet and sighed. Her heart sank.

'I'm sorry.' He lifted his face sadly. 'I'm so sorry. Don't take this the wrong way, but I can't live here. If we're going to get married, I've got to live in Eastonbirt. I'll never survive here.'

And so it was that she became Maryam Black, with a Mrs at the beginning of her name. Her mother cried at the hurried wedding; her little sisters giggled, shoved pillows up their bridesmaids' dresses and paraded around the kitchen, hands jammed in the small of their backs, making ouchy faces. *Oooh, the baby's kicking. Ooh, stop it, baby – you're kicking my heart. You can't kick when I'm walking up the aisle.* Her dad was stoic. *It's not even two hours' drive to Eastonbirt. I've already worked out my route. Now they've opened that new road from Gloucester we'll be up and down it like rats up a drainpipe, you see if we're not.*

Eastonbirt was in a valley cut into the Cotswold plains. If you stood at the top of the escarpment and looked across to the other side you could see all of flat, golden Gloucestershire, then Oxfordshire, tilted to the east. Beyond it, way, way, way beyond it, was London, where the people who owned half the houses in the village spent most of their time. She'd never seen so many beautiful houses unlived in. The shops all catered to these weekend visitors – cupcakes and distressed furniture, bunting, and artisan chocolate in flavours of chilli and pepper.

They moved to Eastonbirt just two months before the baby was due. Rhory's mother had been dead for three years, and his father was still so sick of heart that he didn't want to live in the family home and had moved to a flat in Bicester. Maryam was surprised by him, his normality. He kept Toby jugs and china sculptures of horses, just as her own dad did. He wore slippers in the carpeted flat and she couldn't believe he was really the father of someone as exotic as Rhory. But he was kind to her, and talked to her soothingly, as if he pitied her – the ugly duckling who'd married out of her league and would never be able to relax.

The family house vacated by Rhory's father was going to be their home. It was a rambling stone cottage named 'the Bake-house', which sat halfway up the hills on the hems of the park. The garden was an unenclosed space opening straight into the trees. Maryam didn't know what to make of the park. Sometimes when Rhory was out at work (he'd quickly found a job working for a cabinet-maker) she would stand in the windows and stare at it. There was a blur at the top of it where the trees met the sky. And under that a labyrinth, a place walkers got lost, a place she hesitated to set foot in. Vast and uncharted, it was never going to be her friend. Never.

She should have spent her final two months before the birth making baby clothes, resting and eating. But the Bakehouse was dark and draughty, with her father-in-law's used furniture, and red carpets that had lines of dirt going up the centre. So instead she set about making the house into their home. She stripped back the carpet to the floorboards, hired a sander and stayed up into the night varnishing the floor. She crawled around on all fours, liking the way the baby lolled downwards in her belly, taking the weight off her organs. The Aga was thick with grease, so she used a knife to scrape it off, collected it in a pan and padded down to the treeline to drop the chunks of fat in the woods for foxes to eat.

The old shutters she encrusted with fragments of mirrors; she broke up old tiles and set them in harlequins into the gables until it was a colourful little gingerbread house of a place. She made valances and pennant-shaped blinds from offcuts of lace from the local charity shops. When Rhory brought home furniture commissions she learned how to do the upholstery.

'You could make a business of it,' Rhory said. 'You know, when the baby's old enough.'

The baby arrived. Arran. Long and flexible, breathing calmly in spite of the fierce labour. Already able to open his eyes and focus. He was more beautiful than Rhory, if that was possible, and she was slightly intimidated by him. The nurses all crowded round. *He's so good-looking! Just like his dad. Look at that face!* The other mothers watched in sullen silence. A beautiful baby absorbed all the light in the ward, stole from every new soul in the hospital. One of the mothers made a point of going over to the bed to watch Maryam change Arran's nappy. She obliged, wondering if it was the woman's way of reassuring herself that he functioned the same as other babies.

She made Arran's clothes from charity shop fabric, sitting at the sewing machine whenever she wasn't breastfeeding. She stencilled dinosaurs on his nursery walls. The summer died outside the window; the edges of the leaves became old and crisp. She thought about the Swami and what he'd said: *All will be well. The baby will be happy.*

At three months old, Arran had an infection. Something minor in retrospect – upper respiratory – but it was the first time she'd understood that she was smaller than the universe – that she was only a part of the chain and that the little red-faced baby, fists clenched up at his cheeks, was more important than her own existence. The doctors had muttered about emergency numbers and not being afraid to dial 999. The thought that he might not survive could have knocked her down and sent her sprawling faster than a speeding truck.

He lived. He bawled his way through one night in the big double bed, between her and Rhory, their sheets thrown off because although it was nearly November the nurses had said to keep him cool. In the morning she and Rhory awoke frozen and blue, a puffy pink baby snoozing peacefully between them.

She looked at her husband on the other pillow. His eyes were bloodshot from lack of sleep. He blinked at her. Smiled and mouthed, 'Morning, babes. Long night. You OK?'

She began to cry. She rolled her head away from him and pushed her face into the pillow, her elbows mounted on each side like eagle wings. Bawling her eyes out into the pillow, on and on. She felt him shift behind her, his tentative palm cold against her back, meant to be comforting.

It was ten minutes before she lifted her face and rubbed the snot from her nose. Arran was still asleep between them and Rhory was watching her.

'I'm sorry,' she said, her voice thick and nasal. 'I'm sorry. Please don't look at me like that.'

'I'm trying to understand. I know things are wrong. I know you're depressed.'

She pressed her fingers into her eyes and struggled up, bolstering the pillows behind her head.

'Is it because of Arran?'

She nodded minutely. 'A little,' she ventured. 'A little.'

'You're not happy with him?'

'I love him. I adore him.' She lowered her eyes to look at the baby fast asleep on his back, his arms up above his head. No signs of fever. Just his ribcage moving up and down. 'He looks just like you.'

'He looks like you too.'

'But mostly you.'

Outside it was raining. An autumn day, a lot like the day she'd first met Rhory. The steady drip drip drip from the eaves, the fat pearls of water that hung in the gables. It reminded her of Wales and the girls who adored Rhory so much.

'Did you marry me because you had to?' she blurted out. 'Did you only marry me because of Arran?'

That jolted Rhory. 'Sorry?'

'I never understood why me. I never understood why you didn't choose one of the other girls in the village. Or someone from Oxford. Or London. You could have, you know. You could have had anyone.'

'I didn't want anyone. I wanted you.'

'But why?'

He shook his head, mystified as to how to answer her. 'Because I . . . ' he began. Then he dug his elbow into the pillow and leaned his face into his palm, looking at her very steadily. 'Because you are dignified. Because you're calm. Because you make everything around you beautiful and easy. Because you're smoking in bed, because you're not crazy, because you make polenta bread to die for – and mostly? Mostly, because you're grounded. You see the world for what it is. There's nothing in your head that doesn't have weight.'

In her cotton pyjamas, soaked in dried-up breast milk and Arran's baby sweat, her face sleep-creased, the rain plinking outside the window, a vital part of Maryam changed at that moment. He meant it. He really meant what he was saying. It was like a fast-forwarded movie – an animation of a metamorphosis.

Grounded. She was grounded and serious and that was what people respected in her. Whatever had happened in Wales, whatever had happened the day she'd walked out of town to see the husband of the woman with the shipping containers and the chickens, she would never mention it to Rhory. He could never know. Never.

Alex

That night Arran and I sat at the edge of Lake Tarquil – the biggest of the lakes, a brooding monster of a thing that stretched for miles. We were using a catapult we'd constructed to shoot stones into the glassy centre of the water. The cata-. pult was beautiful. As fourteen-year-olds Arran and I had built it together in his dad's workshop using the scrap wood left over from Rhory Black's jobs. It still shot stones as far into the middle of the lake, just as it had back in the day when Arran and I were still kids and spent hours roaming the park.

Tonight wasn't exactly the same – him in his suit, his tie unloosened, shirt-sleeves rolled up, posh shoes – and me in my Force-issue blue sports shirt, a little bit of sick on my shoes because earlier I'd had to arrest a woman in Stroud who'd been drunk. She'd been throwing all the heavy pieces of furniture she could lift out of her third-storey window on to passers-by. I'd managed to calm her down and get her into the car, where she'd puked up all over me. It had reassured me that human nature and madness weren't any different out here in Gloucestershire from in London.

Our lives had changed. We weren't Huck Finn and Tom Sawyer any more, but the old habits still stuck hard. Him still totally, stratospherically fit. And me, just me. Short, freckled and ordinary.

'Are you gonna tell me what's in the box?' Arran nodded down at the crossbow I'd lifted from the waste at Evil Tower. 'Or do I have to guess?'

'You have to guess. Because I'm not going to tell you.'

'Jesus.' He slotted another of the pebbles into the sling and fired it out into the lake. 'You haven't changed. Friggin' Katana.'

'Katana? Nope. Sorry. Too old and cynical to be doing superhero stuff.'

'You *what*? You didn't just say the words "too old and cynical to do superheroes".'

'Well, sure, I'm still a card-carrying member of the Outsiders, but some of my kendo powers may have been modified by age. Course, I can uncouple a speeding train with one hand while shooting a Luger with the other, but I've also learned to reason with people.'

'Reason with people?' He kept a straight face. 'I don't understand.'

'Of course you don't. It's a human power.'

We went on throwing stones with the catapult. Arran muttered darkly about how he'd have to train up his baby sister to step into my shoes as his wingman. Because to his way of thinking, he said, it sounded as though I'd jacked in the position. He had taken off his jacket, rolling it into a type of bolster that he used to brace the catapult. The lake was flawless and still, like a mirror, reflecting the late sun, dragonflies darting to and fro across the surface. Early evenings in London kind of got forgotten, missed, because you could never see the sky – or at least not the full dome of it, with the changing sheets of weather moving around. Here, it was like constantly being in contact with heaven.

'What about your Achilles' heel?' Arran wasn't giving up on his superhero stuff. He was stuck in throwback mode, trying to relive our childhoods. 'What's your kryptonite?'

'I don't have kryptonite. I told you, I'm not a superhero any more.'

The truth was, I'd never admit to Arran that *he* was my kryptonite. Ever since we'd gone skinny-dipping aged fourteen and in the glint of moonlight as he emerged from the water I'd caught sight of his penis – not shrivelled the way you'd expect from the cold, but half-erect, swinging and long – a switch in my head had been thrown and I'd known. Just known. I remember thinking seriously, *Mum, I can reassure you: I'm not, as you have long suspected, a lesbian.* Except I couldn't say anything. He was out of my league, several classes above my punching weight; his girlfriends were satiny and nicely clipped, with smooth hair and long legs.

'Something's happened,' I said after a while now. 'Something I can't explain.'

He stopped what he was doing and turned to me.

'I keep thinking.'

'Ouch, bad – especially for a cop. You start thinking too much and before long you realise what a full-on cock-up the British judicial system is. What you're a card-carrying representative of. And that way, as the man says, lies madness.'

'I'm serious. Anyway – you're as much a part of the system now as I am.'

It was true. Whatever strange and unholy power had taken us after the crash, it had driven us both in the same directions. From the outside Arran looked like an investment banker – all slick suit and nice black Audi. But the truth was, he worked for the police. A civilian, true, an IT trainer in the forensic unit at Gloucester, but it didn't matter if he didn't carry around a warrant card; he was a civil servant like me, the coin came from the same grubby hand, so there was no point in him mouthing off about the service.

I pulled the photograph out from my back pocket. It was creased and crumpled. No point in protecting it; there'd be no usable forensics on it after Mum had put it through the shredder.

'This came. I thought you might know something about it.'

He lowered the slingshot and leaned over to look at it.

'It turned up in the post, no writing, no explanation. Can you see a face? Here, in the lower window?'

'A face?' he said warily, the way you'd talk to someone who was borderline insane and holding a grenade. 'Where?'

'It was here. In this window. Photoshopped in, of course – but it was completely fucking creepy. Scared the shit out of me. My amazingly clever mother contrived to shred it.'

'What sort of face?'

I rubbed my calves, uncomfortable. 'Don't laugh, but . . . remember the bonehead? In the woods?'

'Of course. You and Minnie shitting yourselves.'

'Technically we did not shit ourselves.'

Arran laughed. He put down the slingshot, clicked on his phone and held the screen up to illuminate his face from underneath. 'The bonehead. *I'll eat your kidneys, little child.*'

I shook my head and lowered my face. I could have told him that while the face in the window could have been my imagination at work, Bamber growling and scared in the woods that same night hadn't been something I'd invented. But Arran's goof-faced little mongrel, Tumble, had been missing for weeks, and it would be pretty insensitive of me to labour the point, so I tried to force out a laugh. Tried to make light of it all.

Catching the false note in my laugh, he lowered the phone. 'I'm sorry. Not funny?'

'Not funny.'

Maryam

Arran turned out to be a dark, full-lipped child, with a steady gaze that would make even strangers treat him with respect. Maryam relished his babyhood. She played peekaboo with him, taught him how to eat sliced bananas and how to pull himself up to standing. She wriggled her fingers through the holes in the *Hungry Caterpillar* book; she held him and smelled his clean washed hair. She cooked polenta bread and taught herself how to make Moroccan food in a tagine Rhory brought home one day from a house auction.

When Arran was six months old, Rhory's best friend Fenton arrived back in Eastonbirt. He'd spent three years in London getting an accountancy qualification and was back now to start up his own business. He was older than Rhory, prematurely balding, and seemed to come from an entirely different generation: more sensible, more buttoned-up and correct. Maryam was tongue-tied around him the way she would have been if he were a head teacher. But the men's friendship was old and solid. They made a strange pair at the Ragged Stall pub every Friday night – the carpenter and the accountant. Surely there was a joke in there somewhere.

Fenton had brought back his own family from London. Lois, his wife, was older than all of them, nearly thirty.

'Lois is from Surrey,' Rhory warned Maryam. 'You'd better make sure there are napkins on the dinner table.'

'I'm from Surrey,' Lois said when they met, holding out a polite hand. 'But don't let that put you off.'

She was as tall as Maryam, and imposing, with the stiff neck and the broad pink face of a playing card queen, hair a frizzy halo of blonde, and long, muscled legs that looked immaculate in a skirt. In the summers she wore a thin chiffon scarf around her neck, as if she were gliding through the perfume department at Harrods, and in the winter it was pashminas – making her more regal, more serious. She had a baby of five months old too, a sturdy, blonde-haired, pink-skinned girl called Sophie May who had been sitting upright from four months and taking solids from three. A miracle megababy.

Maryam in her Afghan coats and knitted peasant clothing might never have had the courage to speak to Lois if it hadn't been for the babies. But from the start Lois was determined that Arran and Sophie May were going to be firm friends. She encouraged Maryam to come up to the big mock-Georgian house she and Fenton lived in, with its neat lawns, the family's BMW and Lois's little runaround in the driveway. Maryam was timid, but she forced herself to go. She was the woman with her feet on the ground. That was what Rhory loved about her. So she put Arran's stuff in his buggy and pushed him up the hill.

The house was so different from the Bakehouse, so ordered and spotless. Fenton's office was in the annexe that connected the house to the garage, with a sign on the interior door that said *Man Cave* in jaunty letters. He never seemed to move from there or make a sound, so the two women and the babies were alone in the vast carpeted rooms with the dark wood furniture.

Lois served strong tea and huge frosted cakes from the cupcake shop in the high street. She was posh but kind, and as long as they were talking about babies Maryam felt safe in her company. Sophie May had all the modern toys – play mats and tunnels and balls and Fisher Price eggs – and, while she and Arran crawled their way around the lounge, Maryam and

Lois whiled away long summer afternoons, discussing naps and teeth, comparing sleepsuits and breast milk and weight and all the other commonplaces that were the vital markers of a successful day with a baby.

Winter arrived, lengthened and then dwindled. The point on the escarpment where the sun rose daily inched its way south-wards, moving towards spring, and the trees began to look silvery at the places the new leaves were ready to bud. The two fat babies grew fatter and stronger and learned how to crawl, how to walk and talk. As the summer grew drowsy Arran was the first to speak, aged just thirteen months. 'Sophie May won't be far behind,' said Lois. And then, her eyes fixed on Sophie May sitting on the floor in the sun, pulling the fur off a toy rabbit, 'I'll never love anyone as much as I love her. Never.'

Maryam was confused. 'Not even Fenton?'

'Not even Fenton. You know how it is.'

But Maryam didn't know how it was. She loved Rhory as much as she loved Arran. She wouldn't be able to choose between the two.

Her son grew long in the limb and suntanned from days in the garden. He went to nursery with Sophie May, Lois made sure of it, and after nursery they'd go back to the Hansels', or to the Bakehouse, where Maryam made carrot and cinnamon cake, or sparkling ginger snaps stuffed with cream. The two men finished work and went to the pub and the women shared bottles of prosecco. Sophie May was spirited. She often hit Arran with her toys. When he'd had enough he'd sit cross-legged in a fury, his back to her until she wrapped her arms round his neck and said wispily, 'Sorry, Arran. Sophie May sorry.'

It all went too fast. The next thing Maryam knew, the baby days were all gone and Arran was trying on clothes for his first day at school. Tall and sombre in the St Winifred's purple sweater, on the first morning he took Sophie May's hand and led her into the school.

'Look at them, they'll never be separated.' At the school gates Lois was regal, her hair done in a swept-up-do, watching Arran and her daughter merge into the playground colours. There was Minnie Frobisher and Jessop Jarvis. And the feisty little Mullins girl who lived with her posh mother in the biggest house in the valley. 'It's all so beautiful,' she said. 'So beautiful.'

Maryam was silent. The other mothers were laughing and smiling, waving gleefully at their children. She had a scarf wrapped tight around her neck so no one could see the cold round stone in her throat trying to push its way through her skin. Some things could never be regained or restarted or replaced.

'Do you ever think about having another baby?' she murmured later that day, back in the mock-Georgian house, the Wedgwood teapot on a stand between them. 'Does that ever occur to you?'

Lois shot her a curious look. 'Not at all. Never. Fenton and I agreed: just the one. I'm going back to work soon – part-time.'

'Work?'

'For Fenton. I do his admin – he's been farming it out while we waited for Sophie May to start school, but now I can get back to it. What about you?'

Maryam studied her hands. The bitten nails, the charity bracelets piled up on her wrists. It hadn't occurred to her that suddenly she'd be in a void like this.

'Maryam?'

She raised her eyes. Lois was smiling at her sadly.

'I know. It's not easy. But if you're not going to have more children, then why not go back to work?'

'Back to work?'

'Yes. Why not?'

Where did Maryam begin to answer that? *Because all I've ever done is pull pints in my parents' pub?*

'What about your sewing? And what you've done to the Bakehouse? Interior design – you'd make a fortune round here.'

Maryam stared at Lois. Interior design. 'But I . . . ' She looked down at her thrown-together outfit. The chunky cardigan with the mismatched buttons. Her cord skirt, boots from eBay with a broken zip. 'Me?'

'Exactly. You're the perfect Stroud girl. Slightly hippy, slightly arty. A bit of a bohemian. You're the sort of person who makes this area what it is.'

Maryam fiddled with the buttons on the cardigan. She stroked the cord skirt flat along her round thighs. There was a flower she'd embroidered on to the skirt using a slip of beaded brown lace from an old blouse of her mother's. She'd done it without thinking. She liked it, but the idea that it might have wider appeal, that someone as urbane and stylish as Lois might appreciate it? Never. Never ever.

Lois leaned over and grabbed Maryam's hand. 'In fact – Fenton's going to give you your first commission. His office needs a makeover. You've just been appointed.'

Lois was right. The interior design business that Maryam started so haltingly and nervously was a success. At first it was frightening, but she remembered Rhory's words: *you're grounded.* Taking deep breaths, keeping calm and playing the role, she set about building her network. Fenton was delighted with the look she chose for his office – smart beige and petrol-blue stripes. Grey blinds and neutral walls. Soon the word got round about the boho Welsh girl who drove everywhere in a customised battered Vauxhall decorated in brown and orange diamonds, the inside festooned with jingling beads and trims. The car was a quirky moving advertisement for her trade. She specialised in putting beading on blinds, in trimming curtains with a little extra something – a row of yellow bobbles on the leading edge of a grey curtain. A lime-green braid across the middle of a pink cushion. Her work was competent and creative, but, more importantly, she was not beautiful or chic enough to pose a threat to the rich ladies, whom she recognised as posh because of their kindness, their lack of regional accents.

She made tentative, stressful trips to London, to the fabric fairs at Chelsea Harbour, and came home laden with fabric books, the brands tripping off her tongue – Colefax and Fowler, Designer's Guild, Romo – as if they were family names.

Rhory now had his own furniture-making business. He introduced her to his clients, and she recommended him to hers. For a while money came easily and in abundance. They holidayed in Corfu and Egypt. Once Morocco, in a medina, the Berber blue entrancing her and making its way into future designs, becoming a signature. Rhory found the money to set up his workshop in the garage and construct an additional room for Maryam's use. Attached to the side of the Bakehouse, it was built using reclaimed timber, bricks, and specialist panes of glass with inbuilt UV protection. The new room served as a living or summer room for the family, but it was also Maryam's private den and workroom. There was a separate annexe leading from it where she kept her sewing station and stored the fabrics. She began working on a design using as a theme old plans of Eastonbirt Park, taken from the historical society website. She borrowed the patterns that made up the old arboretum which, like the mansion, had been abandoned and forgotten decades ago. Maryam loved the alleys, the half-moon-shaped plantings, the carefully hand-drawn patios, borders and irrigation systems. She could work them into her images.

'So,' her customers would ask, 'no plans to have another baby?'

'Oh, no. Far too much to be getting on with.'

She was a liar. What she wanted, *all* she wanted, was another child. Arran had been too easy to conceive, so why hadn't another baby come along? A little girl with Rhory's bee-stung upper lip? Or another Arran – a strong boy who already stood head and shoulders above the other boys in the class? But month after month her period came. At her school they'd called it the Curse because of what it did to gym classes and tight jeans. Only now was she understanding its true biblical meaning. It was the curse of not being pregnant.

The seasons came and went, the shadows around the Bake-house lengthened and shrank, the leaves changed colour, fell and grew their new clothes in the springtime. Soon Arran was trying on uniform for his senior school and Sophie May had breasts under her sports tops. By year eight the kids were already talking about who was dating whom and rumours went round that one of the girls further up the school in year ten was pregnant. Someone Maryam's age was going to be a grandmother. Would that be her fate too: to be a grandmother before she had another child of her own?

She plucked up the courage and told Rhory. They attended a fertility clinic and both had tests. Maryam's age really wasn't a problem; at thirty-two she was still very much in her fertile years, and there was nothing physically wrong with either of them – nothing at all. Their best chance of conceiving was to 'just keep making love naturally as ever'. The consultant's smile was so confident that Maryam went away with renewed faith. But six months later she was still getting her periods, and now was feeling the steady and fierce ticking of the clock chipping away at her from inside. She was worn away, egg-shell-fragile. Was it right that her first son's voice should have broken before the second child came along?

It was Arran's first year in sixth form when she finally gave in. She called her mother and asked about the Swami. He'd long left his shoo-in wife and moved to Bristol. Maryam tracked him down on Facebook and late one March afternoon, when she was supposed to be finishing a set of silk pleat curtains, instead on impulse she drove over there, using the country roads because the motorway still made her nervous.

The flat was in an unremarkable Victorian semi, painted pale green. There was a small sign propped in the window with a Yantra drawn on it. The Swami was still the same good-looking man, though now there was grey in his beard and he carried a soft stomach under his clothes. He wore ruby silk robes over jeans which, he explained as he invited her in, was all about practicality: it was too cold to be bare-legged in wintry Britain.

Inside, the place was centrally heated and very warm, which helped, and she found it easy to relax with the Swami, who watched her from the opposite purple velour sofa, his jeans-clad legs crossed, his hands resting lightly on his calves.

'Maryam?'

'Yes.'

'I have never forgotten you. From the first time I saw you, I knew you were special.'

She was astonished, embarrassed. She had no idea how to respond.

'It is not often that I see a soul like yours come through my door. I carry you here in my heart.' He placed his hands piously over his chest. 'Tell me – is that baby good and strong?'

'He's . . . he's amazing. Seventeen now. And lovely, so strong and happy and handsome.'

A moment's silence. The Swami's mouth twitched slightly. 'But?''

'There haven't been any more children.'

'I see.' He drew his hand down his beard and let out a long sigh. Uncrossing his legs, he got to his feet. 'May I touch you?'

'Yes.'

'On the sofa, please.'

She lay on the couch. It smelled of tobacco and was itchy under the backs of her arms. He'd put his hands on her before all those years ago, but that didn't make it feel any less strange. She closed her eyes and pulled down the waistband of her skirt, tugging the high-waisted kickers down too. He stood next to her, placing his palms sideways on her abdomen, just below the navel. For a long time he didn't speak. There was nothing, just the sound of them both breathing in and out in the small room.

'Oils. You need oils.'

She opened her eyes. He took his hands off and went to the corner of the room where there was a glass-fronted cabinet with row after row of decanters, one of which he uncorked. He poured oil from a larger glass jar into a tiny vial and held it up to the light.

'This time it is different, Maryam. I am sorry, but it has to be different. The first time was all very natural, a result of love. Not this time.'

'What do you mean?'

'You need intervention. Here is sandalwood and rose otto. Very precious. You need to pay attention to your sacral chakra, the seat of Shakti. Rub it in twice a day, my friend. I will show you how.'

He came back to her and instantly she closed her eyes. Her heart was thundering. What did he mean, it was different? Intervention? She heard him breathing, wanted to open her eyes. The smell of the oil was bitter, ammoniac, making her eyes water. He rubbed it slowly into her stomach, clockwise, his hands cold and patient.

Then it was over. She opened her eyes. He was back at the cabinet, putting crystals into a small silk bag. 'Sit up, please.'

She pulled the skirt back up and swung her legs round.

'You need to do this every day. Every single day – do you understand?'

'Yes.'

He handed her the bag and sat down opposite her, his face serious.

'Maryam – it is important you know things. You must know the ways of the spirits. There are spirits here, just as there are spirits in my own country – they are in the woods, in the sky and the clouds, everywhere around you. Some of them are good and some are not. Many of the female spirits are so jealous of a baby that they will wish you harm. If you are fortunate enough to fall pregnant this time, the spirits will know that it was not destined. They will know that there has been intervention and they will want their price.'

'I don't understand.'

'With these oils, this intervention, you are borrowing from the spirit world. Like a bank – you take good from it and you create a vacuum. The spirits will refill that vacuum. They will take from you in ways you will not always see, subtly and secretively. You will put everything down to bad luck, but actually it will be them. Punishing you for having a child they did not intend you to have.'

She held up a hand to her throat, her voice very fragile and wavery. 'But I . . . what should I do?'

'When you conceive your child – and, if you follow my instructions, you will – you must be cautious. Very cautious. Think about the place you live. Are there spirits there? Legends?'

'Um – there's supposed to be an apparition, I think. In the park at the bottom of my garden. The local people talk about it.'

'Then be aware of it. Be-ware. Keep open your own third eye and defend yourself. Here . . . ' He held up a bag of tiny gleaming stones and, leaning over, handed them to her. 'These are moonstone and selenite. Use nazars if you must. But at all costs protect yourself, protect your house.'

She left, clutching her essential oils and crystals in her hemp bag. He was crazy, she thought. Completely crazy. At home she locked the oils in a hexagonal cupboard Rhory had made for her workroom. She hid the key. Rhory mustn't know the insane mission she'd just been on.

Two days later she woke feeling ill. She crawled into the bathroom and immediately felt the need to squat. She sat on the toilet, her knees up, hugging them, shivering. A spasm that seemed to originate in the deepest place imaginable roiled through her, making her eyes water, her chest convulse. Something slid out into the toilet. Feverishly she jumped off the seat and looked in the bowl. A bloodied, solid shape the size of a golfball. Not her period – that had happened a week ago – so what was this clot? She let out a half-sob, and wiped between her legs. There wasn't much blood on the tissue – whatever had been there was now all in the toilet.

'Maryam? You alright?' Rhory on the other side of the door. 'Maryam? What's up?'

'Nothing.'

The oils – perhaps they had tipped her system over some kind of edge. Or had the Swami dislodged something? She stared at the clot for a while, alarmed, watching spirals of red emanate from it and swirl in the water. As she watched, it broke down, resolving into a bowl of watery blood. Shakily she flushed it away, cleaned herself hurriedly, found a pair of knickers and pushed a sanitary towel into them. Outside the bathroom window the trees were bending and whispering in the wind. She went to the window and gazed out at them.

The place you live – are there spirits there?
You take good from it and you create a vacuum . . .
They will want their price.

The winter after she saw the Swami was long and arduous. Eastonbirt was snowed in for two days and the shops ran low on supplies. The Christmas tree on the green in front of the Ragged Stall couldn't be removed so it lay on its side, shedding brown needles. The village made an appearance on the local news, a helicopter shot of queuing traffic and salt-white lakes, men dragging bags of rock salt up the hills on children's sledges. Rhory worked from home and Maryam got order after order for quilt covers and double-backed curtains. The houses around here were draughty and hard to heat, they needed good ways to block out the cold.

At night, when the heating was off and everyone was in bed, she pulled on her alpaca cardigan and went downstairs. There, night after night, she crouched in her workroom in the dark, rubbing oil first into her belly, then into the place on her forehead where she imagined the third eye to rest.

What did the Bakehouse look like from the park? How much of the family could be seen? In the mornings she stood at the back door drinking weak tea. There were no footprints on the snow in the garden. Only those of deer and foxes.

Spring came. And with it a blue cross on a test stick.

She raced down the stairs and buried it deep at the bottom of the wheelie bin, taking alarmed steps back from it, her hands on her thudding heart. It was something dangerous, something conjured by her imagination and meddling where she shouldn't. But a week later there was still no blood and the cross on the second stick was there. Positive. You are positively pregnant, Maryam, she thought. It's happened. For whatever reason, it's happened. Do you feel safe to keep going? Can you call it coincidence?

She stared at her own face in the mirror and thought about pregnancy hormones and madness. The worst kind of madness. She kept rubbing oils into her stomach and it kept growing bigger. She didn't tell Rhory. It was a secret, but she was hiding it for a different reason from before, from when she'd hidden the pregnancy with Arran. This time she'd cheated to have the baby.

Rhory noticed one morning when he was brushing his teeth. He paused, and, in the mirror, watched her get out of the shower, his eyes going down to her stomach.

He lowered the toothbrush. She wrapped a towel around herself guiltily. But he came to her, pulled her towards him, worked his hand worked down between their bodies, palms running across her stomach.

'You're different.'

She squeezed her eyes shut. She mustn't be ashamed. She'd done nothing wrong. It was over a year since she'd seen the Swami – this could have happened naturally.

'Is it what I think?'

'Yes. It is.'

He held her head between his hands and kissed her face all over. Laughing, his teeth minty and white. Crouching down and rubbing his head against her stomach. 'Fucking awesome. I told you it would happen. I told you it would. This is literally the best thing ever.'

Maryam closed her eyes. Her fingers were white bones drooping at her sides. She pictured light around them both, the bedroom, glowing like a Yuletide tableau – she the Virgin Mary, blessed by God. But a coldness too. Just outside the range of the warm glow, in the parkland at the end of the garden, there was darkness. A figure-shaped patch of nothing in the trees.

Alex

Crickets started up in the trees. It was a new sound in the west of England and not something you heard often, except when it got really hot. The lake stretched out in front of us, fat and silent, as if glutted and content with what it had taken from us. The pink of the sky and the cobwebby clouds reflected in it.

Arran raised the catapult and took aim across the water. Changed his mind and scoped his hand horizontally, taking in the silent shoreline, the trees crowding down into the water. He let the stone go, zinging across the lake, out into the dark. Then he lowered the slingshot and looked at me.

'Why did you think I would know about the photo?'

I shrugged. 'I dunno. Was thinking that maybe I'd said something when I was lying on the road. When you were taking care of me.'

'Oh, you said some things, believe me. Like threatening to kill me when I tried to go anywhere near your hand. You were rank.'

I gave a small, embarrassed smile, and gazed across the lake at the crash site. It was a hundred yards to our right, up at the head of Lake Tarquil. In the half-light I could see the reflective arrows on the crash barriers the council had put up. The slipway had been cordoned off with a single bar that could be lifted for fishermen and maintenance crews. The road was quiet – every few minutes a solitary car crossed the causeway.

'Arran, I know we've gone over this a million times, but what do you remember?'

'Do we *have* to do this?'

'Yes.'

He sighed. 'OK, I remember swimming.'

'We all know you swam. I mean, the main thing you did that night was swim.' He'd been the night's hero – he still got fan mail from girls who'd seen his face on the news. Jessop Jarvis and Keith Brown owed their lives to him, though people privately wondered if Keith Brown would have been better off left in the wreckage. He was on life support in Gloucester and his days were ticked off by nurses monitoring bowel movements, bedsore-prevention turns and ventilator infection assessments.

'I remember taking care of you.'

'Did I say anything else? Anything about seeing the bonehead?'

Arran lowered the catapult and stared at me. Goosebumps broke out all over the side of my face where his gaze was focused. We'd grown up together, and if you asked him he'd probably say he was never more at ease than when we were together. True for me too. Except he thought I had my feet on the ground. He thought I was non-neurotic.

'Don't look at me like that. I really thought I saw something – someone. The bonehead, looking at me.'

He grinned. 'Dope. Well trippy.'

Trippy. He was right: it had been a hallucination. So why wouldn't it go away?

'Except what if I *did* see someone? And what if I kind of translated them into something creepy because I was so out of it.'

'Maybe a paramedic,' Arran suggested. 'The place was crawling with them.'

'I mean before they all arrived.'

Arran frowned. 'There wasn't anyone.'

'Really?'

'Really.'

He pulled the piece of paper towards him and studied it with the light of his phone. 'If there was a face here, then who do you think sent it?'

'I don't know. There's nothing in the room downstairs that could look like that, nothing at all. I suppose someone is trying to scare me.'

'Why?'

I gave a long, loud sigh. 'Because I'm back? Christ knows.'

I got up, brushed off my trousers, and pulled the crossbow case towards me. It had stupid Pokémon GO stickers all over it, which kind of destroyed its badass cred. 'OK,' I announced. 'Arran Black, now is your time.' I unclicked the fasteners. 'But it's going to turn us to the dark side. Put us on the wrong side of the law. Funny place to be for two police employees.' I opened the case and showed it to him. 'A crossbow. Totally illegal to use, especially if we use proper bolts. But I don't know . . . ' I gazed out across the lake. 'I think it could be just the thing to get our miserable little pebbles to the other side. What do you think?'

Arran followed my gaze. He was immediately sucked in. 'OK, let's do it.'

We pulled the crossbow out of the case. It was cheap and unreliable – he knew that from the weight – but he was enthusiastic enough not to pick holes and we decided to try it without the pebbles lashed to the target bolts – just to get an idea of how powerful it was. Arran took first shot, standing legs astride, his head raised nobly. 'Make sure you remember how I looked today, firing the last flaming arrow that brought down a civilisation.'

'Stop showing off.' I held up my phone, videoing him. 'Get on with it.'

He clicked off the safety and let the bowstring go. It made a pathetic, plasticky twang, but, to give the crossbow credit, the bolt launched high and long – sped with a weird thwacking noise, low over the lake, its shadow racing across the water surface. I got to my feet to watch it, slightly awed. It was going far, much further than the catapult had managed.

'Dope.' Arran was smiling. 'Fucking check it out. It made the other side.'

He was right. It hadn't landed in the water. There had been no splash and no tinkle of water – it had gone into the brush on the far shore.

I grabbed the crossbow from him and slotted the target bolt into the groove, adjusting it so the fletching was lined up. 'I'm going further.'

I hoisted the rickety plastic thing on my shoulder, squinted – I was left-eye dominant according to the police school at Hendon – and let the bolt fly. It soared, going to the left of Arran's shot, but still way, way over the lake. The sound rang out across the water and a cloud of birds rose from the forest where it landed.

I lowered the crossbow and we both stood in silence, staring in awe at the distance we'd covered.

'That was so fucking illegal,' I breathed.

'Swe-eeet.' He clapped my arm. 'Come on – let's see who got furthest.'

Maryam

Rhory hadn't been able to contain his excitement at the pregnancy. Every one of his clients knew about it within days. Lois and Fenton brought round congratulations cards, and even the woman in the cake shop knew. Poor Arran was nineteen and due to start college in September. It was too horrible to think of his parents making babies. Too gross. Whenever the new baby was mentioned he'd sigh and leave the room.

Maybe Rhory took pity on him, forgotten in the excitement, or maybe it was just his own excitement brimming over, but one day he arrived home with a puppy.

'A puppy?'

'The baby will love it. Here.' He set the straggly creature down on the lawn. It shook itself, then sat down and studiously licked its forelegs. 'Meet Tumble.'

Tumble turned out to be a scruffy but obedient little soul. His paws were so big they seemed to trip him up at every step and his clumsy, bounding run made his ears fly out either side of his head like aircraft wings. Maryam was fiercely protective of him. He had a little cage that he sat in on her business trips. He was as quiet as a mouse when she went into the mansions to measure and quote, sift through sample books. He greeted her on her return with three excited turns inside the cage.

In the evenings of her second trimester, after meals when she couldn't sit down for the way the baby and the food were starting to fight for space in her ribcage, Maryam took Tumble for walks. Sometimes they'd stay in the garden or wander along the driveway; other times she took him into the parkland, letting him run after smells and rustles in the undergrowth. She would examine the trees, looking up at the patterns their branches made, always remembering what the Swami had said. She'd like to go back to him and ask him what he meant about spirits taking something back, but she didn't. It meant more money and more time, and shouldn't she be conserving both of those?

One night after the walk, at about six months into the pregnancy, she was leaning over to snap on Tumble's lead when something in the trees they'd just walked through shifted. She froze, bent over, hands on the collar.

It had been a flash of something white or cream in the trees. Human-shaped. She'd caught it just out of the corner of her eye. There had been eyes. She was sure.

She clipped the lead on, and slowly raised her chin.

The woods were silent and very dark. The land sloped down from the back garden and the light from the moon barely reached through the foliage.

'Hello?' she whispered. 'Hello?'

Silence. Tumble lowered his chin and thrust himself forward on his front legs, his backside up. On high alert.

'It's alright,' she told him, pressing her hands on to his haunches. 'Don't worry.'

She straightened, her heart thudding loudly. The extra surge of blood stimulated the baby – it began to roll and turn under her ribs. The tree trunks were hazy, yellow-grey, the space between them purple. What had she seen?

She glanced back at the house. Rhory and Arran were in the living room, watching rugby on catch-up. She whipped her head back in time to see something move. A human shape, the slippery impression of a white dress, yellowish. Black eye sockets, a sealed mouth. Then stillness.

At her shins Tumble growled, straining at the lead.

She led him a few steps down to the edge of the lawn, where the rough ground of the park began. Holding the lead tight, she leaned forward, trying to extend her body into the trees without actually setting foot in their shrouded realm. A path led through the forest about ten yards down and often hikers would walk along it. You'd see them in the summer months, earnest and dressed in North Face kit, talking about contour lines and rest stops. In this light the path was only visible because of the lack of vegetation surrounding it, a vague blurred absence of dark.

If the figure had been there earlier, it wasn't any more.

She stretched her ears into the darkened trees, trying to detect a breath or footfall. But all she could hear was birdsong, the forest's sleepy preparation for night.

Tumble had stopped growling. He was looking up at her, waiting for instructions. She closed her eyes and took several long breaths. 'Nothing happened, Tumble. Nothing. Everything's OK.'

'Can I ask you something really random? Really out there?'

It was late afternoon in autumn, a week after she'd seen the apparition in the woods. Fenton and Rhory were at the pub, Arran was out with friends, Sophie May was at the cinema and Lois and Maryam were in the garden, wrapped in blankets, drinking hot chocolate from big mugs. Tumble was getting bigger every day; now he was almost as tall as her knees. He was lying on his side in the grass, thoughtfully chewing the laces of Maryam's leather shoes.

Her stomach too. That was growing solid and round. Less than three months to go.

'Go on, then,' Lois said. 'Sounds interesting.'

'Don't laugh. But . . . do you believe in ghosts?'

Lois gave her a sideways look, half-smiling as if she wasn't sure if this was a joke or not. 'What? Like dead people?'

'Or . . . entities. Beings. Presences.'

'I like a good ghost story. Fenton took me to see *The Woman in Black* – I didn't sleep for weeks. And *Blair Witch*? Eww – no, thanks. Too much for the heart.'

Maryam bent over, cautiously, trying not to squash the baby, and brushed at the strap on her shoe where Tumble had left a rime of saliva. It was that time of year when the trees had gone crisp and brown as if burned by the departed sun. Already the dead leaves were piling on the ground; in the mornings when they let Tumble out he'd run in there to chase foxes and badgers, and the only way to keep track of him was to listen to the crunch and scatter of dry leaves.

What did a spirit look like? Mothy, she thought, with a tail that slipped into nothing and got caught in the branches.

'Umm . . . ' She rubbed her nose, not knowing where to start. 'Rhory told me once that the park was haunted.' She jerked her chin in the direction of the trees. 'He said there's a story about a woman out there.'

'Yes, Sophie May told me that too. The ghost of a prostitute. Is that what you heard?'

'Something like that.'

'The kids said she was a gypsy and a prostitute and she took one of her clients into the park and he killed her – dumped her body.' Lois was watching the trees now, her face in profile as if the mention had got her thinking how close the woods were. 'No one knows where, but there's more to the rumour.'

The skin on Maryam's arms pricked up into little bumps. She pulled the blanket tighter around her. 'What else?'

'Nasty things about how he went back to the body. Even though her head had decomposed, he continued to . . . er . . . *do* things to her, if you get my meaning.' Lois rolled her shoulders in a delicious shiver. 'It must be great living this close to the park – I'm jealous. There's something exciting about being this close to nature.'

Maryam sipped her hot chocolate. Her eyes were pricking with concentration. A mummified woman. A bone face. A spectre. Out there in the trees?

Abruptly she put her mug down and gathered Tumble up on to her lap, holding him tight, crushing him into her bulging stomach. 'Shall we go inside now? I'm getting cold.'

Alex

Arran and I went round to the far side of the lake to search for our bolts, but it took ages. It was getting late and the going was difficult. Lots of dried-out creepers at waist-height, clinging to our clothing. It wasn't bad for me, but for Arran in his smart suit it was a pain in the butt. Eventually we came to the place the bolts had fallen. I found mine easily – the dart was luminescent pink and had landed in a tangle of ivy on the side of a fallen tree trunk. Arran's was nowhere to be seen.

'Do you know where we are?' Arran stood a few feet away, his back to the lake, his hands dug into the small of his spine, looking inward at the tangle of trees. 'I've never been here before.'

I fitted the dart back into the foam casing of the crossbow case and stepped over a snarl of brambles to stand next to him. The woods were dark and unfamiliar. Strange to think that in all the years we'd lived and grown up in Eastonbirt I'd never crossed over on to this side of the park. It was so abandoned and overgrown. Impassable. 'What do you think?'

'I dunno. Maybe the arboretum? See that tree there? The big one – looks like it's got wings.'

I did. It was tall and spreading and though I didn't truly understand trees, in spite of having grown up here, I could nonetheless tell it was different from the others. As if it was not accidentally there but planned.

'What is it?'

'I think it's a yew. And don't push me on that – but we did a module on poisoning and yew berries are toxic. Also juniper.'

He made his way through the bramble until he reached the tree. 'Look at it. It's huge.' He took a branch in his hand and rubbed the leaves between his fingers, then sniffed them. 'I don't think it's supposed to grow here. It must be here for a reason.'

There were no paths around us – no way to leave or move forward. The arboretum had been forgotten and was buried deep in the landscape like the castle in *Sleeping Beauty*, the vines and the thorns crawling up around it.

'Do you think we can get further?'

He stood on tiptoes and peered into the morass of bindweed and bramble. 'Not a hope. Most of the trees are probably dead anyway.'

We continued along the shoreline until we happened upon Arran's target bolt, face-down in a nettle patch. He retrieved it cautiously, avoiding the nettles. Then we stood for a while and marvelled at the lake. It was inky dark now. The water was still and glassy.

But this wasn't the old days. We both had jobs to do and needed to sleep. We weren't going to fire the crossbow again, and we weren't going to slog all the way back to the other side of the lake. There was no more conversation. I hoisted up the crossbow case and we began to walk wearily back to the road that led to the footpath.

'You won't believe it,' I said as we mooched along, kicking stones as we went, 'but Traffic offered me a placement. Just like that. I didn't even apply for it.'

Arran slowed; he turned and fixed me with his eyes.

'What?' I said. 'What's the look?'

'Just a sad realisation that nothing changes.'

I cocked my head on one side, not immediately getting his meaning. 'I'm sorry?'

'My mate at Gloucestershire has been after that placement for years . . . no disrespect but he's way more qualified.'

I stared at Arran. And then I got it. A thump in the chest. 'Fuck's sake. They chose me because I'm a woman.'

'Would be my guess. That, and you've come back from London all sexy 'cos you've had two years in the Met and they probably can't believe their luck and don't know why you came back, which is pretty much a mystery to me too – so they're thinking "overqualified, overexposed, overambitious. Female. She's gotta be kept sweet".'

I walked on another twenty steps, absorbing this. 'I can't believe it.'

'I wouldn't knock it.'

'Well, I am knocking it. It's shit.' Suddenly it all felt like a treachery.

A while later, we reached the road, the place where the footpaths divided. 'OK,' I said, 'I'm going home.'

'See you next time.' Arran held up his fist to bump mine, his customary way of saying goodbye. We never set a date, or made arrangements to meet again; we just said 'see you' and trusted the rest to fate.

'Yeah, see you next time.'

He turned and wandered off in the direction of the Bakehouse. It was nearly ten p.m. but the sky was still pale pink, like the inside of a mouth. I watched him go, casually loafing his way back up the path to the Bakehouse, arms swinging a little, pulling leaves off the branches as he went.

Kryptonite would never quite sum it up. Kryptonite was shiny, intergalactic and emitted a glow. My thing for Arran was more of a . . . toad, a squat, dark thing that sat just out of reach in the side of my mind. I'd learned to pretend it wasn't there, and that seemed to work. Most of the time.

Maryam

Once it started it was quick – all within weeks. An avalanche.

Maryam's dad fell down the steps in the Monmouth pub, broke four bones and punctured a lung. He lasted four days in hospital before he died. 'Terrible debts,' her mother said at the funeral, crying into a lipstick-smeared hanky. 'How am I going to live with it? I'll have to be a bankrupt. None of your sisters making a penny – all out on the dole. What am I going to do?'

Maryam and Rhory applied for a second mortgage to pay the debts, but when the surveyor came he found dry rot in the attic. 'You're looking at nine, ten thousand pounds? It's probably pre-existing so the insurance won't cover it. The best you can do is sue the original surveyors. Have you got a copy of your survey . . .? Phew, forty years ago? That long?'

And all the redecoration too. That would be thousands. Rhory opened a bottle of wine at two p.m. He filled the glass and drank it all in one go. His face was pale, his ears red. Stunned, Maryam poured herself a glass – the first in the entire pregnancy. She carried it into her workroom and stood at the window, scanning the trees.

'Spirit, spirit,' she muttered. 'Is this you taking your price?'

She hung charms around the Bakehouse, things no one would recognise as symbolic – a Hand of Fatima here, a nazar there, an eight-sided mirror in the bathroom. On the legs of the beds she tied red wool. A dreamcatcher in the window of the baby's room. No one in the family need know how often she sat staring at the woods, imagining a dead prostitute. A body missing in the woods. Mummified, the head eaten back to the bone.

There was no information about the prostitute online, nothing on Reddit, no entries in 'Gloucestershire's most haunted' or on Nextdoor. Maryam got up the courage to drop it into conversation with clients who knew Eastonbirt. She mentioned it laughingly, as if all she wanted was a thrilling nugget of gossip. People either laughed, told her she wasn't to believe the nonsense children talked, or they'd sidle up closer and whisper about the time their uncle John saw her in the wood. *Floating half a foot above the lake, she was. White dress. Bone face. Eaten away by the rats is what my uncle said.*

After she went missing there were more deaths in the woods. Did you hear about them? Young men it was, wandering off the path, falling down cliffs. You know what she was doing, don't you? She was luring them back to the gully where her body was. Wanted them to find her. Give her a proper burial.

She was a gypsy. A Roma. No one cared much – they said it was good riddance – a Roma prostitute? Not the sort of person who's wanted round here. No wonder they didn't search for her body too hard.

It was 1900 when she died.

She went missing in 1947 just after the war.

Oh, it wasn't all that long ago – I remember it. In the '80s, I think.

You know what he did to her body after, don't you? And her face all gone but he still went ahead anyway. Must be a man thing.

The baby was a girl, said the hospital, and she had a habit of sucking her thumb for the scans. The ultrasound operators laughed and said she was going to be an actress – *proper little poser, loves the camera.* She got hiccups in the womb, making Maryam's tummy jump like a live frog. She pointed it out in the NCT pre-natal class and let everyone put their hands on her belly to feel the little spasms. After the thirty-week class she and Rhory were so caught up in discussing transitions and birth plans that neither of them gave it much thought that Arran wasn't back when they got home. He was a grown man, out at a reunion party. There were no clock-watchers for him any more.

Rhory let Tumble out for a pee and Maryam served up the cassoulet that had been sitting on the Aga all night. Duck breast, white beans, succulent chunks of celery in the white bowls. They ate in easy silence, laughing when Tumble came bowling back into the house, tail wagging, mouth open.

The edges of the valley were sharp, so although the crash site was close they didn't hear the sounds from the lake. No screech of brakes or long yawing creak as the coach went down. The first they knew was Rhory's phone ringing, lying face-up on the table among the debris of the dinner, the screen flashing white and alarmed.

It was quicker to the causeway on foot than by road. They raced through the trees, Maryam going as fast as she dared, keeping her palms on the tree trunks, terrified she'd fall on her stomach. Sirens wailed mournfully across the park and the blue lights were visible through the trees. Up ahead of her Rhory was bellowing, 'Arran! Arran!'

The scene when they burst out on to the road was from a nightmare. Car headlights, queuing from both directions, engines running, brought to a standstill by the cop cars and ambulances, still arriving and weaving their way between the traffic. Screaming, someone shouting orders and in the distance the clack-clack of helicopter rotors. The coach was upside down, unbelievably deep in the water, only recognisable from the light of the passenger compartment, surreally still shining though it was submerged. It showed eerily green through the lake water, like a neglected aquarium.

There was a fish-like smell of electrical short circuits and burning rubber in the air. In Maryam's belly the baby did a long, nauseating somersault.

'There he is!' Rhory said. 'He's there.'

A drenched group of teenagers stood clotted together in a miserable huddle on the verge, their faces pale and streaked in the blue flashing lights. None of them could take their eyes off the coach. The girls were crying. Others were crouched over prostrate forms on the tarmac.

Arran was inside the trees on the other side of the road, kneeling next to a girl who lay in a ball. He was too absorbed in talking to her to hear his parents.

'Arran! *Arran!*'

Maryam and Rhory began to run, pushing their way past bewildered officers and dazed teenagers. He glanced up at them, face blank, and went straight back to the girl on the ground as if he hadn't recognised or registered his own parents. The girl was Alex Mullins. Her eyes were half-closed, her mouth was blue with cold, her clothing was torn and saturated. Her left hand had been reworked into an unrecognisable shape.

Other parents were arriving now, some pushing forward and screaming, running in frantic zigzags from group to group. Onlookers were standing at the edges of the police cordon, taking photographs. When the paramedics came for Alex, at last Arran straightened. He turned woodenly to his parents, head down, hair dripping, shaking.

'Come on, son.' Rhory threw his jacket around Arran's shoulders. 'Come on. Let's get you out of here.'

The ambulance crews were overworked. Arran was unhurt so he sat in a police car to get warm, between his parents on the back seat, his head on Maryam's shoulder, the lake water soaking into her sweater. He smelt of algae and beer. A whiff of burnt rubber in his hair.

He said nothing in answer to their questions. Was he hurt? Who else had been on the coach? And how many were alive? Rhory was exchanging frantic texts with Fenton, biting his lip and staring into the flashing blue lights. 'Sophie May?' Maryam asked Arran quietly, and in reply he dug his face further into her neck. She put a hand on the side of his head and pulled him to her. They fell silent and just sat – waiting.

She couldn't watch Fenton and Lois arrive, over at the far cordon. She couldn't watch the police speaking to them, drawing them to one side. Then the bodies coming out. The slick of wet hair splayed out on the road in the blue lights. Maryam turned her face to the darkened window and stared into the trees. It took a moment for her eyes to adjust but when she did she saw, higher up the valley, someone in the trees watching the crash scene. A slight figure in white, light coming off her in odd angles that made her appear to be in a tree, not at ground level.

Maryam's throat clenched. A small, shocked noise came out. She reached blindly for the door handle. But in that moment the figure was gone. Startled, like a deer, it slipped silently down from the branch. Lowered its face and slid away into the shadows, so unnaturally smooth it could have been gliding on ice.

That November day two and a half years ago, a giant hand had squeezed Eastonbirt as hard as possible, the village's young oozing out between the knuckles. Seven dead, one with life-altering injuries, one on permanent life support. Another with blades for legs. Victoria Mullins founded the Dandelion charity for those injured in this and other accidents, and everyone in the community pitched in. Each shop had a collection tin, with images of the teenagers in the windows. Huge baskets of flowers appeared at the edge of the lake, slowly rotting to be replaced by more and more. When the police tents had gone, the press packs and gawkers had dissipated and the bus had been lifted out of the water, the inquests began. Maryam made a maternity dress in black, putting in clever darts that she could adjust. With each session she let the seams out a fraction to accommodate the baby.

She would not allow the park spirit to believe it had destroyed her dignity.

Sophie May was dead. Trapped in the wreckage in spite of Arran's attempts. Lois was beyond inconsolable. She'd become something Maryam didn't recognise. If you visited, she and Fenton were granite statues, sitting in their huge living room at the dining table, not speaking, their hands folded formally, two untouched glasses of red wine on the table. Both were always immaculately dressed – Fenton in his accountant's suit and Lois in a skirt, floral blouse, nude tights, proper court shoes and her pastel-coloured scarf. Behind them, mounted above the fireplace, was a blown-up picture of Sophie May in a black dress at a charity ball. Candles burned at its base day and night.

Her funeral was the biggest the village had seen. Lois conjured a preacher from London who was like something risen from an Easter triptych; he stood with his arms open, his palms facing the heavens, head back. Sophie May's class-mates all wore white – that was the request posted on her Facebook memorial page – and the white ash coffin had an artist's impression of Sophie May on both ends. Lois and Fenton cried soberly, as if they didn't have the energy to stop the tears coming out. They didn't hold hands or touch for the entire service.

One day Maryam went into Lois's kitchen to get a glass of water and saw that the door to the utility room was open. This was the place she kept her huge freezers full of ice cream and the massive top-loading washing machine that would take a fifteen-kilo load. Maryam tiptoed to the door and poked her head around it. Sophie May's clothes were hanging out to dry – jeans, T-shirts, skirts, knickers and bras. A second pile sat on the ironing board.

'She was at the top of the set in all her arts subjects,' Lois explained with an apologetic smile. 'She was taking a year off to see the world – we'd already taken her to Italy – but Cardiff had made her an offer, you know. All those children at school and only she got the offer to Cardiff. And it wasn't favouritism because of her looks – they offered her the place even before she sent the photograph.'

The house was always clean, but a smell developed in the kitchen. Maryam couldn't place it. Was it the smell of food going off, or just the smell of defeat? Despair? There wouldn't be another child for Lois. She was forty-nine now. No fertility doctor could beat those odds.

Rhory played his part by taking Fenton out to the pub three times a week. Lois had lost interest in her job and Maryam, recalling how encouraging her friend had been all those years ago about starting a business, tried to divert Lois, taking her out of the big house and over to the Bakehouse as often as possible, where she mixed up exotic cocktails, mojitos and daiquiris. Lois always brought with her a photograph album of Sophie May – the memories she'd been putting together alone at her table in the big house. A page for each week of her life: notes from teachers; first birthday cards; a lock of hair tied with a ribbon. Already she'd filled six volumes.

The dead Roma spirit hadn't taken Arran in the crash, but it had taken Sophie May. And it had taken Maryam's father. Would that be all she took in return for the baby? Was that the end of her harvest?

And, if not, was there anything Maryam could do to change it?

Alex

The next morning I sat groggily at the breakfast bar in my navy trousers and polo shirt, a huge cup of coffee from Mum's posh cappuccino-maker in front of me. I flicked idly through the Facebook and Twitter feeds on my phone (I'd given up Snapchat when I went to London; it had suddenly seemed so childish) while Mum clipped around the kitchen in her high heels, putting the dishwasher on, giving the occasional surface a last-minute shine and sparkle. I could feel her thoughts – *sit up, stop slouching, put on some make-up, grow out your hair* – but she managed to keep them to herself, which for Mum was a major achievement. A change from her comments when I was a teenager dressing in combats and fleeces. *On a positive note, at least, dressing like a lesbian provides an interesting conversation. I mean, the laughs you must have when you reveal you're actually heterosexual.*

'Where are you going?' I asked out of politeness more than genuine curiosity. 'You look nice.'

'Thank you.' She crossed from the kitchen into the living area and checked over her appearance in the mirror over the fireplace. An oyster-grey frock coat and pearls, every inch the lady who sat on numerous charity committees. 'I'm meeting Lois Hansel to discuss the memorial bench.' She stopped at the huge sliding windows. 'Where is he? Bamber?'

She'd never wanted a pet, she didn't like the mess and the hair, but I'd pestered and pestered. I'd named him Bamber after a song I loved from Monty Python which had the name

'Bamber Gascoigne' in it; Mum kept showing me pictures of a television presenter from forty years ago, and saying, *This, this is Bamber Gascoigne. Do you really want a dog named after him?* When I went off to London to join the Met, Mum spent the first year complaining about having to walk him, then slowly her complaints turned into little stories about how Bamber had done such and such in the park today, and how he was so well-behaved compared to other dogs – some of which hadn't been neutered and would hump everything in sight whereas Bamber never so much as licked his genitals in public. Then how he liked chicken more than liver, how he carried Hat so lovingly, and how he adored having his ears scratched. One day, about ten days into my second year in Hammersmith, it had dawned on me that he wasn't really my dog any more. He'd morphed into Mum's dog.

'He should be back by now. It's been over an hour.'

We stood on the deck and watched the silent trees. Some with ivy winding up them, some soft and drooping.

'I'm sure he's fine. Chasing the foxes.'

'No.' An edge of panic crept into Mum's voice. 'No – it's too long.' She looked at her watch. 'Why wasn't I paying attention? It's an hour and ten minutes. The Blacks' dog is missing somewhere out there. He ran away just like this.'

'Easy solution here, Mum. We walk Bamber on a lead, instead of letting him run wild.'

She scrutinised the trees. 'He's never done this before.'

'Mum, he has! This isn't the first time, it isn't even the second; it's probably the hundredth, or two hundredth. He likes this time of day.'

'No. Something's wrong.'

I said nothing. Pretty much every morning we had this charade – Mum panicking because Bamber wasn't back. And always he came back and always she continued to let him run into the trees. As if to prove my point, at that very moment, pounding out of the woods, he appeared, his tongue lolling out happily. He cantered up the steps to the deck.

'You bad boy,' Mum said delightedly, bending over and patting her calves to get him to come to her. 'You naughty boy – got Mummy worried.'

'See?' I eyed him as he rolled on his back, destroying the rope chew toy he loved. He was filthy from his romp in the wood, getting it all over Mum's tights. 'What did I say? He always comes back.'

She brushed her ankles. 'Thank you. Anyway – it appears your dog is in need of some grooming.'

'My dog? He's your dog when he's clean and well-behaved and my dog when he's running away or filthy. How does that work?'

She was amused, but hid it well – the tiniest hint of a smile. Mum and I would never openly say it, but we loved each other.

I sighed and waved my hand at her. 'OK, OK, you go. I'll deal with it.'

When she'd gone, zipping away in her little white Audi TT, with the roof down, I whiled away a few more minutes, drinking coffee, eating an almond croissant Mum had warmed in the oven. Bamber bounded around the garden killing his rope chew and I caught up on things on my phone. I'd only been back in the area for four weeks but already I'd had numerous invites to go out and hang. Maybe Arran and my sergeant had been right – maybe I had been 'rolled in London stardust' – because I didn't remember ever being that popular before.

What had Arran said about my sergeant? *They don't know why you came back.* The girls in the estate agents had said it too: *Why have you come back?* Why? Good question.

I scrolled down the list of friends. Most were from London, but lots were from here, and I focused on the group who had been on the bus that day. There had been fourteen of us, including Michaela's dad, Mike, who'd been driving. Only seven of us survived: four unharmed or with relatively minor injuries – me, Michaela, Arran and Ozone Winters – and three others with major injuries: Keith who was on life support, Jarvis Jessop, who'd had his lower legs amputated, and Minnie Frobisher, who hadn't been so lucky and was in a wheelchair. Of the seven dead, the only active memorialised page was Sophie May Hansel's, which was maintained by her parents and showed Sophie May in full-on seductive pose – a black mini skirt and orange T-shirt, her long straw-coloured hair hanging over her shoulder.

Minnie's page had been updated only yesterday with a post of a new ironic *Hello Kitty* T-shirt and a meme of Jessica Lange smoking, the words *Boo hoo hoo hoo* under her face. Jessop's page showed him wearing shorts, grinning delightedly at the new paint job on his blades. Apart from his new legs, the rest of his posts revolved around his life at university in Dublin; he had finally returned to his course, or rather started it over again, almost a year after the accident. On Ozone's page the activity was less intense. The profile pic still showed him at about seventeen, along with his sister, cuddling their puppy.

Chaos. The dog's name popped into my head. The most hysterical piece of bad naming, because Chaos was in fact the mildest-mannered Labrador imaginable. But then, I'd named my dog after a random ageing TV quiz host, so who was I to talk?

I sent Ozone a message, and then sent one to Minnie Frobisher, who still lived in the area. Minnie's acceptance pinged straight back. God, I was a shit not to have kept up with these people – really, who did I think I was, getting all London on them and ignoring them?

Back in town. I'm a Bluelivesmatter now (you probs heard?) but I haven't grown an extra head and it'd be dope to catch up mebbe?

Bish, came the reply. *Name the place and time!*

What r ur days like?

I'm @ the Sun College in the day, home w/OAP parents after. 17 Playford Av, Glos. PS pls don't judge, cuz my wheels aren't goals, rn. Kk?

Wot no bling?

Soz what can I say I'm the scrapes.

I'll live w/it.

I made a note in my diary of the address and did a quick Facebook surf to see if I could remember Minnie's sister's name, just so I had something warm to say when we met. Ozone hadn't responded – I got the feeling he wouldn't – so eventually I rinsed out the cup and swapped my work boots for flip-flops, tied one of Mum's Cath Kidston aprons over my work kit and went into the garden, where the sun was just cresting the treeline, the grass already crunchy-hot underfoot.

Bamber was still tearing apart the chew toy, in a frenzy of circles and growls. He was the funniest of dogs. Hat was immaculate and revered, but when it came to a random dog chew he could destroy it in nanoseconds. And splatter the gooey remnants throughout his coat. He also loved rolling in the fox shit that could always be found just inside the trees at the end of the garden.

'The state of you.' I planted my hands on my hips, and glared balefully at him. 'Yes.' I pointed at the apron. 'Because it's going to get messy. Because you're a complete pain in the butt. Get it?'

He dropped the toy and looked me, tongue out, tail wagging ferociously. He half-knew he was in trouble, also half-knew how biased I was. I held up a warning finger. 'It's the hose for you. No looks.'

Bamber did a few excited victory laps of the garden while I unwound the garden hose. The hose, in sunny weather, was more of a treat than a punishment, and when I turned on the water he squatted down on his haunches, ready to attack the stream. I let him duck in and out of it for a while, then I had to get mean.

'Now sit down.' I grabbed his collar and brought him down to a sit. 'Just behave yourself.'

He obliged and sat on his haunches, occasionally snapping his head round to nip at the water, while I squirted a handful of dog shampoo and got to work lathering.

The birds were singing and chattering in the trees. From here I could see about a hundred yards into the parkland, before it got too obscured by greenery. Different in the winter when the trees were grey scarecrows. Such an easy place to imagine as haunted. When you're half-conscious it's common to hallucinate things. Just not so easy to get rid of the images later.

Soon the lawn was waterlogged, islands of soapy foam floating everywhere. I hosed him down. 'You look like a water rat,' I told him. 'A complete vole, an apology of an animal. Let's get those ears sorted.'

I found a nugget of something in the fur on his back that didn't want to shift. A stick or something had got caught and the water alone wouldn't rinse it out. 'Bamber, seriously, what have you been doing to yourself?'

I dragged him over to a dry piece of grass and sat down with my knees apart, legs crossed like a Buddha, pulling him closer. He was still wet but, with that miraculous animal's way of being able to dry off in about five seconds, by the time I'd got him seated and stopped his squirming his fur was already springing up in tufts. I began to tease away at the knot in his coat. 'What is this, you tart? What the hell have you picked up now?'

It seemed to be a tiny plait in his fur – tied off at the end with a very slim scrap of braid. I unplaited it, pulled the ribbon out and examined it. Mum's idea of cuteness. That or the groomers'.

'Ugh – that's slightly gay, Bamber, if you don't mind me saying.' I rinsed it off and chucked the ribbon into the bushes then continued to massage out the clump of fur. He nuzzled his face against my calves, leaving plenty of dog hairs I'd be picking off later, then settled on his side and lowered his face to rest on my calves. I got his point. It was shaping up to be a dry, warm day, with no clouds in the sky. Anyone in London would have given a kidney to be here today, with all the trees and the smells of grass, and the sounds of birds.

I know now that I should have been more grateful to have been me, that day, in the sun, with Bamber.

Maryam

Maryam kept her secret. Held it reluctantly, hanging off her as heavy as the baby weight. Rhory must never know about it, however unhinged she became. Whatever happened, she would never tell him the truth about how their lives were being bartered and traded by the spirit world. About the crash; Sophie May's death; Dad; the debts and the problems with the roof – about how she'd brought it upon them, for the sake of the baby.

It turned out not to be the end of the spirit's harvest. The spirit, perverse and cruel, had more in store.

Rhory lost his biggest client, a man in Birdlip who'd commissioned an entertainment space, a job that was meant to fill the year and could be worth over forty thousand pounds. In moments it went from a dead certainty to a financial disaster. No more entertainment space, no more holidays in Morocco for the Blacks, no more cuts of lamb from the organic butcher. She stopped buying IAMS for Tumble and switched to Aldi own-brand.

When her waters broke it all happened fast. Minty arrived fully awake and blinking, lots of hair, and hands that gripped like pincers. She had been so easy and determined that the doctors shrugged and said she could go straight home as far as they were concerned. So she was wrapped up and taken back to the Bakehouse to meet her brother and her dog.

Welcome to the world, Araminta Black, Minty for short. Black-haired and as tauntingly beautiful as her dad and older brother. A tiny version of Arran, with a smaller nose and puffier lips, she thrived, doubling her weight in weeks. Her cry was like a lamb's, a long and protracted 'ah ah ah ah' sound that made Arran laugh and Tumble flatten his ears guiltily, as if he was somehow responsible for her distress. Maryam lay on the bed with her and stared, running her fingers over her brow, round her hairline. Checking she was properly human and had no goat genes, nothing to mark her out as bewitched or fey.

There was no celebration; times were lean. Maryam's sisters drove up for the day and remarked that she didn't seem happy. Everything was OK, she told them. She was tired, that was all. 'Give my love to Mum.'

They kissed the baby goodbye and promised they'd send love to Mum and would ask her to visit the new baby. It would be a tonic for her after losing Dad. And hadn't they tried to get her to come and see Maryam this time, but failed?

She'd never know for sure if the message got back, because the next thing the spirits took was her mother. Before she'd even seen Minty.

Suicide. Not tidy – she was found half-alive and taken unconscious to hospital, where she took longer to die than her husband, sepsis crawling along her arms in red spiders. Maryam breastfed Minty next to the bed while the nurse changed her mother's soiled sheets. Maryam dragged out the black cotton funeral dress and nipped it in to fit her shrinking post-baby waist. Poor Minty, still a baby, wearing navy instead of pink. People around her crying instead of smiling.

Rhory changed. He seemed angry with everything. He shouted at Tumble and even snapped at Minty. One night he took the car without telling anyone where he was going and came back with the smell of hashish on his clothes. Maryam held Minty at her breast and pretended to be feeding her even when she wasn't. It was her excuse not to face the things that were happening. The way their family was unstitching itself.

April evolved fussy and rainy. A tile came off the roof and the rain soaked all the replaced timbers. A damp patch appeared in the ceiling above Minty's cot, shaped like a heart. Maryam moved the cot to the other corner of the room

Lois had lost interest in her job since Sophie May had died. Instead she and Maryam volunteered their time to the Dandelion charity. Weekly they'd visit Victoria Mullins in the big glass and aluminium house on the other side of the village for meetings with the other trustees. The house was so different from the Bakehouse – so precise, honed and light-filled. Only the garden was similar, a lush green striped lawn that led down to the edge of the park. Victoria Mullins woke every day to the same vista of trees, the same teeming undercurrent of wildlife and insects as Maryam. Did she ever see spirits in the trees? Maryam wondered. There was a dog, Bamber, who sat under the table during the meetings, a straw hat next to him. She watched him as he moved around the house and saw he was calm, not anxious about the park.

The charity's first project was to co-fund with the council the building of a play park for special needs children. It was on the escarpment overlooking Lake Tarquil, not far from the crash site – part civic area, part memorial, Maryam thought. She and Lois volunteered to stuff envelopes with leaflets asking for donations and reminding people to visit the park.

They did it over dinner at the Bakehouse, one spring evening. Lois brought over two crates full of envelopes, a bottle of wine and a velour teddy bear for Minty, who was four months old.

'I remember this stage so well.' She stood next to Minty's cot. 'Look at that little face. She's sleeping exactly the way Sophie May did at that age. Arms above her head.'

'She's a good sleeper. Same as Arran.'

'Here, little Minty. A present.' She put the teddy next to Minty's face, adjusted it, then gave a long sigh and leaned back, folding her arms and shaking her head. 'You are so lucky, Maryam. So lucky. I'd give the world to be in your shoes.'

Maryam gave a pallid smile and mumbled, 'I know, I know.'

She was guilty of tainted reproduction. A beautiful sweet child, gained dishonestly. Yet she was expected to be happy.

They carried the crates of leaflets and letters into the garden. Maryam had made a rose and emerald embroidered tablecloth, which was spread out on the table under the apple tree. On it were quiches with chives, frittata made from eggs laid by the neighbours' hens, a jug of mint julep and long gruyère cheese sticks to soak up the alcohol. Tumble, now an adolescent, was lying drowsily next to the table, all four legs stretched out. Long as an otter.

The two women filled plates and glasses and set to stuffing envelopes. Lois's bare arms in the short-sleeved blouse were thick and freckled. She kept her pink tongue wedged between her teeth in concentration. The greying roots of her hair had been allowed to grow in since Sophie May had died.

She looked up and caught Maryam looking at her. She opened her mouth to speak, then changed her mind and lowered the envelope she was sealing. 'OK. What's going on?'

'I'm sorry?'

'What's going on? You look terrible. There's something you're not saying.'

'I'm fine. Everything's fine.' She took a huge slug of mint julep, put the glass down and continued folding leaflets, her hands shaking.

Lois didn't go back to work. She just stared at Maryam, challengingly, until the colour rose in her face and she had to stop what she was doing.

'Please, please don't look at me like that.'

'Then tell me.'

Maryam rubbed her arms nervously, biting her lip. 'Promise you won't tell Fenton?'

'Of course. Not in a million years.'

'OK, OK.'

How was she to explain this? This black magic, this beautiful child whose entry into the world had been bought by Maryam from the spirits and was being paid for in blood? The night of the crash, inside the police car, eyes hazed with tears, blue lights flashing. Arran soaking his way into her sweater and, in the woods where no one else would notice, a blurred human figure with dark eyes watching them all in silence. The feeling that they were being watched. And later, the flicker of a face in the woods that day with Tumble. Only thirty yards away from where they sat now.

She refilled their glasses and placed hers neatly in front of her. The ice had melted. She used a finger to move the sodden mint leaves around the glass. 'Have you . . . have you ever seen something you can't explain?'

'Beg your pardon?'

'I know it sounds crazy, but I have. Twice now.'

Lois dropped her chin in her hands and stared at Maryam, letting her eyes roam all over her face. 'Seen something?'

'Yes – over there in the trees. I didn't imagine it.'

Lois turned to look in the direction she'd pointed. Then she turned back, her face tight. 'What do you think you've seen?'

'There is something out there – I don't know what – but if there's a myth about the woods being haunted then where do you think it's come from? I've seen things I can't explain and suddenly, everything is going wrong for us. My parents have died, Rhory's business is a disaster. It's like something is in the park and it's just trying to reach out and get us. Make my life a misery. It's as if this place has an energy that brings bad things.'

Lois didn't stop looking at Maryam. There were spidery veins either side of her nose that seemed to get deeper red. Angrier. Eventually she said, 'Actually, I'm sorry. I think I've got to go home.'

'Lois?'

She shook her head tightly. Got to her feet, leaflets and envelopes fluttering down around her, grabbed up her keys and her bags. 'I'll call,' she said stiffly. 'I'll be in touch to get the crates back.'

'Lois?'

But Lois was walking away, a little unsteadily, hitching her bag on to her shoulder.

Maryam breathed out. Lowered her face, utterly ashamed. She'd chosen the wrong time, completely the wrong time, to bring this up. Her parents and Rhory's job and the rotting joists in the Bakehouse were nothing compared to losing a daughter. All this time and she still hadn't learned proper Shires manners. Surrey manners, Cotswolds manners. Inside, she was still a pig-slaughtering, axe-wielding girl from the wrong side of the border.

Alex

'I'm sorry if this causes any repercussions or awkwardness.' Later that day I stood in my sergeant's office, shoulders back and army-rigid. 'That is not my intention.'

She had been interrupted in the middle of a budget-planning submission and was seated at her desk as usual. 'I beg your pardon?'

'I said I don't want to appear ungrateful, and I apologise in advance for any problems this may cause you.'

Sergeant Johnson considered me for a while, narrowing her Cleopatra eyes. Then she said drily, 'Can you hear what you sound like, PC Mullins? This is not an *Midsomer Murders* box set. Please do me the honour of behaving like a human being and not an extra acting the role of cop. Just spit it out.'

'OK.' I lowered my head and scuffed my boots back and forth on the floor. She was right – I was behaving like a twat. 'This is awkward, though. It's the Traffic placement.'

'What about it?'

'I don't want it.'

'Why?'

'Because they're only offering it to me because I'm a woman. And probably because they think I'm a lesbian, which I'm not.'

'So? I only got my promotion 'cos I'm female and black.'

I blinked. 'No! That's not the reason you did. You're smart, I've watched you.'

'Yes, I'm smart, but so are all the other people who tried to get this post. I got it because I look good. Female, black. Added bonus of good legs in a skirt. My photo's on the home page of the Billboard and I like it. I'm not going to complain. Are you?'

I hesitated. 'OK – so I know I'm privileged. My mum is minted, and that means that, honestly, I can choose. And I choose not to take a training post that came to me because I'm a girl. I'm letting it go to someone who really deserves it.'

'You're crazy. Everyone wants a job in Traffic. You know that.'

'I do. But it's still my decision.'

My sergeant was wrong when she said she only got the post because she was a black female. She didn't recognise her own dignity. She was far too proud and principled to argue with me any more. Instead she narrowed her eyes and considered me very carefully.

'I need to know something from you.'

'Go ahead.'

'I need to know why you came back.'

Only twenty-four hours ago I wouldn't have known how to answer her. Now I did. I was back because I couldn't forget what I saw that night.

'Tell me something.'

She raised her eyebrows. Challenging. 'Yes?'

'Have you ever heard of the bonehead.'

'The bo . . .? You what?'

'It's a local legend. A ghost. A prostitute who got murdered – the killer went back and had sex with the body.'

'Because that's my answer to why I'm staying. I believe that behind every urban legend there is a grain of truth. Something that can be drilled down on. Have you ever heard of the Bunnyman bridge?'

'Where is this *going*, Alex?'

'Bunnyman is urban legend on steroids. It's in America and people travel for miles to see the bridge, where this guy is supposed to be dressed as a bunny and basically tortures and kills people. Skins them.'

'Just what we need.'

'But if you look at it you find there are some local events that support it. Like a man in a rabbit costume threatening people with an axe – which is real, it's in the police ledgers – and from that grows a legend.' I nodded. I was pleased with myself for managing to put it into words. 'That's what I want to do about the bonehead. I want to find out why anyone around here would believe there's a ghost in the park.'

There was a long pause while she regarded me. From the corridor came the sound of the Response and Investigation team coming back from a job, laughing and heading for the locker room. She said, 'Alex, I'm going to repeat to you what I think you just told me. OK? Just so we're both clear?'

'OK.'

'You've just told me that you're turning down a place in the Traffic unit so you can stay here and play like you're from that Snopes.com website?'

I lowered my eyes. When she put it like that it sounded so lame. But I nodded. Muttered something about how I knew she'd understand. I left the room feeling childish and empty. Out into the empty Dettol-scented corridor, where the receptionist at the desk had her head down. I walked past her and all she did was lift a hand to say hi, not breaking off from the conversation she was having in her earpiece.

Seriously? Had I given up a Traffic placement for this? Staying in Stroud just to satisfy myself I wasn't mad?

Maryam

Alex Mullins was back in the village. She'd been away in London for two years and her return had brought back a shifting, dazzling sparkle that had changed Arran. Last night he had spent the evening at the lake with her the way they used to as children. Maryam thought they'd always been just friends; now she wasn't so sure. She noticed he spent more time in the bathroom and his bedroom was tidier. He was polite, and had even kissed Maryam's cheek a couple of times.

She stood at the sink, up to her elbows in soapsuds, and gazed out of the window at the full, fat trees. It was the time of year when they sprouted exuberantly, seeming to double in size almost overnight. A fringe of fresh, fleshy nettles lined the garden perimeter. It was a rare afternoon when she and Rhory were both working from home. A big treat. She'd made tomato and vodka soup for lunch, Rhory had brought home French bread and they'd eaten in the garden with Minty cross-legged in the grass, eating cheese and apple.

After lunch, Rhory had gone to his workshop while Maryam had brought Minty to the kitchen and washed up. Minty was in her high chair, studiously pushing her fist into the little plastic bowl of sliced bananas. This should feel right, but it didn't. It was empty, with no Tumble at her calves, getting under her feet. No smell of dog food, no chewed tennis ball gathering hairs in the corner . . .

Six weeks ago Arran had come jubilantly into the garden, holding his phone up with his Facebook page to show Alex's message from London. Maryam should have responded better to him, but she was anxious about something outside his control and she wasn't able to unstick her fear.

He was disappointed by her lukewarm reaction.

'Aren't you lit? She's coming back.'

'Of course, of course. She's lovely.'

'What, then?'

Maryam shook her head quickly, not letting herself glance towards the treeline where Rhory was standing with his back to them, his hands plugged into his hips. 'Nothing. We're so happy for you. Go and send her our love, tell her good luck with the move. Ask her to come for a meal when she gets back.'

Arran was too preoccupied to question more. Nor to notice anything odd about his dad. He went back into the kitchen, his head bent over the phone. When he stopped at the fridge to get a beer he turned sideways and she got a glimpse of the edge of his face, a delighted grin.

'He OK?' Rhory came back to the table and sat down. 'Looks excited.'

'Alex Mullins is coming back from London.'

'Cool.' Rhory picked up his own beer, held it up to her and gave her a brave smile. 'Cheers.' But instead of drinking from it he sighed, put the beer down. He put his forefingers to his temples. 'Fuck. Fuck, I'm worried now.'

'Me too.'

He got up and came to her, resting his hands on her shoulders. They were both silent for a while, their heads turned to the trees. It was Tumble's habit to sleep in the afternoon; then, as the sun drew closer to the top of the escarpment, he'd spend half an hour or so rooting among the brush on the floor of the forest. He rarely went far, and always came bounding back in time for supper. Until tonight. Until an hour ago, when Maryam had thought she'd heard him barking. She'd come out of the house to find an empty garden and Rhory in his workshop, oblivious.

'Weren't you watching for him?'

'No.' He had come out of the workshop, wiping his hands with a rag. 'Why would I? He was just loafing around the trees. He's not a puppy.'

'But didn't you check he'd come back?'

'He always comes back. He will when it gets boring out there.'

But it hadn't got boring and he hadn't come back. Together Maryam and Rhory had combed the garden, calling and whistling, throwing Tumble's favourite toy into the leaves to tempt him out. The forest had just given back its complacent insect buzz of early summer and eventually, after an hour and a half, they'd given up. They'd brought drinks out into the garden and sat in defeat at the table, staring into the trees.

Now Arran had gone inside, the two of them were still for a little longer, not speaking, watching the shadows rolling in like a tide, the first cool breeze scamper over the lawn. A woodpecker inched its way up a trunk only a few yards inside the wood, as if nature didn't care about this human drama and intended to keep getting on with things regardless. From the den came a Spotify advert, then an old song. Blur, 'In the Country'. Rhory used to like Blur. He used to play them on his CD player all the time when they'd first arrived here at the Bakehouse.

Maryam put her hand over his where it rested on her shoulder, and lifted her chin to look up into his face. 'You need to remember exactly. The last place you saw him.'

'I don't know.' He was vague. His face grey and clenched as a stone. 'Somewhere in there.'

'But where exactly?'

'I don't know. Does it matter?'

'I don't know if it matters.' She got to her feet. 'I don't know.'

'Where are you going?'

'I don't know that either.'

She walked down the lawn, dazed. Further into the beginning of the park. The grey shape of the path was ahead of her, about twenty feet down the slope, slightly obscured by the frosting of wild garlic and dying bluebells. Her feet were clodded, heavy. Dread lay thick in her chest.

'What's happening?' Rhory was behind her. 'What's happening.'

'I just need to know where you saw him. Was it down here?'

'Yes. I mean . . . probably. Why?'

She breathed in hard through her nose. They had stopped at the place she'd seen the figure that day. The very place. The swollen-jointed old trunk reaching arthritically upwards. A smatter of acid-green leaves. The path, worn and trodden. A pile of horse manure pressed into the ground by a passing pair of trainers or Wellington boots.

'Maryam?' Rhory's face had a dull, clouded look, as if his blood wasn't pumping right. 'What is it?'

But she didn't know what to say.

Alex

I got off shift at five and drove slowly, trawling through a hot afternoon, marvelling at the innocence of Gloucestershire in the sunlight, everyone so ordinary and clear-skinned and trouble-free – even in Stroud, with the streets full of OAPs and students from the art college, trailing around, their hair dyed in shades of lime and raspberry, toting huge portfolios emblazoned with Japanese Manga stickers. It was difficult to imagine there being anything to be afraid of out here. Except maybe boredom, the tyranny of safety.

I was driving past Vibe Hairdressers, near the A46, when the door opened and Michaela Lewis stepped out on to the pavement. I'd forgotten she worked there. She was a mess. Her purple polyester dress was tight in the wrong places and her pasty white legs had bites all over them. Her salon customers must have been confused by her hair, which was dyed aubergine, the roots showing down the parting. She pulled a cigarette out of her fake leather bag and lit it as she marched down the street.

I pulled the car over.

'Hey.' I leaned across the passenger seat and rolled down the window. 'Michaela!'

She came to an almost cartoon-like stop. Juddering slightly with the shock of seeing me. 'Alex? Shut *uuup*! Alex, it's you?'

I slung the door open and she chucked her cigarette into the gutter and jumped in. 'Oh, my God, for fuck's sake! I swear . . . I was ignoring you 'cos I thought you were some randomer trying to hook up or something.' She stared at me, running her eyes up and down my uniform. 'I mean, I knew you were back and everything.'

'And you knew what I was doing for a living?'

'Yeah – I knew what you were doing and all that – but I never expected you to . . . oh, come here . . . ' She leaned across to me, her arms wide. We hugged. She smelled of night buses and fabric conditioner. I could feel her shoulderblades under my fingers like flat slates under thin sand. 'My God, I missed you,' she said.

'I missed you too.'

We separated and grinned. She looked older, much older than I remembered her. I could see her jawbones under the white skin. Her heavy eye make-up was crusted in black dots in the corners of her eyes.

'Where are you going?' I asked.

'Just home. Finished my shift.'

'Me too. I'll drive you.'

'That would make my day. A lift home.'

And so off we went, me and Michaela, the skeleton girl who was my age but looked a hundred. I glanced down at her hands as I drove – I could see the veins and the sinews. As if she was only being held together by the pockmarked casing of her skin. Her dad had been the driver of the coach that day. His body wasn't brought to the surface until forty-eight hours after the crash, then it was tested for drugs and alcohol, all negative. The investigation was never able to establish that the coach company had been negligent about the maintenance or safety record of the coach, nor had it found Mike Lewis culpable. No one would ever know for sure what had caused the accident.

'What's it been like,' I asked. 'You know. With your mum?'

'Mum? Oh, like, a total fucking nightmare.'

'How?'

She leaned forward and scratched the scabs on her legs distractedly. 'Dunno. Maybe Dad was like a buffer or something between us. I never really thought about it before. Now me and Mum, we're like . . . ' She fisted her hands and bumped knuckles together. 'Always aggro together.'

'She's on her own. My dad died before I could remember him so it's not so bad for me, but I've still had to live with the single mother syndrome. The one where they're going through the menopause and screaming and tearing their hair out.'

'Even though she's loaded?'

'Yeah – even though she's minted she's still doing that hormone thing. Cleaning lots. Obsessing about our dog.'

Michaela scrunched up her face and massaged her hair. 'What is it about them? They turn into frigging she-devils.'

'Same.' I cheered in the way I used to when we were squad teenagers. 'Same.'

'Least my mum's got a boyfriend. Bristol. So I've got the flat to myself most nights. Good wifi in the tower – they did some kind of deal.'

'Cool.'

'Did I tell you I had a tattoo done – here on my wrist. Do you like it?'

'Love it. It's a salt cellar?'

'Salt protects against evil.' She held it up to face me. 'Evil evil, get away from me, evil.'

I laughed, acted scared, pretended I was going to lose control of the steering wheel. I turned up an old Halsey track I loved. We wound down the windows and let the wind blow into our faces. Perhaps for a few minutes we got close to being happy.

'I can't believe it's been two and a half years,' I said. 'How does that happen.'

'Was it dope? London? I always want to know.'

'Yeah – it's kind of . . . I don't know. Made me miss here.'

The streets out to Eastonbirt were eerily calm. No school traffic, no lorries. It was the way I imagined it would be if World War Three had been announced. Then we turned off the escarpment and began to wind down, down, down into the valley, through the huge stone gates and into Eastonbirt Park. Closing in on the causeway. *That* causeway, with *that* bend.

In the passenger seat Michaela became silent. Until the crash no one had given much thought to the way the road meandered along next to the lake. It looked a gentle-enough slope into the water and it didn't seem possible that a coach could roll and sink to such a depth. I slowed the car down and we both lowered our chins slightly to peer down into the water. It reflected back the hazy reflected shape of my car, but nothing else. There was nothing to see.

'You OK?' I asked.

'Not really.'

'How come?'

'Don't laugh, but I'm totally paranoid. Every time I leave the flat I'm like, I just want to put a bag over my head. I'm like, everyone's throwing shade, pointing at me, giving it: *Her father killed all those kids. Probably drunk.*'

'No way. No one thinks that. I promise you. He didn't do one thing wrong, Michaela. Not one thing.'

'You think?' She rubbed her thin white arms nervously. 'You really think?'

'I know. The coroner said it too. It was never an issue. I mean, never.' The road began its slow climb back from the bottom of the valley into the village. 'And anyway, I don't remember it all, it was like one long hallucination, but I'm paranoid too.'

'You?'

'Yeah. I mean, I still think I saw weird shit that night.'

'Weird shit? Like?'

I gave a nervous laugh. 'Honest? I was out of it. But I swear I saw someone on the road that night. I know you saw a deer cross the road, but my head was so messed up with what they gave me in the hospital for my hand that even today I still think I saw a person.'

'*What?*'

'Lame, but when you're pumped full of drugs you hallucinate things.'

'But it was a deer. I saw a deer.'

'I know – I'm not saying it wasn't a deer, I'm just, like, what I saw was someone else on the road that night.'

I realised then Michaela had stopped scratching her legs and had gone very still.

'Yeah,' I said. 'It's like, totally makes no sense, does it?'

We drove into the village in silence. I'd crossed a line without even seeing it.

'You can drop me here.'

I steered to the side of the road. She gathered up her little handbag, got out. 'Bye, then,' I said with forced cheeriness.

'Bye.'

There was an awkward moment while she stood on the side of the road, as if she wanted to say something but couldn't. She half-took a step towards the car, then stepped back. Eventually she dug in her bag for a cigarette and turned away to light it. I decided the conversation must be over. I put the car into gear, heading off down the high street.

Except I wasn't ready to leave it. Her nervousness had left a gap in my mind.

I reached the top of the street and instead of heading straight over the roundabout towards my house I circled, once, twice, then drove a few hundred yards back in the opposite direction.

I was thinking about one of the inquests I'd attended. There had been so many – all held at the same court in Gloucester – a modern building, clean and airy, yet as solemn and hushed as a funeral parlour, as if maybe there were dead bodies some- where behind the smart wooden panelling. This particular inquest came back to me now because Michaela had been on the stand. She was wearing black court shoes in a shiny pat- ent, her face was make-up-free, her hair pulled back off her face, and she kept a handkerchief pressed to her puffy nose. Her eyes didn't leave the coroner, half-shy, half-willing to play her part – as if he was a coach giving directions and Michaela was determined to follow every instruction to the letter. It was when the coroner asked her about the road conditions that something in her face had changed.

'Do you know why he swerved?'

'No.'

'Do you think he saw something in the road?'

'Maybe.'

'Maybe?'

'Yes, I . . . ' She had trailed off, her attention rolling off briefly to the other side of the court where all the survivors were huddled in the public seats. 'Dad might have seen something in the road . . . '

'Might have seen?'

'Probably saw,' she'd corrected hesitantly. 'Probably.'

'I appreciate how difficult this is for you, Miss Lewis, but did you see what your father saw?'

'Um, yes.' Her eyes had drifted back to us onlookers, in her face a hint of fear mixed with defensiveness. 'Yes,' she'd said eventually, emphatic. 'Yes. It was a deer.'

It all came back to me with a rush as I drove through quiet, familiar little Eastonbirt. I got to the place I'd dropped Michaela. I pulled into a double yellow line and put on my hazards. I could see her on the pavement up ahead. She was a hundred yards ahead of me, walking very quickly and very hunched, past all the shop fronts. Then she turned and dived into one. I didn't have to drive forward to know which shop – it was the off-licence.

The vodka and Coke bottles in her bin. The sore, scratched look to her face and legs.

Michaela never used to be like that.

It came to me fast and clean. She'd lied about the crash in the inquest. And she was still lying now.

Maryam

You lose a child and every single person in a thousand-mile radius knows. Everyone comes out to search, the Pope gives you his blessing. You lose a dog and no one could care less.

The police weren't interested. The RSPCA put a notice on its Facebook page and the local vets all displayed their posters – along with several other 'missing pet' notices – but after that it had been up to Maryam and Rhory to hunt. They'd leafleted the whole village and put up more posters all over the park. Every time the phone rang her heart had rapped – angry knuckles under her breastbone. But Tumble hadn't been seen. No dead dogs, no living dogs. He'd disappeared into thin air.

Maryam had lost track of time. Returning to the present, shaking herself out of the trance, she looked quickly around the kitchen. The washing-up suds were still dripping down her arms. The trees were still thick and silent out of the window. The nettles, the ivy-wrapped trunks. The meadowsweet and mares' tails. Carpets of dying wild garlic stretching off between the tree trunks in every direction. Minty was still in the high chair, humming to herself, playing squidgy games with the banana.

Letting the water out of the sink, she wiped down her arms with a tea towel. She and Rhory had silently gone past the point of still hoping they'd find Tumble. Neither of them wanted to pull the dead remains of any more badgers from rocky fissures. The search was over.

She lifted Minty out of the high chair and gave her a quick sponge-down, holding her at the sink and running the tap on her hands to swill away the banana. 'Come on, sweetheart. Let's have a walk.'

'Walk walk.'

'That's right. You like walking. Let's get those shoes on.'

They went out of the kitchen and into the garden, Maryam going slowly, holding Minty's hand. Minty had been walking since before her first birthday. She had sturdy legs and a ferocious determination to be ahead of everyone, but even she seemed anxious when they got to the edge of the wood. Maryam had to coax her across the border between the garden and the trees.

'It's OK. It's a lovely forest. Lots of trees.'

'Bunnies?'

'Lots of bunnies too. Let's look for bunnies.'

Minty hesitated, but then she pulled herself together and, frowning, took a brave step into the wood. They went on further into the trees, stopping every now and then for a difficult section.

Eventually Maryam got to the tree where she'd seen the image and which from Rhory's account was the last place Tumble had been. She stopped, and stared up into the branches, diamonds of blue sky shining through. A normal-enough oak tree. Gnarled and old but nothing to mark it out as unusual.

'Mummy, Mummy.' Minty clasped her arms around Maryam's legs, pressed her face into her thigh. 'Mummy.'

'Come here.'

She picked her up and settled her, wedged her against her hip. Minty gave a deep sigh, wound her arms around her mother's neck, dropped the side of her face on to her collarbone and stared out at the trees solemnly, as if this was all so wearying, such old and tragic news.

Maryam turned and manoeuvred her feet over the old roots, then leaned slowly back against the tree trunk. 'Let's just stop here for a bit. Have a rest.'

They were both silent for a while, faces still, blinking at the silent forest, waiting for something. This tree was bigger than its neighbours and there was a magical kind of symmetry to the arrangement of the surrounding trees, as if they'd grown in a circle around it. Not as formal as the arboretum, but even so it was a miraculous accident of nature to see this pattern, this reverence. What about this place was significant to the spirit?

Maryam tilted her head and looked back up the slope. They hadn't come that far at all. The Bakehouse was still just visible through the trees. It looked so welcoming – warm and comforting, like a castle in the middle of an enchanted forest, higher from this vantage point, making it taller and more majestic than in real life.

And that was when she realised. The thing she'd been missing that made her fear even worse. She stiffened.

'Mummy?'

'Yes. Come on, darling. Let's go back.'

She hurried back up the slope, crushing the wild garlic underfoot, the bitter smell in the air, Minty grizzling and scared. 'Mummy, Mummy.'

'It's alright, darling. Shhh.'

In the house she settled Minty down in her high chair again, switched on the TV to CBeebies and found her favourite toy, a chewed old plastic horse that Minty carried everywhere. When Minty had calmed down and was transfixed by the TV, the plastic horse held fast against her cheek, Maryam padded around the house in a silent, frantic hunt. Through all the ground-floor rooms she went, opening cabinets, searching through piles of mail, through all her upholstery inventories and the stack of papers they kept in a kitchen drawer that included utilities bills and the family's passports.

She was looking for a single sheet of paper. Something she hadn't given a thought to in weeks and had forgotten all about until just now, looking at the Bakehouse from down in the woods.

It had been morning, everyone rushing with coffee and Minty's nursery bag to be packed, and Rhory had torn open the mail, glanced at one sheet of paper and held it up to Maryam.

A photograph of the house.

'An estate agent – a new gimmick. We're not selling the Bakehouse so they can swing.'

She'd barely glanced at it, accepting his explanation. But now she couldn't get it out of her head. The photographer, if she was remembering correctly, must have taken the photograph from that oak tree, the place she and Minty had been standing in just now. Why had it never struck her as odd? An estate agent going down into the parkland to take a photo instead of taking it from the road? Yes, it made the house look more imposing and grand from that angle, but there was something unnerving about the idea of a photographer out in the woods.

Where was the photo? If she could find it she'd know for sure.

Nothing.

She slammed a drawer shut and stood, her hand pressed against her hot forehead, surveying everything in the downstairs study. It was all remarkably ordered, unusually tidy. She didn't recall Rhory being this neat with things.

When he came in from the workshop at coffee time she questioned him. 'You remember that photo the estate agent sent?'

'Uh huh,' he answered automatically, not looking at her. He was clutching a handful of dowel plates. He'd bruised a finger from a mallet the other day and now it was blue and green. 'I mean . . . no? What photo?'

'A few weeks ago – a photo came in the post. Of the house. You said it was from an estate agent?'

'I'm not sure – don't remember.' Distracted he began rubbing the plates with an oil-soaked cloth. 'I binned it probably. Is there any coffee?'

'You never bin things.'

'Well, I don't know – maybe I did. I don't remember.' He raised his head and squinted at her. 'Why? What is it?'

She shook her head. She didn't have the words. 'You don't remember what you did with the piece of paper?'

'No. I mean, I don't even remember what you're talking about. Vaguely I guess, something, but junk mail. Why would I remember that?'

'Because someone is . . . '

'Someone is what?'

She sat down at the table, exhausted. She ran her hands down her face. 'We *could* move one day. Into Stroud, maybe. I was looking on Rightmove – there are some lovely places.'

'Why would you want to do that?'

'There's a nursery there for Minty. A really nice one.'

'We've got a really nice nursery. And an amazing primary school. St Winifred's. It was good enough for me and for Arran so why wouldn't it be . . . ' He tilted his chin down and looked at her seriously. 'What's this about?'

Maryam took a deep, deep breath. Held it for a long time, then let it all out at once. 'I don't like it here any more. The woods frighten me.'

'You what?'

'I said the woods frighten me. I think something is trying to . . . Something is . . . '

A fleshy sensation rose inside, pressed hard against her throat, and to her shame Maryam began to cry. She couldn't stop it happening. She snatched up a tea towel and held it to her face, turning away from Rhory in mortification. Minty lowered her cup from her mouth and stared at her mother.

'Jesus,' Rhory muttered, jumping to his feet. He put his arms round her and kissed the top of her head, muttered, 'Shhh, shhh,' comfortingly into her hair.

It was the worst. All the things he valued in her: her common sense, her calm. Her rationality. She was shattering his illusion, second by tiny, shrill second.

'It's my fault. It's all my fault: my parents, your job, the house. Even Tumble – it's my fault.'

'What? What are you talking about?'

She held the tea towel tight against her eyes and shook her head. 'I don't want to live here any more, I want to move. Something is in those woods watching us, and it hates me.' She tightened her fists. 'It hates me *this* much. It wants to hurt me. It took away Tumble and I don't know what it's done with him!' She wiped her eyes furiously with the tea towel, knowing how insane it sounded. 'You won't understand; you won't believe me.'

Rhory was silent. From the high chair Minty's eyes were big and round, not knowing what to do in the light of her parents' behaviour. From the radio came the tinny music of the news starting up. The day was rolling itself forward. The world and the laws of space and time didn't care that her life had come to a frozen stop.

Eventually he spoke. 'That thing above the kitchen door?'

She glanced up at the place he was looking, her nose red and swollen. It was a nazar. And above the Aga was the Hand of Fatima. He'd never noticed them before.

'What is it?'

'It's a decoration,' she said, holding her breath. 'Just something pretty.'

But Rhory wasn't fooled. He was silent a little longer, a muddiness in his eyes, a million emotions crossing his mind at the same time. Then at last he breathed out, an expression of weariness coming over him. He rubbed a hand across his face. 'You bounced back so well with Arran, but this time, with your parents and everything . . .?'

'What?'

'There's no shame in depression, Maryam. No shame. I've been down myself, really down with this work shit going on. I wouldn't judge.'

So that was how it was. The crazy lady. Postpartum and maybe even perimenopausal – name it, she fell into the category.

Alex

The personal device Gloucestershire Constabulary gave me was different from the London ones and actually a little easier to navigate. The next morning when I checked, at almost the crack of dawn, the first job on the coms line was a burglary at Sun College, so far up in the northwest that no one in Cheltenham or Evesham had picked up. If I left now I might just squeeze in before morning rush hour. I got on to coms and confirmed I'd attend.

Sun College was a conglomeration of buildings on a wooded slope between Stroud and Cheltenham. From the road you couldn't see it, hidden by trees and the heft of the land, but once I'd negotiated the little driveways, followed the signs, it was like being in a small village – there were car parks and reception buildings and theatres and playing fields and cafés. There was a lime-green line running down the centres of the walkways for the visually impaired, and matching signposts in jaunty lettering, saying: 'Sun Theatre', 'Music Therapy Centre', 'Cookery', 'Gardening', etc. The buildings were all new, timber trims and glass, with sweeping roofs and porthole windows that gave them all an ark-like appearance, as if there should have been animals marching two by two, instead of wheelchairs and carers and nurses moving from one building to the next.

The break-in turned out to be a pile of broken glass in the cafeteria with one very sorry-looking employee standing next to it. Last night, he'd locked up then realised he'd left his phone in the cafeteria. He hadn't been able to get through to the senior security staff's mobiles so he made the decision to break the glass, get the phone, and pay the bill for the glass. He'd left messages, but no one had alerted security before they turned up this morning to unlock and found glass on the floor.

By the time I arrived, the whole thing had blown over and there were just lots of red faces.

I made the report, then sent Minnie a quick text. She was here already, at the netball court for a pre-breakfast training session. From the village's café I got two cappuccinos to go, two croissants, then trotted down there. I turned down the volume on my radio, and slightly fiddled it out of my ear so I'd only hear the chatter if it got urgent or if my name was called.

Minnie was on the court with three other wheelchair-users, in the middle of a ferocious drill, passing the ball between them and throwing their wheelchairs around the place. I'd always known she was the prettiest of all of us, but sitting in her wheelchair, with the early morning light piercing through the trees, dressed in a striped beach-ready T-shirt, full-on suntan, her black hair caught in a ponytail, she was mega mega pretty. Prettier than the Kardashians and twice as sassy, flinging the wheelchair around corners, calling out to the boys and throwing gang salutes.

When she saw me at the edge of the court she squealed at the top of her voice, 'Police Officer Mullins!'

She threw the ball over her shoulder, not caring where it landed, and came tearing across the court, her arms going like pistons. Her little pink tank top was the tightest thing imaginable next to a swimsuit. 'Alex, Alex! Look at you. You look like something out of *Fireman* frickin' *Sam*.' She grabbed my wrists and inspected me, looking me up and down as if to check all of me had made it back from the city. 'That pic you posted your first day in London – I swear you were the only white person on the street.'

'Yeah, London. I mean – you know, you're lucky I didn't get chopped up and sold for bush meat. I'm one of the very few who made it out alive.'

'Stop teasing me.'

'Stop being a racist.'

'Am not – I can't be – I'm immune. Mum's Jamaican, I cannot, therefore, be a racist.'

'Come here and give me a hug, you half-Jamaican racist.' I leaned over and hugged her, even though I was in uniform. She smelled of strawberries and vape liquid. 'You look awesome.'

'I know,' she glinted. 'All of those boys wanna do the bad thang with me. Watch their faces fall when they realise I'm not playing any more. I'll be gone five minutes tops and they'll be hitting my phone up.'

We went back into the main complex, Minnie using her electric motor, which was totally noiseless and smooth. We sat with our breakfasts under a huge cypress tree that, for some reason this early in summer, had dropped needles and turned the grass in its shade a sand brown. She kept flicking her hair over her shoulder in a way that I envied. The crash had severed a nerve in her spine, but she informed me it hadn't messed with her sex drive, which apparently was second to none.

'Not that I'm hitting on you, Alex. Much as I like you.'

I coughed and stirred a little cinnamon and cocoa powder into my cappuccino. 'Yeah – about that. I'm not a lesbian.'

'That's OK,' she smiled. 'It's a free country. You can be what you want to be.'

'Right. And like I said – me? Not a lesbian. It's just I can't be bothered with nails.' I waggled my bad hand at her.

She gave a sympathetic smile. 'Well, I'm sorry to gloat about my hands, but they kind of make up for what happened to my feet. And I LOVE my fingernails.' Minnie pushed out her fingers and twisted them from side to side, admiring the glitter nail job. 'I love them.'

'They're so goals. I like orange. Do you remember Harley Quinn? How Giacomo puked on your dress?'

'I know – for fuck's sake, what is wrong with men? He never even said sorry or anything. So I'm like – don't react. Keep the dignity.'

'That's the one. Keep the dignity.' I licked the froth off the spoon carefully and squinted sideways at her. 'What's it been like, Minnie?'

She shrugged. 'Oh, it sucks, of course. The first year was the worst. They kept talking about neuroplasticity and shit.'

'Neuro what . . .?'

'The idea that you can regrow neural pathways to take over from the pathways that have been cut. The idea that they might be able to get me walking, get me out of the chair.'

'And?'

'They stopped talking about it twelve months ago.'

'Oh?'

'Yes, oh.' She smiled. 'But, weirdly, that's when it started to get better – the moment they basically told me to give up hope. Turns out hope is shit. Hope sucks dick. Anyway, now I treat the whole thing like a gift. Something that makes me stand out from the crowd.'

'Minnie, you always stood out.'

'Seriously, though, I've figured that not being able to walk gives me extra points for every effort I make. I swear it won't be long before I get my PhD, years before half my friends.'

Then she stopped talking and tucked her hands out of sight under her armpits. She leaned forward in the chair, suddenly quiet and serious.

'Why are you here, Alex? Is it 'cos of your mum?'

Mum's charity was giving thousands and thousands a year to Sun College, so I could see her reasoning. 'No. It's not the charity, but it is the crash.'

'The crash? You're in uniform.'

I tugged at the cuticle on my thumb, the one on the left hand. For some reason since the accident the cuticles just seemed to grow extra-thick. A disgusting habit, but I couldn't stop it when I was thinking hard, just pushing at it and moving it around over the nail. 'Minnie, you've been happy staying in Eastonbirt since the crash, right?'

'Weird question, but yeah. Why?'

'Nothing made you want to leave? No one sent you any mail about it? No weird pictures? Anything negative?'

'Not at all. All positive. Six hundred Instagram followers because of it. Apart from that, life goes on. Mum's still working at Loxton's Chase, Dad still for the council. We're happy. I'm happy. As happy as you can be when you've lost the use of your legs.'

I put the cup down on the grass and pushed the hair out of my face. 'OK – so I guess there's something else on my mind. I keep thinking there's something about the accident that still doesn't feel quite right.'

'Meaning?'

I couldn't just come out with it. *I think I saw a ghost, a person – something. But not a deer.* I hedged. 'Not so much the report as the testimonies. You were at the inquests. You were there when Michaela Lewis was on the stand?'

'Yes, I was. Not nice listening.'

'Did you think she was telling the truth?'

Minnie made a face. 'Sorry?'

'Did she seem transparent when she was on the stand?'

'Transparent.' Minnie pondered the word. Her brown eyes rolled up and her bright nails clicked up and down on her knees. Eventually she said, 'No. Not really. Now I'm thinking about it she was proper secretive. Looking back.'

'What do you think she was lying about?'

Minnie put her elbows on the wheelchair rests and made a steeple of her hands, pressing her mouth down on to her fingertips and giving this serious thought. 'I don't know, but I don't think she really saw a deer.'

'Why would she lie?'

'Who knows? I suppose to get her dad off the hook. I mean – if she thought he'd fallen asleep or something. I never saw this deer – not that I was looking, but I never saw no deer. Did you?'

I couldn't answer. Didn't want to answer. Minnie watched me in silence, while lower down the slope the college students were arriving. People went by in wheelchairs, some of them full of energy, duking it out for speed, others slower, keeping their heads lowered cautiously.

'Alex?'

I stopped picking at my hand. I placed it on my knee, looking down at it. I couldn't answer the question. If I could have answered it, then I probably wouldn't have been sitting there on the grass in Sun College, groping around in my head for an answer.

Maryam

She woke up to find Rhory had already showered and dressed for work. She roused Minty and carried her around the house until she found her husband in the kitchen, frying bacon with the radio on. Arran sat at the table with a bleary look on his face, his tie askew, a cup of coffee in front of him.

'Morning, boys.' Maryam slotted Minty into her high chair and did up the food-stained buckle. 'Sleep well?'

They both grunted a sleepy acknowledgement and continued with what they were doing. The radio was on – something about inflation and the economy. More bad news. More and more.

'Eggs,' she said brightly. 'I think I'll scramble some eggs to go with the bacon. Arran?'

'I'm late, Mum – I'll have to grab something at work.' He pushed the chair back, gave her a quick peck on the cheek and headed for the door, grabbing keys from the huge bowl on the side table where all their belongings ended up: spare change, keys, paperclips. Maryam watched him in the hallway pulling on his jacket, taking his phone off charge. It wouldn't be long before he found his own place, and then even a few monosyllabic minutes in the kitchen would be a luxury she'd hanker for.

'Eggs, Rhory?'

'Please.'

'Please,' echoed Minty brightly. She was holding her plastic horse and dancing it across her breakfast tray, singing little songs to it. Now she began to chant in time to its cantering. 'Please please please.'

Working alongside Rhory at the Aga, this seemed like a normal household. The eggs came together beautifully, not sticking or running away into milky veins; the bacon was crispy, the radio played her favourite Nirvana song, the sun was shining, and the clematis on the old shed, which for years had stubbornly refused to flower, had suddenly burst into spectacular bloom. Impossible to remember her fear of those woods, to believe anything out there could be watching them, trying to hurt them. If she leaned back a little and peered to the bottom of the garden she could see that already the sun was picking out the leaves and the shadows between the trunks.

When they'd eaten and cleared up, and Minty was drinking juice from her sippy cup, Rhory sat down and opened up his computer, the screen facing him so Maryam couldn't see it. She poured herself another mug of coffee and leaned back against the Aga, watching him.

'I'm OK now,' she said. 'I feel much better.'

He raised his eyes and let them move cautiously over her face.

'I'm going to see a doctor today. And I'll . . . change the decorations. They're upsetting to you.'

He nodded slowly, gravely.

'Well, then . . . ' She smiled brightly, turned away and emptied the coffee pot into the sink, hiding her exhaustion from him. She hadn't slept last night. 'That's all sorted, then.'

She wiped the worktops down and hung up the tea towels. Transferred the empty eggshells in the cartons to the recycling. She knew psychotropic drugs could do nothing to turn back the clock. What could SSRIs or anxiolytics do to stop the spirit tormenting her?

So what then, Maryam? she thought. What are *you* going to do?

Maryam

Maryam – with her heavy, slow frame, her long black squaw's hair, her striped tights and velvet hats. Moving steadily through life. The solid one, the sensible one. Pretending yesterday hadn't happened, that she hadn't admitted her weakness to Rhory. Trying so hard, in her shaky little Vauxhall, battered but vibrant. Flashing brown and orange, brown and orange. Trundling up the road to the nursery, Minty on the back seat. Ignoring everything around.

It still hadn't rained, but today the sun had gone and it was a heavy, cloud-covered day. The cows were out on the common above the village, which had an ancient law allowing farmers to graze cattle in the summer months. Unsuspecting out-of-town boy racers tore across the cattle grid, past the warning signs, and were full of indignation when their customised Nissans ploughed into a solid-beamed Belted Galloway, while the villagers were wiser and knew to add time to journeys, knowing the cows were apt to cross the road at the drop of a hat, no warning, no Green Cross Code. If, one morning, she passed an ominous shape draped in a tarpaulin on the edge of the road, she knew there'd been a collision and she'd need a story ready for the back seat.

That? Oh, that's just a pile of bricks; they're going to make a building here, I think.

Or, *It's just a haystack covered in plastic, nothing to worry about.*

No dead cows today. But the live ones were unnerving. Everywhere they were hunched in big huddles, something she hadn't seen before. Animals had instincts for bad spirits that humans didn't. She didn't like this protective clumping-together of nature.

She dropped Minty at the nursery, jumped into the car, wound back down the hill into the village. She parked up and walked down the high street, her tasselled bag slung over her shoulder, head up, chin forward. Appear strong. Whatever you feel like inside, make the outside a fortress. Past the stripy awnings of the new cupcake shop, past the florist where the lavender and hydrangeas were being watered by a girl in a bright yellow apron, past cafés with chalked blackboards announcing the day's specials. *Huevos rancheros* on sourdough with dukkah, smoky Virgin Marys, buttermilk pancakes.

There weren't many estate agents, but even one was a hurdle for her that felt like scaling a wall. She had to stand in the doorway taking deep breaths before she opened the door and went inside. How could it be that there were so many pretty girls in one village – it was like a slap to the eyes. Every one who glanced up and smiled was groomed and glowing – the sort of girl Maryam had taught herself not to envy or stare at. Was Rhory aware that these girls were everywhere?

She steeled herself to ask. But they hadn't sent out a picture of a house without accompanying text. It wasn't their policy.

'I'm just a temp,' said the receptionist. She leaned back in her chair and called into the back office, where three heads raised from the computer monitors. 'Did someone else call about a picture of their house coming through the post?'

'I don't know.'

'I thought I heard Janey saying someone had been in?'

'I don't know.'

'So we definitely don't send stuff out without text? Photographs of property?'

'Never.'

'And none of the other agents?'

'I don't know. I've never heard of it.'

'I'm sorry.' The girl swung her chair back to face Maryam. Gleaming teeth and hair. 'It wasn't us. You might want to try some of the Stroud offices. They have lots of different marketing techniques.'

Maryam couldn't face the Stroud offices and she couldn't face any more of the agents in Eastonbirt. Instead she sat in the Vauxhall and ate a wrapped sandwich she'd bought from the Co-op. She chewed slowly, watching people walking by. All these people who were younger than her, but somehow seemed to have lived here longer than she had. Was it true what Lois had said all those years ago: that she was one of the people who made Eastonbirt what it was? An integral stitch in its fabric? It didn't feel to her that she was an organic part of the place.

Not many sewing jobs to complete that afternoon. Really she should put in some more work on the tapestry she'd been developing from the arboretum design, but instead, back at the Bakehouse she spent the afternoon creeping around the cool stone rooms, pulling down the charms, the mirrors and the red threads. She sat with them in the workroom and found ways to disguise them: a thread hidden up high on the bed leg where the duvet would fall and cover it, the beaded blue and white nazars concealed carefully in drawers, poked out of sight into the folds of the curtains.

Important to go along as normal. She was unflappable and calm; nothing was happening that she couldn't cope with. She collected Minty from nursery and at home made avocado and alfalfa sprout sandwiches, a side salad with pomegranate seeds and feta cheese, strawberries for dessert. Arran came home early and sat on the bench at the table under the apple tree, drinking a beer in his shirt sleeves. At his feet Minty, wearing just her shorts, jumped her plastic toy horse round an improvised showjumping ring. Arran told Minty enormous, amusing lies about how he used to have a horse, how he'd been a great rider and won the biggest horse race on the planet.

When the food was ready Maryam cleared a space and lifted Minty up so she was sitting on the table. 'Special treat, Minty. No high chair.'

'No eye-che. No Tumble.'

Maryam paused and studied her little girl, with her downy hair – all Rhory – and that incredible pushed-up mouth. 'You're right, baby.' She hitched up Minty's shorts, which were drooping down around her nappy. 'There's no Tumble any more. Now, do you want cheese?'

Minty didn't ask about Tumble again. She accepted the cheese. Maryam hoiked her on to her lap and began to finger-feed her food. Minty didn't like the alfalfa sprout, she made a face, and Maryam held out a napkin for her to spit out a mouthful. Rhory got home and he brought out a beer and sat with them. Slowly they began to lapse into something like a family. Idly conversing.

Maryam picked up a strawberry and smelled it. It smelled of all the summer days they'd spent together, all crushed into one tiny fruit. For a moment she wanted to cry for how perfect their lives must appear from the outside.

Alex

The next day there was a message from Ozone. *Come and see me? I live in Cheltenham now.* I got back to him and said I'd be there around six.

The address was in an estate on the outskirts of the town and, driving along trying to find his number, I thought how it must look like a giant amoeba from above, it was so tentacled and spreading, lots of pod-shaped offcuts and house after red-brick house, all with hung tiled walls, PVC windows and beaten lead roofs. The lawns were neat, the pampas grass and hydrangea well tended; some of the narrow driveways had caravans wedged on them, while others had tiny runarounds, Smart cars gleaming on the tarmac in reds and blues. Ozone's house had a neat lawn with a pollarded tree surrounded by stones in the centre, and a huge camper van taking up the hard standing.

As I walked up to the house, a man peered down from the roof of the van. He was holding a dripping sponge in one hand and a bucket in the other.

'Hi,' I said shielding my eyes from the evening sun and looking up at him.

'Hi.'

There was an awkward moment. I had a feeling I'd seen him before, but he looked in his forties maybe, so slightly creepy if he was Ozone's boyfriend.

'I'm here to see Ozone.'

'He's inside.'

'Thank you.' I hesitated, then, feeling totally lame, walked to the glass-enclosed porch. I knocked and waited, staring at a row of geraniums in pots along the sill. Outside I could hear birdsong. Fuck, but life was different in the provinces. Seriously, was it possible a housing estate could be this quiet at rush hour?

'Alex, fuck's sake, hon.' Ozone opened the door. He'd cut his hair and dyed it that purple-grey everyone in London had two or three years ago. There was a stud in his nose and he wore a black vest, cargo pants and bare feet. 'Come in.'

He led me into a living room where there was a fake fire-place, lots of leather furniture and family photographs in gilt frames on the sideboard. There was a glass display case with a whole load of crystal animals – the sort of thing mum would call '*charriviste*' (her blending of 'chav' and '*arriviste*') and I'd have to agree with her – the style wasn't what I'd expect from Ozone.

'Been here long?'

'Two years. How long've you been back?'

'Nearly five weeks. Old country bumpkin now. The Londoners told me I was running away to become a woolly.'

'A what?'

'A woolly. It's what they call rural police.'

'Oooh,' he said. 'I see.'

We both stood for a while, awkwardly, not knowing quite what to say. Ozone and I had never been really close so it must have seemed weird me contacting him out of the blue. I gave him a grimace. 'Actually, I'm sorry, Ozone, but I'm sort of here to ask you some questions. About the crash. I think the investigation missed something.'

He made a face. 'What? Is this you as bill or you as Alex asking? You're not in uniform.'

'It's me as Alex. I just . . . ' I scratched my head, trying to find the words. 'There are things about that night I just can't get into the right place in my brain. Like, did you see the deer that Michaela said went in front of the coach?'

'I was on the other side and I wasn't looking out. The police already asked me all this.'

'You really haven't got any memory? Don't remember seeing anything that didn't come up in the inquest?'

'No.' He frowned. 'Why?'

'I dunno. Just something bothering me.' I chewed my lip. 'Do you ever have . . . dreams about it?'

'No. I never did. I think I was the lucky one.'

The door opened then and a woman in her forties wearing a floral blouse and khaki slacks came into the room. She was about my height – a fox-like face, brittle yellow hair and eyebrows that were so waxed and dyed and shaped they didn't seem to belong to her face at all. Like stick-on plastic replicas.

'Oh,' she said. 'I'm sorry, Ian. I didn't know you were with someone.'

I got it then – this was Ozone's mum. The guy outside I'd recognised because it was his father – he'd changed a lot, put on weight. So this would be Ozone's parents' house, and that explained the crystal animals with the weird red eyes.

'Hi. We met a long time ago. I'm . . . ' I swept my hair back from my face. 'I'm Alex Mullins. Me and Ozone were at school together.'

'Yes. I remember you. You were in the crash.'

'That's right.'

She kept shaking my hand, staring at my face as if trying to find the polite words. Then she flinched and let go of me hurriedly. 'Oh, I'm sorry, your hand. I'd forgotten.'

'That's alright, it's my left hand.' I held it up quickly to show her. I'd learned to give a quick flash of the scarring rather than hide it, or force people to look more closely than they wanted. Some people cringed, others asked openly to examine the skin, but most people did exactly what Mrs Winters did: they smiled and changed the subject.

'Would you like a cup of tea?'

'That would be great. Thank you.'

'Sugar?'

'Just milk.'

'Of course.' She made to leave the room but paused halfway out of the door, cleared her throat and said in a weird, quiet voice, 'Um – Ian, sorry, Ozone, have you got a moment? Give me a hand with the tea.'

'Sure.'

I was left in the living room on my own. I didn't know what to do. I wandered around the room, studying the sorts of things that would only interest a tomboy like me. The electrical fittings and the gas-flame-effect marble fireplace. The fact that the plaster was cracking in the places the screws held up the plasterboards.

The big French doors to the garden were open so I went over and looked out. I could see Ozone and his mum talking in the kitchen as they made tea, the steam of the kettle misting up the glass. Something was wrong here; I was missing something. I scanned the garden: very neat, very trimmed. What was it about the stillness of the grass in the sunshine that was wrong? In the shade of a large sycamore a cat slept on a striped deckchair.

I went and sat on one of the leather sofas, feeling its high-pitched squeak under me. *Charriviste*. It was only when I'd gone to London that I'd realised what a complete and utter snob Mum had tried to make me. Growing up I'd had a sense of it, but it was Hammersmith that firmly put me in my place. I'd had some corners knocked off me in the Met, and I hoped it had made up for how insufferable I must have been growing up with my huge country home and the holidays in Bali and Mozambique.

What was I missing? The fake marble fireplace. The photos of Ozone and his sister on the mantelpiece . . .

'Alex.' Ozone appeared in the doorway. He was on his own, but in the hallway behind him I could see his mum and his dad, who must have come in from the front garden.

I twisted in my seat and dropped my hand over the back of the sofa. 'Everything OK?'

'Um.' He carefully shut the door behind him and came over to the sofa, almost tiptoeing. He sat next to me with his knees very neatly together, as if he was in a headmistress's office. 'Look, Alex, don't take this the wrong way. Mum and Dad, they . . . we've got a kind of rule in our family. We don't talk about the crash.'

'Oh. OK. That's weird.'

'I don't argue with them. Things . . . happened after the crash and we decided to move away. Mum especially – she wants to forget it ever happened.'

'Things happened? What things?'

'I don't know. Mum never talks about it. But . . . oh, God, please don't get this wrong, but would you mind not staying for tea after all?'

I opened my mouth then closed it. I could feel myself going bright red. I'd been told to leave people's houses before, in terms a lot harsher than this polite request, but somehow this hurt more than any of the yobs and muppets in the Hammersmith tower blocks. 'No.' I got up. 'Of course not. I'm sorry – I didn't mean to cause any problems.'

'I'm the one who should be sorry.'

'That's OK. Just – if you remember anything about that night, will you call me?'

'I'll try.' He smiled weakly and got up to open the door. When I went into the hallway Mr and Mrs Winters were standing there, hands together, heads slightly lowered, as if the undertakers had arrived and were leaving the house with the corpse of a family member.

'I'm sorry,' Ozone's dad murmured as I passed. 'I hope you understand.'

I nodded. 'Yeah – of course.'

But I didn't understand. Not at all. I hadn't got even the faintest grasp on the complexity of all the things the Winters family were dealing with.

Alex

That night, sitting on the sofa after Mum had gone to bed, I flicked robotically through Ozone's Facebook pics, trying to see what I was missing. He led the sort of provincial gay life I imagined was typical – parents OK-ish about it, desperately trying to show willing by welcoming his boyfriends into family life. One or two pictures of his mum, dressed in a fierce Ana Matronic PVC dress, her husband's arms around her waist. Smiling into the camera.

What are you hiding? What is it?

Bamber shot to his feet growling, his head towards the window. He ran to the glass door and stood there, his muzzle up against it, his butt moving from side to side.

'Jesus.' I put down my phone and rocked forward to my feet. Padded over to him, grabbing him by the collar. 'What's going on, Mr Ninja? What's out there?'

Usually he'd bark and get more excited, but tonight he didn't, he just kept wiggling his hindquarters, agitated.

I let go of him and, not taking my eyes off the window, backtracked to the wall where the light switches were. I threw the four switches that turned off the living room, the hallway and the kitchen downlighters. The room went black. Bamber's and my reflections disappeared.

'Shhh, Bamber, shhh.'

He stopped his agitated whining, but instead of staying at the window, he turned and ran away, his paws tickertackering on the floor. He stood next to me, close to my calves. I hadn't known him do that since he was a puppy.

'Jesus,' I crouched and put my hand on his back. He was hot and bristling. 'Bamber – what the fuck?'

Slowly, from the other side of the window, the shapes in the garden began to emerge from the black and become familiar. I could just make out the line of the trees at the edge of the park, only about forty yards away at the end of the garden. The blurred shape of the deck railings materialised two yards from the window.

'OK,' I whispered. 'OK, boy, shhh.' Stealthily, not rising from my crouch, I crawled my hand up the wall to the switch plate. I knew the switches upside down – I'd lived here for years. I could pick out the exact two that would throw the entire garden into luminescence.

'Bamber – you've got to stay still. Don't move.'

I dropped the switches. The light flooded the deck and the garden beyond it. There were a few insects circling, but nothing on the deck.

I jumped up and ran to the window, Bamber at my heels. I threw the big glass-paned door sideways on its hinges, the way I'd seen the support groups in London do on a drugs arrest, and stood in the space, my feet planted, my head thrust forward.

'What?' I bellowed, with forced aggression. 'What. The. Fuck?'

Nothing. The garden was silent and still. The lines in the grass Mum's gardeners made with the lawn mower shone grey and black in the yellow light. The crickets were awake, their electric buzz zapping through the air, like in the tropics.

Bamber and I stood there in our little gap, looking out at the trees, waiting with pent-up adrenaline for something to happen.

Nothing happened.

Maryam

It had been Lois who'd made the peace with Maryam. Not long after Tumble disappeared, she'd arrived one evening with a card and a huge cake, frosted and dotted with strawberries. She'd apologised, said she'd been insensitive. Maryam had wanted to hug her, but thought that might be too Welsh, too effusive, so instead she'd apologised too. She didn't deny she felt cursed, make light of it or say she must have imagined what she was seeing, but she did admit she'd been wrong and self-pitying.

'It must have been a touch of postpartum depression,' she'd said valiantly. 'Even two years down the line, I suppose it's not too late for it to strike.'

Lois had become invaluable to Victoria Mullins' charity, and was always running little errands for her. It was good, Maryam thought; it kept her out of the house. The playground the charity had funded was now an established part of the community. On Thursdays and Fridays Lois came over to the Bakehouse and together they walked Minty up there to play.

They went slowly, Maryam pushing the chair, laden like camels on an exotic desert trail, with the nappy bag and a rucksack and water bottles. They went past the crash site in silence, past the motionless lake with the mayflies sleeking along the surface. One or two cars passed, giving them a wide berth. On the far side of the lake the ground began to climb back up out of the valley. Maryam leant into the buggy as the hill steepened, following Lois, watching her freckled calves tighten and release with every step.

'Low lows. Want Horky.' Minty, dressed in a yellow crocheted dress and ankle socks, got bored quickly and began leaning out of the buggy and pulling at Lois's skirt. 'Low lows. Want Horky.'

'Horky?' Lois slowed and tilted her head down to look at Minty. 'Horky? Now let me think. Hmm . . . ' She put her finger on her mouth as if contemplating this. 'I'm not sure I know who Horky is.'

Minty giggled. 'Low lows silly.'

'Isn't she?' agreed Maryam. 'Very silly.'

'Horky is horky.'

'Horky? Now let me guess what sort of animal Horky is.'

'Horky. Horky.' She placed both hands on her knees and frowned crossly at Lois. 'Horky.'

'I'm still trying to guess. Is Horky a giraffe?'

'No!' Minty squealed delightedly. 'Horky is horky.'

'I know! A pig.'

'No no no!'

'A pussycat? Meow meow?'

'No no no!' Minty began to bang her hands up and down on her knees. She was getting to the point where she'd be cross, so Maryam reached inside her cardigan pocket and pulled out the little plastic horse Minty carried everywhere. She slipped it in a closed fist to Lois, who transformed the movement into a conjurer's display.

'Well, look what I've found. A horsey!'

'Horky!' Minty leaned forward delightedly.'Horky, Horky!'

The game continued all the way up the hill until they got to the play park, which sat on a notch of ground that gazed back over the Eastonbirt valley. It was empty today, and there was an unused look to it, like a newly delivered car, everything gleaming with anticipation. Built with both able-bodied and special needs children in mind, it had a witch's hat rope ladder, wobble walks, monkey bars and hanging logs, all on a rubberised surface. There was a scent garden for the visually impaired, handrails leading to each area, and a bespoke toilet unit where a teenager could be wheeled in, to use the toilet or have a change of clothes.

They got Minty into one of the swings, slotted her legs into the basket arrangement and snapped it shut. A few pushes and she was content to swing back and forth, holding Horky out in front of her so he could see the view. The two women wandered to the edge of the park and leaned on the railings. Below them was a small area, freshly concreted. Surrounded by yellow and black caution tape, it had slots ready to accommodate a bench that was about to be erected there.

A memorial to Sophie May.

Lois was raising money on JustGiving for a bench to be placed up here, overlooking the lake. Lois's grief was endless, and her notion of what was appropriate for her daughter was also limitless. Every time she reached the target she'd decide on a more elaborate design for the bench, which in turn cost more money, which translated into more fundraising. Eventually she had settled for a teak bench with a cast-iron curlicue Lutyens-style back. It would be unveiled by Victoria Mullins this weekend.

'We got another Like on that picture I posted.' Lois pulled out her phone and began swiping through the photos. 'See. Minnie Frobisher. It was at lunchtime so she must have been at work. But the JustGiving page has only gone up two pounds this week. Have you any idea why?'

'Not really.'

'I've put up a new picture of her, just to get the interest going. What do you think?'

Maryam tucked her hair behind her ears and leaned over to look at it. 'It's beautiful.'

'It was taken in Tuscany.'

'The summer just before?'

'The summer just before. She was so tanned.'

Maryam had seen the photo before. In fact she'd seen it several times over the last few years – Sophie May standing in front of the Duomo in Florence, wearing a spaghetti-strap top and frilled denim shorts. It was unbearable what Lois and Fenton had been through. Sophie May Hansel. Nineteen. Killed, the coroner said, instantly. In the impact and not from drowning, as some of the other teenagers had.

Lois had become preoccupied with Sophie May's Facebook memorial page. It had over a thousand followers and every day Lois posted something: a photo or a memory or a poem illustrated with little line-drawn angels praying. Occasionally it was something Lois had seen or done that she thought Sophie May would have liked.

'Fenton took it. Look.' Lois leaned over and pushed the phone towards Maryam. There Sophie May was, smiling into the camera. 'Look at her face.'

'Beautiful.'

'Oh, yes.' Lois lowered the phone, a look of wonder on her face. 'That's something I don't think I'd realised until all these people started responding, talking about her beauty. It's brought it home to me how beautiful my daughter is.'

'Very beautiful.'

'So beautiful, and that seems to wake people up. Maybe I shouldn't be surprised that her memorial page is so over-subscribed.'

'Absolutely. I completely—' Maryam broke off. 'Did you hear that?'

'What?'

'Over there in the trees.' She pushed herself upright. Suddenly alert. 'Barking.'

'What? No, I didn't.'

In a trance Maryam ducked under the railings and headed into the trees. A path meandered a few feet below the play park, leading along the side of the escarpment. She joined it and followed it in the direction she'd heard the noise, her pulse pounding. 'Tumble?'

Deeper in the trees the sunshine was stolen by the foliage, and even a few hundred yards from the brilliance of the play park it felt like evening, darkness, clotted and cold among the branches.

A fox, startled by her, broke cover and raced ahead down the slopes, ducking under bracken, bouncing itself off trees in its desperation to flee. She stared at it. A fox? Was that the noise she'd heard?

Silence.

Tentatively she took a few more steps along the path. It occurred to her that this wasn't far from where she and Rhory had found the badger. Here was a stream that ran down the side of the escarpment in branching rivulets, like fingers holding the rock back against the cliff. A tree, clinging despairingly to the rock, its roots exposed and fragile. Malevolent spirits could mimic the voices of loved ones – she was sure she'd read that somewhere. Was this the plan? The husband leaves the insane wife. Checks her lovingly into a hospital then flees, new wife in tow.

She licked her lips, her tongue thick and dry. Not insane; she was not insane.

Turning, slow and regretful, she trudged back up the slope, hands rammed into her pockets. She came round the corner to the play park and there was Lois, white-faced, holding Minty who was crying.

Maryam picked up her pace. 'What is it?'

'She was scared. You left so quickly. I got her out of the swing for a cuddle but when I put her down she thought she saw you in the woods. She had a little run into the trees to find you and . . . '

'I'm sorry.' Maryam got her breath back. 'Come here, pickle.' She took Minty and looped her legs round her hips. Ran her hand across Minty's forehead, pushing her hair up into a little exclamation mark. 'It's OK. I didn't go anywhere.'

Lois balled her fists and swung them back and forward at her sides, tipping to and fro from her toes to her heels, like a guilty schoolgirl trying to act casual. 'I'm sorry,' she mouthed.

'It's OK. Don't worry. No harm.'

Minty was clinging on to her neck with vicelike arms, sensing that if she pulled back she'd see her mother's face and risk a telling-off.

'Minty? Are you alright?'

The toddler nodded hotly against Maryam's neck. 'Minty walk. Walk.'

'It's alright darling – it's alright. Next time make sure someone walks with you. OK?'

''K.'

'Those trees are . . . you could trip over and fall, that's all. Now give Mummy a big hug.'

She did, grizzling and squirming with tiredness. She'd clearly shocked herself.

They walked back to the house in silence, Lois pushing the chair, apologising every few feet. 'She wasn't gone long, I hardly lost sight of her, she thought she'd seen you in the trees.'

'It's OK, it's not a problem. But Lois?'

'What?'

'Please don't tell Fenton I went looking for Tumble. Will you do that for me? Keep it to yourself? He'll tell Rhory and it will get complicated. I don't want Rhory thinking I'm imagining things.'

Alex

After work I had a quick run through the shower, pulled on shorts and trainers, and headed off across the park in the direction of the tower block, hands deep in my hoodie pockets. Evil Tower's thin, bitter shadow was long at this time of evening – so long that it reached across the village and just fingered the end of Lake Tarquil. I passed through the shadow, then back into the evening sunshine, on up through the fields below the village.

The off-licence was opposite the entrance to the tower. It had been here for years, and must have changed hands ten times that I could remember. The woman who owned it now, a small Sri Lankan lady, was shy and a little abrupt. Probably used to people ignoring her, or worse, trying out titbits of Urdu on her because they had that absolute naïvety about Asian people. How had I never noticed before just how damned white Eastonbirt was?

I meandered around the off-licence, passing the time of day and pretending to read the labels on the bottles. It had been a hot day, so most people who came in bought Pimm's and rosé wine. I recognised a few of them and kept a low profile, taking the chance while the woman served them to bend my knees a little and scrutinise the entry to the tower. I didn't know what floor Michaela lived on, but she saved me the problem by suddenly appearing in the shop, over at the spirits aisle.

She wore a puffa jacket, which must have been way too hot on a day like this. Her legs were bare, though, rammed into knock-off Converse high tops, calves so white and thin the veins stood out like cables. She hadn't noticed me. I got a little nearer, my back to her, pretending to be opening the fridge.

'Can I have a bag?' She stood tiredly at the pay desk while the woman rang up the purchases. A litre bottle of vodka, three packets of crisps and two bottles of Coke.

'Fourteen pounds eighty, dear.'

'Fourteen . . . I thought this was on offer.' She gestured back to the shelf where a card was on display. 'Says twelve forty-nine.'

'No, dear, that was for the gin. See?'

'Oh,' she said lowering her head and wrinkling her face. She dug in her handbag for more change and came out with a handful of coins, counted them out on the counter. She shook her head when she saw how much she had. 'Um . . . don't supposed you've got a penny pot?'

'I'm sorry dear – it never works. People steal.'

'Hey, Michaela.' I said.

She turned round in surprise and found me standing there with a two-litre bottle of vodka. 'Oh.' She looked as if she was about to smile, then the faint spark in her eye died and she gave me a small, downtrodden nod. 'Soz about the other day. I must have been on one.'

'No worries.'

'Yeah, well, I'm sorry,' she mumbled, then turned back to the coins on the counter.

I watched for a while then stood a little closer. 'Looks like we've got the same taste. Good old Glen's. You can take your Cirocs and your Absoluts any day, it's all the same stuff, just in a prettier package.'

She smiled reluctantly. 'Yeah.'

'Tell you what, for old times' sake, why don't I pay for this?' I held up the two bottles for the woman. 'Cancel that payment. I'll get these.'

'No,' said Michaela, 'I couldn't.'

'Oh, Michaela, come on. Do you know what my salary was in London?'

She shook her head.

'Well, it was lots. I mean ridiculous amounts.' That was a lie, it had been twenty-nine thousand a year, including London allowance, but that wasn't the point. My mum was minted and I had plenty more spare cash than she did. 'So go on. For old times.'

Eventually she gave in. We wandered out of the off-licence together with our thin plastic bags, into the early evening sun. 'I'm sorry about the other day,' she said again. 'It wasn't what I expected to hear.'

'That's OK. I've got a big mouth anyway.'

'Do you want to come upstairs for a bit? My mum is in Bristol. As per.'

Her place was two floors higher than the boys with the drone. Another weird little letterbox slotted high in the sky, exactly the same layout except Michaela's flat was much scruffier than the boys' place and smelled of smoke. The window was dirty and smeared; the tiny balcony was wedged with an old bike and an ice box.

'Wow,' I said. 'Views are even better up here.'

'I know.' She was in the kitchenette, pouring the vodka into glasses, the flickering fluorescent downlighter under the cupboard making her face a pale green. 'When you live here you get used to it.'

I pushed past a stained leather recliner, a filled ashtray on the armrest, and went to the window. There were shabby lace curtains hanging in the corners, and I could tell by the flies and cobwebs collecting up there that they hadn't been drawn in months. Beyond the glass was the park, stretching its vast tentacles up the sides of the valley, going on forever. The shadow of the tower getting longer and longer across the trees and the lakes.

'*Kampei.*'

I turned and found Michaela holding out a glass that had red glass hearts curled around the stems, something about a wedding written in gold paint across the bowl.

'That's Chinese for cheers.'

I took the glass and saluted her. 'Wow. Chinese at seven in the evening. Life goals.'

She tipped the drink back in one. I did the same. 'That is so fucking awesome.' I twirled the glass round, peering into it as if the secret of life was hidden in the bottom. "What did you put in it?'

'Just lemon, voddy and Coke.'

'Soooo good.'

'Another?'

'Yup. And I'm going to do it this time.' I made to take the glasses from her. She hesitated, confused. 'It's OK,' I said, 'I'm not trying to be rude, I loved the taste, but how about I make it a bit stronger?'

She relaxed her hold, allowing me to take the glasses. She went to sit on the sofa, lighting a cigarette from a packet she'd fished out from under a cushion. 'To be honest I knew I made that one a little weak.'

I wasn't trying to lie to Michaela or pretend to be something I wasn't, but I had to be less than honest that evening. While she was smoking her cigarette and rubbing her feet, sore from a day in the hairdresser's, I was in the kitchenette with my back to her, filling up the wedding glasses with eighty per cent voddy to twenty per cent Coke for her, and five per cent voddy to ninety-five per cent Coke for me.

'Don't let me get drunk.' I handed her the glass where she was sitting on the sofa, her feet up on a dirty fluffy cube foot rest. 'Or I'll go home and Mum will be on my back telling me I'm always drunk and I've brought a problem back with me from London.'

'God, I get you. I mean, like totally saaaaame.' She held up her glass and knocked it back in one. I did the same then took her glass and headed back to the kitchenette for a refill. She took it and again drank it all in one; I tipped back mine (pure Coke now) and held out my hand for her glass. 'Another?'

'Fuck, yes.' She slammed the glass into my hand and gave a sassy smile, flirtatious brows. 'Like, I do it for the turn-up, know what I'm saying?'

'Totally.'

And so went the evening. Me acting and poor Michaela falling slowly, but steadily, into the trap. The evening grew long over the park; the trees developed huge, dignified shadows stretching up the valley. Moths came to batter against the window, so high above the ground that they were dew-laden. Michaela and I talked about everything – about the crushes we'd had at school, about diets and who was hotter, Kim Kardashian or Gigi, which shops in Gloucester might sell vintage Juicy Couture trackies. Everything Michaela said reminded me of the gap that had opened up since I went to London – or was it just the gap that'd always been there? Hadn't I noticed before that she only had one toilet and had to hang her clothes on the front of the wardrobe, whereas I, to my shame, had a walk-in wardrobe full of spaces I couldn't fill? And four toilets I could choose from. I was a little ashamed to find myself getting cross when she couldn't stop talking about the price of dresses in New Look, instead of caring about what was happening between the United States and Russia and what moderate British Muslims thought about Afghanistan and how much the Shard was charging people to go up to the top.

I'm not proud of how I was that night, not at all.

'Chaela,' I said at nine o'clock, when almost two-thirds of the bottle had gone. I sat up straight on the sofa and tapped her on the foot. She was getting bleary by then and lying back with her feet up on the sofa next to me, twiddling her hair in front of her eyes and talking about nothing in particular.

'Wha'?' she said.

'I'm sorry I upset you. About the deer and that. I feel like you must think I'm nuts.'

She slowly sat up and groped for another cigarette. Lit it, unsteady with the flame, and took a long draw. 'You know what's weird?'

'What?'

She got herself into a sitting position, feet wide like a man's, elbows on knees. 'No one at my hairdresser's even knows I was in that crash.'

'No one in London knew 'bout me either. Why is that? Don't we wanna talk about it?'

'I dunno.' She blew out the smoke and shook her head ruefully. 'I mean, honest to God, Alex, there are things I never told anyone that I'm, like, literally terrified anyone might find out.'

There was a long, long silence while she stared at me with bloodshot eyes. Then abruptly her mouth turned down at the corners, her brow crumpled and tears rolled down her cheeks. I put my glass down hurriedly and shuffled over to her.

'Shit. Michaela, I'm a fat-mouth. What did I say? I'm so, so sorry.'

'No, it's OK.' She rubbed her nose with the back of her hand and pressed her fingers into her eyes. 'It's OK, I swear it's not your fault.'

'I didn't mean to upset you.'

'You didn't. It's just . . . oh fuck. Oh fuck, oh fuck, oh fuck.'

She kept crying and pushing the tears off her face, sucking on her cigarette in between sobs. I jumped up and hastily found some tissues, made another drink and brought it for her. She grabbed the tissues and the drink. Took tiny sips, deep breaths in between, slowly getting a grip.

'Michaela? Whatever I've said, I'm literally dying here, I'm so sorry.'

'No, don't be sorry. It's me should be sorry. About what I said the other day – you were right. I never saw a deer.' She sat back abruptly, the tissue held over her face, shaking her head. 'I'm never supposed to tell any one this. It's been like this fucking secret inside me all this time.'

I sat down next to her and waited for the tears to subside. She sipped at the drink until she'd calmed herself down, and eventually that time-honoured cop technique of not speaking, not interrupting, paid off. Slowly she began to relax.

'It was Dad,' she sniffed. 'He was up to something, but I don't know what. Whoever you saw that night, they . . . they'd been coming for him for a long time. They ran him off the road.'

I took a long, silent breath, my mouth open so she didn't hear my shock. I was right. There *had* been someone else on the road. I wasn't going mad.

'Someone was coming for your dad?'

'It was like this huge family secret. I wasn't supposed to know but I did. Mum used to yell about it when she thought I wasn't listening, going on about how Dad had brought it all on us.' Michaela rubbed her arms as if they'd suddenly become cold. She dropped her hands and looked at me, her nose red and swollen, mascara running down her face. 'She and Dad kept arguing about . . . about a place where people were – were having sex in cars, at a spot somewhere in Eastonbirt. I didn't fully understand it at the time, but I kept hearing them shouting the same things. Something was going on. One night I walked in on Dad, right here. He was staring out of the window at the park and . . . ' She slung the remainder of the vodka into her mouth. Drooped forward, red-eyed. Shaking her head. 'And he was crying.'

'Jesus.'

She put the glass down, stood unsteadily and made her uncertain way to the window. Beyond her the sun was so low, the last orange rays were picking out all the smears and dirt on the glass. Part of me was glad it was so opaque – a shield between us and the park, spreading its hands out across the darkening valley.

'Look at all them trees, Alex.' She put her palms on the glass. 'Going on for miles. And somewhere underneath them all a place. A room, somewhere under the ground. That's where they come from.'

My skin prickled. 'Under the ground?'

She nodded. 'There's a place. A bunker, Dad called it.'

'A *bunker*? Where?'

'I don't know. I just know if I ever find a place in the park where steps lead down I've got to never go down there. I've got to run away as fast as I can.'

'Michaela?'

'Yes.'

'Who? Who was after your dad?'

There was another endless silence. She didn't turn to me and her voice was muffled when she spoke. 'The bonehead. The hooker in the park. It's her.'

I stared at her, not sure if she was being serious. I said tentatively, 'You know the bonehead is a myth, don't you? A ghost story?'

She gestured blearily to the window where the last of the sun had flattened itself out across the escarpment. As if she hadn't heard me speak she said, 'She's out there somewhere. Somewhere under all of that, she's waiting.'

Maryam

The main bathroom on the landing of the Bakehouse was painted half lime-green and half orange. It had all Arran's things in a basket at one end of the bath, all Minty's toys at the other. Funny, sweet, and odd for them, with such a huge age difference, to be sharing a bathroom. More than once strangers had taken Arran for Minty's father.

That evening Maryam set Minty down on the floor of the bathroom and peeled off her dress. It was sunflower-yellow, with a little lace collar made from a wedding veil she'd got in the Eastonbirt charity shop and daisies she'd crocheted across the front. So many people had complimented it over the months.

'Not sure we'll get another wear out of this, my darling.' She examined it. It was covered in grass stains and mud. To look at it, you'd think someone had dragged her along the ground on her back. 'Have you been lying on the ground, you mucky pup?'

'Puppy, puppy,' Minty sang. 'Where Tumble?'

Maryam sighed. She'd thought this was over. How did she answer this? How did she begin to give breadth and height to the enormous thing wedging itself deep in this family? Lois had said, quite solemnly, that Minty had seen Maryam in the woods and had run in there to greet her. At the time Maryam must have been almost a quarter of a mile away, hidden completely from the play park around the edge of a cleft in the escarpment.

Madness, madness, you move as slow as a cloud.

'Sweetie.' She put her hands on Minty's arms and looked her in the eye. 'Mummy's got to tell you something. Tumble loves it here, he loved you, he loved Arran and Horky, but he . . . ' She searched for an idea. 'He didn't like the grass outside. It made him sneeze, so he's gone to a nice new house where he won't sneeze. Another lovely, lovely family.'

Minty plugged a thumb into her mouth and watched Maryam cautiously.

'Darling, he's much happier now he's stopped sneezing.'

'Sneezy?'

'Yes. Sneezing. He can't ever come back here, darling. He can't because he'll sneeze and it will make him very ill. He's happier where he is.'

Minty's pout fattened. 'No Tumble.'

'No more Tumble. I'm sorry.'

Minty gave a long, heartfelt sigh. It must have been something she'd learned from someone else because it was so exaggerated, so theatrical, that Maryam had to stop herself smiling. She became efficient: put the dress in the wicker laundry hamper and got Minty's pink comb from the windowsill. 'Time to brush your hair.'

She put the comb in and found a little braid up near the nape of Minty's neck, tied off with gingham ribbon. She examined the braid for a moment, surprised. It was hidden by the fall of her hair over the top and was so tiny it was almost invisible. Lois must have done it while they were playing. Or Arran, or Rhory.

'I'm going to have to take this out now,' she said, untangling it. 'Just for bedtime.' She pocketed the ribbon, smoothed Minty's hair and tucked it behind her ears. Then she helped her step with her pudgy little feet into her sleepsuit, the yellow one with the two Minions pictured running away, underneath them the words *I didn't do it* . . . She buttoned it up and turned Minty to face her, her hands on her shoulders. 'You are so beautiful.'

Minty smiled and waggled her horse at Maryam. 'Horky bed.'

'Are you sleepy, Horky?' Mayram put her nose to the little animal's face and nuzzled it. 'You're such a clever horse.'

Minty squealed with delight and crinkled her face into a grin. They took turns kissing Horky and laughing. Maryam knew how selfish she was. She knew she should be thanking fate daily for the beauty of her life with her little girl and yet . . .

And yet.

Alex

I thought I didn't have a runaway imagination, thought I was good at putting things in sensible boxes, but that night, leaving Michaela's, my imagination had taken hold and wasn't letting go. Mike Lewis had talked about the bonehead as if she was real. Did that mean he'd believed he'd seen a ghost, or was it a closer clue to my theory that any urban legend had some roots in fact? Had Mike known something that I could add to the myth to make sense of it? And what was this bunker Michaela was so afraid of?

I walked back the long way, through the village and along the road, rather than taking the short cut through the park. The streets of Eastonbirt had an abandoned feeling. One or two summer parties were just audible from the bigger houses on the hill, but the centre of town itself was silent. My head was pounding.

By the time I got home the stars were out, pinpoints in the clear sky. The porch light was on but Mum had gone to bed, and Bamber greeted me at the door, holding Hat gently in his mouth, his backside wagging from side to side, delighted to find that there was another visitor after he'd thought lights were out for the night.

I followed him into the kitchen, throwing down my keys and kicking off my sweaty trainers. I went to the fridge and this time had a drink for real – one of Mum's bottles of Cristal was already open. I downed two glasses straight off, standing there at the breakfast counter, seeing my ghostly white face reflected in the black pane of glass.

It had been bizarre, and an affront to all the things I'd convinced myself were important – like lying, and self-respect – to have tricked poor Michaela, who was an alcoholic aged twenty-one and who was scared and worried about her mother, but kept talking and feeding me information. It was all wrong but I'd done it anyway. I wasn't sure how it made me feel.

The champagne hit my stomach. I drew a glass of water from the expensive ice-maker in the front of the fridge, carried it into the living area and collapsed on Mum's elegant grey sofa. Bamber followed, sitting patiently at my feet, Hat on the ground in front of him.

I lifted my backside and felt around in my rear pocket for the piece of paper I'd brought home with me. Michaela had drawn this from memory – a box-like room. The way she'd imagined it from what Mike Lewis had told her.

I smoothed out the paper and examined it more closely. Under the picture were some notes I'd scribbled the moment I'd got into the lift to jog my memory. 'Parents arguing. Dogging. Bunker.'

'What the fuck?' I asked Bamber, who was watching me curiously, head on one side. 'Am I a ghost whisperer now, or what?'

He gave a huge sigh and settled down, his chin on his paws, watching me with his crazy hairy eyebrows quirking up and down, side to side.

'Come on.'

I got up and went downstairs to Mum's gym. Bamber followed me carefully, one step at a time. I clicked on the light

and stood in the doorway. Mum hadn't drawn the curtains
– reflected in the black glass was the yellow oblong of the
door, with me standing in it, short and pale-skinned. Bamber
pushed past me into the room. He walked around a couple of
times without much interest, occasionally giving one of the
machines a half-hearted sniff. Then he sighed and sat down in
the middle of the room, looking at me as if waiting for me to
explain why we were there, and what was so important.

'Nothing,' I said, clicking off the light. 'Absolutely nothing.'

Maryam

The next morning Maryam walked into the kitchen and found Rhory at the computer. Surprised, he quickly shut down the browser window. 'Maryam.' He closed the laptop and smiled guiltily at her. 'OK?'

She put Minty into her high chair, gave her some apple slices to nibble, and continued with what she had come in to do – getting the Aga warmed up in preparation for the porridge she'd promised Minty. But with every notch of the dials, every checking on the heat, her attention was on Rhory and his computer. He was hiding something. For the first time in their marriage he was behaving as if he had a secret.

Keep calm, keep calm.

'I, uh . . . ' Rhory rubbed his nose. 'Did you go to the doctor's?'

'Yes.'

'And?'

'She agrees. It's postpartum depression. A mild case. I've got pills.'

'Pills? That's not like you.'

Maryam shrugged. 'Sometimes you have to adjust. You have to take the care that's offered.'

'Yes.' He let his eyes trail wonderingly over her. 'Yes.'

She continued with measuring out the oats, chopping the apple, tipping out the raisins, the brown sugar, trying not to look over and meet his eyes. What if he asked to see the pills? He wouldn't do that, would he?

After a while he scraped back the chair and grabbed his keys from the bowl next to the door. 'I'm going to head out. Don't want to be late.'

'Are you going to work?'

He paused, his hand on the doorknob, and turned back to look at her. 'Of course. Where else would I be going?'

She gave a half-smile. 'I don't know. Have a good time.'

She stood for a while, watching him go out of the front door and to the car. He wore jeans and a grey T-shirt she'd never seen before. As always, his hard arms and chest were tanned from all the time he spent outdoors working on his roofs and sheds and garden furniture. He had a single leather thong around his neck. Had he at last, after all this time, noticed how beautiful he was? And how plain and big and ugly his wife was?

She went to his computer and started it up. The browser history had been deleted for the past twenty-four hours. She stared at it for a long time, the screen fizzing white and grey in her head.

No. She wasn't going to lose her head. She wasn't. She threw the tea towel over her shoulder and set to work mixing in the raisins. In her chair Minty studiously fed apple to the horse, wagging her finger at him, lisping, 'Horky eat, Horky eat.' The sun was coming up. The shadows of the trees grew shorter in the garden.

Maryam closed the back door, locking it tight.

Alex

I had a habit of always keeping the window open overnight, even back when I'd lived in Hammersmith where the rush hour started at six a.m. In Mum's house my bedroom was up on the second floor, under the eaves, and I liked the fresh air coming through the window. That night I didn't sleep well – every sound from the woods unnerved me, made me restless – but when I woke the sun was up and the woods were benign and innocent. When I peered down into the garden Bamber was sitting calmly on the lawn next to Mum, who had put on a white one-piece swimsuit and sunglasses, and was reading the newspaper under a huge patio umbrella.

The trees beyond them were unmoving in the morning heat. Innocent-looking. You'd never think anything was going on under that benign surface.

I called Arran and arranged to meet him for lunch.

The café was a narrowboat moored in the Gloucester docks, a giant red teapot mounted on top of it. On the deck were various chairs and tables, in multicoloured ice-cream shades: pistachio, strawberry and cream. Arran was waiting for me at a table painted tangerine with a jar full of heather in the centre. He was wearing a well-fitted, expensive suit and his dark hair had been trimmed, the sideburns shaved neatly. I knew, from the way he self-consciously fingered the lapels as I came along the pavement, that he wasn't comfortable with the way he was dressed. He was certainly attracting attention from some of the women on board.

A calm, long-haired woman in a mirrored skirt ran the café; the menu had organic bacon sandwiches and gluten-free cakes lined up under glass domes. I had a spicy bean burger and edamame salad and Arran made a joke about hamster food and about going to work every day to get away from the hippy cooking at home, but changed his mind when the apple and caraway seed cake turned up in front of him, so newly baked it was still warm. We sipped huge, frothy cappuccinos and he told me about the project he was working on.

We'd always been this relaxed together. Always.

'Arran,' I said after a while. 'Good news. I'm not going mad.'

He paused, the cup to his mouth, regarding me over the lip. 'Shame.' He lowered the cup. Set it in the saucer. 'I like you a little insane.'

'I spoke to Michaela last night.'

'Michaela Lewis? I thought she'd drunk herself to death.'

'Not yet. She's got a job in a hairdresser's. She's just about keeping herself alive.' I picked up a teaspoon and idly tapped its handle on the table. 'She told me some things.'

He raised his eyebrows.

'But it's between you and me, OK? I gave her my word.'

'Goes no further.'

I glanced around to check no one was listening. The café was filling up. There was a couple at the next table both wearing dreadlocks and those long Turkish trousers that were so popular. They had a baby in a striped cotton baby sling who had been sick and they were arguing, as they mopped her up, about whether her food should be chopped up smaller.

I put my elbows on the table and leaned across to Arran so I could speak in a low voice. 'There *was* someone out there that night, someone who ran the coach off the road. It wasn't a deer.'

Arran folded his arms. His narrow expression said he was going to be hard to convince.

'Now, Michaela, like, *literally* still believes in ghosts. She swears it was the bonehead. And whatever sarcastic look you're going to give me, first of all – and look me in the eye here – *I am not a believer*. OK? I'm not going head-fuck on you.'

Arran screwed up his face. It was plain he was trying hard to accept this ludicrous notion. 'This is a proper fairy story, Alex, but for the sake of all the times you covered my arse when we were playing paintballs, or shared your flags with me, or helped me change a tyre, I'm going to make the effort, for the sake of our friendship. Just don't expect the serious look all the time, OK?'

'That's fine. I'll ignore the sniggers. So apparently Mike Lewis had a problem – someone after him. Any ideas?'

Arran shook his head.

'Do you know anything about rumours of dogging?'

'Uh – yeah. Of course I do.'

I fixed him with a stare. 'You're laughing already? You couldn't have kept a straight face for just a few minutes?'

'The rumours are real. You know Parson's Pike?'

'Of course I do. It's a scenic point.' Parson's Pike was an outcrop of rock on the Cotswold escarpment which peered out west, towards the lowlands of the Severn and Wales.

He gave me a pitying look. 'Serious? You don't know?'

'No.'

'If you're asking about dogging, that's where it happens now.'

I stared at him, feeling the weight of something in my head shift. Mike Lewis. Dogging. Someone coming after him. Secrets. Michaela's mother yelling when she thought she couldn't be overheard. Arguing with her dad.

'I forget you've been away for so long.' Arran smiled at my ignorance. 'They moved up there after the kids' playground got put down on the site in the park. Remember?'

'The Dandelion playground? Mum's place?'

'Yup.'

'I'd forgotten.' The Dandelion Play Park had been funded by Mum's charity. It included access for disabled children and a scent garden for the blind. The place allocated by the Trust, a hectare not far from the lakes, had once been a dogging site and now I remembered all the fuss at the time, the long-winded emails back and forward from the Trust and the council and the charity administrators about how to move the men on from their preferred site. It had never occurred to me that the doggers would have to find somewhere else. Naïve or what?

'I suppose there has to be one in every smart Cotswold, town right?'

'One can only assume.'

Dogging was one of those things that I'd learned about in London in the Force when we'd occasionally have to go out and do drive-bys (sometimes we did it just for the vibe of watching people fleeing, pulling up their trousers). Until then I'd only ever heard people joking about it, never really believed it. I'd had vague pictures of couples doing it doggy-style in the woods, hadn't known that the 'dog' part of it was from the excuse men gave their wives: *Just out to walk the dog, darling*.

In reality it wasn't the dangerous, murky thing I'd imagined; it was just depressing. A lot of lonely men and one or two women, mostly pissed, or high, and either paid for it, or plain desperate to impress on their men how sexually liberated they were.

Michaela talking about a ghost and her dad with a secret? Where did that fit in? My elusive element of truth at the bottom of the bonehead legend.

'Her dad told her not to go down any steps in the park. He said there's an underground room out there somewhere.' I tapped my spoon a little harder. 'So on the one hand we've got a bunch of pervs shagging strangers, and on the other we've got an underground place, somewhere out in the park. What do you think?'

'I don't know.'

'Well, I think I should start with the doggers.'

He raised an eyebrow. 'Rad. Never thought it would be more conservative just doing a Tinder date?'

'I'm serious. I'm going to. Except I can't do it on job time. I've got to be inventive.'

'Inventive? Sounds risky.'

'It is. We'll take my car.'

'You what?'

'Tonight. We're going up there.'

He sighed and rubbed his face. 'Alex, if you get caught you'll get into about a hundred different types of trouble.'

'I know. Are you on?'

Maryam

Her iPhone on the dashboard. The number in red. *Call Bristol Swami home?*

Call Bristol Swami home?

Maryam in the driver's seat, sitting on clenched fists. Not trusting herself. She dragged one hand out from under her and clicked the Home button. The screen dissolved. Shaking, she wound down the window and stared out of the car.

It was early afternoon. The back seat was piled high with samples: wallpapers and paint charts, upholstery fabric books and trim boards. Today was the day of the week she reserved to discuss colour schemes with clients, usually the thing she loved the most: the click of pleasure when a fabric held against a paint chart made a light come on in a client's eye. But Rhory's browser history, cleared? If she'd been born here in Eastonbirt, or born beautiful, the history wouldn't have been cleared. She was sure of it.

After her last client she'd driven here to Stroud, to an anonymous car park behind a supermarket, where all the lorries thundered by, bringing goods into town from the far-flung fields of Spain and South Africa. Where flattened cardboard boxes were stacked in wire cages. Where the bittersweet smell of meat hung in the air and the swill of water from the supermarket cold store room ran out on to the tarmac.

On the front seat was a tub of pills. She'd found an old plastic medicine pot at the back of a cupboard, empty, still with her name printed on the label from some long-ago prescription.

In a chemist she'd found the most anonymous-looking aspi-rins possible, had disposed of the box and blister packs and shovelled the pills into the pot. If Rhory ever asked, she'd pro-duce these. Lies locked you tighter than the truth, but what else could she do?

No one would see her here. No one. She picked up the phone again, looked at it, then turned it face-down. Stared at the young man, younger than Arran, dressed in green and white overalls, throwing a pile of moulded fruit trays on top of the boxes. Then turned the phone back over and hit the Call button.

Three rings, no more. Then, 'Hello?'

She held her breath, not daring to speak.

'Hello? Who's there?'

'It's . . . ' Her voice was congested and cracked. 'Maryam. From Wales.'

A long silence. Then he said, in a calm voice, 'Hello, Maryam. Can I help you?'

'Yes, I . . . I need to talk. I'm in so much trouble. Everything you said has happened.'

'Come and see me straight away – I've got an appointment available this evening.'

'No. No, I can't.'

'You must.'

'You don't understand – I can't.' The moment she went to Bristol Rhory would know. The way blood poisoning could creep up a blood vessel, visible on the surface of the skin – somehow he'd track her madness all the way down the M5, the M32, straight into the heart of the city. 'My parents are both dead, my dog has disappeared, I've seen something stalking me in the trees where I live and now my daughter is seeing things too. I want to make it stop. Please make it stop.'

'Maryam – come and see me. I beg you. Come and see me.'

'Can't we just talk? On the phone?'

'I don't do telephone consultations.'

She began to cry. Tears puddling in her eyes and mucus coming out of her nose. She hadn't a handkerchief so she had to wipe her nose on the sleeve of her Paisley blouse. 'I can't come down, please, I can't. Just please make it stop.'

'OK, OK, look, quietly now. I'll tell you one thing.'

'Yes?'

'Listen carefully. If you can find the place the spirit is coming from, you can approach it – tell it to stop.'

She sniffed up the mucus, rubbed her eyes. 'I don't under-stand.'

'You heard me. Find the place it lives, then face off with it. Tell it to stop.'

'But I . . .'

'I'm sorry – I can't continue. I don't do telephone consul-tations; they can be dangerous. You can make an appointment – Like me on Facebook and I'll send you some information.'

The phone went down.

Maryam, in her scruffy Vauxhall, wound the window up so the boy in the overalls wouldn't hear her, shoved her hand into her mouth, and sobbed.

Alex

As soon as all the Response and Investigation team had left the locker room, I hastily shoved my tac vest into a holdall. Checked my radio was powered down and pushed it in too. Technically they were personal issue, so it wasn't exactly illegal me having them off duty, even so I marched out of the station as though I had a gun to my back, ramrod-straight, with a wide, false smile pasted on my face.

I was tired and sweaty and had only half an hour to collect Arran. When I got home, though, I found Mum on the lawn, staring into the woods, her hands on her hips and a look of despair on her face. She was dressed in long polka-dot gloves and a wipe-clean apron with a picture of an ice-cream cone on it.

'What?' I called, though I knew the answer. Bamber. 'What's up now?'

'All I can say is, he must despise the chicken he gets at night. And the clean sofa he feels he has a right to.' She flipped her hand in the direction of the park. 'Well, if that's what he wants to do, he knows what I have to say about it.'

'He'll be fine, Mum. He's a dog. Being fine is what he does.'

'Really? Really?'

'Yes. Oh, God – Mum, yes, he'll be fine.'

'I can't understand it. He's never done this before.'

I bit my tongue, and left her to it. I could hear her yelling for him across the garden as I went upstairs. I showered and dressed in combats and a T-shirt, pausing in front of the mirror and leaning in to study my face. Wide and freckled.

Dark lashes but not a lot else going for me. What the hell did I think I was doing? I was going to be laughed at. I opened the drawers in the bathroom and rummaged through them until I found some bits of make-up left over from my teenage days. I shovelled them into the holdall with all my police kit, then, at the last minute, threw in a ridiculous rape alarm I used to carry around at fourteen. The battery was probably dead.

Arran was waiting at the top of the driveway to the Bakehouse. He was wearing commando black, with walking boots and his own rucksack over his shoulder. When he slid into the passenger seat he smelled of aftershave. Not something I'd ever smelled on him before.

'Arran – this can never go any further, OK? This is serious shit I'm playing with at work.'

'I know it. Believe me, I know it.' He put on the seatbelt. As I drove, he spread out on the dashboard a huge printed map. 'Meanwhile I'm officially the geological king. Look at this – it's the cliffs under Parson's Pike. Off a cavers' website.'

'Wow! Found anything?'

'Not really. In fact, it's disappointing. There's absolutely nothing in the car park itself, Dad and me looked round it when we were searching for Tumble. Plenty of condoms and knickers but no underground rooms. The only place we might find something is this ridge.' He ran a finger along a contour line. 'But honestly? I don't think so.'

We parked down the escarpment next to Loxton's Chase, a pub only a few hundred yards away from the Parson's Pike car park, and made our way through the overgrown grass to the place under the scenic point where the land fell away. There was a little dip in the bushes from which you could look back and see the entire tan stripe of rock under the clifftop; no trees or shrubs, just a naked geological display of strata.

I had no clear idea of what we were looking for. Steps, Michaela had said. That implied something man-made. We found a rough ledge about twenty feet below, not a proper pathway but maybe a fox or badger run – and managed to creep along it. Every few yards we stopped to inspect the stone, checking we weren't missing any holes among the vegetation. Behind us, fifty miles to the west over the Brecon Beacons the sun was silently sliding into the horizon. It would be picking out the mountains on the east coast of America, but it was done with England. The shadows around the trees had got long and molten and headlights had started to appear in the car park on the top of the cliff.

The doggers.

Arran didn't say anything, but I could tell he didn't really believe there was such a thing as a bunker. An underground room. He said this was near the place his parents had found a dead badger when they were looking for Tumble, but that had been in a natural crack between rocks, not steps.

We searched for an hour, then it was too dark to keep going. We stood for a while, peering off the edge down into the trees, both lost in thought. We'd searched just one tiny section of the escarpment. Below us were acres and acres of uncharted land. A dozen places a dog could die. A hundred places a woman's body could lie and become mummified. A thousand holes that could lead to an underground room. The park could swallow anything and keep it secret for years. A dog. A Roma prostitute. A dead man's secret.

By the time we got back to the car the whole escarpment was swallowed in darkness and Loxton's Chase pub was lit up like a beacon.

'Plan B?' he said, getting into the passenger's seat. 'There are plenty of cars up at the car park now.'

I sat breathing slowly to calm myself. I'd seen the number of cars. 'Yes. I mean – I suppose it was always going to happen.' I leaned over the back of the seat, pulled over my holdall and began unpacking my police kit – the radio, and my tac vest. 'This – ' I waggled the radio at him ' – stays off regardless, OK? I'd rather dial 999 than use it. It's for show, nothing else.'

'Fair enough. What's the plan?'

'We've got to go in there as though we're part of it.'

'Yes, I knew that,' he said. 'I've researched the etiquette, so I'll start the thing.'

'You've *researched* it?'

'Weird that I don't just know what to do – is that what you're saying?'

I grinned. 'I'm sorry.'

'I'm driving – it'll look wrong you driving. And . . . er . . . ' He looked pointedly down at my black fleece and combat trousers.

'I know. I'm sorted.'

I dragged the bits of make-up from the holdall, flipped down the visor and used the little mirror to put on some make-up. I darkened my eyebrows, drew a line across the top of my lashes, and outlined my lips in red.

Arran was silent as I worked. When I was finished, I pulled off the fleece to reveal a thin black vest.

He looked at me steadily for a long time.

'What?' I said. 'This is role-playing. Nothing else. Role-playing.'

He shook his head. Looked bitterly out of the window at the darkening branches. My insides turned over slowly. Was he disgusted by me? Was it all too weird for him?

'Arran?'

'Nothing.' He pulled out his phone and switched it to silent. 'Right – if we're going to do this, now is the time.'

Maryam

It was the day of the week the Hansels always came over together: Fenton to take Rhory to the pub and Lois just to sit and chat with Maryam. Arran had gone out early, but Minty was still awake. Maryam carried her out on to the drive at the front to greet them.

'Low lows.'

'That's right, sweetie. That's Lois. Lois's car.'

'Low's car. Green.'

Maryam tucked her chin down to look at her daughter. 'That's exactly right. Lois's car is green. You clever girl, you nearly made a sentence.'

Minty smiled shyly and dug her face against Maryam's neck, pleased with the praise but self-conscious too. Arran had never been shy with praise. It was amazing to Maryam how two children could look so much like brother and sister yet behave so differently. Maryam kissed her hair.

'Clever Minty.'

Fenton got out and let Lois reverse her lime-green Beetle so that it wasn't blocking the driveway. He looked pale and a little shaken. He was wearing a white striped shirt open at the neck tucked into cord trousers. There were sweat circles under his arms.

When he saw Maryam watching he held up a hand in greeting. 'Hi, Maryam. Hi, Minty.'

'Are you OK?'

'Fine, thanks. Absolutely fine. Rhory?'

'In the back garden.'

She watched him walk to the side of the house. He wasn't fine. There was something crooked about his body, as if he was holding himself very carefully over a spike that would impale him if he relaxed. But there was no time to think about it because Lois was out of the car, looking neither ill nor worried. She wore a pale pink scarf and kitten heels. She held out her arms. 'Minty? A hug for Auntie Lois?'

Maryam held Minty out. Obediently she looped octopus arms around Lois's neck and leaned her head on her shoulder.

'Now then,' Lois said, carrying her into the house, 'tell me, is that the sleepsuit I bought you? This one with the sheep on it? Do you count those sheep when you go to sleep? Hmmm? Baaa?'

'Baa,' Minty said. Then, because she was proud of herself, 'Low's car green.'

'Her first sentence, I think,' said Maryam.

'You clever little thing. You are a clever little sausage, aren't you? And are you ready for bed now? Feeling sleepy?'

'Low's car green.'

'That's right. What do you think of my pearls, Minty? Pretty, aren't they? That's it, gently. Don't pull too hard now.'

In the workroom, all the cushions Maryam had been working on were draped over the surfaces. The tapestry she'd started based on the old arboretum design was hanging over a chair. While she made a space on the seats, Lois untangled Minty's hand from the pearls and set her down on the floor. The moment she found her feet on the ground she began to run round in excited circles. 'Tea tie, Lows. Tea tie.'

'It's gone teatime, you little monkey. Long gone. It's time for mummies to have their treats now.' Laid out on the table in the centre were three oval dishes Maryam had assembled:

some baklava she'd made last week, some medjool dates, and on the third dish a block of weird Basque cheese one of Rhory's clients had given them. There was also a bowl of fig chutney from the figs in the garden. A bottle of sauvignon stood with two squat glasses next to it. Lois rubbed her hands together. 'Yummy yummy, Minty's mummy always gives me happy tummy.'

'Yummy yummy,' Minty echoed. 'Yummy yummy.'

'Time to go to bed now, Minty. You've said hello to Lois, now it's time for byebyes.'

'No no no.' She jumped up and down on the spot. The feet on her sleepsuit pulled off her toes and flopped around as she danced in a circle, moving her hands up and down. 'No no no bed!'

From the sofa Lois raised her eyebrows at Maryam. 'Can't she sleep here? It can't hurt, can it? She used to do it all the time.'

'Minty sleep here! Sleep here.'

Maryam gave a long sigh. Two sentences in one day. Minty was learning to argue. 'OK.' She held up her hands. 'I give in. Let's get you comfortable.'

Minty scrambled on to the sofa next to Lois and lay down obediently, head resting on her lap. Maryam fetched a hand-stitched quilt she'd bought in a shop in Eastonbirt; one day she intended to unpick it and use the fabric in a project. For the time being it was a perfect throw. She tucked Minty up, pushed Horky into her arms. 'That's it. Close those eyes now.'

It took a while for Minty to be convinced that Lois and Maryam were serious – she really was going to have to go to sleep. But eventually she stopped wriggling and moving around and pushed Horky up against her face, her thumb in her mouth, her eyes closed.

While she slowly calmed herself, the two women spoke in a mixture of sign language and whispers. Maryam filled glasses in silence, held one to Lois to drink so Minty wouldn't be disturbed. Hand-fed her a couple of snacks. They both tried hard not to laugh.

Eventually Lois put a hand on Minty's head, watched her for a few breaths, then winked at Maryam. 'Mission accomplished, I think.'

'Let's put her on the other end of the sofa. I'll take her up when I go to bed. She'd sleep through a nuclear attack, this child.'

Together the women carefully laid her sideways across two sofa cushions. Minty grumbled faintly in her sleep as Maryam tucked a blanket around her and pushed Horky down between her arms.

Maryam filled glasses. She made another plate of dates for Lois. Then she sat, cross-legged, her head on one side. 'Is Fenton OK?'

'I'm sorry?'

'Fenton looks . . . ' She shook her head. 'I don't know. Earlier I thought he looked unwell.'

Lois smiled dismissively. 'Oh, no, he's fine. Just being a baby. You know what men are like.'

'I guess.'

A few more minutes ticked by; they exchanged desultory information. The dress code for the unveiling of the bench at the weekend. Victoria wanted everyone to wear something orange to represent the charity, whereas Lois thought it was hyper-controlling to dictate what people wore and shouldn't it be black for a memorial? Meanwhile, had Maryam heard? The Ragged Stall had been downgraded by Environmental Health. Who knew what they'd found? Lois had heard it was rat droppings.

Maryam smiled and responded, but what she really wanted to say was, *What did you see near the play park the other day? When Minty ran into the trees after me, did you see anything?* She wanted to tell Lois what was happening, share the burden. But if Lois told Fenton, Fenton would tell Rhory and they'd come full circle back to Maryam, the mad woman, and *Aren't the pills helping, darling? Do we need a second opinion – should I come with you to the doctor?*

She stood. 'I'll get us some more wine.'

In the kitchen she put the cooled leftovers from dinner into Tupperware, dumped all the pots in the sink and got another bottle of wine from the fridge. The back door was open; the two men hadn't gone to the pub yet, they were still at the table, opposite each other, hunched over, deep in conversation – a look of intensity she'd never seen between them before.

She stopped and watched them for a while. On the table the plate of food she'd made for them was untouched. There were four beer bottles and a glass of water. Fenton was drawn and grey, as if he'd had a tremendous shock. Meanwhile Rhory was talking slowly and reassuringly. From time to time they both turned to look into the trees.

Her pulse began to race. It was hard to be sure from this angle but it seemed to her that they were focusing on the exact place in the woods where Tumble had gone missing. The place she'd seen the apparition.

Shakily she draped the tea towel over the Aga. She ran the tap, scooped up a handful of water into her mouth, splashed a little on her face, patted it dry. Feeling a little clearer, she headed out into the garden. Both men hastily turned to her, their faces wallpapered with fake smiles, eyes dim and unfocused because that was the way with most humans: they found it hard to lie with their eyes.

'Maryam. OK?'

'Yes. Just coming to get the tablecloth.'

'You sure you're OK? You look shaken.'

'Do I?'

'Yes – do you need to sit down?'

She took a long breath, half closing her eyes to keep herself steady. 'Nope. All fine. As I said, just the tablecloth.'

She collected it up, shook it, and took it back inside, closing the door behind her. She leaned on the door and put cold hands on her burning cheeks.

Alex

Arran drove in silence, back up the escarpment towards the viewpoint. Eastonbirt was behind us, the lights just coming on and reflecting in the giant lakes. We steered down a skinny single track, trees crouching in an arch overhead, then suddenly we were out in the car park at the top of the escarpment, the whole night revealed to us, sky peppered with stars and uplit clouds. Cars were ranged along the tarmac, each separated by three or four spaces, all facing out across the panorama.

I checked my phone mounted on the dashboard. It was jumping between 4G and 5G. The sweat gathered under my arms. 'Shit. I can't believe this is happening.'

'It's happening.'

Arran drove to the end of the lot. The ground was bumpy and little stones clinked against the underside of the car. There were about eight cars in total, all with just their brake lights on, no headlights. He brought my little Kia to a halt parallel to the others, facing out over the great gulp of night sky. It was a good position. He'd left enough room to swing the car around and accelerate away if things went wrong.

The other vehicles were darkened, the windows closed. A couple of solitary shapes in the drivers' seats.

'What now?' I hissed, smelling my own, tense breath in the closed car. 'What do we do?'

'Lock your door.'

I did.

He unbuckled his belt. 'Right – show your face, but don't meet anyone's eyes. Keep your focus on the dashboard. OK?'

I found a spot on the dash that I could stare at and lifted my chin. 'OK.'

He reached up to switch on the interior light. Instantly the forms in the other cars began to stir. A door opened and a stocky white guy with a shaved head got out, beginning to walk towards us.

'Fuck. Fuck.'

'Yeah,' Arran muttered. 'Fuck's sake . . . '

Before the sentence was out of his mouth the man had opened the back door. 'Hi.' He poked his head into the interior. 'Alright?'

'Hi,' we both said robotically. 'Get in.'

He was in the car and on the back seat already unzipping his trousers when he realised his mistake. He stopped what he was doing and raised his eyes to meet ours in the rear-view mirror. Instantly his face fell.

'What? *What?*'

Arran flashed his staff card – the one that had POLICE written big, and STAFF written small enough to be invisible in the dim light. 'I'm Sergeant Black.'

The guy dropped back into the seat, shaking his head, defeated. 'Nice. Except you can't do me for anything.'

'We're not here to "do" anyone for anything. We're just recceing the area because next week there's going to be a huge ANRS trial in the area.'

'A what?'

'Automatic Numberplate Recognition System,' I said, meeting his eyes in the rear-view mirror. He was in his forties, I guessed, with a thick neck and a row of studs in his right ear. 'What happens is, we take a data set from everyone who comes into the car park, and then we ask their permission to use their personal details with a trial of the software.'

'You what?'

'No problem if you don't want to talk about it – I can understand now might not be a good time. Shall we come and see you at home some time? Maybe a weekend or a . . . '

'OK, OK, enough.' He held up a hand to shut me up and addressed Arran. 'What do you want, mate?'

'Nothing. Just conversation.'

'Yeah, come on. Out with it.'

I fished in my pocket and pulled out my phone, swiping through until I found a photograph of Mike Lewis. I twisted in the seat and held it straight out, right in front of the dude's face so he couldn't ignore it. 'Know him?' It was the official one from the bus company ID, and then I swiped it to show one from Michaela's Facebook page. 'Do you know him?'

'No.'

'You sure? You're not looking. Here, I'll hold it closer. Never met him?'

He pushed the phone away from his face, and turned his head to one side. 'What if I have?'

'He's dead, so you can't really hurt him any more. But something was bothering him.'

'Oh, was it?'

'Yeah – something was happening up here that scared him. A woman in the woods at night. White dress. Strange face. Ring any bells?'

The guy rubbed his nose and ducked a little in the seat to glance out of the darkened windows as if wondering if we were being observed. Wondering if he could lie.

I smiled at him in the rear-view mirror. 'As I said, maybe this is a bit uncomfortable out here in the dark. Your house would be a much more relaxed environment for—'

'I said stop it. I'm talking, OK?' He began to tap his fingers on the seat, glancing side to side again. Then he said, 'OK – I tell you what. There is someone who might know. The one who told me about it. He's usually here tonight. Maybe a bit later. Keyhole Raj.'

'Keyhole Raj? What sort of a name is that?'

'You don't want to know.'

'You're probably right,' Arran said, screwing up his face. 'OK – so we wait.'

'Fine by me. He should turn up.'

We sat in silence while the dashboard clock clicked through the minutes. The guy leaned forward uncomfortably, rubbing his shins and lifting his chin to look out of the window. It was eerie hearing him breathe behind us. I could smell his after-shave now, and washing powder and the scent of cooking. By slightly tilting my head I could see through the gap in the seats, the side of his chunky leg, in denim. I saw a meaty hand and wrist, pale blond hairs and tattoos snaking up his arm. He was clenching and unclenching his fist.

'Shame,' he said, meeting my eyes in the mirror. 'I mean. big shame you're a cop, 'cos the tits and that. We could've . . . '

'Shut it.' Arran twisted round in the driver's seat and pushed himself into the space between the seats. 'When you're up to your neck you be like: *I'm sorry, I recognise the shit lake I'm swimming in and I'm not going to make more trouble.*' He jabbed a finger into the guy's face. 'Hear? You don't open your fuck-ing mouth.'

'OK, OK. Sorry.' He held up his hands and subsided in the seat. 'Truly, mate, I'm sorry. Didn't mean to go there.'

Arran turned back in the driver's seat, facing forward. He adjusted the rear-view mirror with precision, making the point that he could monitor the guy's movements. I was beyond embarrassed. I dipped my chin and tried not to meet anyone's eyes.

Headlights waxed and waned on the A417 and from time to time a car would swing into the lay-by. Each time the dude would straighten up and peer over his shoulder at the owner, then shake his head and settle back into his place. Cars circled us, but we sat like mourners, our heads lowered, as still as we could. One or two men wandered by, hands in pockets, shadows in the forest, stopping slightly to peer inside. My work ASP baton was lodged in next to the hand-brake within easy reach if the circling got too much. I let my hand rest on it. It was the way I imagined bush rangers in Africa would be, hands on weapons, keeping calm while the hyenas stalked.

'OK, that's him.' The man in the back straightened up as a set of headlights pulled to a stop not far from us. 'That's definitely him. Switch on your overhead.'

Arran clicked on the interior light. I lowered my hands so my face could be seen and half-closed my eyelids. There were a few beats of silence then footsteps on the gravel. Someone approaching the car.

Behind me, the man rolled down the window and leaned out. 'Keyhole. Care to join us?'

'I'm invited?'

'Yes, you're invited.'

I dared to look sideways at Raj. I had time to get the basics – he was Asian and medium height, very good-looking, with nicely cut hair and a catalogue-model suit. Then he was open-ing the door and getting into the back. Before any of us knew what was happening the tattooed guy had jumped out the other side, slammed the door and was backing away rapidly, holding his hands up, saying, 'Sorry, mate, sorry.'

I spun in the seat and thrust the warrant card in Raj's face. 'Don't get out, sir. Not yet. Just a quick chat. I really wouldn't get out if I were you.'

He stayed in his half-tensed position for a few more seconds, then, with a long exhalation of breath, slumped in the seat, shaking his head. In the dim light from his headlights I could make out a little more. He was the whole package: crisp white shirt and silk tie in pale orange and tan stripes. If I'd subconsciously stereotyped a dogger it wasn't anything like this. I half-expected him to start trying to sell me insurance. Instead he just sat there in the back seat, sweating, embarrassed, desperate to be anywhere but where he was now.

'Lovely night for a drive.' Arran folded his arms and casually wound down the window to gaze out at all the trees and the hills. 'Though it seems to me maybe you're not here for the views.'

Raj was silent, debating his options.

'There's a huge operation going on in the park – lots of police officers. Every car within the boundaries of the park is going to be PNC-checked. It's not what any of us want to do – it's orders from on high. You know, the monkeys on the top branches.'

Raj's shoulders drooped a little, his head hung a little lower. He twisted his wedding ring around his finger. 'Please,' he whimpered, 'I need to go. I'm going to be late.'

'Another time, then?'

'No. No.' He twisted the ring agitatedly, any remaining confidence seeping out of him. He was trembling like a child. He had lots to hide and we'd scared him. 'I'll deny speaking to you if I'm ever hauled up in front of a magistrate. I've got a mortgage to service, for fuck's sake – I can't get fired.'

'As far as we're concerned, after we go our separate ways this conversation never happened.' I held out my hands to show they were empty then twisted in the seat, unzipping my tac vest and opening it for Keyhole to see my radio was turned off. A magician proving to the audience there was no trick there. If he'd known more about the police he'd have known a dead radio meant I wasn't on duty and was doing this under the radar.

When five minutes had passed and there were no distant sirens, Keyhole seemed to trust us. 'What's the quickest way to move on from this? What do you need to know?'

I fumbled out a notepad. 'What do I call you?'

'Do you need that?'

'Yes. I've got to have a name. Keyhole Raj won't cut it.'

He hesitated. 'OK then . . . Patel. Raj Patel.'

As I wrote it down I could feel Arran smiling next to me. Raj Patel was a name like John Doe. All three of us knew he was lying. 'So, Raj, tell me, do you know this face?'

He took the phone and held it down on his knees, squinting at it, zooming in and out and fiddling with the brightness control. For a long time his expression didn't change or give anything away.

'Well?'

He pushed the phone back at me. 'He's dead, isn't he? I saw his face in the paper after the coach crash. I hadn't known his name until then.' He spoke into the window, misting the glass. 'But I'd seen him around.'

'He was part of this scene?'

'No – not exactly – something else, down there.' He made a circling gesture to indicate the park below us. 'Somewhere down there. He owed someone money.'

I stared at the dashboard, not wanting to move or speak while this sank in. Then I recovered myself, nodded, pretending this was exactly what I already knew. 'Yes. There's been a lot of chatter.'

'What sort of chatter?'

I could feel Arran's eyes on me, and I could almost hear the sarcastic comments that would roll through his thoughts when I said the word 'bonehead'. I did it anyway. 'Chatter about the bonehead.'

Raj visibly jolted back in his seat. There was a long pause while he moved his shoulders around as if he was trying to remove something that was sitting on his neck. He cleared his throat, sat forward in the seat, talking in a low whisper, casting his eyes from side to side, checking the darkened car park for anyone watching us.

'How do you know that?'

'As I said. A lot of chatter.'

He pressed his finger to his mouth, as if testing what he could safely say. Then he took it away. His eyes in the rear-view were dull, non-reflective. 'OK, so I've known about it for four years. I've seen a picture of her but I've never met her.'

'Her?'

'She's a hooker, works the park. People talk about her.'

'And what do they say?'

'Nothing. I mean – I dunno. They say she's got a pimp.' He lowered his chin and checked out of the windows. This was making him deeply uncomfortable. I could smell fear on him in this closed space. 'She's the first point of contact. Meaning no Tinder, no phone calls. The punter finds her in the woods

– a fixed time, a fixed place, down on the Eastonbirt Road. He follows her – meets her pimp. Then they do the business.'

'Why do you call her bonehead?'

'Because of the clingfilm round her head.'

Next to me Arran stiffened. I took a long slow breath through my nose. My eyes were stinging. From the woods nearby came the needling sound of an owl staking out its territory.

'Yes,' I said eventually. 'We heard about the clingfilm. She can breathe, can't she?'

'Of course. It's only a look. There's an urban legend about a woman murdered in the park who was a hooker – this is just a real hooker cashing in on the legend. But you knew that, didn't you?'

I lowered my face, allowing myself a moment of satisfaction. Everything I'd said about there always being a kernel of truth under these legends was being proved right . . . though here it sounded more as if the reality had grown from the legend, rather than the other way round. Still, I was strangely relieved. There *had* been someone on the road the night of the crash. I wasn't delusional.

'It's a bizarre way to hook up. It is just sex they're paying for?'

Raj gave a low, mirthless laugh. 'I think it's more than that. Though I suppose "sex" is the nearest you can get to describing what happens.'

I raised my eyes to his in the mirror. He was looking back at me steadily, almost sadly. Sweat had broken out on his forehead.

'What? What happens?'

He didn't answer for a long, long time as if he couldn't trust himself. 'I don't know for sure – I've never been there. But when you consider how secretive they are, how much money changes hands, the fact that her face is wrapped in clingfilm? You can guess at extreme S&M. Maybe worse.'

I let out a long stream of air from my nostrils. Next to me Arran rubbed his nose hard, his eyes lowered. Gnats battered softly against the windscreen and the brake lights from the other cars lit his face in a weird red glow.

'Where do you know all this from?'

Raj shifted uncomfortably in the back seat. The upholstery creaked. 'Mostly from him – Mike Lewis. I'd see him up here from time to time. Once he told me about the woman. How he was going to find her. He showed me a picture of her, freakish cow. And of the bunker she operated in.'

My spine stiffened slightly. 'A bunker?'

'That's where it happens. It's somewhere out there . . . ' He waved a hand in the direction of the park. 'But it's well hidden. Underground, I think.'

I had to pinch my knees hard to avoid looking over at Arran. Exactly what Michaela had said. A bunker. Under the ground.

'You'll be lucky to find her. She's stopped operating. Or gone very quiet.'

'How do you know?'

'Rumours. An incident happened one night, something bad, so they stopped. Although, as we all know, things like that never really stop. Not forever. Now, am I free to go? I've told you all I know, and I do know a little about my rights.'

'Of course.' I reached numbly into the back and pushed open the door. Relieved, Raj began to pull himself out of the car.

'Just one thing,' I said as he was about to close the door. 'You don't have any clue where this "bunker" is?'

Raj glanced over his shoulder to make sure he couldn't be overheard. He leaned back so his face was in the door-opening. 'No. In the picture she was in front of . . . columns, I think. White columns. But I've looked – believe me, I've searched this place.' He waved his hand out to indicate the park. 'And I have no idea where the photo was taken.' Then he was gone, pulling his car keys out and heading straight back to the smart Jaguar.

Arran and I said nothing, we sat in silence, digesting what had been said while Raj's car pulled out of the car park. It was Arran who finally broke the silence.

'I'm really sorry,' he muttered. 'You were right. I take it all back.'

Maryam

It was late, but Lois was still at the Bakehouse. Minty was fast asleep on the sofa. Two bottles of wine had been opened and Maryam went to the kitchen for a third. As she came back into the hallway the front door opened and Arran let himself in, throwing his car keys into the ceramic bowl and stripping off his jacket.

'Is that for me?' he said, eyeing the bottle. 'I need it.'

'Where have you been?'

He shook his head. 'Nowhere. Just a work thing.'

He wasn't dressed for work. He looked as if he'd been at the gym, or at the pub. He had a whiff of the forest on him. Maryam said nothing. She got him a glass and he followed her into the workroom, where Lois was standing at the window, looking out at the treeline. She turned when they came in and Maryam felt Arran stiffen next to her.

'Arran!' Lois's face broke into a smile. 'It's been too long.'

Maryam reached out and squeezed her son's arm. 'Just stay for a few moments,' she murmured. 'Just one drink.'

Arran slightly lowered his eyelids, enough to signal his secret protest to Maryam. Since the crash he hadn't enjoyed conversations with Lois. Briefly she thought he was going to say no. But he didn't. He simply set the glasses down and began pouring drinks.

'Mrs Hansel.' He held out a glass to Lois.

'Thank you, Arran.'

He sat down in Rhory's chair, his feet apart, elbows on his knees, his glass cradled between both hands. It was plain he was hoping to avoid speaking, hoping just to drink his wine, stay until it was reasonably polite to leave. Maryam knew that every time Sophie May was mentioned, his normally calm face would crease uncomfortably and his neck would grow dark and red.

'How's work?' Lois turned so she was catty-corner to him on the sofa, her knees drawn up together, her body bent over like an excitable schoolgirl, fidgety and expectant. 'Still enjoying it?'

'Yeah,' Arran said. 'Good. You know. For work.'

'I'm not really working for my husband any more. I've started working for the Dandelion charity.'

'Mum said. You enjoying it?'

'It takes my mind off of things. You know.' Arran didn't reply. Lois repeated, 'You know. It's a good way of keeping my mind off things?'

'Yes. Yes, it must be.' He stared into his glass. 'Must be.'

Maryam tried hard not to speak. It was always the same between these two. On the one hand Arran's reticence, and on the other hand Lois's inability to recognise his discomfort. All Lois wanted was someone to share the memories with. Maryam was mildly irritated with Arran for ignoring her.

'Have you seen the memorial page? I've updated it.'

'I've been busy at work.'

'I was wondering if you could repost for me. You've got so many friends. A share would be such a help.'

Maryam saw Arran deliberately avoid meeting Lois's eyes. 'I'll see what I can do.'

'See this new picture?' She held out her phone to him. 'Did Sophie May ever show you that one herself?'

'I don't know.'

'Didn't she? I'm sure she must have. Look how pretty she is in this one. Do you like the dress?'

'I guess.'

'Maybe you could share this picture. I'm sure all your friends – I mean the boys – if they see her in that dress they might be inclined to . . . you know.' She made a cheeky little clicking noise in her throat and winked broadly. 'Dig a little deeper?'

This time Arran answered with a grunt. He shot Maryam a despairing look.

Lois tired of waiting for him to look at the phone. She clicked it off and placed it, rather pointedly, face-down on the table. She sat back in her chair, folded her arms and crossed her legs – beating out a nervous little rhythm with her foot. A long silence rolled out where no one met anyone else's eyes.

'Nice that Alex is back from London now,' she said eventually. 'Arran? I suppose you must have seen something of her?'

'A little.'

'Always were as thick as thieves, you two.' She smiled. 'In a brother-and-sister-type way.'

'Maybe.'

'I was talking about her to Fenton the other day. We were both wondering if she's made up her mind yet?'

Arran raised his eyes sullenly. 'Made up her mind? About what?'

'You know. About whether she's . . . you know.'

'She's not a lesbian, if that's what you're asking.'

Surprised at his vehemence, Lois sat back a little. 'Of course not – I didn't mean to be . . . ' She looked around, flustered. Found her wine and drained the glass, patting her mouth with the back of her hand. 'I meant nothing by that. It's lovely to see you again, Arran – looking so handsome. Doing so well. I see you've got a new car?'

Arran raised his hands and placed his thumb and forefinger over his eyes and squeezed them exhaustedly. He sat like that for a minute or so then lowered his hand and stared at his mother. 'Mum? I'm tired. It's been a long day. I'd love to just go to bed if that's OK?'

'If you must.' Maryam was shocked at how prim and tight she sounded. Like a starchy old Victorian nanny. 'Take Minty up too, will you?'

'Of course.' He scooped his little sister up, his hand under her bottom, her head lolling dreamily on his shoulder, and headed for the door. 'Night,' he said without looking back. 'Night.'

The two women sat in silence. Maryam was so embarrassed by Arran's behaviour, she couldn't look Lois in the eye.

'I didn't mean to say the wrong thing.'

'It wasn't you, it was him. Ignore him.'

'I feel terrible – I've upset him.'

'You haven't. He's like this all the time.' Maryam picked at her nails, the way she used to as a girl, afraid of the teachers. 'Lois,' she said eventually, 'did you tell Fenton anything? About what I've been telling you recently. My . . . my problems.'

Lois peered at Maryam thoughtfully. 'I'm sorry? Say that again.'

'Have you told Fenton anything?' Her face was getting red. 'About the things I've been . . . seeing?'

'God – you told me not to say anything and I didn't. I haven't said a word. Don't you trust me? I don't tell Fenton anything, can't you see that?'

Maryam's hands, hanging at her sides, were filled with blood. Her veins must be so thin, she could feel the blood in them stretching and waning. Stretch, wane, stretch, wane. Did she believe Lois? She ran her tongue round her lips.

'Lois, am I going mad? Because that's what Rhory thinks.'

'Rhory can think a lot of things. It doesn't make them right.'

'Everything is going wrong. Everything is . . . ' She caught herself in time and smoothed down her hair, pulled the sleeves of her blouse neatly down to her wrists, calming herself. No. Don't go back over it all. Instead she looked Lois in the eye, leaned forward and whispered, 'Just tell me one thing.'

'Of course. No judgement.'

'Fenton's told you all the local stories, hasn't he? About the woman in the park. The prostitute. The bonehead. Did he ever tell you any more about her? Did he tell you where she's been seen? Or exactly what part of the park her spirit is supposed to live?'

Lois's face twisted momentarily, trying to normalise the oddness of this question. She put her finger on her lip and nodded, playing for time. Then she lowered her hand.

'I don't remember anything much. I'd speak to Fenton and ask him again, but that's not an option, is it? So I'll tell you the only thing I remember. The only thing, and until just now I hadn't even given it a thought. But . . . '

'But?'

'I remember him saying something about a row of columns. You'd have to ask him if you wanted it clearer, but that's what I remember. A row of columns.'

'Thank you. Thank you.' Maryam sat back on the sofa and put her forefingers to her eyes. 'And please can we forget this conversation ever happened?'

Alex

It was late when I got back, but the lights were still on and Bamber didn't greet me.

'Mum?' I hung up my fleece in the hallway. 'Mum?''

She was sitting in the living room wearing her white waffle nightgown and white flip-flops. There was a nearly empty bottle of wine and her face, free of make-up, was swollen from crying.

'Mum?'

'Christ,' she sniffed, touching a handkerchief to her nose. 'Alex. Why is he doing this? I'm going crazy.'

At her feet lay Hat, Bamber's toy, abandoned. The plate-glass windows stood wide open to the night, moths circling around the opening. Above every uplighter crawled one or two flies.

'He's gone again?'

'No. He never came back.'

I lowered myself to the sofa and sat for a minute, staring out at the line of trees, black against the navy-blue sky. Somewhere in the woods a fox was killing its prey – I recognised that desperate scream from childhood nights when my window was open. Bamber had never gone missing for more than an hour or so. Until this week I'd loved the park. Now I hated its presence. I was starting to believe it was trying to take things from me.

I ran upstairs and in my room quickly changed into jeans and sturdy trainers. Downstairs in the utility room was a large Maglite, which weighed nearly two pounds and sent a beam

a that could light things up at fifty yards. I went back into
the living room, where Mum was standing on the deck like a
ghost, half-heartedly rattling a box of dog treats in the hope
Bamber would hear.

'Stay here,' I told her.

'For heaven's sake, Alex.'

'What?'

'Be careful.'

'I'm alright, Mum. I promise.'

I snatched up Hat and marched down the steps, across the
grass and into the woods. The slope down was steep in places
and everywhere were exposed tree roots I had to avoid being
tripped by. 'Bamber!' I called as I walked. 'Bamber? Where the
hell are you? Bamber?'

The trees were quiet and still. The fox had stopped making
noise and any other wildlife out here was scared into silence
by my presence. In the dark the trees seemed thicker and
heavier. In London I'd been to drug raids where the suspects
had firearms and knives. There was nothing to be afraid of
here. I repeated it to myself as I went. Nothing to be afraid
of. A couple of perverts in the bushes. Nothing I couldn't
deal with.

Almost every week of policing in Hammersmith I'd had
to attend a homeless woman who wandered the bus garage.
Privately, when the inspectors weren't listening, the rank and
file called her 'Spazzy Annie' because whatever drug she was
on caused her periodically to throw herself in a screaming,
hollering ball around the ground, frenzied as though she was
being burnt, her belongings scattered across the pavement.
People would back away, alarmed at the violence, but all it
took was a cop to step up to her and say sharply, over the
yelling, 'Annie! That's enough.' Then she'd subside and crawl

back to the wall and collect her belongings, smoothing back her hair and adjusting her clothes.

As I walked into the woods, every step pushing the sense of unease deeper and deeper, I wondered how it was that the human race kept up this strange, unspoken dance that protected the boundaries between violence and peace? There was an order, lines that weren't stepped over. A pattern ingrained in us all. Even Spazzy Annie knew when to stay on the right side of the line. What was it out there in the dark trees that had stopped respecting that boundary? A secret club, an underground place, unimaginable for the things that had happened there. I pictured something black, sinewy and low, stretching out from the bunker, twining around tree trunks, pulling living things down into it.

Not Bamber. Please not Bamber.

I wasn't far from the lakes now; the moon was reflected in them. I stopped, exhausted, my feet sore and swollen. I checked my watch. I'd been out here for almost two hours. 'Bamber?' I called, desperately. 'Bamber? Please? PLEASE!'

Bamber, please! came the echo, but no bounding or panting or joyfully crazy Bamber leaping out of the undergrowth, covered in burrs and bits of stick. No orange tennis balls. Nothing. No one.

Huge against the night sky loomed the tower block, as dark and all encompassing as a mountain, its concrete flanks stained with years of rain and wind, vertical lines of lights delineating the stairwell in the centre, and one or two other horizontal lights scattered around the block: the living rooms of residents still awake. I wondered how I'd appear to them. Like an ant. A frantic insect scurrying across the forest floor.

They must feel like gods up there, I thought emptily. Like gods. Maybe they all understood exactly what was happening down here.

Maryam

Maryam? Maryam . . .?

She woke in the darkness, thinking someone had spoken her name. Lying on her side, she blinked a couple of times until the room swam into focus. Moonlight came through the thin curtains and lay on the floor. What had woken her? Had she heard a noise coming from the park?

Out of habit she rolled over towards Rhory, and that was when she realised what had woken her. He wasn't there. The duvet was thrown back and the sheets on his side of the bed were just an empty, crumpled terrain, lit blue by the moon.

She sat up, rubbing her eyes. The bathroom door was closed but something told her he wasn't in there. She got up and padded to the door, knocked, and, when there was no answer, opened it. 'Rhory?'

No light, only the answering glint of sparkling ceramic from the bath and toilet. She went on to the landing; Arran's light was on. She knocked gently and peered around the door. He was lying on his stomach on the bed, his hair dishevelled. His boots were unlaced on the painted floorboards, and there was a slight woody smell in the room.

'Arran? You OK? It's the middle of the night.'

'Yes.' He was intent on something on his laptop – it appeared to be a map of the park.

'Don't stay up all night.'

'I won't. Remember my twenty-first birthday? Sort of indicates I'm old enough to manage my own sleeping patterns?'

She tiptoed back on to the landing and checked on Minty. Sleeping soundly. Maryam stood at her cot and ran a hand over her warm little head, making her snuffle and stir. She'd taken her ridiculous plastic horse to bed with her and Maryam gently moved it out of the cot and placed it on the shelf nearby.

Where was Rhory? He'd come home from the pub last night; she'd lain awake waiting for his key in the door – so where was he now?

She crept down the stairs, expecting to see the light on in the kitchen with Rhory hunched over his computer, but the den was dark and so were the kitchen, living room and conservatory. The clock in the kitchen said 3.10. All the doors were locked, but keys were missing and in the hallway she found a space on the flagstoned floor where Rhory's wellington boots belonged. The peg where his sailcloth waterproof hung was also empty.

In the kitchen she poured herself a glass of water and took it through to the workshop. She stood at the window, watching the line of trees that marked the edge of the park. The night had become windy. There were leaves and twigs dancing across the garden, the trees moving their old arms like sorrowful priests. Her own reflection – with her slightly hooked nose, her wide shoulders – stared back at her.

It occurred to her that they should have checked the Bakehouse for ley lines before they'd moved in. Ley lines could make all sorts of bad things happen – they harnessed energy, good and bad, so she'd heard. They could draw spirits and souls to places beyond the grave. Maybe the Bakehouse was built on a pagan burial ground. Why hadn't she thought of any of this before? Why hadn't she done any research? She should be more proactive – as the Swami said, she should go and find the bonehead. Seek her out.

She double-checked the door was locked, giving it two rat-tles to be sure. Then she adjusted the Hand of Fatima hanging out of sight above the door. Her phone was on the table in the conservatory where she'd left it the night before and she checked it, but there were no messages from Rhory, no sug-gestion of where he could be. She scrolled through, found his number and stared at it for a while, wondering what would happen if she called it. A text, she decided. A text was better.

Hello, darling, just checking you're OK. It's dark, don't like the look of that wind. M x

She deleted the word 'checking' and replaced it with 'won-dering if'. Then she deleted the bit about the weather; he'd think she didn't trust him to know what the weather was like. The phone had an app they'd installed that would tell you where all the phones on their accounts were – but if she pinged his phone to find out where he was, an alert would come up on his phone and he'd know she was suspicious. She typed in the words *I love you xxxx*. Then she deleted the whole thing, tapped in Lois's number, and sat for a while considering that. Three a.m. She couldn't call her now. Just couldn't.

She switched it off and placed it screen-down on the table. She went to the hexagonal cabinet and pulled out her oils, lin-ing them up. The day she'd brought all these oils home she'd been full of hope. Now she was just scared and cold and old. Possibly mad.

She mixed a few drops in her Moroccan jar and pressed it into her brow chakra – the ajna – and sat in contemplation for a while, asking for guidance, for help.

After five minutes she opened her eyes. Nothing had come to her; nothing was different. She was as empty and dry as before, a husk. She crawled on to the sofa, tucking her feet up, pulling the quilted throw over herself, and stayed there, sipping the water. The door to the fabric store was slightly open so the tapestry of the arboretum was just visible, slopped over two chairs.

Trees planted in complex, significant patterns. Geometrics. The stunning counterpoise of a circle against a crescent, or at right angles to a formal line. Colonnades. Columns.

She blinked, a tiny snapshot of the pattern. Blink, blink, blink.

It must have been an hour that passed, or more, because the sky had started to go creamy pink above the park when there was a sudden movement in the trees. A shape, watery and pale as the moon, coming up the lawn towards her. She stiffened and was halfway off the sofa when she realised it was Rhory, walking determinedly towards the house, the wind blowing his jacket against him. She subsided into the chair as he went past the side of the house, and presently she heard the back door open.

He wasn't loud as he came in, but the house was so hushed she could hear every movement. She heard him taking off his wellingtons and the clatter of the jacket zip against the wall as he hung it up. He went into the kitchen and she heard him switch on the kettle.

She didn't move. She didn't know what she was going to say. Presumably he was making himself a hot drink. The fridge opened, closed, there was a pause and she saw his shape coming down the corridor towards the conservatory.

The shadows must have hidden her presence, because his surprise at finding her there was clear from his expression. He took a breath, then let it out. 'Oh,' he murmured. 'Maryam.'

'Rhory.'

'You're up early.'

'Yes,' she said. 'So are you.'

'I've been in the park.'

She didn't nod or respond.

'I've been looking for Tumble.'

'Tumble?'

'I know we agreed we'd given up, but I thought I . . . I thought maybe I'd heard him barking . . . '

She stared at him. He was lying. She was sure he was lying. There was a hooded look to his eyes. A horrible balance. The panic came up in her and she had to swallow hard to keep it down. 'I see.'

'Well,' he said, 'I'd better get some sleep. Got to be up in no time for work.'

He turned and left the room and went upstairs. Stunned, she sat there, staring at the empty doorway, not believing anything about what had just happened.

The snapshot of the tapestry stayed with her. Long colonnades and circular plantings. She'd downloaded the plan of the arboretum on to her phone and studied it carefully. It showed an entrance somewhere near the crash site, so later that morning she drove down there.

Lake Tarquil glinted contentedly. It had always had the power to torment. A *No Trespassing* sign hung from the bar barrier, and mounted on a stand next to it was a lifebuoy in a red plastic case, instructions written on it in four different languages. That had appeared after the crash too. Funny, because a lifebuoy wouldn't have saved any of the teenagers who'd died. They'd all been trapped in the coach wreckage.

She wound down the window and peered out. The only other car on the verge belonged to a family. The man had a toddler in a rucksack on his back. He and his wife both wore shorts and hiking boots. They were standing there, not talking, studiously eating bananas as if they had discussed it before they married and among other agreed points of protocol had noted that bananas were the right thing to eat before a hike. She envied them their commonality – their commitment to following the rule of cordial family life. No one would look at her and Rhory, Beauty and the Beast, and think of them as a harmonious family.

At last finding her courage, she got out and began arranging the hessian bag over her shoulder. The banana family hadn't even looked at her, and somehow she found that depressing, that she could be on such a mission so full of bravado and courage, yet still not be noticed. They should be looking at her in wonder – as if she were a sky-bound firework, or a ship's flare.

She locked the car and walked along the edge of the lake with the hessian bag banging at her side. There were so many routes through Eastonbirt – the park was huge enough that you could walk for miles and get totally lost. There were big signs everywhere with vague maps of the paths and warnings not to stray from them, and emergency numbers for the National Trust ranger who made her slow way round the place each day in an open-topped Jeep. Quite often Maryam would see the ranger come bumping out of the park, two or three relieved-looking ramblers in the back clinging to the roll bars. There wasn't a lot of phone signal in the park either. It seemed extraordinary that you could be in England, one of the world's most populated countries, and be as out of touch as if you were in the Himalayas or the Atlas mountains.

She stopped on the shore, and, when she was certain the banana family weren't watching, headed along the road to the place she'd noted on the arboretum plans. The woods were dense – no one ever tried to negotiate that part of the park; it was a notoriously impassable, bound solid with rhododendrons. The National Trust was trying to raise money to create a task force that would go in and poison all the roots, then they'd be able to uncover the remains of the arboretum.

A tractor went past on the road behind her, throwing up clods of earth, leaving the pungent scent of horses. The driver was a young man about Arran's age wearing a tiny straw boater as if he were at a regatta and not high up in a tractor cab. She pulled her crocheted cardigan up around her shoulders, wishing it had a hood.

Then she took a step into the rhododendron forest. The path was littered with the usual detritus: a few Coke cans, some tissue paper with something dubious-looking on it, even one of Tumble's missing posters fallen from its tree and trampled; dew had got inside the laminate and made the ink run. She stopped and stared at the poster. Tumble . . .

That badger, stretched out and stinking. Had it gone into the crevice to die because it was old or injured? Or had it become trapped in there and starved to death?

She picked up the poster and crumpled it into her sleeve, raising her chin to scan the surroundings. Plenty of people had been here but it wasn't a thoroughfare, more a blunt little appendix ending after a few yards in impenetrable bush. The birds were singing further in the trees, but she could see nothing, the thicket was so dense. At foot-level a pair of abandoned shoes were trapped under some barbed wire. She crouched and peered at them. They were limp and sodden, half-covered by leaves, with the defeated look of discarded rubbish. How had someone left a pair of trainers in the middle of a wood without noticing? Arran had told her that trainers hanging in a tree, or from an overhead line, meant a drug-dealer was there. But these were old and had been there for a long time, judging from the mildew.

She got down on hands and knees, dug her elbows into the ground and tried to see what was on the other side of the tangle. Just visible beyond the twined shrubs, only a few feet away, there appeared to be a small clearing. Heart thumping, she scrambled to her feet and pushed her elbows into the thicket. Spiders, insects and leaf bark cascaded on to her bare skin, into her hair, the twigs scratched at her forearms, but eventually the branches released her and, taking a deep breath, she stepped into small glade of tall trees.

The sunlight was coming down in shafts, picking out swirling dust and insects. There was grass underfoot and no traffic noise, the thicket was so dense. Already she'd lost her sense of direction, but she knew she was in the arboretum. Maryam pulled out her phone and checked for a signal. The pulsing blue light on the map showed her almost on top of Lake Tarquil. As long as she kept the lake to her left and didn't let it slip behind her, she'd have a way of getting her bearings.

From the clearing there seemed to be several exits. One had the strange appearance of having been trodden recently. But that couldn't be right – no one came here. She followed it cautiously, carefully picking over brambles and sticks, trying to protect her bare legs from the thorns. For as long as she'd lived in Eastonbirt people had told her not to go into the old arboretum; it was no-man's-land unless you had a machete or a chainsaw. It had never occurred to her that there were ways through like this, routes, if you were prepared to duck and dive, double back and push through bits of thicket, elbows held up, face lowered, using the top of your head to part the branches.

The going was slow and within an hour, though the lake was still to her left, she had no memory of which route she'd taken.

She was thirsty and her hair was crawling with insects and leaves. She was losing heart. What on earth had she expected?

She was just about to turn and head back when she pushed through a barricade of rhododendrons and found herself in an extraordinary corridor of trees with pale, papery skin. So uniformly planted, in two perfect lines. A colonnade. They were ash, very old. Some of them were dead, some dying – but the spaces between them were even and the living trunks were so smooth and regular in their size, they had an almost architectural symmetry, like the columns in a Greek palace, white and ethereal in the greenish light.

She stopped wandering around and stood in the centre, quite still, dwarfed by the majesty of those slim white trees reaching up to the sky. Was this it? The home of the bone-faced prostitute?

What now?

She scrutinised the margins, the gaps between the trunks, gripped by a sense that she was being observed. The buzz of insects among the long stalks. Her attention splayed out from her third eye like tendrils, snaking away in every direction.

Face her, the Swami had said, *face her and tell her to stop.*

Maryam had no idea why, but she began to speak in a very low, rhythmic chant.

'Speak to me, please. I know you're there.'

Her voice was flattened by the humid air, but she persisted.

'Speak to me, speak to me. Are you going to take my husband away from me?'

The trees were silent. Over her head a skylark swam upwards in a vortex. Maryam shuffled around to face the opposite direction. All around the outer perimeter of the trees the undergrowth was thick and dense, trapping the light. It felt oddly enclosed, as if it was a sanctuary of some sort.

'Was that you at my house? Was that you at the crash? What do you look like close up? Show me yourself close up.'

A noise. A crack of branch or a dry leaf crunched under-foot. Gathering all the energy and courage she had, she began to speak again. 'I'm here to tell you something. I'm here to warn you never to get between me and my husband.'

She opened her eyes. The echoes bounced back to her through the woods but beneath them was silence. Not a snap of twig or a rustle of leaf. Everything around her was the same. Nothing had changed.

Alex

In all the messages I exchanged with Arran overnight – all the theories about Parson's Pike, all the possible places in the park he thought we should search for columns – I didn't mention Bamber. It would mean talking about Arran's missing dog and I didn't want to prod at that. Besides, Bamber would be back by the morning. He would. He had to be.

But he wasn't. And that was when I knew that all the things I'd tried overnight to avoid thinking about or believing were probably true. I had to drink four cups of black coffee straight before I could find the willpower to leave the house.

It was a baking hot day. Arran and I met near the lakes, with phones fully charged for GPS reception, bottles of water and tubes of suntan lotion. He was dressed in a surfer's T-shirt and cargo trousers that made him look more like the old Arran I knew. Still I was too sad and full of fear to be comforted by anything from my childhood.

'You OK?' he asked. 'Sorry – but you look like shit.'

'Thanks. I didn't sleep.'

'Oh?'

'Come on.' We went past all the cars and the ice-cream stall, not yet opened, its bright striped awning rolled up, until we reached the entrance to the car park. There were three notice-boards, one containing a map showing some of the routes through the park, another a faded illustration of all the trees and wildlife to be found there. The third was protected by a glass door – astonishingly, it hadn't been vandalised – inside which were pinned a variety of notices: planning permission notifications, minicab business cards, flyers from the Gloucestershire Wildlife Trust. Under a note advertising pilates and yoga in Eastonbirt Village Hall was a sad and faded A4 print out. Tumble – the Blacks' dog, who'd been missing for weeks.

I unpinned it and refastened it so it was on top of the other notices.

'Tumble,' Arran said. 'Suppose I'll never see him again.'

'He went into the park. Didn't he?'

'Presumably. We've got him on the RSPCA website, on Nextdoor and on Facebook. Nothing. Not a whisper. He vanished.'

I pulled my own laminated poster out of my rucksack and pinned it up next to Tumble's. 'Bamber – our dog. He's gone too.'

Arran stared at the poster. His mouth open a little.

'Disappeared. In the park. Last night.'

He glanced around himself at the lakes and the woods running up the side of the valley. Then he rubbed his arms, as if on this brilliant sunny day he was suddenly cold. 'That's . . . what? A coincidence? Isn't it?'

'You tell me.'

Neither of us spoke for a while. We simply stood there regarding each other, both of us pondering what all this meant. A picture of Mum's house mailed to us. A place in the forest that had scared the crap out of my dog. And now he was missing. Arran's dog too.

Coincidence?

'Do you have a good feeling about this?' Arran's pupils were hard and dilated.

'No. I have not one shred of good feeling about it. I think our dogs have been stolen and I think the bonehead woman and her pimp are behind it.'

'Why would they kidnap . . .?' He broke off and closed his eyes. Took a few deep breaths. 'Actually, don't answer that. I can fill in too many of the blank spaces. Shit.' He kicked the bottom of the noticeboard, hard. 'Shit, I fucking hate people.'

We'd both had the fight knocked out of us, we were both numb, and for a while we simply stood there, dazed by it all. Though it was still early, people were arriving at the lake. Their kids, their walking boots, their water bottles. Their dogs. All alive and bounding around. What if the bonehead is here? I thought, watching the faces passing, oblivious to me and Arran. What if two of these men and women are the pimp and the prostitute who do unspeakable things? I recalled what Raj had said last night in the car. *An incident happened one night, something bad, so they stopped.*

An incident? The faces marched past me, men in middle age, some balding, some ruddy and thick-necked. Others young and fresh-eyed. There'd been a cop in the Met police addicted to chemsex with men he met on Grindr. It had caused his death. What did that sort of ferocious sex drive lead to? *What sort of fucking incident?*

'We've got to find the bunker.' I lifted up my rucksack. 'We've got to find it now.'

We walked down the long track into the park. It hadn't rained all summer, and sometimes it felt as if Eastonbirt was in some awful oven, being slowly cooked alive. The leaves were brittle on the branches, some already beginning to fall, and the earth had dried to a bone-grey crust. The path was cracked into so many sections it looked like broken eggshell.

We moved from the columns at the entrance of the old park, all the way down the mansion driveway, stopping at the ruined Greek temple that had been one of the follies from the estate. We walked around it twice, kicking aside leaves, lifting up crumbling stones, searching for steps.

'Columns, check. Steps. No check. Let's keep going.'

We clambered off the drive to look under ledges and roll away boulders. We even stood for a long time on the edge of the lake, watching the damselfly nymphs and the fish swimming lazily. Bamber could swim, so it was unlikely he'd come to harm here. I couldn't get the image of him in an underground vault out of my head.

The last place we checked was the derelict mansion. We got there mid-afternoon. In spite of the way walkers thronged the rest of the park, somehow they always gave the old mansion a wide berth. It was as silent and empty as ever, its huge buttresses and window sockets yawning at the trees that surrounded it. One face of the building had disappeared entirely, and all that remained was a twenty-yard row of footstones, moist and pocked with debris.

Tentatively we picked our way passed the flimsy safety tape that fenced it off from the public. In the ruins the smell of bat guano from the decaying rafters was overpowering. A tree grew in the centre of the entrance hall, reaching its arms upwards, stretching through the ruined ceilings to the sky. We stared up at the decaying gargoyles. We scoured the rooms, studying the damp covered plaster, the stairwells that started but ended nowhere. I ran my hands along the buttresses and the mullions, went into the tiny forgotten rooms where the weeds grew high around abandoned beer bottles and covered every inch of the floor, looking for steps going down.

There were only two columns in the entire house. Both were topped with unfeasibly ornate Corinthian capitals. They stood at the end of the entrance hall on either side of the front door, so the only place they could be observed was from inside the shell of the house. Arran and I stopped in front of them and considered all the angles a photo could be taken from. Then we stamped across the ground, hoping to find an entrance. A hidden trapdoor or something. There was nothing. All we found were more broken beer bottles and weeds. A sodden sleeping bag under several seasons' worth of leaf matter.

A noise came from the main hallway. A tinkling of metal. A sound of plastic being trodden on. We moved quietly into the corridor, Arran's finger to his lips. Listened for the sound again. To our right was the dining room with its vaulted ceiling and vast stone fireplace. Another tinkle, then a lone fox stalked through the crumbling corridor. Casually looking for a quiet place to eat the prey that dangled from its jaws. A pigeon still twitching, feebly moving its wings.

Arran let out his breath and dropped his head back against the wall. 'Nothing. There's nothing here.'

'Nope.'

I breathed for a few more minutes, swallowing the need to cry. Then I said, 'Why us?'

'What?'

'If they've taken our dogs, does it mean we're being targeted by someone? And if so, why? What connects us?'

'I don't know. The coach crash?'

'There were other people on the coach.'

He shook his head. He sat down on the ground and pulled out his water bottle. Drank it all down. Wiped his brow with the back of his hand. 'I'm out of suggestions.'

I looked at him sadly. I was out of suggestions too. I was tired. All I wanted to do was sleep. Maybe if I was lucky I'd wake up to find it was all a dream.

'Come on.' I picked up my rucksack. 'Let's call it a day.'

Maryam

The day arrived to unveil the memorial bench for Sophie May. It should have been a good, respectful and focused day; instead Maryam felt out of control from start to finish. Arran had been odd for several days and first thing in the morning he'd eaten breakfast then gone out into the woods. By the time she and Rhory and Minty were ready to go, he still wasn't back.

Rhory texted him, irritated. *C U @ the play park* came the reply, and when Rhory'd asked, *What's happening? You're supposed to be here*, he simply got the same reply again. *C U @ the play park.*

Rhory drove. He was trying extra-hard to be civil – he hadn't complained about having to wear the orange waistcoat under his suit, he'd gelled back his dark hair, greying at the sideburns, and he'd put on aftershave – he looked completely and utterly gorgeous. Minty was in the back seat, wearing the dress Maryam had stitched and seamed from a piece of orange chiffon. Maryam wore an orange velvet hat, but she felt robotic and cold as the car jolted down through the village and out on to the valley road.

The roads were empty, the village was quiet and the walkers weren't out in their throngs yet. Rhory took the curve faster than she would, zipping past the entrance to the arboretum. She put her finger to her forehead and lowered her chin as they rattled over the causeway. Something in those woods had been stirred. She had drawn its attention, issued it a challenge. It would be watching her now, decoding every emotion, finding victory in her despair, weakness in her strength.

There were several cars at the car park next to the play area, and room for several more. Over the path that led to the park a huge fluttering banner, in the charity's trademark orange, yelled *Welcome to the Dandelion Play Park.* When she got out of the car, leaning into the back to unbuckle Minty, she felt the sodden silence of the trees behind her. Could her expression be read from forty yards away? Would the ghost of a Roma prostitute read emotion from a distance? Maryam thought the answer was yes. As she straightened out Minty's dress and pulled her out of the car, the hairs on her arms stood up, stiff and bristling.

'Come on. Let's do it.'

They walked up the little lane under the banner. The play area had been transformed for today's unveiling: every piece of equipment was adorned with orange ribbons and there were two bearded young men in black taking photographs of all the guests. Already it was filling up with people – the various parents and local village councillors and church goers. Quite a few of Arran's friends. Victoria Mullins, Alex Mullins and Lois were standing in the small cleared area around the bench. The bench itself was covered in a large orange sheet with the name of the charity emblazoned on it. It was weighted around the hems because attached to the top were eight helium balloons ready to lift the sheet when the time came. One of the balloons had lost its gas and lay limply, bouncing half-heartedly against the shroud.

Victoria was dressed in a black linen trouser suit with orange buttons, there was an orange bow in her hair, and Lois wore a plain black polyester dress that made her look rumpled in comparison. Alex, in embroidered denim culottes and a blouse in flame orange, was pretty, Maryam realised. Very pretty. She blinked at her, surprised. It was funny: Sophie May had always been considered so gorgeous that Alex had sort of blended into the background. Not any more.

Maryam followed Rhory to the back of the crowd, where Fenton sat awkwardly on one of the toddlers' spring-mounted horses. So low down, he looked fragile and small. His thinning hair was gelled back, showing the pink of his scalp. His ears looked bulbous: thick and red. The edge of his shirt collar, which was orange, had a telltale line of dark red where sweat had soaked into it, and there were bluish shadows under his eyes.

'I'm just going to stay out here, out of sight. If that's OK.' He ran a hand over his gelled hair. The veins over his knuckles were red and inflamed.

'That's OK.' Rhory patted his friend on the shoulder. 'We've got your back. You stay here.'

A new group of people arrived from the car park. Maryam recognised most of them. There was Michaela Lewis and her mother, the Browns, Mr and Mr Jarvis, and Minnie Frobisher, speeding along in her wheelchair, accompanied by a whip-thin young man wearing jeans and an orange T-shirt emblazoned with words Maryam didn't understand.

EAT/SLEEP/RAVE/REPEA . . . NAH. EAT/SLEEP/EAT/SLEEP.

'We're going to have to talk to everyone,' Rhory said. 'Press the flesh. Do the done thing.'

'I know.'

'Come on, then.'

They joined the group. Rhory was not a natural socialiser, but he was better than she was. He was able to shake hands, smile, ask what was happening with all of them. Maryam stood next to him like the weak schoolfriend, one hand holding Minty tight, the other clenched at her side, a smile pasted on. From the corner of her right eye she could see the edge of the escarpment, the footpath where Minty had imagined seeing her moving through the trees. To her left, half a mile away in the valley, was the rough snarl of trees that concealed the arboretum.

Nowhere to hide. Set your shoulders wide, lift your chin and draw back your face muscles so you look calm.

Minnie Frobisher's mother was there. Jan Frobisher, sleek and shiny with her guttural laugh and her cornrowed hair. Wearing a tight leopardskin dress, stretchy orange panels at the waist, high heels, and stud earrings complex as tiny meringues. Maryam didn't know Jan well, but she'd always liked her. She waited for Rhory to greet her before she said hello.

'Hey.' Jan stretched up on tiptoe and kissed Rhory on the side of the face, smiling blindingly. 'I don't believe it, Rhory – twice in one week?' She dropped back down and wheeled her face round to Maryam, reaching her arms out. 'Maryam. How are you?'

'I'm, I'm . . .' She stuttered forward into Jan's arms. Felt the firm squash of her breasts, smelled the scent of her hair, the peppermint of her breath. Her heart was racing. What did she mean, twice in one week? *Twice in one week.* She rocked back on her heels and stared at Jan, her pulse saying *tick, tick, tick! Someone's making a fool of you.* 'I'm great. You?'

'Good, good. All going great.'

Rhory had a hand on Jan's arm and was moving her away to meet someone else. Maryam, rooted to the spot, watched them go. Her face like fire, her throat moving and moving, trying to calm itself. Eventually she turned away and found Fenton watching her. He flinched and turned his eyes to focus on something else. His face was wine-coloured, hiding something.

She pulled her cardigan around her and lifted Minty. Rhory hadn't mentioned seeing Jan. He'd have said something if she'd been one of his clients. He'd have mentioned it.

Alex

The day of the unveiling I got dressed in something orange to represent the charity. I felt like an idiot but Mum needed my support. I found the place at the Dandelion Play Park she wanted me to stand in, and arranged myself the best way I could. Acting out respect and dignity even though inside I was aching. Imagining the things that could be happening to Bamber.

I hadn't spent much time up at the play area before. On one early visit home from London Mum had taken me there and showed me what the charity was going to do, lots of architect's plans and stuff, but I'd never really thought about the land itself. Now I realised it was very exposed and flat. The view down the valley to the crash site was only obscured slightly by the treetops on the level below us.

It had never crossed my mind that the people who used to come here for sex had had to move their operation. What would that be like, to turn up and find the thing you were used to had changed? To a lot of people addicted to benign stuff it would be like turning up to the supermarket and finding Tesco's had stopped selling vape pens or prosecco. Or cream buns and chocolate. Did it, should it, make any difference that their addiction was sex? I scanned the trunks and the shadows between them. Could someone be out there now? How much would they hate us all, taking away what they wanted?

Michaela was there with her mum, smiling shyly, overwhelmed by the number of people. Her hair had been done for the event and she had a bag slung over her shoulder. It was slim, except for the tiny bulge at the bottom in the shape of a bottle. I gave her a quick wave and she waved back. Minnie was the star attraction, as always. She wore a turquoise vintage '80s dress and tore the wheelchair into the play area, followed by her mum in a sassy orange leopardprint dress, and a totally hot guy in a cool T-shirt who slouched in, completely fazed by the event. When they'd found their place he stood there fidgeting and shooting embarrassed glances at us all, as if this was all overload and what he really wanted was to hide behind Minnie's chair.

It was weird. All these people from my past gathered together, all slightly the same, but all slightly changed by the past two and a half years.

No Arran yet, but his mum was there. I hadn't seen her for ages. She'd always been so exotic in my mind, so flamboyant, and uncaring about what people thought. Her face was a little subdued, but everything around her was still as dignified as I remembered. She wore a peach-coloured velvet cap over her hair, peacock feathers on her handbag. Walking next to Maryam was Arran's sister, Minty. She'd grown since I'd last seen her. She too was dressed like a troubadour or a nine-teenth-century vaudeville star – mesmerising in an orange dress. I'd have given the world to have that style. It was one of those things passed down through the generations, and some-thing that had completely missed me and Mum.

Arran's dad was there too. He was eclipsed by his wife, somehow, but he was good-looking like Arran, self-possessed. He stood with his hands in his pockets, talking to Sophie May's dad, Fenton, who was sitting on one of the springy horses meant for the toddlers. Fenton's wife, Lois, stood at the front of the group with my mum, on either side of the shrouded bench.

'Hello,' Mum said into the handheld mic, looking up at the crowd. 'Thank you all for coming.'

Everyone stopped talking and turned to look at her. She was nervous. Her face was odd and swollen, as if she'd tried to bolt it together after a painful operation. She'd tried to stay professional all day but she was a wreck, only just holding it together. Two days without Bamber. 'What if he comes home while we're at the park?' she'd said. 'Shall we leave the doors open?' I'd had to be fierce with her – tell her no. The thought of leaving the house unlocked for anyone or anything to walk in from the park made me sick.

'Hello,' she said bravely. 'And can I take a moment to ask you to look around and notice just how many people are here? What a wonderful response from the community.'

She wasn't a natural speaker but she gave it her best. She'd been rehearsing this speech all week. Using a section from St John's gospel about the Lord coming back to take people to his table, and a seven-hundred-year-old line written by the Persian poet Rumi: 'Whatever sorrow shaketh from your heart, far better things will take their place.'

Everyone nodded appreciatively; a smatter of applause ran through the group. I tried not to turn and look at the surrounding trees.

In the middle of the speech Arran arrived. He was dressed in a suit but he was leaden-faced and agitated, less at ease than Fenton even, which was saying something. He shouldered his way through the crowd, glancing at the faces as if searching for someone. The moment he saw me, he came to a halt and stared at me. With an abrupt nod he discreetly opened his jacket, pointed to his mobile phone in the inside pocket. Mimed texting by moving his thumb up and down to indicate he'd texted me.

I couldn't get my phone out while Mum was still talking. I was in the firing line of the lenses, right at the front. And I was on duty as the perfect poster girl for Mum's charity. I'd survived the crash and gone on to join the police force and become a fully functioning member of society. I gave a tiny nod, moved my eyes away from his, straightened my shoulders and kept my face neutral. My eyes were on the shrouded bench, where Mum and Lois were organising themselves. The photographers turned from the onlookers and focused on Mum. My smile fixed, chin up and not looking down, I rummaged in my bag. Found the phone and risked glancing at the screen.

Six messages from Arran had come through while my phone had been on silent. *Six*.

The last said in caps: *URGENT. CALL ME FFXSAKE.*

I shoved it back in my bag quickly. Raised my chin. I couldn't stand here and read through his messages in front of everyone; I had to keep my attention on the ceremony. I dared shoot my attention across at Arran. He was staring at me meaningfully.

'What?' I mouthed to him across the crowd. 'What the fuck?'

'Have to talk.'

'As soon as this is over?' I made a sarcastic scan of the crowd to remind him how many people were here and how important this was. 'Can't it wait?'

He thought about it then gave a single, resentful nod. Folded his arms and raised his eyes to the overhead branches, feigning listening to what Mum was saying. But he couldn't keep his anxiety in check. He tipped back and forward on his heels, back and forward.

'Every child who has been damaged by trauma, every one who hasn't got a voice, they are the children we are here today to give a voice to.'

I clapped pallidly. I closed my eyes and tried to keep up with what she was saying. I tried to listen to all the stuff about Sophie May, about how inspirational she'd been. But I was drifting. I was floating through the woods surrounding the playground. People out there watching? The men who got moved on by this playground. The men who used to come here to fuck each other. Where were they now? And did they have a vendetta against our families?

Maryam

It was ice and phlegm. It was a clot in her throat, a lock on her eyes. Rhory so furtive and fidgety next to her. Jan Frobisher a few paces away, watching Maryam nervously. Knowing something was wrong. Rhory had done a thing he wasn't proud of. He'd lied to her.

The only power she had was a silent face, so she shut everything down, placed a screen in front of her eyes, made herself unreadable. Anyone looking would see only features: eyes, nose, mouth. No emotion.

The parents and well-wishers stood in a horseshoe around the shrouded bench, listening to Victoria Mullins talk. Maryam's eyes phased in and out of focus, one minute a haze of dots, the next a row of faces. Fizzing slots of orange clothing below wan expressions. Mouths smiling, heads tilted back, listening and remembering. Arran had arrived as he'd promised, dressed smartly and clean-shaven. He was look-ing at Alex Mullins, frowning at her. She gave him a puzzled look in reply. She shook her head briefly, mouthed 'What?'; he said something else, held up his phone. They were conversing somehow, in a secret code Maryam didn't understand.

Alex and Arran. They'd played together at primary school – had spent years making dens and bonfires in the park. Nothing would come between those two. What would happen when Arran got a girlfriend, or Alex a boyfriend? How would their friendship weather that storm? She was glad for Alex that it hadn't turned into a crush. Arran was too beautiful for his own good; better he marry someone who was completely unimpressed by his looks. She didn't wish on any girl the marriage she'd had, a life lived eclipsed by the persistent glow and power of a husband's good looks. Of course Rhory wanted to cheat on her. Of course. Why wouldn't he?

Lois released the shroud from its moorings, letting the balloons start to lift. There was a two-minute silence, not just for Sophie May but for all the children killed or injured in the crash. Minty whispered and twisted impatiently, tugging at Maryam's leg until she had to be shushed. Then, mercifully, the ceremony was complete. People broke into loose groups, chatting and hugging, introducing family members, friends. Men coughed and cleared their throats, slapped each other on their backs; women fumbled in handbags for phones, tissues. Alex Mullins helped Lois gather the sheet to the side, untangling the helium balloons and popping them, pressing and rolling them against her thighs to deflate them.

Maryam rubbed her eyes with her knuckles. Minty leaned against her calf, fingers in her mouth, gazing at the adults behaving so strangely. Then, from the back of the crowd, near the edge of the play area, came a small disturbance. A few people moved quickly sideways, someone pushing a path between them. It was Fenton, walking unsteadily towards the trees. A second later Rhory broke free from the group he'd been standing with and followed.

Maryam stared after them. She couldn't see Fenton's face, but from the way Rhory was hurrying after him, head down in concern, she guessed Fenton was ill.

'Come on.' She lifted Minty and carried her to where Arran stood, his face grey and serious. 'Arran – look after your sister.'

Arran took Minty without questioning and Maryam headed through the crowd after the two men. The cork wedge sandals were difficult to walk in, and she had to use the tree trunks to steady herself. After the sunshine and noise of conversation the woods felt quiet and still. They smelled of dried-out pine needles and leaf mould. She could see Rhory and Fenton, about forty feet ahead in a grassy copse. Fenton was bent over, one hand wedged against a tree. He sweating profusely and his face was pale from pain. Rhory had his arm over his shoulders and was holding his jacket, talking to him intently.

Ashamed of witnessing what felt like something so private, she hovered, self-conscious, and waited.

Fenton began to retch. She heard the hot splatter of vomit.

'Maryam?'

She turned. Lois was a few feet behind her on the path. She was clutching her handbag, which was unzipped, a stack of well-wishers' cards wedged in it. Her face was dazed. 'What's happening?'

'It's, uh . . . '

She turned to look into the woods. Further in the trees Fenton vomited more.

'What's wrong with him?' Maryam whispered under her breath. 'I thought he was ill the other day. Isn't he any better?'

'Nothing's wrong with him.'

Maryam glanced in surprise at Lois. Her voice was firm, uncharacteristically blunt. And her face was fixed.

'There is nothing wrong with him. It's probably just something he ate. Will you hold this?'

She handed her bulging handbag to Maryam, smoothed down her crumpled, badly fitting dress, and set out across the woods to the men. Maryam watched Lois reach Fenton, exchange a stiff sentence with Rhory, then bend to consult her husband.

She couldn't hear what they were saying, but she knew she was being fenced out of something important. A wasp buzzed around her head, trying to land on her arms. She swatted at it. Stunned, it settled at her feet on a blade of grass, lifting its wings as if to recover itself. She squatted down and dropped Lois's heavy handbag down on top of it.

Then she began to cry.

Alex

After the service I had to help Mum organise the shroud and pack up the microphones. Then I went looking for Arran. I found him holding Minty in his arms, surrounded by a bunch of teenage girls who were asking him if he had been the one who'd saved all those people in the crash and could they have a selfie, and could they hold Minty? When I arrived they all shrank back a little, as if I were a teacher or something, come to break up the fun. It took me a moment or two to realise they thought we were a couple. That Minty was our child.

'She's lovely, she is,' said one of the girls. 'Aren't you cute, eh? Is that your little toy horse? Let me see it?'

Arran eyed me seriously. He looked awful this close up. Just terrible.

'Um . . . Arran?' I said loudly. 'Can we talk?'

He put Minty down and let the gang of girls lead her to the swings. Then he beckoned me to the edge of the play park, where the grass was long and seed-heavy.

'What're all the texts about? What's happening?'

'Uh.' He rubbed his eyes and glanced around to make sure we weren't being watched. 'Will you come over to my house?'

'What, now? Yeah, sure. Why?'

'I found Tumble.'

'Sweeet!'

'No. Not.'

My smile died. 'Arran?'

He lifted his eyes to mine. They were bloodshot.

'Jesus. What is it?'

'I'll show you.'

Minty must have got bored playing with the girls in the park because we eventually found her with Maryam, who was walking towards us holding her. 'She was in the woods,' Maryam said as she passed. 'I wish you hadn't let her wander off like that.'

I watched them go, Minty eyeing us over her mother's retreating shoulder, her thumb stuck in her mouth. I got the impression I'd just been told off in the nicest possible way.

'Don't worry about Mum,' said Arran. 'She's not good at the moment.'

'How come?'

'Postpartum depression. Dad's worried about her; she's on pills. I'm not going to tell her about Tumble. We've got to keep this to ourselves.' He put his hands in his pockets and looked down at his feet. I was about to ask him if he was OK when he let out a long sigh and lifted his head again. 'Shall we go?'

I told Mum I'd walk home from Arran's, then we got in his car and drove out to the Bakehouse. It had been a long time since I'd last been there and it hadn't changed much. The fancy gables painted in grey and white, the shutters Arran's dad had custom-built, with their sweetheart holes in them, open and draped in oddments: paper flower leis Maryam had made, glittery scarves, shrivelled daisy chains and a string of plastic beads. It was all just as I remembered. The Blacks were the artiest family I'd ever known. As a kid I'd dreamed Mum would one day wake up a bohemian and we'd be able to scrap all the highly polished granite surfaces, the downlighters and the windows that got cleaned every fortnight.

Arran stopped at the top of the driveway and checked no one was home yet. His face was very pinched. 'Sorry. I don't want any of them knowing you're here.'

'Thanks!'

'I don't mean that. I mean I don't want them to know what's happened.'

I rubbed my nose with the back of my arm. Since we'd left the play park I'd been feeling sick with nerves, and I kept having to swallow hard to get a taste out of my mouth.

We went round the side of the house to the back. I'd forgotten how Arran's garden was exactly like ours – about an acre of lawn then a sudden merge into the purply evening trees of the parkland. No fence, no barrier. We'd lived like this for two decades and none of us had given it a second thought. In retrospect, how stupid had we been?

Arran headed into the trees, using his elbows to push away the branches. I crashed after him, glancing over my shoulder at the house. My breath felt sour in my nose and my mouth.

He stopped about twenty yards into the woods. His hand was on an old oak tree that stood in a natural clearing. 'Here,' he said. 'This is where I found him.'

I came up close to the tree and peered at the black lettering scrawled down the bark. Spray paint. It took me a moment to read it, the writing was so uneven.

GET OUT.

Goosebumps came up all over me. My throat was tight. Arran stepped forward and ran his hand over the bark. 'Look.'

There was a nail there. Hammered into the trunk. A scrap of fur clinging to it.

'Shit. Shit.'

I folded my arms, twisting round, side to side, trying to get some perspective on why it had been here. Why this place specifically? To my left the trees dropped away in a long, slow dip – down towards the lakes. To my right the land lifted up towards the Bakehouse. The fairytale gables were visible through the thick branches. It felt familiar, but I didn't know why.

'Do you want to see the rest?'

I glanced up at Arran. He was chewing the inside of his mouth, not meeting my eyes.

'Do you want to see it?' he repeated.

'Yes. Yes – of course.'

We walked back up the slope, the leaf mulch around our feet slowing our legs. It was still afternoon but the dark of the woods was clinging to us as we came out on to the lawn. The house was silent – the rest of the family still wasn't back.

'In here.' The little workshop's door was open and we both ducked inside. I hadn't been in there for years and years. It was like a bomb shelter, long and low, brick-built and white-washed. On every wall implements hung. There was a saw horse and row after row of furniture varnish – an entire shelf rack filled with templates for corner joists.

Arran walked ahead of me, his finger still to his mouth. 'Here.'

He'd stopped next to a closed plastic crate on the floor.

It was pink, which seemed totally inappropriate – the colour of fun. I knew what was inside. I knew it wasn't going to be fun at all.

'Open it, then.'

He did, and I crouched down next to the crate to look. I'd got used to smells in London – one cop had told me that the trick to good policing was to have no sense of smell – so the choking scent that came up didn't put me off. Arran put his hands in and pulled it out and that was when I cracked a bit.

'OK.' My throat was moving up and down. I put my hand over my mouth, took in a breath and held it down hard against my lungs to stop myself retching. 'OK.'

'You going to puke?'

'No.' I breathed deeply, wiping my eyes and nose with the back of my hand until I had it under control. I'd seen more horrible things than this in London; the new cops always got sent out to investigate the smells coming from flats, and why there were circulars bulging out of the unemptied letterbox. But this was too close to home.

Squatting, I spread the body out over the crate. The place the dog's eyes had been were empty. The place his nose should have been was gone. His skull was pared back to the bone. The rest of the skin was intact. My eyes got heavy.

'Just the head is skinned,' Arran said. 'The rest has been mummified. You noticed that?'

'Of course. How could I not?'

'It means it's been kept somewhere warm and dry. Like dry-curing meat.'

I stood and found a stool to sit on. Put my hands on my knees and lowered my face. My eyes were watering. 'I'm going mad. Now I really know I'm going mad. Why the fuck are they doing this? *Why?*'

'I don't know.'

I lifted my eyes to him. 'You don't think it's because of the charity? Your mum is always helping my mum.'

'I don't know. Maybe.'

The sound of a car crunching on the driveway. Then voices. Adults talking tiredly, subdued. Minty babbling away. A door opening and closing.

Arran went to the door, looked out, then came back into the shed. 'I can't keep it here.'

'No, of course you can't. Have you got a bin liner?'

'I can find one. Why?'

'Mum's got a freezer in the garage. Hasn't used it in years. We'll put it there.'

Arran rummaged around in a couple of drawers and came back over to me, carrying a roll of bin liners. 'I'll double this up.'

He wafted one up and down to open it while I picked up what remained of Tumble. He had been a hairy mutt who came up to a person's knee – a little like Bamber, which made the whole thing worse. His skin was scratchy against my inner arms and palms.

'What's that?' I asked, pointing to a place on the edge of the skin that roughly corresponded to the abdomen. It had an oddly definite outline.

'I cut out a sample. I'm taking it into work, talk to the lab guys.'

'You can't do that.'

'I'm going to. I don't know how I'll get it finessed, but I'll do it somehow.'

I nodded. I had a flashback of us as kids out here in the same workshop: we'd been trying to dig in the garden and he had broken his dad's spade. He'd looked me in the eye and said: *I will get this sorted. I don't know how, but I will.* And he had. He'd mended it and his dad had never noticed. Arran had always had that confidence.

I shovelled the remains into the bin liner Arran was holding, folding down the parts of the skin that were hard. His paws and his tail. Next to me Arran rubbed his temples frantically. I got up and put my hand on his shoulder.

'It's OK. I promise. We'll work it out.'

Maryam

'That's it. Gently now.'

It was almost seven p.m. and Minty was still awake. She'd been fussy and difficult because she hadn't had her afternoon nap. Maryam didn't have the energy for a battle over bedtime, so she'd let her stay up. They were making chocolate chip cookies.

'Very, very gently. You put the eggs in.'

Minty stood on a chair so she was level with the mixing bowl on the kitchen table. She was in her *Minions* sleepsuit again, an apron printed in cherries tied around her. Maryam was still wearing her dress from the fundraiser and a tired old Limoncello-printed apron Rhory had bought her in a tourist shop in Rome. A million years ago. When she'd thought she was safe.

'You did that beautifully. Now, then, here's a spoon.'

'Spoon,' Minty echoed. 'Spoon.'

'Yes, that's right. Now, with the spoon can you very carefully stir, like this? See? Nice and gentle.'

Minty began to stir the mixture, making it splatter all over the table. Rhory, who was sitting morosely at the end, a glass of Cragganmore in front of him, watched in silence.

Maryam took a breath. Wiped the hair out of her eyes with the back of a flour-covered hand and said in a strained voice, 'You can tell me now. This is a good time. She's occupied.'

Rhory shifted forward in his chair and peered up at her, his mouth puckered.

'Now,' she repeated. 'Now is a good time.'

'There's nothing to say. She works behind the bar.'

'Not at the Ragged Stall. She doesn't work there.'

'No. She's at Loxton's Chase.'

Maryam was holding Minty's hand to guide her stirring, and now she tried not to tighten her grip. She believed the Bakehouse smelt different – as if someone had been in here while they'd been at the play park. How else could you explain the abrupt and inexplicable shifts that life was taking daily? Loxton's Chase was a country pub out on the side of the escarpment near Parson's Pike. Rhory hated that pub – he hated the beer. He always said he could taste the bleach they used to clean the pipes.

'You never go to Loxton's Chase. It's a pub for the hunt people.'

'Well, I did. One night this week, that's all. It's not a crime.'

Minty looked up and smiled toothily. 'Minty make cookies.'

'That's right.' Maryam kissed her on the head and carried her to the sink, where she held her kneeling on the sink edge, and ran the tap to rinse the biscuit batter off her hands. She carried her back to the chair and wiped the table a little. Then she pulled over the last of the bowls in which she'd carefully measured out the ingredients. 'Chocolate chips now – the best bit. Here we go.' Carefully she helped Minty hold the bowl – so huge in her little hands – and tip the chocolate into the mix. 'Yum yum. Looks good. Yum yum.'

'I hope we're bringing these children up right,' Rhory said suddenly. He was staring at Minty, a strangely haunted expression on his face. 'I really, really hope we're getting it right.'

'We're doing our best. That's all we can do.'

'Spoon,' Minty said. 'Lickie.'

The cookie batter had raw eggs in it. Maryam had heard somewhere that it was a sin to let your child eat raw eggs, but if it made Minty happy then Maryam was going to be a sinner. She handed her the spoon. Minty took it and scrambled up to sit on the table, carefully running her finger up the laden spoon and licking the batter off slowly, almost thoughtfully.

Maryam sat down, tired. Her arms were itchy where she'd picked up insect bites in the woods earlier.

'What's wrong with Fenton?' she asked. 'He wasn't drinking, was he?'

'Not at all.'

'Then?'

'I have no idea.'

'Maybe food poisoning?'

'No.'

'How can you be sure?'

Rhory raised his eyes. 'I don't know. Why does it matter?'

'If it's not food poisoning then it's probably a virus. It might be infectious. He's had contact with Minty recently. We ought to know.'

'That's not what it is, OK?' Rhory pushed back the chair and stood. He tipped more whisky into his glass, picked it up and left the room. A moment or two later she heard him going into the living room. Soon the television was on. Rugby. She wanted to call after him: *Is what's wrong with Fenton something to do with Loxton's Chase? Did you go up there with him?*

Back to Minty, who had finished licking the spoon so thoroughly that it was now shiny enough for her to be able to examine her own distorted reflection. 'Come on, pickle, let's get you to bed. The cookies will be ready in the morning.'

This time Minty didn't argue. She dropped the spoon, stretched out her arms and allowed Maryam to lift her up. She was so drowsy by the time they got upstairs that Maryam had to hold her in one arm and clean her teeth – slapdash considering the sugar she'd scoffed during the day. Her nappy was dry so didn't need changing and Maryam just laid her straight in her cot, tucked Horky into her arms and stood for a while, stroking her warm little head.

There was another little plait in her hair, hidden up in the nape of her neck. This time it was tied off with an orange ribbon. Gently, so as not to wake her, Maryam stealthily unpicked it. She turned it over and over in her fingertips. It was strange the way the braids were never on the top of Minty's head and only visible if you ran your hands through her hair. It was either Rhory or Lois doing it and there was something vaguely sinister about it. She was going to ask them. There were lots of questions getting ripe for the asking around Lois and Rhory. Lots of things that needed to be cleaned out. They were keeping something quiet and it concerned Fenton.

The sound of someone in the kitchen. She pushed the ribbon into her cardigan pocket and went silently on to the landing. Arran was down in the hallway hanging up his coat. He gave her a wan smile as she came tiptoeing down the stairs.

'Hi.' He had changed from the fundraiser outfit to black jeans, Vans and a thin shirt. 'Where's Dad?'

'Watching the rugby. Where've you been?'

'Work.'

'Work? I thought I saw you in the shed earlier.'

'Yeah, I . . . something cropped up and I had to go to Gloucester. Don't worry about it.'

They went into the kitchen and he got a beer from the fridge. He didn't use a glass, but downed it in one. Maryam watched him in silence. Arran had never been a big drinker – until he was fifteen he'd hated the taste of beer and even now he had to be coaxed to drink even a tiny glass of wine. He took another from the fridge then sat down next to Maryam, watching her silently. She smiled at him and he smiled back, sadly.

'Do you want to eat? There's some frittata I can heat up.'

'No. Thank you.'

'Are you OK. You look . . . Do you feel OK?'

'I guess.'

'Tell me, because we still don't know what's wrong with Fenton. It could be food poisoning. It could be something infectious.'

Arran tapped the side of the bottle, watching her thoughtfully, as if he was deciding what he could or couldn't say.

'Arran, what? What is it?'

'Nothing.' He shook his head, turned away. 'There's been a spate of burglaries in the village. They're talking about it at work. I think it's serious. Keep everything locked. Everything – all the doors, the windows. The police think they're coming in from the park.'

'No one's said anything.'

'Just . . . just please do it.'

He got up and left the kitchen with his beer, closing the door and leaving her to wonder what felt worse – the idea of burglars coming in from the park, or the niggling sensation that her son had just lied to her.

Alex

It had never seemed right to me that the remains of a living thing could be wheeled carelessly into a freezer. Packed away like a carton of frozen food. Except that was the way it was; that was the only way. I'd seen it done to humans before, in those '80s-built mortuaries in London, and now I had to do it to Arran's dog. I folded his skin inside the bin liner into a neat, shoebox-sized package, secured it with brown box tape, and placed him deep into the freezer in Mum's garage under all the industrial-sized packets of frozen peas and broccoli.

It was nasty. Really nasty, and beyond anything I'd ever dealt with.

The next morning I showered and dressed as normal, drank cappuccino from Mum's fancy Nespresso machine and carefully dodged her questions. I knew she wouldn't check the freezer – she hadn't in years – but even so I felt odd leaving Tumble in there. As I reversed out of the garage, the white rectangle of the box got smaller and smaller in my line of sight. Some things were wrong, and some things were necessary because of the way the world was engineered.

I had the conversation with my sergeant in her office overlooking the little bakery where all the bready smells wafted in, making acid rise in my throat. I put my phone on the table in front of her.

'These are the photographs.'

She searched my face then lowered her eyes to the screen. Scrolled through them. 'And this is what you called me about yesterday? On my day off?'

'I'm sorry. I know I shouldn't have. I understand you didn't want to speak about it then.'

'Don't let it happen again.' She squinted at the phone, pinch-zooming the photo. 'I'm not an animal person – I can't tell what this is.'

'It's a dog. Isn't that obvious?'

'Not to me, it isn't. I just see bone and fur.'

I looked down at my feet. I hadn't slept all night. Arran and I had made a pact that we weren't going to tell our mothers and that made it worse. I'd had to lie to Mum, tell her there'd been burglaries in the village and we needed to lock every door, every window. She'd obeyed, meekly. She must have been too tired to argue.

'Yes, but with your permission I'll submit samples for DNA testing to the lab. That will be conclusive.'

There was a long pause. Then the sergeant said, 'PC Mullins. Let me just go over this in clearer detail. A dog – missing?'

'That's correct. And returned.'

'Granted, that is fairly perverse.'

'The dog was taken from its house. It's been missing for almost two months. Its . . . remains, its coat, whatever you want to call this – turn up in about the same place it was last seen, nailed to a tree. The words "GET OUT" on the tree trunk. See? That is fucked-up. Whatever perspective you look at it from, it's fucked-up.'

'Extremely unpleasant. However – allow me to tell you the level of tolerance the chief has for animal-related crime.'

My shoulders slumped. I knew where this was going – the joke was that even in England prosecuting people for cruelty to animals was incredibly hard and usually wasn't the police's remit anyway. Usually it fell to the RSPCA. The police notoriously had to turn a blind eye to incidents like this. Often I thought it was because they really didn't know what law they were enforcing.

'If a horse's head turned up in someone's bed, the chief constable would want to see the rest of the horse to establish there'd been a crime. He wouldn't crime it until the last possible minute. The bar is extremely high – always has been with animals.'

I took a long, long breath. Mum said when I was little I used to have major tantrums that she cured by betting me I couldn't hold my breath. I didn't have any memory of the game, but I did now have a habit of holding my breath when I wanted to get angry.

'OK.' Eventually I let my breath out and subsided. 'I'm sorry. You're right.'

'I am. I'm usually—'

'It was a shock.'

'I'm sure it was, but—'

'And I can't let it go. It's connected to something going on in the park I've been concentrating on and I—'

'Alex! Shut up.'

I closed my mouth, stunned. She was shaking her head and peering up at me as if I were some fascinating but obscure specimen that had been offered to her to study.

'If you would shut your pie hole and listen for one flat second you might be pleased to hear that I'll put someone on it.'

'Someone? Me, you mean.'

'Since when would you be allowed to investigate a case that you are involved in?'

'Then who?'

'Whoever is the next on the coms queue.'

'But it could be anyone.'

'Yes, anyone. You don't get to pick and choose.'

I closed my eyes and tried to keep calm. 'OK,' I said. 'What about the DNA tests?'

'Don't push it.'

I left the office, my heart thundering, and went into the ladies' to splash some water on my face and try to get some perspective. I looked at myself in the mirror. I looked red and feverish. Mum had told me they had no idea what was wrong with Fenton – maybe it was infectious, or maybe not. I leaned over the sink and tried to retch. Tumble. A dog I hadn't really known in life, except as a puppy. But Bamber? Bamber, Bamber – where are you? I thought. Where are you? What is happening to you now?

Tears came out of my eyes and plinked into the sink. I had to tear off acres of tissue from the dispenser to blot my face.

When, at last, I was able to throw up, I felt better. I washed my face, sluiced out my mouth and slipped a piece of chewing gum between my teeth. Arran had a piece of Tumble's hide wrapped in plastic. His day off, but he had spent the morning on the phone trying to talk the lab guys he trained in IT to slip a few DNA tests into the rota at the lab.

What was it going to prove? That the piece of fur was a dog? And what else?

As Arran had said, we were pissing in the wind. But sometimes even that felt better than doing nothing at all.

Maryam

Arran was on a late shift and he stayed in his bedroom muttering on his phone until gone ten. Rhory had taken Minty to nursery and continued on to work. Maryam stayed in the workroom and rolled a new part of the tapestry on to the frame, listening to the sounds of the house around her. When she'd come down this morning all the doors except the front door had been bolted from the inside. She'd tried to open the window in her workroom and found she couldn't.

The Bakehouse. A little prison. A glittery unhappy ginger-bread prison up on the side of the park.

Movements overhead. Arran was getting up. She went into the kitchen and began brewing coffee, slopping the thick sliced bread she'd soaked in egg batter into the frying pan. French toast with spicy crab apple jelly made from their own tree in the back garden. Crazy combination, but it was a family favourite.

Arran pulled back his chair and spooned jelly on to the toast. He hadn't shaved and there was a dead feel to him. A lack of energy.

'The doors are all locked.' She poured coffee and set the milk jug next to him. 'I couldn't get out of the workroom. Are you telling us the truth about the burglaries or is it something worse?'

Arran paused mid-forkful and raised his eyes to her.

'Just tell me. If you're lying, just say it. I've never got angry with you for the truth, so it's easier just to come out with it.'

Beaten, he lowered the toast to the plate. He pushed the plate out of the way and rested his elbows on the table. The big clock above the stone fireplace clicked through almost a minute before he spoke.

'Mum, have you ever thought about leaving here?'

'Leaving?'

'Yes – Eastonbirt? You didn't grow up around here; it's only Dad who's really got roots here. Maybe you both could do with a fresh start. I know you haven't been happy recently. Dad told me . . . about the pills. I'm sorry.'

She paused, the coffee halfway to the Aga. Her pulse was slow and thick. 'He told you?'

'Yes.' He was staring at her as if he was very sad. 'Dad said you've seen things. In the park. Things that made you nervous.'

So it was all out. All out in the open. Arran. Arran. Strong and level. Could she trust him with this?

She put down the pot, pulled back a chair and sat close to him, at a diagonal, her head lowered. 'I'm sorry,' she said softly. 'I'm sorry. I have seen things that haven't made sense. I haven't known what to do.'

'There's no shame, no embarrassment. You're not going mad. But you do need to tell me what you've seen.'

'Tell you? No. I don't think I can.'

'You can.'

'You'll tell your dad.'

'No. You have my word. I want to know. Mum, I *need* to know.'

The clock ticked some more. Maryam used her palms to smooth her arms, where the hairs had all stood up to attention. Her body hair had always been darker than she'd wanted, conjuring the impression of a man. Or an ape. She'd tried bleaching for a while but it had made her hair sturdier and more resilient. Now it was on high alert, like live wires.

'OK. I . . . don't laugh, but . . . I saw a woman in the trees. The night of the crash, when you were in the police car with us. I can't explain how she got there, but she was in the trees and she was . . . ' Maryam shook her head. 'I don't know. She was watching us. Me.'

'What did she look like?'

Maryam blinked and lifted her eyes. Arran hadn't laughed. He was taking this seriously. 'That's the part I can't explain. She was . . . um . . . dressed in white. But it was her face that was weird. It was almost shiny. Like bone.' She closed her eyes and put cool fingertips to her hot forehead. 'I can't believe I'm telling you this. You'll think I'm mad.'

'I won't. Trust me, I won't.'

'Because I do know what they say about the park. About that thing. You know, they call it the bonehead.'

'Yes. I know.'

'So maybe I did make it all up in my head. Imagined I was in some kind of urban legend – the woman who got murdered. I'm delusional. I probably am.'

'I don't think you are.'

She lowered her hands and frowned at him.

'Really,' he said, 'I don't.'

'I saw her again.' She nodded to the back door. 'Out there at the end of the garden, where the path starts. There's a big tree there. It's the place Tumble went missing.'

Arran sucked in a breath, whistling it across his teeth. 'And you didn't tell this to Dad.'

'No. He thinks I'm going insane as it is. I'm not going to confirm he's right.'

Arran's eyes raced across her face. He leaned in and spoke intensely. 'Listen carefully, Mum, really carefully. You're not going mad.'

'I am.'

'No. You are not. You've seen someone. A human being. A real person. She's flesh and blood. She's a sex worker, Mum, someone local – a hooker. Just like in the legend, but real.'

Maryam watched her son's mouth moving. His beautiful Rhory mouth. Nothing coming out of it could be right. It was an alien language – a collection of phonemes that hadn't been fitted together in the correct order.

Seeing her confusion, he reached across the table and covered her hand. There was a pitying light in his eyes that made her feel suddenly ancient. As if they were discussing her care home options and he was giving her a gentle lecture about remembering to take her pills and to stop arguing with the nice lady who brought her breakfast every morning.

'But no. You don't understand. It wasn't a human being I saw . . . '

'You saw a real person, Mum. She's part of a bunch of pervs who operate in the park. They've got some kind of fetish about the bonehead legend, so that's how she dresses to meet her clients.'

'But her . . . face. It *was* like bone. Just like the story.'

'A trick. She wraps her head in clingfilm. It's a kink some people have. You don't want to know.'

Maryam let all her breath out and stared at her hands, limp in her lap. She was nearly forty-two and she couldn't tell the difference between a hooker and a ghost. No spirits in the wood? What then of the Swami and his predictions? Was this really postpartum depression, or the perimenopause? What next? Was she going to grow hairs from her chin so everyone could laugh and call her the Old Witch in the Bakehouse?

'I thought she'd been stalking me. I thought I was being punished for . . . ' She bit off the words. 'What I mean is, for months, years, things have been going wrong. The crash, Grandma and Grandpa. Dad's work. Tumble. I thought it was that woman doing it. The bonehead.'

She glanced up at the place the Hand of Fatima was wedged secretly into the door frame. She thought of the oils, Minty's birth. It couldn't all be explained away this easily.

'Arran, you're saying there's nothing to be afraid of. But you've locked all the doors. The only one not bolted is the front door. Because of Dad leaving for work.'

'I'm not saying that. I'm not telling you there's nothing to be afraid of.'

'You're not?'

'No.'

'Then what?'

A long, long silence. The distant sound of a lawnmower sailed in through the open window. Upstairs, Minty had woken up and was wailing.

'Arran? Please speak to me. You're scaring me.'

He rubbed his mouth self-consciously, the way he used to when he was little and was telling a lie. 'I'm saying, let me deal with things. And in the meantime keep the doors locked. Watch everything. Don't let Minty in the garden on her own. Don't you go in the garden after dark on your own. And never leave here or go to bed without locking the place.'

Alex

I couldn't do anything more that day, so I picked up a few token jobs to make my queue look normal if it was scrutinised. I went to some abandoned cars near the Thames and Severn Canal, out to a post office owner in Rodborough who was battling graffiti on the walls, and I drove two community support officers to a primary school in King's Stanley where I introduced them to a row of scrubbed, eager faces who sat cross-legged on the floor, unblinking, while the officers dutifully rolled out a plastic zebra crossing, handed out posters depicting the message *Keep your eyes on the road, not on your phone* in emojis, and allowed the children to examine their hats and the handcuffs I lent them.

I sat with a patient smile on my face, hoping no one could tell I wasn't listening. One of the teachers knew who I was and during the talk, without introducing herself or even speaking, she sidled up to me and squeezed my arm affectionately – as if to convey, *I know your pain.*

I'd got used to that approach. Ever since the crash I'd been everyone's property.

'How are you getting along, then?' she whispered with a smile, pressing her hands together between her knees like an overenthusiastic schoolgirl. 'Is it strange being back in the boonies?'

'It's nice. Really nice.' I couldn't press any enthusiasm into my voice. I looked around the classroom walls at the artwork, hoping to find something to change the subject. Along one side of the room were pinned twenty or so sheets of dull red construction paper, in a long snake shape. On them was depicted a tableau of men leading livestock to market. The title, in individual letters cut from vivid yellow paper, read: *Our lives in Gloucestershire. What Do the Farmers Do?* At the front of the parade was a man leading a horse pulling a caravan.

My attention stayed on that horse. Something about it was important.

'I bet things are really quiet here, aren't they? After Hammersmith? I had a cousin who lived in Hammersmith. She told me people used to leave used needles on her doorstep. Do you think she was making it up, Alex?'

'What's that horse there for?' I asked, lifting my finger to point at the picture.

The teacher glanced up at it. 'Which horse?'

'The one at the front. It's got a plait in its mane.'

'Oh, yes – probably shouldn't have let the kids leave that up there.' She gave an embarrassed giggle. 'We could get into trouble with that.'

'Why?'

'It's a . . . ' She hesitated, then said in an over-careful tone, 'A traveller's horse. By which I mean . . . ' She shuffled closer to me and held her hand up to shield her mouth. 'By which I mean a gypsy horse, except of course you're not supposed to say that any more, are you?'

'What makes it a traveller's horse?'

'Lots of things. But mostly the plait.'

The plait. I stared at the plait. There, in the classroom lit brightly and full of smells and colour, I was back seven days ago in the garden, sleepily lathering Bamber. I could feel on my fingertips the grittiness of his fur as I tried to tease the braid out of his hair. He'd been alive, incredibly alive – full of everything. His head so perfect and covered with skin and hair.

Then there was Tumble. As I was lifting his pathetic remains into the bin liner last night, I'd felt something gritty in his coat. I'd thought it was a stick. Ignored it.

A muscle-deep ache of dismay crept over me.

'What the significance of the plait?'

She laughed again, with the embarrassed humility of someone who'd grown up on the land and was faintly ashamed of having to explain these traditions to the sophisticated urban folk. 'You never heard of it, Alex? We used to talk about it as kids – about how the gypsies would come and choose a horse in the field? And if they liked it and planned to come back later they'd plait its mane?'

'If they "liked it"?'

'Yes. If they wanted to steal it. They'd mark it in the daytime, come back at night and find the good horse by feel. You never heard that? A plait is a warning that your horse is going to get stolen.'

I was icy cold. Frozen in my seat. 'No,' I managed to say. 'I've never heard that.'

She laughed and ran her hands through her hair. 'You're not that much younger than me. Don't you remember the dead woman in the woods? The one who got mummified?'

'Of course I remember it.'

'Then you know there's a legend around that too? That the bonehead was a gypsy. And that if she wants something she'll mark it first by plaiting its hair? I'm full of these legends – my own fault, I studied classics at university – big mistake. Alex? Are you OK?'

'I'm fine, thank you.' I stood. 'Thank you so much, you've been very kind. I hope the children have enjoyed it.'

'We're very grateful, Alex. Very grateful to you and your officers.' She grabbed my hand and shook it as hard as she could, smiling into my face. 'I'm so sorry. I didn't mean to upset you with whatever I said.'

Maryam

It seemed to Maryam that she was living life from inside a hardened bubble. Hours of cooking and cleaning; dressing Minty; driving; cutting fabric and threading the sewing machine. She still hadn't absorbed what Arran had said. She wanted to ask him again, but he was difficult to pin down, and secretive. Every time she caught sight of him these days he'd be gone, slipping away either to work or to Alex Mullins' house. Maryam thought Alex was somehow involved in all this. Was that what she and Arran talked about late into the nights? The men and the women in the park who knew how to grind themselves against an unfamiliar pelvis without caring. The ones who wanted to connect flesh to flesh more than anything else.

The Hansels came over to the Bakehouse for an early tea. Fenton claimed to be feeling better but he didn't look it. If anything he looked worse, his skin washed so pale the veins were visible under it. He'd only been in the house five minutes when he disappeared into the toilet at the end of the stone corridor.

Lois said nothing and wandered off to play with Minty, while Maryam and Rhory stayed in the kitchen getting dinner ready, the back door open so warm air could come into the house. Tonight it was going to be a mass of finger food: tiny fajitas she'd shaped carefully, small enough to pick up and stuff with cheese, chorizo, avocado chunks. A whole bowl of chopped green tomatoes from the farmer's market in Stroud. Pimm's with cucumber and mint and strawberries.

She and Rhory worked in silence. Lately he had been as evasive as Arran. How could it be possible to occupy the same space as another human being, to share his bed, and yet know nothing, absolutely nothing, about what he thought? She had so many questions to ask. Where did she start?

After a few minutes there was the sound of the toilet flushing. The door slammed and Fenton came into the kitchen, wiping his hands. 'Can I help?'

'Sure.' Rhory handed him plates and glasses. 'On the table.'

The two men tramped back and forth between the house and the table under the apple tree, which was covered in the vibrant emerald and rose tablecloth. Rhory was buoyant, stopping to make jokes. Maryam watched them carefully, semi-ashamed to be noting where Fenton put his hands, what he touched. She also monitored the two men carefully for an exchange of secrets that would exclude her.

'All your doors are locked.' Lois came out of the workroom holding Minty's hand. 'We just tried to go out of the workshop – it's all bolted. That's not like you.'

'There've been some burglaries,' Rhory said. 'I'd lock yours, even up where you are in the village. Smart thinking, you know.'

'Burglaries?' She sounded unconvinced. 'It's the first I've heard of it.'

'Maybe the police are trying not to alarm anyone. We only know because Arran heard it at work.'

He left the kitchen carrying a tray full of warm crusty bread, butter and beer bottles. Lois sat Minty on the table, handed her Horky, then went to the fridge to get a bottle of wine. She put it on the tray then rummaged through the kitchen cabinets for Maryam's wine cooler. 'It all sounds a bit strange to me. Burglaries. I haven't heard any thing about it.'

'Everything is strange.'

'Tell me about it.' She stopped next to the oddment bowl where the family threw everything – keys and paperclips and rubber bands – and peered down into it. 'Those are pretty.'

Maryam glanced up. She was looking at the ribbons from Minty's plaits. Gingham in orange, and gingham in blue. 'Oh, I forgot to give those back to you. They're from the braids in her hair. So sweet.'

Lois fingered the ribbons, frowning. 'What braids?'

'You put braids in Minty's hair? Here? At the back of her head.'

'Not me. Someone else.'

'Oh, then Rhory, probably. He likes doing things like that.' She grabbed a pile of clean napkins from the top drawer and added them to the tray. She picked it up to carry it out, but changed her mind and lowered it to the table. At the bottom of the lawn the men were sitting under the tree, Rhory leaning forward in his seat, holding his beer bottle, peering at Fenton, who sat crumpled in on himself on the little bench. He looked terrible.

'Lois,' Maryam said carefully, not taking her eyes off the men. 'Fenton and Rhory – they tell each other everything, don't they?'

'Yes, I mean I think so.'

'Do you think it's important that you tell your partner everything?'

'No.' She put the bottle in the cooler and wrapped it in a tea towel. 'Not at all. I don't tell Fenton everything. It would be a disaster.'

'Can I ask you something weird? Does Fenton ever go out of the house at night and . . . and . . . ' She sighed. 'And lie about where he's been?'

Lois stopped what she was doing and frowned at Maryam. 'I beg your pardon?'

Just as she was about to repeat the question, Minty began to wriggle. She rolled herself on to her stomach and tried to struggle down off the table. Maryam let go of the tray, caught her in time and lowered her to the floor. She ran off into the garden and before Maryam could ask again, Lois followed her, carrying the wine, her peach-coloured scarf flapping behind her.

Maryam stared after her. It was as if no one in the world would stand still long enough to give a simple answer.

She took out the tray and Rhory helped arrange the food on the table. Minty floated around them, dancing and singing. She came to a stop a few yards from Fenton and regarded him seriously. His mouth was flaky and dry, his skin pale. Whatever it was making him so unwell must surely be contagious. Why was no one else reacting to this? Was she the only one who had noticed?

She hoped Minty would simply stand there and show him the horse. Instead she crawled on his lap.

'Hello, Minty,' he said wearily. 'Hello.'

'Oh, Minty,' said Lois. 'I really wouldn't, darling. He's not very nice to be around at the moment.'

But she plopped herself down, and although he appeared to be uncomfortable under her weight, as if it pained him, he said nothing and tried to raise a smile, nodding and talking when she held up the horse for inspection.

Maryam stood for a while, fiddling with her charity bracelets awkwardly. Then Rhory reached over and touched her arm – nodding meaningfully at her place at the table as if to remind her of her manners. 'It's OK. He's not a leper,' he murmured. 'Eat. Be sociable.'

She sat at the table and poured wine, made up little plates for everyone, trying to arrange them prettily. Rhory lapsed into a monologue about UK and American politics, using phrases like 'fiscal versus monetary policy' which Maryam couldn't understand.

'Lois,' Fenton said suddenly, cutting Rhory off mid-flow. 'Lois.' He turned his head creepily to his wife. His nose and the tips of his ears were blue, as if there was no blood getting to them. He was breathing quietly, but very fast. Minty slid off his lap and stood, her hand in her mouth, watching him in curiosity. Without a word, he got up and lumbered away into the trees.

'Mate?' Alarmed, Rhory jumped up. 'Fenton? Mate?'

Maryam stood and walked after him into the trees, followed by Lois.

'Is he OK?'

'I don't know.'

Fenton had stopped in the trees. He had simply sat down as if his legs had been cut from under him. Rhory was crouched next to him, anxiously peering into his face.

'Shall I call a doctor?' Maryam said. 'Rhory – call a doctor, for God's sake. Where's your phone?'

'No.' Fenton half-raised his hand and moved it in a circling motion. Tears were streaming down his face. There was a small rope of saliva hanging from his lose bottom lip, and, Maryam noticed, bruises covering his forearms. 'Please don't. Just let me keep . . . Let me keep going down this path.'

'This path? What path?'

'Just leave me.' He gave a sudden jolt like someone who was falling asleep and Rhory seemed to grasp the seriousness of the situation. He stepped forward and grabbed him by the shoulders.

'Mate, what the fuck? This has gone too far . . . '

But Fenton's head jerked and he lay down on the ground, his shirt rucked up to reveal his skinny white belly. His chest convulsed in a cough and he brought up a stream of something black and sticky. Like tar in the grass.

'999,' Rhory muttered. 'Now.' He fished out his phone and threw it to Maryam. She caught it shakily. 'And tell them he lost consciousness. They'll come quicker.'

Alex

The sky was turquoise where the moon shone down on the clouds. Midnight. I'd waited up until I was sure Mum was asleep. She had a satin face mask and earplugs so usually nothing woke her, but you could never be sure.

I didn't switch on the lights. Instead I relied on my phone, creeping through the house. It was so cold in the garage that my teeth chattered, the chill seeping up through my socks.

Tumble. Jesus, Jesus. Not a dog any more. Inside the bin liner he'd frozen to a pile of folded, frosted tissue. I had to lift the whole thing out and place it on the garage floor, where it slowly defrosted and left brown sludgy tracks across the concrete floor.

I hadn't known this dog very well in life, but the skin and fur were familiar – every inch of it made me think about Bamber. I squatted down and used the palms of my hands to flatten Tumble out on the floor, arrange his legs and paws to four corners. He looked like one of those gross lionskins you'd see in '70s movies.

I found the plait quickly. It was in the same place Bamber's had been. My hands stayed on it, my mind ticking along. Maybe Tumble's hair had been too matted for the Blacks to notice, but there was the same little fabric ribbon that had been in Bamber's coat.

I scrunched it into a ball and got up. I wanted to puke again. Wearily I refolded the skin into its place in the freezer. I took the ribbon to my bedroom – placing it on the bedside table. Then I sat in the window and watched the trees.

They would mark a horse if they 'liked' it. Because it would be good in the field. What would a sex club be marking a dog for?

I wasn't even going to say the words to myself.

'Bamber?' My voice was pathetic in the dark night, thin and feathery. 'Bamber . . .'

Maryam

The darkness on the edge of the park. The prostitute in the white dress who looked like a ghost, a rotting body. The black of Fenton's vomit. Tar. Dead blood. He was in the acute wing at Gloucester Royal hospital and couldn't speak to anyone.

But no one would tell Maryam what was wrong with him.

'They don't know yet.' Rhory and Lois got back from the hospital at midnight, both moving slowly, both pale and pinched. 'Until the doctors say, we just don't know.'

'They must know something.'

'Nothing.'

Lois was exhausted. A changed person. She didn't smile or make conversation, but went wordlessly into the workroom, her mouth locked, her eyes lowered. When Maryam went in to tell her she could stay in the guest room, Lois nodded, got up and went robotically up the stairs. Later when Maryam took her in a spare nightie and toothbrush, she found Lois lying facing the wall, not speaking.

Rhory was filled with nervous energy. He went around the house locking doors and windows. Then he checked each one again and pushed furniture against doors. He stood for a long time at the window in the workroom, peering out into the darkness. Maryam sat on the sofa behind him and watched him for a while. He was agitated, his fingers twitching at his sides. Eventually she said, 'There was a lot of blood when Fenton was sick. The internet says that's internal bleeding.'

'And that's why you should never use the internet to diagnose something.'

'Yes, but what else could it be? And how can he have internal bleeding?'

Rhory didn't answer that. He continued staring at the park. His breath steamed up the window. Eventually he spoke, in a low wooden voice. 'Growing up, I never thought about the park. I never realised how close it was.' He put his hands on the pane and rested his forehead against the glass. 'Naïve. Naïve. I look at it now and wonder how it hasn't crawled right up the garden and into the house.'

'Please don't,' Maryam shivered. 'Please.'

Alex

The next day, after I'd done all the morning's paperwork, I approached the police receptionist. I cleared my throat and checked over my shoulder. All the doors to the sergeants' offices were closed, and although the incident room door was open there was no one in there.

There was a trick I'd learned in London to get yourself assigned to a case. I didn't know if it would work here or not, but I gave it a go.

'Um, I was thinking – if someone, uh, kinda, you know, opened an incident record. And somehow left off their name?'

She didn't miss a beat. 'Of course.' She put down the inventory she was working on and swivelled her chair round to the computer, tapping in a few words as if this was something that happened every day. 'I'll raise it as what? Anonymous phone call?'

Without any external reports the quickest solution was to anonymously raise an incident; it would get assigned to the next person in the line who picked it up, which I was ready to do, and as long as I didn't 'crime' it, i.e., assign it a crime reference number, I could probably buy a day or two of my own time without any of the sergeants picking up on it.

'What do you want me to write?'

'Report of theft at business in Eastonbirt.'

'No worries.' A few more taps of the keys, and she was finished. Seconds later when I checked my Samsung there it was, incident number 060617/011 suspicious circumstances, theft. I logged a line saying I'd attend, meaning control would have me shown as 'committed but deployable' until I signed back on. I thanked her, got my radio from the wall-charging unit, buttoned down my epaulettes, and was ready to get on the road to Eastonbirt.

I stuck the phone in its dashboard holster and as I neared the village I called Mum.

'Alex? Are you on duty? I thought you couldn't call when you're at work.'

'I can't.' I slowed at a pedestrian crossing to allow a man with a fleet of dogs to cross. A professional dog-walker in hiking gear, little 'camel' water suck tubes dangling out of his rucksack straps. The dogs were all healthy and tall – Weimaraners, Greyhounds. 'I'm in a work car, but I just wanted to ask a question.' I tried to soften my voice. I hadn't slept, not one moment. All night I'd had my thoughts on that ribbon. 'Mum. About Bamber. Random, but did you ever do things to his fur?'

'Do things to his fur? Well, I comb it, of course. Every day. Alex, you've been in London two years, you've forgotten what it's like in the countryside. Things get matted. Animals get filthy.'

'I haven't forgotten. I promise you that.' The dog-walker had finished crossing so I put the car into gear and continued on. 'I was thinking about putting ribbons in his hair. Is that something you've ever done?'

'A ribbon? You mean on his head, for example?'

'Not on his head – just anywhere. A gingham ribbon?'

'What sort of a question is that?'

'A stupid one. Forget it.'

Mum went suddenly silent. The line hummed. Then there was a sharp intake of breath and she said, 'Oh, good God, you've found him. That's what you're saying.'

'No – I . . . '

'Or you've found *something*. A dead dog and it's in some sort of state that you can't tell me about and so you're asking about ribbons and—'

'No. *No.* Mum, please. I'm just asking a question. Please try not to read too much into it. Just tell me, did you ever put ribbons or anything, anything, into Bamber's fur?'

'Not ribbons. No. Not ribbons. Please tell me what's going on.'

I managed to calm her, finish the call and park up in Eastonbirt. The high street looked so normal. It was another hot day and the florist was using a spray to spritz the outdoor display of potted flowers, the water running down on to the pavement in streams. People were sitting at the little café under the umbrellas, numbered wooden spoons on the tables, their newspapers unfurled.

I got out of the car, tucking my radio out of sight. The groomer's was one of those places with a single window and a tiny door with a bell on the back. The whitewashed walls had been decorated with paw prints, and the wraparound reception desk bore a silhouette of a poodle on its front panel.

'Hi.'

The man behind the desk had dyed ginger hair sprayed into a Tintin spike, geek glasses, and a diamante chain acting as a belt for his black skinny jeans. 'Hello,' he said giving my uniform a cursory up and down. 'Am I in trouble?'

I put my phone on the counter with a picture of Bamber on the screen.

'Ah.' He leant over and tickled Bamber's screen head. 'Bamber. My Monday morning pooch.'

'I'm Victoria Mullins' daughter, Alex.'

'Of course you are. Now I remember. You know something? Bamber and your mum, they make it worth getting into work, bless them. Look on the wall, see?' He waved a hand behind him at the collection of client photos in a montage. In every one he was pictured holding each dog up to the camera. A shot in the bottom corner showed him grinning with Bamber in his arms. The groomer was wearing Bamber's Mexican hat. 'He let me wear Hat. Personally,' he smiled, 'I took it as a huge honour.'

'He's missing.'

The man's face fell. 'Oh. Oh, no. I'm so sorry.'

'Yes.'

'Is there anything we can do? Put up a poster? We'd be happy to?'

'You're kind. But for now, you can tell me something.' I glanced around the room. There was a wall of cages, small ones on the top and big on the bottom. Two huge grooming tables dominated the centre of the floor and there were three or four lighted display cases with various products lit up. 'When you groom dogs, do you ever do anything extra with their coats? I mean fancy things – ribbons.'

'Oh, the poodle topknot. It's making an ironic comeback, the celeb pampered pooch look. Maybe since Dame Rivers passed.'

'I'm thinking more a small plait in the coat. Here.' I tapped my back. 'Just a tiny one.'

He frowned. 'Not exactly. Bit random.'

'Do you use any gingham ribbon for the dogs?'

'Not that I can think.' He opened a drawer and shuffled through before coming up with a sample board of several different ribbons. He stroked one or two of them. 'No, not really gingham. Why?'

'Bamber came home last week with a plait in his hair – it was tied with gingham. I assumed it was you.'

The man leaned forward and pressed his hand flat against his chest. 'I swear I don't know. But what I would say is that we have a lot of part-timers. Some of them have their own little signatures – it's their way of showing love. There's Katya and Bogumila and Sapphire and . . . oh, the list goes on. It wouldn't surprise me if one of them went that extra mile. Bamber's one of the favourites.'

'Who did him last week?'

He shrugged. 'Probably all of them. They're my little coven.'

'Can you ask them?'

'I will. Katya's gone back to Gdansk for a holiday but Sapphire will be here later and – oh, there's Jade too, and . . . ' He trailed off. 'Look – there are lots. Can you leave it with me?'

'Sure.'

I stood for a while, regarding him. If I said, *Do you ever hear stories about bestiality? Is that something you've ever given a thought to?* what would he say? What would he tell me?

Eventually I didn't have the courage. Instead I placed my business card on the counter.

I felt empty. Sapphire and Katya and Bogumila and Jade . . . they weren't the answer. I knew that already. I went back into the open and I stood for a while breathing in slowly, watching the world going about its business in the high street.

Who are you? I thought. And have you killed my dog yet?

Maryam

Lois was no better the following day. She appeared in the kitchen, bleary-eyed and leaden. She hadn't washed or dressed, and was still in the nightie and dressing gown Maryam had lent her.

'Going to work?'

'Yes.' Maryam rinsed out her coffee mug and hauled Minty on to her hip. 'I'll be back at lunchtime. Will you still be here?'

'I'm not going anywhere.'

'Here, then. Spare keys. Make sure if you go out everything stays locked. You know what Arran said. And just help yourself to food – you know where everything is.' She paused in the doorway. 'If you hear what's wrong with Fenton will you call me?'

'Sure,' Lois mumbled vaguely, opening the fridge and staring into it.

Maryam watched her for a little longer. Why couldn't she talk to her friend any more? She no longer knew what she could believe or hold on to, who she could turn to. It was like crawling around outside the walls of a giant mystery where no one would communicate, no one speak plainly.

Eventually she left Lois to it, closing the door behind her.

Another ponderously hot day. A good day for headaches. Minty sat silently in the back seat, holding Horky up to her face, staring out of the window. A cow had been hit on the common, its sinister dark shape covered in a tarpaulin, and when Minty said, 'Mummy?' and pointed questioningly at the hump, Maryam almost burst into tears. She couldn't answer another question about death and disappointment and misery. Maybe later she'd go to the hospital and try to speak to Fenton alone. Would she dare do that?

Little Meadow Nursery was at the top of the common: three terraced cottages knocked into one, with sunflowers painted on the outside and a bumble bee sculpture coming out of the chimney pots. The pre-school boys on the swings at the front gathered to watch Maryam lift Minty out of the car. The attention made Minty shy – she jammed her fingers into her mouth as Maryam carried her up the path. Maryam hadn't paid this month so they went to the nursery office.

She was greeted with a big smile by the head, Amber Carter. 'Hello, Minty. How are you?'

'She had two whole oranges and a croissant for breakfast.'

'Well done, Minty.' Minty thrust out the plastic horse and Amber waved at it. 'Hello, Horky. Did you have your breakfast too?'

'Horky hungry. Hungry.'

Maryam dug in her pocket and pulled out her wallet, giving Amber her card. She watched her jam in the numbers. Out of the back window three young nursery helpers were tidying up the plastic ride-a-long toys littering the scorched grass. 'One of our family friends is ill – might be some sort of stomach virus. We don't know yet.'

Amber didn't look up from the machine. 'OK. I'll keep an eye out. There are one or two in Tulip Room off with something today – maybe it's doing the rounds.'

'But this one is serious. So if there's anything at all, anything, call me.'

'Of course.' She handed Maryam back her card. 'We'll watch you – won't we, Minty? Make sure you're OK.'

Maryam shifted Minty's weight to her other hip and slotted her card back into her wallet. The two gingham ribbons fell out. She remembered then that she still hadn't asked Rhory if it was him putting the plaits in Minty's hair.

Amber picked them up and looked at them in her hand, smiling, waiting for Maryam to explain.

'I meant to ask,' she said, 'It's funny: my friend thought I'd been putting plaits in Minty's hair, and I thought she'd been doing it. So we had one of those weird moments, you know . . . ' She twirled her finger next to her head to indicate confusion. 'I don't suppose one of the staff could have plaited Minty's hair? To make it pretty?'

'Ordinarily we don't encourage the staff to do anything like that. Not until the children get to the Buttercup Room, when they are three and can choose.'

'OK, never mind.' Maryam took the ribbons back. 'Probably my husband. Shall I take Minty down to the Tulip Room?'

'Of course. And we'll keep a close eye on her – make sure no poorly tummy.'

A ghost made real. A spirit made flesh. A belief she'd carried with her like a secret treasure for years. Maryam drove out on to the M5 among all the Mercedes and lorries and horseboxes and white vans, all of them speeding south blindly, ignoring her in her rickety car, with all the zinc pelmets swaying and jingling, elephants jiggling around cheerfully.

She was usually scared of motorways. Not today. She didn't care.

She came off at the Bristol exit and, as if led by blind intuition, steered the Vauxhall down the narrow roads until she recognised the peeling Victorian houses, the Polish shops and the council blocks of St Pauls. It wasn't raining here either, but it had that heavy, overcast look that made it feel as if the storm was creeping towards the city. People moved along the pavements with their heads down, their shoulders hunched as if it was already pouring.

The old Victorian house with the peppermint-painted render and the PVC windows hadn't changed much, though the Yantra sign was weatherworn and streaks of rust ran down the walls from corroded drainpipes. She went into the side street and found a place to park. Bristol was so different from Gloucestershire, where everyone stared at her orange and brown car. Here no one even glanced at her. She blended into the background.

She switched off the engine and looked across the street.

The back garden of the Swami's house had been turned into a parking space, and there, glinting as if newly waxed, its backside turned to the road, was a huge white car that had *Porsche Cayenne* on the back in stark silver letters.

Maryam fumbled for her bag, rummaging out her wallet, pulling out a few ten-pound notes and some change. She didn't have an appointment and the Swami wouldn't speak to her on the phone, so what should she do? Was it acceptable to just walk up to the door and knock? Wait to be let in and then ask if she could speak to him?

Just as she was about to get out of the car, the side door of the house opened and a man stepped out, huge and dressed in low-riding tracksuit bottoms, a brown leather jacket with a canvas hood worn over his face. It took her a moment to recognise him as the Swami. He had a phone pressed to his ear and was laughing, his free hand extended with an electronic key in it. The Porsche's locking system beeped and flashed and he sauntered over to open it. He hesitated a moment before he got in and turned to check the street, as if he suspected he was being watched.

Maryam slid stealthily down in the driver's seat, her head down, pretending to be checking her phone. A moment later she heard an engine fire, and the huge throaty monster of a car swung out of the driveway and passed her, heading for the main road.

She dared to look up and saw the brake lights as the Swami waited for a space in the traffic to turn right. Then he was gone and she was left in her tiny, thin little car, her heart racing.

Arran had been right. Everything she'd feared and worked towards in the last few months, all the things she'd been stupid enough to believe – it all had to be turned over and examined afresh.

Alex

The fanlight I'd mended was holding fine. I stood on a stool and double-checked the lock – turning the key back and forward, then tugging on the handle for good measure.

'I've kept them all locked,' Mum said. 'Because of what you told me about the burglaries.'

'Good. Don't let up – even for a minute, you hear?'

'Are you going to tell me now?'

I turned from the window. She was sitting on the sofa, her legs tucked under her. She was wearing white slacks and a pale spotted blouse, but she didn't look as neat as usual. Since Bamber had gone it was as if she was disintegrating very subtly – like an immaculate silk scarf fraying slightly at the edges.

'Tell you what?'

'You found something. You found Bamber, didn't you?'

I jumped down off the stool and carefully returned it to its place under the kitchen table.

'He's dead, then. Will you at least grant me that knowledge?'

'No. He's . . . oh, God, Mum, I don't know. I'm going out looking for him now. OK?'

'No, you're not. You're lying.'

The blood rushed to my face. It wouldn't matter how old I got, Mum would always be able to have an effect on me. 'I'm not lying. In fact – look. There's Arran now.'

I went to the glass door and opened it. Arran was coming up the steps to the deck, wearing a camo jacket and hiking boots.

'Good timing,' I hissed under my breath. 'You're a lifesaver. Play along.'

'Arran?' On the sofa Mum leaned forward to see him. 'What are you doing here?'

'He's come to help me look for Bamber.' I shot him a tight smile. 'Haven't you?'

'That's right, Mrs Mullins.' He held up a hand to greet her. 'Won't be late.'

She subsided a little on the sofa, not sure now about her instincts. 'OK,' she said warily. 'And will you make sure you send Fenton and Lois Hansel my very best? Ask Lois to send news the moment she hears?'

'I will.'

I closed the glass doors, locking them carefully and drawing the curtains. Then I took Arran down through the garage. 'Does anyone know what's wrong with him?'

'Dad does. But he's not telling anyone.'

'Weird.'

'That's parents for you.'

I opened the freezer and rummaged under the peas, the frozen vegetables. Pulled out the trapped shape and put it on the garage floor.

'I think he, she, *it*, whatever or *who*ever it is – I think they've been planning this for a long time. They put a plait in Bamber's coat.'

Next to me Arran's face was solemn. His mouth set firm. 'Explain.'

'Four days before he disappeared, at least I think it was four days, I was washing him and I found a plait in his hair.'

'A plait?'

'Like a little braid or something. Tied with a ribbon. The way travellers used to with horses they wanted to take.'

'That's fucked-up.'

'Yes. And look.' I pulled on latex gloves and handed a pair to him. Then I unfolded the packet, the white frosting scattering on the floor. The section of Tumble's coat with the braid in was at the top so I didn't have to make Arran look at the entire skin. I pulled back the hair and showed him the place I'd untied the plait. Then I handed him the ribbon.

'The one on Bamber was exactly the same.'

Arran stared down at the ribbon in his palm. The blood had left his face. I think he was trying to picture how it could have happened – how his dog could have got close enough to someone in the park for them to earmark him for abduction.

I collected my big Maglite torch and we went outside. I closed the garage door with the remote control and gave it a rattle to be doubly sure. We went round the side of the house to the back garden and down to the trees.

We'd decided we would search around the edge of the lake first. Maybe we were clutching at straws but Arran had the idea that there might be some holes or crevices in the embankments that had steps. Something we'd missed. The need to find the bonehead's bunker was tightening like a vice.

The woods had gone past that chattery stage when all the animals were getting ready to sleep, or waking to hunt. The leaves were still and silent. Not a breeze or a scrap of cloud in the sky. I was cold and unhappy. I was desperate to find Bamber, also terrified I'd find his body. His skin.

We searched for two hours, until I was so tired I was shivering. Eventually I simply gave up and sat down on the edge of Lake Tarquil. All the stars were reflected in the mirrored surface. I wanted to think of nothing except tracing out the constellations in the water surface. Arran sat next to me, saying nothing. We must have looked a little like the boy in the Dreamworks logo – fishing in a clear blue lake.

I picked up a pebble and launched it at the water. It fell about thirty yards away, making a plop like a fish jumping.

'He's dead,' I said faintly to myself. 'He's dead.'

'You need to be prepared for that, yes.'

I flung a second pebble – this time with more force. It made another two or three yards on the first one.

'Are you still wondering about the "incident" Raj was on about?' Arran said.

'Of course I am.'

'Do you think whatever happened involved our dogs?'

I looked sideways at Arran. 'OK, you can stop reading my mind now.'

I let my gaze wander back over the water, watching the last of the ripples move across it. I thought about the fish moving under the surface, travelling through the dark mud and weeds, winding and crisscrossing. My damaged hand ached.

'What are we missing, Arran? What is out there that we're missing? Is there anywhere we've overlooked?'

'I don't think so.' He fingered out a pebble from under a rock and flung it after mine. It swivelled in the air, plopping down not far from where mine had landed. 'Lois Hansel says you're a lesbian.'

'Yeah, well. Everyone says I'm a lesbian.'

'But you're not.'

'No. Of course I'm not.'

'Because it turns out that I'm a heterosexual.'

I stared at Arran. He was looking out over the lake, his face completely composed. I knew he wasn't gay. It hurt me every day that he was straight, and so fucking beautiful he could make a person cry. It hurt me to think of all the girlfriends I'd have to watch him fall in love with, the babies he'd make with other, better-looking women. I didn't know why he was telling me this now, and I didn't want to hear about who he was in love with. So I stayed silent.

After a short time he lowered his head and began ferreting around for another pebble. 'Anyway. What are we going to do? We can't just wait for Bamber to be returned. Not like Tumble was.'

I ran my hands down my face and stared out at the lake. Something was digging at my brain – something about the Bakehouse.

'What is it?'

I glanced at him. 'Had you ever been at that tree before? Where you found him – had you ever been there before?'

'Why?'

'Just . . . I don't know. Just . . . ' It was something about the Bakehouse. Something about the way it rose up above the treeline from that angle. The photo of Mum's house was in my back pocket. 'You're sure you were never sent a picture of your house?'

He shook his head. 'Nothing I ever saw.'

I narrowed my eyes. Thinking.

'Alex?'

I got up and brushed the dust off the back of my trousers. 'I think I know.'

We walked slowly because it was now completely dark and the place was treacherous in this light. Arran was ahead of me, his torch shining on the ground ahead of us. The battery was getting low so he had the phone on low power and the beam was sickly, hardly worth using. From time to time I gave him instructions: left here, or straight on. I didn't need the photo of the house to compare it. I'd internalised the angle it had been taken from and could navigate until we were nearly at the place.

Soon I could see the top windows of our house, the security light that shone all night looming down from under the gables. My heart was thumping hard and loud. Why hadn't I thought about it earlier: coming back to that point in the woods? It was obvious now I saw it – that must be the fun for the people from the sex club. Their vendetta was all about scaring and intimidating to the point that we felt we had to leave. The sinister photograph of the house to draw attention to a spot in the woods? Of course Bamber would be there.

Arran got to the small clearing ahead of me. I saw his solid back come to a jerking halt. Instantly he twisted back to me, holding up his hands and moving towards me.

'Oh, no,' I said, desperate. 'Oh, please no.'

'Don't look. You don't need to look.'

But I could see. I could see the grey burr of light and shadow around one of the trees. In the dim light glowing from the house beyond the trees I could even see the letters on the tree trunk.

GET OUT.

'Alex, you don't need to look, you don't need to.' He pressed me gently back into the forest the way I'd come. 'I'll deal with it. Just let me deal with it.'

My fight was gone. I backed up against a tree and slithered down it to the ground. I knocked my knuckles into my temples and let the tears come.

Why us? Why us? What had we done to deserve this?

Alex

I'd turned into a warrior. A kind of desperado – thin and drawn from nerves and lack of sleep. I stayed up half the night in my bedroom sitting at the open window, the crossbow from the boys in the tower on my lap, just staring out at the woods. Willing the pimp or the hooker to dare to come near. Willing and waiting. My fingers itching on the bolt. I'd do it. I'd do it in an instant.

Arran had taken away the remains of Bamber and Tumble in twin black dustbin liners. I didn't ask what he was going to do with them. I tried not to think about what was left of Bamber or what had happened to him before he died. Instead I fixed in my mind the bonehead hooker and her pimp. I drew a mental target across their image.

I was going to find them. They were playing a slow and nasty mind game with us, an attempt to get us to leave. If it killed me and cost me my job, I was going to look in their eyes and make them say sorry for everything. They were going to suffer; they were going to question their own sanity the way we'd been questioning ours.

Next morning I got into work early and tracked down the PC who'd been assigned to figure out how our dogs had been killed, how they'd made it back to the trees near our gardens. He was a six-pack gym bunny who smelled of aftershave and chewing gum and couldn't keep his eyes off his own reflection in the window behind me as we talked. I knew he didn't give a shit and I came close to telling him so, only at the last minute recognising the error.

'One thing you should know,' I said, leaning on the desk so my face was so close he had to look at me. 'You need to talk to the doggers in Eastonbirt. Parson's Pike. Go down there – hang out. Try it, it's fun.'

'You are joking, aren't you?'

'No. I'm giving you a lead. It's the best lead you could have. You might try asking if any of them have anything against the Dandelion charity. The charity put a play area slap bang on the old dogging site. Maybe caused tensions?'

I wished I could have saved the look he gave me as I left. Bewilderment and vague resentment all mixed together with grudging admiration that I'd had the balls to talk to him like that. Maybe he'd do something about it rather than checking out gym memberships.

In the street below, I could see all the office workers hurrying to work – skirt suits and trainers, just like in London. Dog-walkers and shop owners mingling with cleaners at the ends of their shifts. One of you, I thought as I waited for the database to load – is it one of you? Is it you walking down the road with your tool bag? Or you with your smart suit and your briefcase? Whoever you are, I'm coming for you. You're going to pay for what you did to my fucking dog.

It took me a while to work out what search terms to use. My sergeant had been right when she said you pretty much had to put a horse's head in the chief's bed before anything relating to animal cruelty was investigated by the police. Everything, it seemed, had higher priority – brake lights, no-right-turn violations and loud parties were more important than the dogs and cats starved and left to rot. Horses that fell dead in the field, they'd been so abused. But no matter how indifferent the police service was, the public didn't stop reporting it. There were plenty of incidents logged. If the past few days had been less traumatic I might have found the reading difficult: a hamster poked through a letterbox with a knife, three cats locked in an abandoned council flat forced to cannibalise each other.

But that day I was hard on the outside and on the inside. I kept reading.

I found what I was looking for after half an hour. A report of the pathetic remains of a pet dog, missing for weeks, being returned to its family doorstep in the dead of night. The moment I read it, I knew. It had happened in Eastonbirt two years ago and the family name had been Winters.

'Ozone,' I murmured, my fingers touching the screen wonderingly. That was what had been missing in their house that day. An immaculate garden, a cat lazing. A photo of a puppy taken only two years previously. And their dog, Chaos? Nowhere.

I fished out my phone and scrolled through, casting glances at the doorway. The sergeant was in the building somewhere and the last thing I needed was for her to come barrelling through now and catch me using the database. The line connected and I stood at the window, my hand in the small of my back.

'Ozone.'

'Alex. I'm sorry – I've been meaning to call. My shits of parents. I'm so sorry. They're so not cool.'

'It's OK. Don't worry. Just . . . ' There was a TV playing in the background. 'Are you at home?'

'I am.'

'Is there any way – any way at all your dad would talk to me?'

A hesitation. 'Now?'

'If he's there. Yes. Now.'

'I don't know. Probably not.'

'Will you give it a try.?'

'OK, but don't get offended if the answer's no. Hang on.'

I heard the familiar sound of a phone being held against a T-shirt or jeans to keep the conversation private. Muffled footsteps, shouts, vague male voices. Someone turned the TV down. Then a shuffling sound and – miraculously – Mr Winters.

'You want to talk to me?'

'I'm sorry – I know this isn't what you want.'

'It isn't.'

'Will you listen at least?'

'It depends.'

'I think I know why you left Eastonbirt.'

'Do you? That's interesting.'

'Did you ever give money to the Dandelion charity?'

'We did. Not long after your mother set it up.'

I dug my thumbnail between my front teeth – thinking this through. 'OK. And at some point did someone put a photo of your house through the door?'

'They did. We reported it.'

'And nothing was done?'

'Nothing was done. I'm surprised they even kept a record of it.'

'They didn't.'

'Then how do you . . . ?' He trailed off.

'Mr Winters – Chaos was stolen from you, wasn't he? In your back garden. Backing on to the park.'

Silence at the other end of the phone. I knew I'd touched another nerve.

'I think he was stolen from you and later returned in the worst way imaginable.' The words were coming out woodenly as I pieced it all together. 'He was stolen from your garden – maybe there was a warning? A plait in his hair?'

'Oh, Jesus . . . ' His voice was weary. I could imagine his face, grey and tired. No wonder he had moved the family away from Eastonbirt – no wonder there was a ban in the Winters household on talking about the reasons they left. 'It's happened again, hasn't it?'

'It's happened again.'

'This time, are the police actually going to do something about it?'

'If I have anything to do with it, they will.'

After the call I sat for some time, my knuckles pressed into my forehead. My bad hand was aching. The charity linked us all together. But there was more. A suspicion crawling around the back of my head. At this count there were three families affected. Mine, Arran's and Ozone's. All of us had been on the coach, and all of us were somehow connected to the Dandelion charity. But other people had been on the coach that day and had donated to the charity, and none of those had been hounded. Michaela hadn't had anything happen since the crash, nor had Minnie, and, as far as I knew, Sophie May's parents hadn't been threatened.

So what was the link?

I got up and went down the corridor. My sergeant was eating breakfast at her desk – a cinnamon doughnut and Starbucks coffee. 'What?' she said, wiping sugar from her mouth but not looking up at me. 'What now?'

'It's been going on for a long time. What's happened to me has happened before. Harassment – things being posted, veiled threats. A dog stolen, its remains returned to the owner. It's a campaign to get people to leave the area. Subtle and warped, but it's working. Once the family leaves, the threats stop.'

She put the napkin down and raised her eyes to me, frowning.

'Yes,' I said. 'It needs to be looked into.'

'It *is* being looked into. By the officer assigned to the case.'

'Please. Please. Let me have just one day. I could make such a difference in one day.'

'Let me think about this. I've got a really complex domestic abuse case, an entire drugs ring to wake first thing in the morning, a Support Unit inspector who fancies me and has made it clear that if his unit is there to issue warrants he expects payback in the sack. I didn't sleep last night because my husband snores because he's fat. And you want me to break every rule in the book, possibly get myself a disciplinary or worse?'

'Um . . . yes,' I said simply.

She twisted the Starbucks cup round and round, idly considering the little wet ring it made on the desk. 'In fact, I'm so busy and stressed that I'll almost certainly ignore the fact that there was a radio missing from the console the other night. And your tactical vest.'

'I'm sorry.'

'I know what you've been up to. I ignored it once; I'll ignore it again. I'm far too busy to be monitoring what happens to personal issue kit. Or what it's used for. I assume I don't need to remind you that if you turn the radio on you'll log in at coms and your gig'll be up.'

'Um – no. You don't need to remind me.'

'And good luck with this, Alex. I mean that. Good luck.'

I took a moment, looking at my feet, my hands behind my back. Then I rocked back on my heels, lifted my chin and said, 'When you told me you got this job 'cos you're black and female and I said no, you got it 'cos you're smart? Guess what?'

'What about it?'

'You were wrong and I was right.'

She swung her swivel chair round away from me, presenting me with her rod-stiff back. 'Thank you, PC Mullins.' She picked up her doughnut and her coffee. 'This conversation is over.'

Maryam

At last came the official news from the hospital. Fenton was suffering from acute peritonitis and had been upgraded to critical. Rhory cancelled his jobs and went to the hospital to wait for news. Minty was at nursery; Arran was at work. Maryam found herself alone at the Bakehouse with Lois.

Lois had spent the past twenty-four hours in silence, in the spare room under a light duvet, or lying on the sofa in the workroom, an open bottle of scotch at her side. Someone, Rhory maybe, had wheeled a TV in and she was lying propped up on her side watching *A Place in the Sun*. She hadn't showered and was already beginning to emit a faint smell.

'Can we talk?' Maryam asked. 'Can we just have a short talk?'

'I don't think it's a good idea. I really don't. I'm sorry.'

She poured herself more scotch and Maryam, feeling as if she'd been dismissed from her own workroom, went upstairs, not sure what to do. She had no appointments until later that day; she couldn't work on the tapestry with Lois there. And she couldn't hide up here, a recluse in her own home.

It was unbearably hot outside; the trees stood silent and thick, as if weary of the heat. She wished she could open the windows, but Arran had scared her so much that she didn't dare. Eventually she couldn't keep still any longer. She cleaned her teeth and got her keys.

Gloucester traffic always felt heavy and anonymous, so she drove more cautiously than usual. All the windscreens appeared mirrored, as if no one wanted to be seen here. Even the hospital had a dangerous feeling, with men slouching near the entrance, hoodies down, pacing and yelling loudly into their phones. A row of patients in dressing gowns stood with their drip stands smoking under a dirty Perspex canopy. They eyed her as she passed and she wondered if they could smell her nerves, even at this distance.

The ward had press-buttons to enter and hand sanitiser at the entrance. She pumped some dutifully on her palms, peering down the corridor. She could see lots of cubicles with glass walls, and inside one or two of them people sitting next to beds, relatives, grave faces. No Rhory.

There was one nurse on the station, so absorbed with what she was doing on a computer that she didn't look up, even though Maryam was sure she knew she was there. Eventually she cleared her throat tentatively.

The nurse still didn't look up. 'Yes?' she said efficiently. Her make-up was flat and yellow. Her cheekbones had sparkling white highlighter on them.

'Um – I'm here to see Fenton Hansel?'

'Yeah, he's . . . wait a moment.' The nurse stood and leaned across her desk, peering down the ward. 'Yeah, the doctor's with him now. You'll have to wait.'

She sat down and went on clicking the mouse.

Maryam shuffled awkwardly from foot to foot. Unconsciously her hand went into the hessian bag and closed around one of the bottles of oil. She snatched it away again. No. She couldn't draw strength from that any more.

'I . . . er . . . ' She cleared her throat. 'I wondered if I could ask a question?'

'What?'

'I've got Mr Hansel's wife staying at my house and she's . . . she's very anxious.'

'Understandably. But he's showing good signs. That's why he's on this ward. Still not talking, but he's breathing unaided.'

'It's good news, but his wife . . . well, she's too shy to ask. But she wants to know if it's infectious.'

'We've told her all this. It's not infectious.'

'And she won't tell you, but she doesn't understand all the science – I think she needs someone to explain it all to her.'

At that the nurse broke away from the computer and lifted her face to eye Maryam carefully. 'What's your name?'

'Maryam Black. My husband's here with Fenton.' She leaned back and squinted down the ward. 'Somewhere. I think. He's been here all morning.'

The nurse pulled a clipboard off a hook, ran her finger down the list and squinted at it. Apparently she found Maryam's name there because she returned it to the hook. 'We've told her what she needs to know – she's seen the hospital admission notes and the chest X-ray. Air under the diaphragm. As well as the peritonitis, an abdominal X-ray showed a pneumoperitoneum.'

'A pneumo . . .? I'm sorry, I think that's the bit Mrs Hansel doesn't understand.'

'Air in the abdominal cavity. Rupture of ascending colon. She knows all about the injury.'

'Injury? There was an injury? Not food poisoning, then?'

The nurse frowned and cocked her head on one side. 'Mrs Black, this has all been communicated by the doctors. Not just to Mrs Hansel but to your husband too. You're on the nominated visitors list but I can't enter into this discussion unless it's with a next of kin.'

'Yes,' Maryam murmured. 'Yes. I mean, I was only trying to get it clearer for Lois. Where's my husband?'

'Probably downstairs. He must have left when the doctors arrived. No visitors if there's a doctors' round.'

Maryam went back down in the lift with a woman and an old man who appeared to be together but stood in silence, not speaking to each other, a fraction too much space between them. As if they'd lost the skill of communicating and lacked the energy to re-learn it.

Outside, it had started to drizzle. While Eastonbirt, only a few miles away, was so dry that its skin was sticking to its bones, Gloucester had rain. The smokers were still huddled suspiciously against the building, surrounded by scattered ash and fag ends. Rhory was not far from them – seated on a bench in a small, tatty garden area with concrete paths and benches, his face creased and anxious, his dark, greying hair sticking up in a vague attempt at a quiff. He must have come down from the ward as she was going up. He wore a leather jacket with the collar turned up and was also smoking. He seemed content to let the drizzle settle on his head and shoulders.

She couldn't remember the last time she'd seen Rhory smoke.

She didn't make eye contact when she sat down, just sat there, clutching the old, worn hemp bag to her chest. Her toenails, she thought, looked very white against her skin – as if she'd accidentally got a suntan in the last few days.

'Smoking?'

Rhory blew a long line of smoke through his nose. 'Yeah.'

A few security men appeared from the hospital wearing hi-vis jackets and talking into their radios. In the distance was the clatter of rotor blades. A helicopter must be on its way.

'I haven't seen you smoke in years.'

'Nope.'

She stared at him. At his beautiful strong neck, the dark hair, the flecks of grey at the temples. He smelled of damp and cigarette smoke and furniture polish. It was a smell that made her think of sex. So unnerving, that the further away from her Rhory seemed to get, the more she thought about sex with him.

He ran a weatherworn hand over his face. 'It's complicated.'

She went cold, because she knew that this was is it. He was going to tell her now.

'Just say it.' Her voice was thin against the noise of the helicopter. 'Say it and get it over with. You're leaving me. Aren't you?'

Rhory turned to stare at her. 'What? What put that into your head?'

'You're not?'

'Of course not.'

'Then why are you being so secretive? What about Loxton's Chase? Jan Frobisher? And, more importantly, where were you really the night you said you were up searching for Tumble?'

Rhory reached in his back pocket for another cigarette and lit it straight from the glowing end of the one in his hand. They used to call it chain-smoking, a detached part of Maryam's brain reminded her, back when everyone smoked.

The helicopter rattled in the distance. The medics and the security men were standing near the helipad, chatting to each other, watching the sky. 'Rhory? Where were you the other night? All night? What are you up to?'

He shook his head, took a bitter drag on the cigarette and blew the smoke out of the corner of his mouth. 'I've been try-ing to protect someone who is so depressed, so off the rails, he can't look after himself.' He tapped cigarette ash on to the damp paving stones and gazed up at the eleven-storey hospital tower, concrete blocks darkened by the drizzle. 'Though it looks like the secret is out now.'

'Secret?'

'Yes. Fenton's secret.'

She bit her lip and tested a few words in her mouth. Eventually she said, 'What put him here, Rhory? In hospital?'

'Oh, Maryam.' Rhory gave a long, exhausted sigh. He ran his hands down his face. 'Fenton is here because . . . ' He raised his eyes wearily to the security men who were gathering in a huge cordon circling the helipad and shook his head. 'Because of sex.'

'Sex?'

'That's what I said.'

'I don't understand. Sex with Lois?'

'Nope.' He stared down at his feet. 'Not sex with Lois.'

At that moment the helicopter appeared overhead, huge against the sky. Instinctively Maryam crossed her arms protectively against her chest, squinting into the blast of air that whipped her hair into her eyes. The noise clattered off the building; the smokers all lowered their faces and dragged their dressing gowns around them.

'Rhory?'

'If I tell you this, I expect it to stay between you and me. Understand?' He squinted up his eyes and watched as the rotors slowed and the medical crew and security converged on the helicopter. 'Fenton is confused. He's always had certain . . . habits. Even before Sophie May died, he had his problems with his marriage and coping with his sexuality. I knew all about it, but I was the only one who did know.'

'His sexuality?'

'He's always liked men. As well as women.'

Maryam's jaw went slack.

'It's not a crime.'

'I know. It's just – I never . . . ' She trailed off and for a while stared blankly at the medics running alongside the casualty on the stretcher. An old lady. Grey hair so thin you could see the scalp under it. Why was she always the last to know – always the ignorant one? She had no third eye. The Swami had lied about that too. 'Lois doesn't know.'

'I'm not sure. Maybe she doesn't know, or maybe she knows but chooses to ignore.'

'I can't believe she knows.'

The helicopter men were getting out and standing around talking. Maybe waiting for another job. On one of the floors high up above them was Lois's husband. A secret so big, so deep.

'Does he have a boyfriend? I mean, someone in particular?'

'No. Have you heard of Grindr?'

'Yes. I mean – oh, seriously? He meets people online? Strangers?'

'Not exactly. He does hook up with strangers, but it's not online; there's no record of it. That's the whole point. But it's similar – it's all about man-on-man, no-holds-barred sex. Sometimes bondage stuff. It happens out in the park.'

She sat back in the seat. Tapped her nails against her teeth. Now it all made sense. The trainers; abandoned belongings in the arboretum. The boneheaded woman with her face wrapped in clingfilm, trawling the night for lonely men. And Fenton had been one of them.

'These are the same people Arran told me about!' she said. 'And I've seen them – in the woods. I thought I was going mad but I wasn't. It's not me that's mad. You have to tell him about this, Rhory. He works for the police. He and Alex are investigating something important to do with this. He needs to know.'

Rhory took a breath to reply, then seemed to think better of it. He looked at her hard and long, as if she were a giant and intricate puzzle he was meant to unravel but had run out of energy for.

'I'm going inside,' he said getting to his feet and jamming the pack of cigarettes in his back jeans pocket. 'The doctors should have gone now.'

Alex

Can you believe it? I got a text from Arran at lunchtime. *Sophie May's dad is caught up in all this. He's got a little secret.*

WTF? I texted back.

You know he's gone to hospital? Well, according to Dad, he visited the bunker last week.

Christ. I sat for a long time, my head throbbing, staring at the screen. Fenton Hansel? Seriously?

I texted back. *What did he say? Did he tell your dad where it is?*

Nope. He's not conscious. Has internal injuries.

What? The sort of injuries I'm picturing?

Sounds like it, from what Dad's saying. Sounds like it got rough. Maybe that was the 'incident'?

I'll come and get you. I'll take the afternoon off.

I logged off duty and went to pick him up. We drove up over the common. This was all so familiar to me – the common dotted with cows, no fencing because of an archaic English law connected with odd commoning traditions I'd never understood, like 'estovers', 'pannage' and 'turbary' – all of which, according to Mum, concerned pigs and acorns and peat. The golfers dragging their bags across the road. The austere stone houses dotted along the ridge. I was wearing my police polo shirt and trousers, and on the back seat, tucked slightly out of sight, was my tac vest, the radio switched off. Also – and I didn't know how I'd had the nerve – I'd taken a man's stab-proof tac vest from the locker room – one of the guys who wouldn't be in for a day or two. I was going to return it.

'Where are we going?'

'I did a PNC check on Keyhole Raj's car. This time a real one. And yes, he does have a lot to hide. Million-pound mortgage, family to support, great, responsible job, etcetera etcetera.'

'Even better. It means he'll talk.'

'He'll talk.'

We went through the impossibly narrow streets of Minchin-hampton, past the old market house with its stone arches, the war memorial.

The million-pound house turned out to be a double-fronted Georgian in weathered Cotswold stone, set just outside the village. I had also figured out from a quick internet search his place of work and already a little about his life patterns. I pulled the car up in a discreet place down the lane from the entrance, and fastened on my police vest, leaving the radio switched off but visible, just for effect.

I didn't want life to be difficult for Raj. I actually felt vaguely sorry for him. But he was all we had and when, just forty minutes later, he turned into the lane that led away from his house, he found Arran and me waiting for him in the middle of the road, arms spread wide.

He stopped the car and stared at Arran, who bent over and smiled at him through the window.

'I want to talk,' Arran shouted. 'Just a few minutes of your time.'

Raj put the car into reverse and Arran had to run along to keep level with him.

'Just a talk!' He aimed a fist at the window. 'Just a fucking talk. Not much to ask.'

Raj swung the car back, shifted into first gear and for a moment Arran looked as if he was preparing to throw himself in front of the car, blocking his way. But instead of driving forward Raj stopped. He took the car out of gear and pulled on the handbrake and pressed the button so the window wound down. He was staring very hard out of the windscreen, the muscles in his handsome jaw twitching.

'Nice,' Arran said breathlessly, leaning into the window. 'Nice.'

'What the hell are you doing here?'

'We need to talk.'

'For fuck's . . . ' He glanced at me, then back over his shoulder at his house. He shook his head, and pressed a button on the central console to unlock the doors. 'If you get in, we're going to drive. I can't be seen talking to you here.'

'Fair enough.'

I locked up my car, tucked in the wing mirrors, and Arran and I jumped into Raj's car – me in the front, Arran in the back. The Jaguar was beautiful. It had expensive champagne leather upholstery and a shiny walnut dashboard like a very old-fashioned car. The latest iPhone was mounted on the dash, a neon flashing aux cord trailing from it, and in the cup-holder was a olive-green thermos flask with a logo in cream saying *Paddle your own canoe.*

Out of habit I did up my seatbelt. Raj accelerated away, twisting down the tiny lanes that were hemmed by the dry-stone walls on either side. For a long time we were silent. He only changed his stony expression to lower his chin and check the mirror before making a left turn, then another left turn and another. His nails were perfectly manicured, he had a Rolex Submariner, and he smelled nice. He wore cufflinks, for Christ's sake; who wore cufflinks any more?

When we'd got on the road to Stroud he pulled into an anonymous industrial estate and stopped the car under a board that showed a map of all the businesses, labelled Units 1 to 24.

'Right – can you walk from here?'

'We can.' I put my forehead on the window pane and squinted down at the pavement. 'But we're not going to yet. We need to talk.'

'Yes, I know,' he said patiently, his eyes flickering to the road, monitoring any cars that slowed. 'I mean when we're finished: can you walk back to your car? I've got to get to work. I've got a huge meeting later this afternoon.'

'I expect you have. In Cheltenham. At Dowliss and Humbert's. A nice life, though, working in conveyancing.'

Raj's expression changed. He took his eyes off the mirror and turned them to look at me stonily. They were very cool and amber-brown. I noticed little bumps on his jawline and upper lip where he'd recently shaved, and decided he somehow wasn't quite as good-looking as I recalled – not so chiselled. He gave me the impression of an egg that had recently been peeled.

'Are you threatening me? Because I thought we had a deal?'

'We do have a deal.'

'Hmm. I notice you're in uniform but your friend isn't. He turned and eyed Arran. 'And I haven't seen his warrant card yet, so I'm assuming this isn't an official visit.'

Arran leaned forward, his elbows on the backs of our seats, trying a different approach. 'Raj, from one human to another . . . we need your help, mate.'

'Didn't I tell you all you needed last time?'

'We thought of some more questions.'

'And if I say no?'

I sighed. 'Please don't do that. Please don't. It will end up being so complicated.'

There was a long, long pause. He looked from me to Arran in the rear-view, then out at the industrial estate car park. 'Not much I can do, is there? I'll give you five minutes – after that it's the end. And I never want to see you again.'

I turned to him in the seat. 'OK. The other day you said something had happened in the bunker that had stopped the club operating.'

'Rumours – that's all. Just rumours.'

'And those rumours . . . did they involve animals?'

He shot me a hard look. 'Animals?'

'Dogs.'

'No.'

'Are you sure? You said the other day that something bad had happened down there, an incident that put them out of business for a while. Nothing to do with dogs?'

'No. It was a man. I haven't heard anything about dogs. And no, I can't tell you more and no, I won't tell you who told me. No matter what pressure you put on me.'

'I'm not asking. But tell us how this man got hurt.'

'I don't know, don't want to know. Apparently he's in good hands now.'

'Good hands?'

'He's safe. So now it's all over.'

'Would you know his name?'

'No, I would not know his name.'

'Does the name Hansel ring any bells?'

'I've said, I'm not giving you any names. Has that sunk in?'

I met Arran's eyes in the rear-view mirror. 'Plaits,' he mouthed.

Yes. I picked up the cue and continued. 'When you talked to your . . . *contacts* about the club, did anyone ever mention to you that they'd put plaits in victims' hair. Before kidnapping them.'

Raj stared at me as if I was a little thick. 'Before doing *what*? Kidnapping . . .? Who said anything about kidnapping? I mean – that'd be weird.'

'Weird.' I tried to laugh, make light of it. 'I love that definition. Weird.'

'Be really careful, constable. I might be a conveyancer, but that doesn't mean I don't understand the principles of criminal law. I'm doing you a favour here. Shall we try to keep that in mind? Who said anything about kidnapping? I never said that.'

'So – a plait? Tied with a ribbon? That doesn't ring any bells?'

'No. It doesn't ring bells at all. We're talking about two totally different things.'

His neck was now a deep puce colour. All the little black bristles where his barber had shaved the back of his neck glistened against the white of his collar. I decided to change tack.

'Have you heard of the Dandelion charity?'

'I dunno. Maybe.'

'It's a charity for children and teens with life-changing injuries.'

'What about it?'

'Do you know if the bonehead – the prostitute – or her pimp, or any of the clients, have got resentment towards the charity at all?'

He shook his head.

'The charity funded the children's play park. And that meant the doggers got moved on, which kind of pissed on everyone's parade.'

'Nope. Nothing.'

'How about the coach crash that happened two and a half years ago? The one in the lake? Do you know if the bonehead has any connection to anyone in that accident?'

'What? No – I swear. I have no idea who she is. Or her pimp. I don't know where they are, *who* they are. I've told you everything I know. Everything.'

A silence descended on the car. We all sat in our own little bubbles, slightly shocked by Raj's vehemence. A van towing a trailer pulled past us, bumped on the rough ground into the estate, the lumber on the trailer bouncing around and trailing sawdust. Presently a smart Audi pulled up outside a unit, and a man and a woman in business suits got out and went inside.

'Raj,' I said eventually in a softer voice, 'the last time we spoke you said there were columns in the picture you saw of this woman. We've been over the park and over it again. There's a huge amount of land to cover and we can't find any columns that match. Are you sure there were columns?'

'A hundred per cent.'

'This is your chance to tell me anything, *anything* that might help us find this place. Any detail, no matter how tiny.'

'I swear, I've told you everything. She was standing in . . . I don't know. Some kind of colonnade.'

I started to reply, but closed my mouth. The word 'colonnade' had started something ticking in my head. 'Colonnade? That's not the same as columns on their own.'

'There isn't much difference – it's just semantics.'

I had to put a finger to my lips and turn away to stop myself speaking. The trailer had stopped and a guy in a T-shirt and a bandana was unloading the timber into a pile outside a rollover door. He was very thin and pale and his face was clenched into a tiny point.

Colonnade. Colonnade.

Eventually I lowered my hand and turned back to Raj with a smile. 'We won't hold you up any more. But I need you to make me a promise.'

'I'm a solicitor, Constable Mullins. You know as well as I do that a verbal promise means nothing.'

'No. Except for the moral undertaking you make. That's something we can only hope for.'

He studied me thoughtfully, as if he was weighing up the option of punching me or shaking my hand. 'What's the promise?'

'That you will be careful. This is now a full-on investigation and if I were you I'd give Eastonbirt Park a miss for a while. Try somewhere else.'

Raj swallowed. He adjusted the flask in its holder so the logo was exactly even between the clasps. 'Thank you,' he said eventually. 'Thank you.'

'That's OK. Just keep your promise.'

'I will.'

We shook hands then. But as he drove away, leaving us standing on the edge of the road, and I asked Arran if he believed him, he just smiled patiently and shook his head.

We turned and began the long walk back to the car.

Maryam

No point in trying to work today and she couldn't go back to the Bakehouse on her own. Lois would be there, and how was she going to look her in the eye? How was she not going to ask – *Did you know? Tell me you haven't known all along about your husband.* So Maryam waited for Rhory to finish with Fenton. When he came out of the huge glass atrium of the hospital she was standing, bedraggled and tired, at the entrance. Waiting.

'I'm sorry. I shouldn't have overreacted.'

Rhory sighed. He pulled her to him and kissed her. They stood like that for a long time, her head on his chest.

'Can we pick up Minty?' she said, her voice muffled against his T-shirt. 'I can't work. Not today.'

'Me neither. Come on.'

They drove in convoy to the nursery. The little boys playing in front of the building all gathered at the railings to stare in awe at Rhory's mud-splattered Land Rover. A proper periscope, as if he were living in the jungle, not in Gloucestershire. The nursery staff were surprised to see Maryam an hour early. Minty blinked shyly at Maryam, as if somehow her being there at an odd time made her unrecognisable as her mother. She hadn't had her nap yet. She was grubby and dishevelled and on the ride home she sat silently in the back seat, holding Horky up to her face, staring out of the window.

At the Bakehouse the world seemed to have spun further off its axis. Arran was home on a work day and wearing odd dark clothes that made him look like some Secret Service commando. He stayed in the kitchen and drank coffee. He was silent and brooding and wouldn't answer her questions as she prepared a quick sandwich for Minty and a cup of tea for Lois, who hadn't moved from her place on the sofa in the workroom.

'Tea,' Maryam said, looking for somewhere to set it down next to her. There was a large glass on the floor, empty, and on Maryam's hexagonal cabinet a half-empty bottle of gin.

'This was Sophie May's favourite programme. She loved it. She'd watch it for hours.'

'That's nice.' Maryam deliberately avoided meeting Lois's eyes. If she did, where would it end, what would they say to each other? Fenton in the park with other men. Where would that subject go?

'I'll put this here, next to you on the floor. I've made Minty a sandwich. Brie and grapes. Did you have any lunch? Would you like one?'

Lois thoughtfully sucked her knuckles and stared at the TV set. 'Yes. No grapes though.'

Minty toddled in from the kitchen, holding her sandwich in one hand, Horky in the other. That got Lois's attention away from the TV. She pushed herself up into a sitting position and held her hands out to Minty. 'Who's this, home from nursery early? Minty Black! And is this Horky I see?'

'Horky hungry.' Minty mimed Horky eating the sandwich. She made a chewing face, puffing out her cheeks. 'Yum yum.'

'Come and sit up here.'

Minty clambered up onto the sofa, making herself comfortable. Lois's smell didn't seem to bother her – she handed her the plastic horse and continued eating, her feet in their red Clarks sandals pushed out in front of her on the sofa.

Lois danced Horky around in the air. 'He looks very pleased with himself. What's he been doing at nursery?'

'Be naughty.'

'Dear, oh, dear. You'll have to tell me all about it.'

Grateful, Maryam went back down the hallway to the kitchen to make another sandwich. But as she started slicing the bread, Arran got up, crossed the kitchen and stood behind her. He took the knife gently from her hand and laid it down on the counter.

'What?'

'Come and sit down, will you, Mum?'

She gave a deep sigh, wiped her hands on the tea towel and came to the table, looking from her husband to her son. 'What?'

Arran held a finger to his mouth and went to the doorway. He glanced down the corridor to make sure Lois wasn't listening, then drew the door until it was only open just a crack, and came back to his seat. Rhory had his elbows on the table, his hands clasped. The atmosphere was the way Maryam imagined a War Cabinet would be, during a top-level security meeting.

'We need to talk, Mum. Do you understand now? What Fenton's been doing? How he ended up in hospital?'

She folded her hands in her lap, hoping that would make her appear serious and prepared to talk maturely. 'Yes. I know he likes men. And that he was going to meet them – strangers – on the common. But I don't completely understand. I'm sorry.' She looked up. 'I know I'm naïve, I know I look ridiculous to you, but will you tell me how it works? How he got peritonitis from doing . . . what he did?'

Arran exchanged an awkward glance with his father. Rhory cleared his throat. He got up and went to the Welsh dresser where the whisky was kept. Since Lois had been here they'd gone through two bottles and now he had to open a fresh one from the collection. He got down the little tumblers and poured them all a tot. Drank his, refilled it, then sat down at the table, meeting her eyes.

'They injured him, Maryam. It got rough, and they injured him so badly that he could die. He didn't go and get medical attention because . . . ' Rhory gritted his teeth and dug a finger in the direction of the doorway. 'Because his life is a living hell. All he ever hears from his wife is about his dead daughter, and yet she's somehow surprised that he's lost the will to live. If you can call his miserable existence a life.'

Maryam had never heard Rhory speak so viciously about Lois. Again she had that sickening sense of an entirely different world existing just beneath the surface of the world she knew.

'They injured him?' Her voice was faint. 'But how? They stabbed him?'

'No, they didn't stab him. They ruptured him.' He squeezed up his eyes as if he couldn't believe he was having to spell it out. 'They ruptured him on the inside. Jesus, Maryam.' He dropped his hand flat on the table with an impatient sigh. 'I'm sorry – I can't go on with this. I can't say these words to you, in front of my son. There are just some lines you don't cross.'

The two men regarded each other silently across the kitchen. It was Arran who spoke eventually. 'Dad, Mum – you need to know something. I didn't want to upset you until I knew for sure. These people Fenton's been involved with . . . we're pretty sure they took Tumble.'

Both she and Rhory shot their heads at him in unison. '*What?*'

'They've got a problem with us, with our family. They want us to leave here. And they're not going to stop until that happens. Dad – everything Mum has seen? Everything she thinks she's imagined? It's not her imagination. She's seen it. Trust me, she has seen it. And the same thing has happened to Alex and Victoria.'

Maryam and Rhory stared at their son. It was Rhory who spoke first. 'How do you know they took Tumble?'

Arran glanced at Maryam meaningfully then back at his father, shaking his head a little. 'Please just believe me.'

'What have they done with him?' Maryam demanded. 'Where is he?'

Arran tightened his mouth and lowered his eyes.

'Arran?'

Silence. Outside the window, birds hung on the feeder, pecking their way through the nuts, not disturbed, because the humans on the other side of the window were so motionless. Maryam's mouth was glued to the roof of her mouth.

'Son . . .?' Rhory said.

He raised his eyes. 'Yes, Dad. Alex Mullins and I are working on it. Please trust me that we're getting there. But I need some help.'

'What sort of help?' Rhory asked.

'You need to speak to Fenton. You need to find out where what happened to him happened. We need a location. Something specific.'

'I can't ask him that. Not the way he is now.'

'You can. You can and you must. We've *got* to know where they're based. I'm serious, Dad. I'm not messing around.'

Rhory let out a long breath. He scraped his chair back and stood. 'OK. I'll go back and see him now.'

'Visiting time is over at 3.30,' Maryam said. 'I don't know if they'll let you in.'

'They'll let me in.' He went to the back door and rattled it, double-checking the lock. Then he went into the hallway and could be heard walking around rattling locks and windows and getting his coat.

'Oh, God,' Maryam said weakly. 'Is this really happening?'

'I'm sorry, Mum. I wish I could have stopped it all.'

Arran got up and went into the hallway, put a hand on his dad's arm. Rhory paused, leaned in to hear what Arran was saying. From her place in the kitchen all she could see was Arran's back and Rhory's face. As he listened, his expression dimmed. It drifted even further downwards, and became solid. His eyes rolled up, caught her looking. Without a word, or acknowledgement he reached past Arran's shoulder and pushed the door closed.

She sat in thrumming silence, staring at the panels of the door. More locked doors, more barriers. More secrets and unnatural fencing-off of knowledge. She heard Rhory's Land Rover crunch out of the gravel driveway. A few moments later Arran was in the doorway, giving her that sorrowful look again. Her head was on creaking cogs as she lifted her chin, her eyes half-closed so she couldn't give away her dismay.

'Was there something else, Arran?'

'No. Nothing important. Dad's dealing with it—' He broke off. 'Mum? What are those?'

'What are what?' She opened her eyes. He was staring at the ribbons she'd dropped on the table with the nappy bag and keys after coming in from the nursery. 'Oh, those. They're nothing. Was there anything else, Arran? Just now you were talking to Dad.'

'Mum. Answer me. Where did you get these?'

'I don't know!' Distracted she picked them up and shoved them in her pocket. 'Dad likes plaiting Minty's hair. It's not that weird. Tell me what you—'

'Stop talking!' He held his hand up, a barrier in front of her eyes. She clicked herself back a step in shock. Arran – eyes red-veined, mouth moving anxiously, neck sinews standing up under the skin. 'Mum – just speak slowly and answer my questions. *What did you just say?*'

Alex

Colonnade

Nothing in the derelict Eastonbirt mansion could possibly be called a colonnade. No passage or grand promenade through the garden. Nothing.

The plans were accessible online through the historical society's website, which coincidentally was maintained by my old history teacher, so I pulled them up on my phone and spent a few minutes sitting in the car, out on the common where the ice-cream van and the prep school kids ran riot at this time of day. It was still mid-afternoon. I'd dropped Arran at the Bakehouse to go and talk to his parents and when we'd parted we'd done that usual thing of smiling, bumping fists and saying, 'See ya.'

See ya, I thought looking out at the grassland, the sky, the beginning of the park just visible. *See ya?* We were both entangled in the most nasty, threatening experience either of us had ever known, and all we could manage was *see ya*. Neither of us admitting how scared we were. Or how we were frantically reassessing, making plans, reaching conclusions.

I put the car into gear and did a U-turn. Wound down the hill into the village, passing all the new developments, the petrol station that had been there since I could remember, the old pub that had become a music venue, then was bought up by property developers and turned into flats. Funny how you could live somewhere so long and only know it in increments – little snapshots. I texted as I drove – another thing I'd be fired for if (or when) I was caught on this adrenaline-pumped mission.

Michaela? U home? @ work?

Home. she pinged back. *Day off.*

Need some chill n chat. Voddy on me. K?

KK!! Do it.

I swung by the Sri Lankan lady to pick up some vodka – I got the Citron; I wanted Michaela to feel better. A litre of Coke and a few packets of crisps. She needed feeding up. The tower was swarming with schoolchildren, all just home and full of energy, kicking footballs all over the place, dogs yapping, music thumping. I got a whiff of ganja on the air and for a fleeting second felt London Calling. London. Everyone in Gloucestershire linked it to stress and fear, yet from my perspective it seemed a haven. A place of dazzling light and anonymity.

There was a parking space right in front of Evil Tower. I parked, leaned into the back of the car and made sure my stolen tactical vests were well hidden in the footwells. I leaped out, the vodka rolled up in a carrier bag under my arm, and headed for the block.

It was just my luck: as I was waiting for the lift, the two laser pen boys appeared in the foyer.

'Am I going to have to ride up with you?'

'Yes,' they said confidently. 'PC Mullins.'

I was used to people taunting me by using my name. It was a code, a banter I'd got used to in London. The implication being they'd noted my name in case they had to sue the police at a later date and win a fortune in compensation. Go Pro cameras were sorting out the Met's problems, but the equipment rollout hadn't reached us in the boonies. I wasn't in the mood for intimidation, or even to chat, but I got into the lift with them, pressed the button for Michaela's floor, and let the doors close.

'Where's our crossbow?' the older one said.

'At the recycling centre.' I kept my eyes on the lights moving up the block.

'Cos we went down to the bins and there was nothing.'

'Hmm, weird. It must have got smashed by going down the chute a hundred miles an hour.'

'We looked. It wasn't there.'

'That's funny. 'Cos I looked too – and I couldn't find it. And I couldn't find the laser pen either. Maybe I should come and have a look in your flat again?' The door opened at their place. 'Shall I?'

'No.' They both slouched out, hands in their pockets. 'Nah.'

The doors closed and I carried on up to Michaela's floor. She was dressed in a short dress of grey towelling, her pale, pockmarked legs naked, feet shoved into black trainers emblazoned with purple lightning flashes. Her aubergine hair was tucked behind her ears, making her appear even thinner than I remembered.

'Hi.' She smiled nervously, her eyes rolling down to the package tucked under my arm. 'Come in.'

The flat hadn't changed much. In the daylight you couldn't see all the fingerprints on the glass, but the stains on the carpet were more noticeable. I went to the kitchenette with the flickering fluorescent lights, and pulled out glasses. I knew the drill. Michaela sat solemnly on the sofa, smoking a cigarette and poking thoughtfully at one of the bites on her ankle.

'You OK?' I took the glasses over. 'You looked great at the play park the other day.'

'Yeah. That was proper sweet. Everyone made a right fuss of me. What about you? You have a good time? Didn't get a chance to talk to you.'

'Yeah it was . . . it was OK.' I took a gulp of my Coke, made a play of wincing as if the vodka was strong. 'Weird, isn't it, how people take notice of you when something shitty has happened.'

'That's what I'm saying.' She downed her drink, got up and went to the kitchen to pour more. 'I mean, the unveiling was like the first any of the stylists even knew my name, and suddenly they're all, *oh, Michaela, will you shampoo my clients next week*, and I'm like serious knocked away by it 'cos they ignored me until then.' She drank down the mix she'd made then filled it up and came to sit on the sofa, her feet curled up. 'What about you?'

I took a moment. 'Well, it's like this. I think people really do notice you after something like the crash happens. So – for example, I think someone's been trying to contact me.'

'For real?'

'Yeah. For real. How about you?'

She shrugged. 'Contact me? Like how?'

'Yeah, like photos and things. I'm talking about maybe the bonehead and her entourage.'

Michaela's face dropped a mile. 'Oh, no, Alex. Not this please. I wasn't never supposed to've told you.'

I put my hand on her arm. 'Don't worry – I've kept it to myself. But I have got to ask you something.' I sipped my drink, buying some time, finding the right formula for my words. 'I know what you saw the night of the crash, but since then, since that night, you've had no . . . threats? No feeling someone is trying to intimidate you? No one hitting up your phone or sending you letters or following you?'

She gaped at me. 'Serious I don't know what you're talking about.'

'OK.' I got up and carried my drink to the window. The park lay below me, baking in the late afternoon heat. Dark green treetops as far as the eye could see. So much land, so many hiding places.

Michaela hadn't been threatened. That fitted the half-theory I'd been toying with. Things grew a little clearer, like a structure rising into focus.

In the crash, Minnie and Jessop had been badly injured, while Michaela had lost her father. The Hansels, though they were deeply involved with Dandelion, had lost a daughter in the crash. None of them, as far as I knew, had been threatened.

The only ones who were the subjects of the vendetta were the ones who'd come out of the crash more or less unscathed.

'I haven't had any threats,' she said. 'I've done what Dad told me, kept myself out of the park. It's down there; I'm up here where I can keep an eye on it.'

'That's a good idea. Keeping an eye on it. A very good . . .' I trailed off. 'Michaela?'

'What?'

'There are patterns in the trees. Have you noticed that?'

'Eh?'

'Can I go on the balcony?'

She got up and unlocked the door. We both went out into the humid afternoon, inching our way around dead plants in pots and a pile of cardboard boxes, long rain-soaked and dried to cracked parchment. The noises from the boys playing football on the green below floated up. There was a hum of traffic from the big A46, a mile away, that could never be heard down in the village. Being on the balcony was like being lifted above the rain canopy of daily life.

'Can you see? There's a circle of different-coloured trees. And a square.'

'Yeah, I think that's the old – um – you know. Weren't they going to make, like, a park for the mansion? I'm talking like hundreds of years ago. Wasn't there meant to be a landscape garden or something?'

'The arboretum,' I whispered. 'The old arboretum.'

'That's the word. Arboretum.'

I fumbled my phone out of my pocket and found the plans of the mansion. They extended out to show where the old landscaper had designed the arbours and the promenades and the terraces, planning miniature temples for the residents to sit and enjoy the specimen trees planted in little clumps. I zoomed in on it, compared it to what I could see from the balcony. A long promenade of trees of a slightly different colour corresponded to what the landscaper had titled *Ladies' Walk*.

Colonnades. Trees in a line could look like columns.

And then I saw something else on the plans that made me start scrolling down for Arran's number.

Before I could reach it the phone rang, making me jump. It was him.

'Christ, you mind-reader.' I turned away from Michaela, who was watching me curiously. 'I was just about to call you – I found something. I need you to . . . ' I stopped. 'Arran? You OK?'

'Not really. I sent my dad to the hospital – he's going to drill down on Fenton, find out if this "incident" that happened in the bunker was what happened to Fenton, or if it was what happened to our dogs.' He paused, then said levelly. 'Oh, and by the way, my sister had plaits in her hair.'

'What?' I gripped the balcony handrail. 'You *what*?'

'Mum thinks Dad put them there. I haven't told her about our dogs and the braids and oh, Jesus, Jesus. This is solid shit.'

'It's OK. Calm down. When did it happen?'

'I don't know – over the past few weeks. Until this blew up, my family was too shagging liberal to lock the doors at night. Maybe the fuckers got into the house somehow. Maybe they've just walked all around our place, found my baby sister in her crib and . . . I don't know. I can't think about it.'

'Call the Stroud station. Ask to be put through to my sergeant.'

'Already have done; they're going to call back.'

'OK. OK. Deep breaths.'

'Alex. I need you here. I really frickin' need you.'

'I'll be there. Ten minutes. And we need to go out.'

'What?'

'Yes. Dress for hiking. I think I've found our columns.'

Maryam

Maryam boiled the kettle, watching the steam come up and blur the window pane. Arran was in the garden making a phone call. The same little boy she'd played conkers with, the boy whose nose she'd wiped, whose dinosaur wallpaper used to scare him at night. The little boy who'd held her hand so tightly the first day of school that he'd left marks in her skin. He was now so tall and grown-up. So serious. As he talked he paced up and down and occasionally she saw the side of his face. His natural tan had left him. His face was tinged with grey, like an old man.

He shoved the phone back into his pocket and came towards the house. A fat bubble of panic lifted under her sternum.

'What? What is it?'

He shook his head. 'Inside.' He stepped into the kitchen and immediately slammed the door behind him, turned and checked it was locked. Gave it an extra shove to be sure, then stood for a moment surveying the back garden.

Arran, who worked for the police and knew all the appalling things that human beings could do to each other. Usually practical and unhysterical. And now afraid. She began to shiver.

'What's happening? What's happening to us?'

'Mum, I've got to go out. Keep the doors locked. Keep your phone on. The police are going to call you.'

'The police? Why? Who put those plaits in Minty's hair?'

He went to one of the dresser drawers and pulled out a small Ziploc freezer bag. He scooped the ribbons into it and put it in his pocket.

'Arran? Speak to me? What is happening?'

'Don't let her out of your sight.' He stopped in the doorway and pinned her gaze. His pupils were dilated like a night animal's. 'Mum? Do you understand? Do not let her out of your sight.'

Alex

The council were doing some maintenance work on the sluice gates, the barriers at the crash site were open, and there was nowhere to park, so we drove to a spot further up the hill. Tucked the car into a lay-by among the trees. We got out and I handed Arran the armoured tac vest I'd sneaked out of the station.

He looked at it seriously. 'Am I going to have to black up, too?'

I pulled a brief smile, acknowledging his attempt at humour. I knew that inside he was shitting himself about leaving his family up at the Bakehouse. There had been two plaits in Minty's hair in the past week. No one knew how it had happened, whether it had been while Minty was playing at the Dandelion Play Park, or whether somehow someone had been able to enter the Bakehouse undetected.

Everything was crashing in on us. My armpits were already prickling with sweat.

'There's a colonnade in the old arboretum. It just never crossed my mind.'

I showed him the photo I'd downloaded on my phone. He stared at it for a moment, then he rummaged inside his pocket for his own phone. He flicked through some documents, scrolled and squeezed, until he found what he was looking for.

'The end of Folly Lake is in the arboretum.' He showed me his phone. On screen was a digital version of the cavers' maps he'd had the other day. 'What if there's a sluice system there? I bet there is.'

I slammed the door and went to the boot of the car. 'Today is the day; this is the hour, the minute. We're going to find them now.'

He came and stood next to me. Inside the boot was the crossbow in its case. We both looked at it in silence for a while, then he shook his head. 'No. You wouldn't. Would you?'

'I don't know.'

'I'm telling you – don't.'

I sighed. 'You're right. You're always right.' I pushed it aside and reached in for my tac vest with my Force-issue ASP – an unfolding baton, cuffs and pepper spray. I let my fingers linger on the crossbow. Then pulled away. Slammed the boot and fastened my vest around me, pulling the Velcro bars tight. 'Come on. If we don't do it now we'll never do it.'

We retraced the road back up the hill until we got to a short track that ended in dense forest and seemed to go nowhere. There was litter: beer cans and bits of tissues hanging in the trees. When I held up the phone, checked my compass and my GPS settings I knew the arboretum was directly ahead of us. Arran raised a foot and stepped on the brambles and roots, pressing them down so we could step over them and push into the undergrowth.

There was a pair of trainers abandoned on the ground, and lots of tissues. We put our heads down and crashed on. The brambles tore at us with every step; before long we both had cuts on our arms, our hair was filled with spiders' webs and leaf matter, but we kept going. My heart was racing a million miles a second, wondering what was hidden in there.

Eventually we came to a less tangled area that marked the edge of the arboretum, and we were able to walk faster. The leaves on the ground were turning a papery gold, they were so dry – even the goosegrass was sickly and yellow. We slowed from time to time to just stare at the specimen trees and the plantings looming up unexpectedly. They reminded us that we were moving through a planned-out area, a landscaper's vision.

Soon I judged we had drawn level with the place where our crossbow darts had landed the other week. We pushed through another huge mass of rhododendron and abruptly found ourselves at the beginning of the colonnade.

'This is it,' I murmured. 'The columns.'

We stared at it in awe. The trees were ash. So evenly planted that, in spite of the occasional one that had succumbed to ivy or disease, in spite of the other younger trees that had sprung up around them, it couldn't be mistaken for anything less than a pre-planned corridor.

I breathed noisily through gritted teeth. 'I wish you'd let me bring the crossbow. I'd feel a lot better.'

Arran didn't answer. He was looking further ahead into the colonnade. He sawed his hand across his throat and dug his finger to indicate the space between two ash trees. I followed him quickly. We got into a huddle, then cautiously peered out.

Someone else was here in the arboretum. It was a man, about forty feet away, his back to us, walking slowly away from us. He was white, thick-set with a shaved head, in jeans and a blue sweatshirt that had the number 89 in luminous yellow on the back.

'What the fu . . .?' I mouthed.

Arran shook his head. 'I dunno.'

After a moment or two we slid ourselves out from the shelter of the trees and slowly, slowly, trying to make as little noise as possible, picked our way cautiously towards him. We were lucky: the ground was dry and crunchy enough that each time he took a step the noise drowned out any sound we made. From time to time he seemed to pause, as if decid-ing where to go. His attitude suggested he wasn't searching for the best path, but watching something ahead of him. And then, just vaguely in the distance – at first no more than a smudge of white in the dark trunks – I saw what. He was fol-lowing someone. A small figure in white, zigzagging between the trees another twenty feet ahead of him. Something oddly malformed about her head.

Arran and I exchanged a look. He nodded. It was her.

I stood on tiptoes and drew Arran to me so I could whisper in his ear. 'He's a punter.'

'Yes. Stick behind me, close.'

Arran pulled up his hood and began to walk slowly with his head down, hands in his pockets. I followed him, my heart pounding, thinking that we must look either very sinister or very stupid. The insects around us thrummed, the sticks broke underfoot, but still the man in front didn't hear us. He was intent on the woman who was little more in my line of sight than a will-o'-the-wisp, flitting frail through the greens and browns.

We slid forward a little further, hugging the line made by the ash trees, ready to melt out of sight should the guy turn. As we neared the end of the colonnade the woman in white stopped abruptly. Arran took my arm and drew me stealthily back against a tree trunk to watch. The man had also stopped – as if waiting for instructions from her.

Now that the woman was still, I could make out more of her shape. What I'd at first taken for a white dress was in fact a grubby white dressing gown, the fluffy sort you could pick up at any supermarket for fifteen quid. On her feet were soiled white sneakers. Her head was, as Raj had told us it would be, wrapped in clingfilm. Though she was half-turned away in three-quarters profile I could see that holes had been torn for ears, nostrils, mouth and eyes.

Bonehead.

Her legs were thin, scabbed, and as we watched she slowly reached down to the hem of the dressing gown and drew it up, pulling it above her waist. She was naked underneath and slowly, inelegantly, she bent over, spreading her sickly white thighs so that the man could see the red slash of her vulva.

It was so primal, so brutal, like the mating ritual of animals where there were no frills, no etiquette. I felt a mixture of pity, embarrassment and vague self-consciousness. I glanced at Arran standing so close to me. My innocent childhood friend. His face was expressionless and it made me wonder how much he'd seen of women, how much of what he was seeing was familiar.

I decided right then, just from his face, that he knew well. Very well. I quickly looked away, and maybe my movement attracted attention because the man in front of us suddenly twisted.

'Hey!'

He was a bull. His head was shaved; his face was red and thick, jutting forward in rage. My instinct was to retreat further, but next to me Arran chose differently. He took a step out into the promenade of trees and began to run towards him.

The man's face changed from aggression to fear. Instead of charging at us, he launched himself sideways, bolting away into the bushes, tripping and flailing. The woman in the dressing gown didn't immediately recognise what was happening, but when she did she darted away in the opposite direction.

'Let him go,' I yelled at Arran. 'We want her.'

I was fit, and fast, but Arran was twice as fast as me. Leaping over the fallen trunks and tangled seas of ivy, he tore away ahead of me. The woman took a left and disappeared behind a huge grove of rhododendron and he followed, not far behind.

I leaped and swore, my heart racing, catching my clothes, ripping my arms. Arran and the woman were about forty yards away. He had closed in on her and was just about to catch up with her when she seemed to disappear completely. Then Arran too – dwindling in size and vanishing.

A few seconds later I reached the point they'd disappeared and stopped, breathing hard. I had reached a derelict, weed-ridden structure of decayed red brick which protruded less than ten inches above the ground and appeared to be connected to the Victorian engineering that went into the building of these lakes. I looked down a set of stone steps into darkness.

We'd been right. There was a sluice system at the bottom of Lake Folly and I was looking at the pumphouse. The bunker, the place of my nightmares, must be part of the mechanical apparatus that kept the lakes functioning.

My eyes began to water.

Arran had followed the woman down the steps. I could hear them down there – him shouting, her yelling at the top of her voice like a mad thing. And another male voice screaming. A Minotaur underground.

I looked at my radio. My hand skimmed over the on-off button. No. I couldn't. Instead I pulled out my retractable ASP baton, flicked it open and cantered down the steps. It was slimy underfoot and smelled of moss and dank water. Natural light filtered down about eight steps, then it was dark, except for a faint glimmer of light through a doorway at the end of the corridor where the yelling was coming from. I went as fast as I could, bracing my bad hand against the slick walls. I was panting now, sweat streaming into my eyes.

I took a breath, ducked my head, and pushed open the door. Instantly I knew I was at the nerve centre.

The room was brick-built, every wall decorated with graffiti and cartoonish figures of naked men engaged in sex acts. Some wore hoods; some didn't. There was a rusting old mangle in one corner and in the other the woman was on the floor, shuffled back up against the wall in fear, her dressing gown hanging open, her hands up defensively, screaming loudly.

In the far corner Arran was also on the floor, in a crabbed, unnatural hunch, his weight on a smaller man who was wearing a purple hoody and jeans. Arran had pulled his arms behind him and was holding on tight.

'Get the fuck off me! Get the fuck off me!' the man was yelling.

I turned to the woman, who was scrabbling at the clingfilm to free her face. I recognised her – but I couldn't say from where. Late thirties and something odd about her eyes, a milky look. The hair escaping from the improvised mask was thin, covered in scraps of plastic. Her naked belly was slack and white, tattooed. The skin draped over her jutting hipbones.

'Get up,' I said, breathlessly. 'Come on. Get the fuck up.' I grabbed her arm and pulled her to her feet, using the gooseneck manoeuvre, then the cross-arm entanglement to twist her hands behind her back. She was so small, thin and fragile, like a child. I pulled her backwards, lost my footing and went down on my butt, pulling her down on top of me. I didn't have the energy to get up. She wasn't struggling so I stayed there with her on my lap, holding her hands tight, ignoring the pain in my injured hand and trying to get my breath back.

Arran had managed to get the man to his feet and held him by the back of his shirt. He pushed him forward – using his whole body to move him in little jumps. Bracing his feet wide and using his trunk to pin the man face-forward into the wall, he grabbed one hand, then the other, and held them there. I'd had no idea Arran knew this sort of technique – it was the sort of thing that we were taught at police college, but civilian staff didn't get trained for this sort of thing. To Arran it seemed to come naturally.

'Now, you fucker. Are you going to co-operate.'

'Have I got any choice?'

'Don't answer a fucking question with another question.' He gave him a shake. 'Answer it with an answer, dickpig.'

'Yes. For fuck's sake, yes. We'll co-operate. Just get my frigging face away from the wall. I can't breathe.'

Maryam

The unfinished tapestry was draped over the back of the sofa in the workroom. All the autumnal colours of the tree plantings and fountains. The symmetrical shapes, a line of trees here, a curlicue there. The neoclassical representations of pagan symbols, sun, moon, mountain. A world condensed into a forgotten landscape plan. Maryam stared at it, resting her eyes. Her head was so tired, she needed something neutral to focus on.

Lois and Minty were with her. They were both drinking a ginger cordial she'd prepared. Minty had hers in her sippy cup and was crouched on the floor, encouraging Horky to drink from it. She had no plaits in her hair now; Maryam had checked every inch of her. There was scotch in Lois's ginger cordial, and Maryam thought it might be time to put some in her own. What else would take the fur out of her mouth? Everything in here was overbright and surreal, as if they were small, bewildered fish moving through a harshly lit aquarium. Batting in confusion at the glass tank-sides.

Arran, please tell me what's happening.

Arran?

Her phone was face-down on the table, and she didn't need to look at it to know the screen was a streamer of blue 'sent' messages.

Rhory. Call me ASAP. Has Arran called you?

Rhory – you REALLY need to call me. I'm going mad here.

No replies.

The doors were locked, the curtains half-closed and the room was hot and drowsy, flies circling in the corner. From time to time Maryam or Lois would go and stand at the window and peer out. It looked completely unchanged, the dry flower beds drooping in the afternoon heat, the insects buzzing in the treeline.

'And he didn't tell you any more?' Lois topped up her glass from the jug. She sloshed some more whisky in. 'Not a clue?'

'No. But he looked scared. Something to do with the plaits.'

'What plaits?'

Maryam glanced at Minty. Then she cupped her hand round her mouth and hissed the words. 'Remember the other day? Those ribbons?' She jabbed her finger in Minty's direction. 'The day Fenton went into hospital? You were looking at those ribbons.'

'What about them? You said Rhory did them.'

'No. It wasn't him. It wasn't anyone at nursery and it wasn't Arran.'

'What?' mouthed Lois. 'What – *seriously*?'

Maryam nodded. She didn't need to mention the time Lois had let Minty had run off into the woods up at the play park. It had been for minutes, seconds, but was the bonehead fast enough to have taken that chance? The plaits had been so tiny they could have been there for a long time without any-one noticing, so they could have been put there days before she found them. Until this week the family had been bad at leaving doors unlocked; they'd trusted the Bakehouse. It couldn't have let someone in. It couldn't have betrayed her like that, could it?

Maryam put her hands to her face and watched Minty, dressed in her still grubby clothes from nursery, hopping Horky along the floor. If someone had been in here, if they'd had enough time alone with her to put a plait in her hair, then what else had they had time to do?

A sudden image popped into her head of a police examination room. Something from one of the new American police dramas where everything was white and tiled and coolly lit. An anonymous doll. A kind doctor asking Minty: *show me on the dolly where he touched you. Can you do that for me?*

'I'm going to choke,' she said suddenly, getting up. 'I'm going to choke.'

'No.' Lois looked up from her drink. 'No, you're not going to choke. That's a panic attack. It's going to be OK. Breathe.'

Maryam obeyed, breathing from the lowest part of her chest possible. Walking to and fro, stretching her arms up and trying to get oxygen inside her.

'Better?'

'Yes. Thank you.' She picked up her phone, checking the signal bars were still strong. 'He said the police were going to call. I should call.'

'No. More breaths. Wait a bit longer. It's going to be OK.'

Maryam tapped her fingers anxiously. She couldn't keep still. She sat down, but got up again and paced around the ground floor. She went into the kitchen and boiled the kettle. Carelessly slopped water into the teapot and took it through with some biscuits. It sat on the table and neither of them drank it. Lois had topped up her glass with more scotch and Maryam couldn't force anything past the dam in her throat. Minty took some of the biscuits and shared them with Horky.

A text came from Rhory. *Should be back in half an hour.* But half an hour passed and there was no sign of the Land Rover.

'He'll be back,' Lois said. 'Try not to worry.'

Maryam said nothing. She carried away the undrunk tea and the plates. The pieces of biscuit Minty had half-chewed and left on the plate. She fetched another jug of ginger cordial for Lois, set it on the table.

'Minty. It's time you had a sleep.'

From her place on the floor Minty raised her eyes and glowered. 'No sleep.'

'You need to. If you were at nursery now Miss Carter would be singing "Sleepy Sheep" and you'd be lying on the floor.'

Minty instantly lay down on the floor, rested her face on her hands and closed her eyes, pretending to sleep.

'Is that where you're going to sleep?' Lois asked. 'Right there?'

'Yes.'

'It's going to be hot there. You'd be better in your bedroom.'

'No. Here.'

It occurred to Maryam then that Minty wasn't at all stupid. She was a genius for atmospheres and knew her family was anxious. She didn't want to be parted from them and Maryam realised she didn't either. The idea of Minty upstairs now, on her own, in this house that couldn't be trusted any more, was impossible.

'OK, let's just open this door here.' She went into the room where the bolts of fabric were kept. It was always cooler in there; there were no windows and parts of the walls were below ground level, making it freezing in the winter but pleasant now. 'I'll get your pillow and duvet from upstairs.'

She went up the stairs, conscious for the first time how much they creaked. If someone had tried to walk up here in the night, go to Minty's room, she and Rhory would have heard it, wouldn't they? Why had it never occurred to her to check all the doors, all the windows, before they went to bed? She'd been so obsessed about a spiritual threat, she hadn't stopped to think about the possibility of a human one.

In the nursery she grabbed Minty's pillow, her sheets and duvet. Before leaving she paused, looking at the low-set leaded windows. The room was in the gables and it looked out over the side of the house. From here Maryam could see the three cars lined up. Arran's Audi, her own junky disordered Vauxhall, and Lois's lime-green Beetle. Where the hell was Rhory? She edged very close to the pane, tilted her head sideways and realised she could just see the woods. From the trees this window would be visible.

She went back downstairs, a pain in her stomach. If she ever ate again it would never move itself down into her intestines. She'd starve to death.

In the workroom Lois had helped herself to more whisky. She was on the sofa, her arm round a sleepy Minty. Maryam set about making a bed on the floor of the fabric room. She put Minty's duvet on the floor to make it softer and wrapped a sheet around it.

'Is it my imagination,' Lois asked, 'or was there something different about Arran just now? Before you got back we were talking and he was very secretive. And then he was in the garden talking on the phone.'

'Probably to the police.' Maryam straightened and came to get Minty. 'Come on, sweetheart. Let's lie you down.'

Minty didn't complain. She allowed herself to be taken to the makeshift bed.

'I'm just going to put a sheet on you – it's very hot, isn't it?'

'Hot,' Minty agreed.

'Let's get you snuggled down.'

As she waited for Minty to get comfortable she cast glances over her shoulder. The garden was still. No movement in the trees. From this angle it would be impossible to see Minty lying here. But later, when Rhory got home, she'd ask him to nail up some planks of wood over the windows. Or, better, she'd ask him to take them to stay with his father in Bicester. She and Minty could sleep on the sofabed.

'There you are, baby.' She stroked the back of Minty's head. Her soft hair lay limp against her skull. 'There you go.'

Minty curled into herself, hugging Horky up to her face. Her breathing got slower, more evenly paced. Maryam pressed her palm against her neck, hoping to soak up a little of her peace, her innocence. Anything to stop her own mind flicking from scenario to scenario. Gradually, by focusing on her breathing, she felt her pulse slow. In creeping increments she found rationales, perspectives. Easier explanations for what was happening. It would all work out well. Arran and Rhory were in control.

She got up, wearily. She felt her way to the sofa opposite Lois and sat down, exhausted. Running a marathon would have the same liquefying feeling. The same surrender to physical exhaustion.

'It'll be OK,' said Lois.

'Yes.'

The two women sat in silence for a while, vaguely listening to Minty sighing in her sleep. Crickets began to croak in the woods. Maryam didn't look out of the window again. The trees were exactly as they had been for years. For years and years and years. Nothing to be afraid of. This was all a nightmare happening to someone else.

Lois leaned over and poured another drink. She sat back, looking at the amber fluid in the tumbler. 'Tell me, has Arran been going to the gym?'

Maryam shuffled upright. 'What? The gym?'

'Yes. He looks a lot fitter than I remember.'

'I don't know. I don't think so.' But now that Lois mentioned it Maryam realised Arran did look different. She'd been too absorbed with everything to notice. Last week he'd asked her opinion on a new shirt, and she'd thought nothing of it. There were new ties on the rack. And a pair of dumbbell weights in vivid shades of orange and green had appeared in his bedroom recently. How hadn't she paid attention to this? 'You're right. I don't know why I didn't think about it before.'

'He's not the old Arran I know. He's changed. She's having an effect on him.'

'She?'

'Alex Mullins. It's like Alex says jump and Arran says how high. I think that was her he was talking to on the phone in the garden just now.'

Maryam pulled her feet up under her and hugged her legs, her chin on her knees. 'Seriously? Do you think he's changed since Alex got back?'

'One hundred per cent. I think he's forgotten all about Sophie May. If you ask me, before we know where we are it'll be Arran and Alex Mullins walking up the aisle.'

Maryam frowned. Lois was still smiling, but there was something *off* about the way she'd referred to Alex – just the tiniest inflection when she'd used her name, a leaning on the second syllable of her name, as if she didn't really believe any-one could actually have been christened Alex. Not seriously.

'That's a bit of a jump.'

'Not at all. I can just see them now: married, parading around Eastonbirt. King and queen of the village. Think of it . . . Alex, in a veil.' She held her hands up in a triangle around her face. 'Tell me, Maryam, seriously, between you and me. Can you imagine Alex Mullins looking quite right in a veil? A veil calls for someone more feminine, doesn't it?'

Lois's attitude needled her. 'Whatever Arran's doing with his life, it's his business.' Maryam was suddenly decisive. 'He's got a right to his privacy.'

If Lois was surprised by Maryam's vehemence she didn't show it. She simply smiled and nodded to herself, sipping her whisky. 'I think you'll be surprised. I really do. I think you'll be surprised.'

Something inside Maryam clicked. How dared Lois make these assumptions about Arran? Being drunk on Rhory's whisky was no excuse.

'I was thinking,' she said quietly, wanting to needle Lois. 'I wonder what Fenton is going to tell us about the person who's done all this.'

Lois blinked. She turned her neck slowly, woodenly, and fixed Maryam with stony eyes.

'It's just that, from what I've heard, Fenton might know quite a lot about what's happening in the park. The bonehead. Whoever she is.'

'Why would my husband know anything about it?'

Maryam stared at Lois. She stared at her the way she'd never had the courage to stare at anyone. It was so peculiar: two women who'd always walked the polite line, suddenly like two wild animals squaring up. Her blood was thumping, thumping. Her face getting hotter. And then, abruptly, she shook her head. 'God. I'm sorry. This is getting to me. All of this is getting to me. It's not you I'm angry with, it's . . . I'm sorry. I'm just scared. Confused.'

Lois closed her eyes slowly then opened them again. For a moment Maryam thought she was going to cry. But then, just as she was about to apologise again, her phone rang. She snatched it up from the table. 'Hello?'

'Mrs Black?' A woman's voice. A Scottish accent. 'This is Sergeant Johnson from Stroud police station. Just wondering if we could send one of my officers over to yours in about half an hour?'

'Of course. Yes, of course. Can you tell me what this is about?'

'Nothing to be worried about – just a quick welfare check on your little girl.'

'My little girl?'

'Yes – and all of you, of course. It's just that your daughter – Araminta, is it . . .?'

'Yes. Minty.'

'Well, she'd be classed as vulnerable, so she comes first for us. Can you keep her in the house for me? Is she somewhere safe? We should be there in about half an hour if that's OK.'

'Yes, I mean I . . . yes, of course. Do you know how to find us?'

'I do.'

As she hung up, a car pulled up outside. Rhory's Land Rover.

She got to her feet and went into the hallway. At last. Maybe he'd have answers.

Alex

I'd had nightmares about this day, but in the end what was most remarkable was how undignified it all turned out to be. How easy and slightly pathetic. Two undernourished people on drugs, who couldn't have put up a fight if their lives depended on it, versus me and Arran. Ending up with me sitting on the floor, this tiny woman on my lap like a ranting, hysterical ventriloquist's dummy, twisting around, getting her naked body tangled in the fluffy dressing gown – and Arran holding the man against the wall.

I knew who the man was – I could tell from the thinning gingery hair, the small, wiry stature. It was Edward Joiner, who used to be a taxi driver and lived in the tower block five floors below Michaela. The woman sitting on top of me thrashing around was his weird, partially sighted wife. The dead prostitute. The thing from my nightmares.

I gave her a good yank and whispered in her ear, 'Just fucking keep still, will you?'

She went limp across me, breathing hard. I kept her skinny wrists in a clasp with one hand and managed, by jacking up my hips, to fumble out my cuffs from my vest.

'Here.' I slid them across the floor to Arran, who tightened his grip on Edward long enough to crouch, snatch them up and lock them on to his wrists.

'Come on, mate.' He dragged Joiner away from the wall and, using his right foot, edged towards him a chair that had been knocked over in the scuffle. He righted it, then guided Edward on to the seat. 'Head down,' he said, pushing Edward's head forward so his arms could swing up behind him. Edward's phone fell out of his pocket and Arran swiped it up and pocketed it in one swift move. Then he looped Edward's arms over the back of the chair and yanked him into an upright sitting position so he was pinioned painfully, his arms stretched behind him around the chair-back. He sat there, shaking his head and puffing out huge indignant breaths that made his lips tremble.

'Take your time, take your time to recover,' said Arran. 'We've got all day.'

He wandered casually around, as if he was totally relaxed, staring at things. Prodding and peering at the way the room had been fitted out. Electric lamps had been crudely hung in places from which wires snaked across the walls, ending at a small red generator jammed in the corner. Everything smelled of salt and ammonia, like the Spearmint Rhino clubs in London. There was a small area that was raised, spotlights hanging above it from the ceiling. Behind the raised area posters had been pasted on the walls depicting women and men in bondage gear, most with their heads wrapped in clingfilm, some in black rubber masks, others in zip-up PVC hoods. Mounted into the stone were 'O'-shaped iron rings.

This was the fetish, then. A kind of subset of S&M. The look of a human head wrapped like that. To what? Ensure anonymity? To free the body to do with it what you wanted? In London I'd known about places like this, but I'd never been inside one.

What about animals? Bestiality?

I scanned everything. No animals depicted, but propped next to the generator were a mop, a bucket, and a white swing bin with a black bin liner. The mop was stained brown.

I stared at it for a while. Then I looked at the lid of the bin, also stained. On the raised area was a further mark. Dried blood. Something had bled here.

'These work?' Arran hooked down a pair of velvet-lined handcuffs from a nail on the wall and dangled them at Edward.

Edward nodded. 'They work. The key's in them.'

Arran fiddled with them, locking them and testing they were sound. He handed them to me and I struggled to my feet. Together we manacled Joiner's wife on to another chair in the same position as her husband. I pulled off the remaining shreds of the clingfilm. She breathed in and out slowly, her eyes lowered. Genuinely ashamed.

'I know them.' I wiped the sweat from my forehead with the back of my hand. 'He's a local knob.'

'Yeah – I recognise him too.' He kicked Edward's feet hard. 'What did you do to my fucking dog, you prick? Eh? What did you fucking do?'

Edward didn't answer. Arran went to his wife and peered into her face.

'She's very short-sighted,' Edward said dully. 'And frankly that's not all that's wrong with her. You won't get anything out of her. She lost it years ago. Meth.'

'Has she got a name?' I asked. 'Do you at least feel the need to name her – considering you're pimping her out?'

'Casey. Casey's her name.'

'Casey.' The woman nodded. 'I'm Casey.'

'And Casey – did you run our coach off the road? Did you do it deliberately?'

'She didn't.' Edward's voice was tight and controlled. 'No – she didn't. Whatever you want to throw at us – and I know you can do a lot – you can't put that one on us. She was there that night – waiting for someone.'

'For a punter?'

'Yeah, she was waiting for a punter. But not Mike Lewis. That was coincidence.'

'Coincidence that she ran him off the road?'

'I just said, she didn't run anyone off the road. That bastard Mike Lewis owed me money. He saw her and . . . well, who knows what a guilty conscience can make a person do.'

I stared at him. Was that really how it had happened? Michaela's dad had spotted Casey Joiner in the place she often waited for clients? Had maybe thought Edward was with her? I could see that the shock could have caused him to veer the coach to one side. It didn't take much on a road like that to destabilise a vehicle of that size. And this pathetic drug-soaked woman on the chair in front of me? She'd stopped on the tarmac that night and got down close to me. To – what? See if I was OK? Or had it been just idle curiosity?

'He owed you money?' Arran said.

'Lots.'

'For the things he'd done down here? With your wife?'

'That is correct.'

'You are scum. Such scum.' Arran circled back to Edward and squatted down in front of him, his elbows on his knees, tossing Edward's phone from hand to hand. 'Right – let's deal with this seriously. Tell me what you did to our dogs and why.'

'We didn't do nothing to your dogs.'

'Yes, you did. And for that you are going to suffer.'

'We didn't touch your dogs. God's honest.'

'Someone saw you – we've got a witness.'

'No, you ain't – that's bollocks. If anyone says we touched your dogs I'm telling you they're lying. I'm going to say it again and this time you're going to listen. I. Have. Not. Touched. Your. Dogs.'

I went to the bin. Looked down at the lid in silence. I didn't want to open it.

'It's not dog blood.'

I glanced up at Edward. 'Not dog blood? Then whose blood?'

'There was an incident here. It got out of hand.'

'Tell us what happened.'

Edward chewed his lip, wondering whether to answer that.

'I can kick your feet as hard as my partner did,' I said. 'Purely in self-defence, of course. Is that what you want?'

'Fuckers,' Edward muttered, shaking his head. 'You're fuckers. I liked you, Alex Mullins, when you were a kid; you weren't all bad, you know. Then you – what? Got it into your head to be a pig?'

'Is that a yes? You'd like another kick?'

'I'm not in the business of giving up people's names. It's their business.'

'But it'll come out. We *will* find out. Whether you tell us or not.'

Arran clicked the home button on Edward's phone and swiped the screen sideways. 'No passcode. You're very accommodating.' He began flicking through photos on the phone. 'I assume I'm going to find what I'm looking for on here. In fact I know I am.'

Edward sighed. He lowered his head, shaking it. On the other chair Casey had begun to cry silently. 'It's OK.' I put my hand on her shoulder. It was so bony, it was like touching a very old woman, I felt a wave of pity. 'It's going to be OK. Don't worry.'

Arran's face was stony as he looked through the photos. I had a vague idea what he was probably looking at; I'd seen things on my first two years of duty that wouldn't leave my mind quickly. Eventually he stopped swiping and handed me the phone.

I took it. Terrified of what I was going to see. 'The dogs?'

'No dogs anywhere.'

My mouth dry, I turned the phone over. On the screen was Fenton Hansel. Dressed in just a grubby T-shirt, kneeling, his stomach resting on a low bench. His legs were bare, his arms loose on either side of the bench so his hands touched the floor, and his face was turned towards the camera. The grey froth of hair was limp and wet and his forehead was twisted into an expression of pain. Behind him a man, bare-chested, wearing a mask, his trousers unzipped so just his shining red penis was visible, was jamming himself into the Fenton's anus. Blood was flowing down his thighs.

'This was the "incident"?' Arran asked.

Edward nodded reluctantly. He was sweating profusely now, his skin shot through with swollen blood vessels. 'That's not me in the mask – it's another of the punters. I paired them up – it got rough.'

'He's bleeding.'

'They used . . . toys as well – that's where all the blood came from. These things happen. We tried to clean it up. I told him to get help – I told him he needed to go to hospital. You know what he said? He refused. He said if he was going to die he was going to die, and maybe that was the best way.'

I used my baton to push open the bin. The insides were stained and dirty and there were blood-covered tissues in the bottom. But no bloodied remains of animals. I let the bin swing closed. I squeezed my nose lightly with my thumb and forefinger. Raised my eyebrows questioningly at Arran. 'You think he's telling the truth?'

'I *am* telling the truth,' Edward interrupted. 'We didn't do your dogs. But . . . '

'But what?'

'Fenton knows who did.'

Maryam

Rhory let himself in quickly, slamming the door behind him and locking it, throwing all the bolts. His face was set tight, his hand on his chest as if he had something hidden in his jacket.

Maryam cornered him instantly. 'What did Fenton tell you?'

He looked her up and down. His face was tired. He threw the keys into the bowl next to the door. 'He said to make sure Minty is in the house.'

'She is. She's sleeping in the fabric room. Has Arran called you? Did he say anything about the plaits in her hair? Why did they scare him so much?'

'Calm down, calm down.' He took her hand and held it to his face. Kissed it once. 'Calmly now. That's it. Shhh. As long as she doesn't go outside, it's OK. Just don't let her go outside. The police are on their way.' He leaned over and glanced down the hallway. 'Is Lois with her?'

'Yes.'

'OK, come in here.' He beckoned her into the kitchen. 'Close the door.' He sat at the table. 'Go on – close it. It's about Fenton, need to keep it quiet.'

Maryam obeyed, doing it as silently as possible so Lois wouldn't hear and be offended. The remains of a hurried breakfast and half-finished cups of coffee were strewn across the table. She cleared a space, put her hands on it and leaned in to look at him. 'What's happening?'

'Fenton is talking.'

'What?'

'Yes. He told me to go to his car and get something. That's why I've been gone so long.'

Rhory pulled an envelope out from inside his jacket. It was padded, the sort accountants used to send documents, and it had the Hansels' company mailing label on it. The top had been sealed and stapled several times. It looked fat and heavy, like a weight sitting in the middle of the table.

'What's in it?'

'I don't know. I didn't have the nerve to open it. Not without you.'

Maryam put her finger on the envelope and drew it across the table to her. Her skin was tingling. 'Shall I do it?'

Just then, from the other side of the house came the noise of a car starting, the crunch of gravel. Maryam and Rory frowned at each other. They left the envelope, got up and went to the hallway. From the window they saw Lois's car reversing out of the driveway. She'd been very silent – neither of them had heard her leave.

Maryam clenched her face up. 'She's drunk.'

'That's all we need.'

'And she and I had a . . . a thing.' Maryam put her fingers on the pane and watched the little lime-green Beetle disappear up the shrub lined driveway. 'Just before you got back.'

'A thing?'

She took two deep breaths. The need to cry had come back to her, cold and hard. 'I let myself get carried away.' She dug her fingernails into the palms of her hands. 'I don't know what was going through my head. I'm making such a mess of this.'

'Come on. You're not making a mess. None of us knows how to deal with this.'

He led her back into the kitchen and she sat down with a jolt, her hands on the table, her head sagging.

'Come on, Maryam. So what if she's upset? In the overall context of what's happening, so fucking what if Lois is pee'd off?'

'You hate her, don't you? You've never said it, but you hate her.'

Rhory didn't answer for a moment. When she raised her head to look at him he had his arms folded over his chest, his face stony.

'It's true isn't it? You've never said it, but I've kind of always known. You like Fenton but you don't like her, even though she's my friend.'

'Maryam, I've never hated her – that's too strong a word. I didn't like her, it's true, and until I knew what she was like to my mate, back when I thought she was making Fenton happy, at least I thought, well, she had her uses.'

'Her *uses*?'

'He's my best mate. I thought she loved him and he loved her. So I never hated her. Now I know all this . . . shit about them, I'm indifferent.'

'I told her about Fenton and the park. At least I probably left her in no doubt about what he's done to end up in hospital. I couldn't help it; I couldn't stop myself!'

'You think she didn't know before?'

'Of course she didn't know.'

'You're wrong.'

Maryam paused. 'What?'

'I said you're wrong – she does know. She's known all along. According to Fenton they've argued about it for months. Years. Ever since she found out. Now.' He nodded at the envelope on the table. 'Are we going to open it or not?'

Alex

It had started to rain while we'd been in the bunker, for the first time in months, and outside the air was full of the musical plink of it falling on dry leaves. Drops hung on the branches, strings of translucent pearls. It felt good to surface and see all the greens and oranges and purples of the trees. As if the world was being washed clean of all the things we'd seen and would never unsee.

I stood there, in a kind of trance, my head throbbing with what Edward Joiner had told us. The rain settled lightly on my shoulders. Arran's T-shirt was wet. He pulled his hood up. He'd put up a good show of being the hard man, but now, his face white, rain trickling off his eyelashes, I remembered him as a boy at nursery. Racing around the playground after a wooden train on wooden rails.

I swallowed and lowered my eyes. We'd decided not to report what we'd seen in the bunker – it would mean the end of both our careers to admit what we'd done this afternoon. One day we'd find a way to let the authorities know what we'd seen today – Edward Joiner wouldn't continue to pimp his wife forever, but that day wasn't today. And we had other things to think about. Another person to pursue.

'No wonder Fenton wants to die.'

'No wonder.'

'What do we do, then?' I looked up. 'What now?'

Arran turned his eyes to me. Rain was plastering his hair to his head. 'What now? I'm the teacher, the nerd. You're the strategist. You tell me what now.'

'I think I make a phone call.'

'Well, then.' He circled his hand in the air, as if to say, *OK, so get on with it.*

'Seriously? Just pick up the phone? Say I want to talk?'

'Unless you've got another suggestion?'

I switched on my phone and scrolled down until I found the number. She answered after two rings.

'Hello?'

'Lois. Hello. It's Alex speaking. Alex Mullins.'

'Yes. My phone told me that.'

I hesitated. 'Can I come and see you?'

'I'm not at home at the moment.'

'Where are you?'

'I'm in the park.'

I came to a halt. Phone to my ear, I stood in the middle of the wilderness and turned slowly, perusing my surroundings. 'In the park?'

'Yes. I'm next to the lake. You know how I like to come here and think. Are you with your boyfriend?'

'My . . .?'

'Arran.'

'Yes, I'm with Arran. Are you on the causeway?'

'I love watching the water.'

I put my hand over the phone and hissed at Arran, 'She's at the crash site.' I twisted round and round to orientate myself, thinking about the direction we'd come through the woods. The trail we'd made was still clear, the vegetation trodden down, and I thought we could be back there in five minutes. 'Can I come and see you, Lois?'

'I'd like that, Alex. I really would.'

'OK. Stay where you are. We can look at some photos together. Maybe post something on Sophie May's JustGiving page?'

'Thank you, Alex. You're a sweet girl.'

I finished the call. Arran was watching me quizzically. 'What're we doing?'

'We're going to talk to her. Come on.'

We trudged back through the wood – the bracken that earlier had been brittle and brown was now drenched. It was raining hard, bouncing from leaves. I stuffed my phone deep in my pocket to keep it dry. My trainers were sodden and slid on the newly wet leaves; puddles were starting to form on the dried-out path and gritty water splashed my calves.

'She's a crazy fucking bitch.' Arran held his hood out over his face so I could hear him speak. 'I've never liked her.'

'Me neither. But I never liked Sophie May either. Speak ill of the dead, I know, but what was there to like?'

'Nothing.'

'Nothing?' I glanced sideways at him. 'She rocked a tight T-shirt.'

'You think? That must be a girl perspective.'

I kept walking. In spite of what I knew lay ahead, I had a moment's glow. It had never dawned on me that he hadn't fancied Sophie May. I'd known he didn't like her, but I'd assumed he'd at least fancied her. Hadn't all the guys?

'What the fuck's been going on in her head?' Arran said. 'Why has she done it?'

'I don't know. To get her own back at her husband's secret fetish? Drive us all away from Eastonbirt so she doesn't have to watch us go on with our lives?'

Arran let out a long exhalation. 'OK. I've got to steady myself here. Because when I see her I'm going to want to kill her.'

'Then don't come near. Let me do it. I'm used to this.'

He nodded. I could tell he was battling hard to hold it together, knowing what Lois had done to Bamber and Tumble.

A wave of tiredness rolled through me. My feet were sore and I had no idea what I was going to say to Lois. But as we crested the lip of the hill, up where the plantation was thickest, things changed. I looked down and saw the yellow smear of the embankment below, the lake glinting like a murky eye. The maintenance trucks had gone, but they must have left the barrier open, because at the top of the slipway was a little green Volkswagen Beetle I recognised as Lois's.

I'd never seen a car that close to the water. Out of nowhere my adrenaline went up a notch.

'Stay back,' I yelled to Arran who started running alongside me. 'Stay back. I know what to do.'

He braked a little and fell behind, letting me canter on down the path, dodging rocks and the chalk-white rivulets that had suddenly sprung up. Lois's car was parked facing the water. The engine was running, the brake lights were on, and there was a small trail of exhaust fumes from the pipe. She was sitting upright in the driver's seat, staring out at the lake. There was something uncharacteristically dishevelled about her. She was dressed in a belted white and blue dress, and her thinning reddish-grey hair had lots of little snarls in it, as if it had started the day in a swept-up style that had somehow come unplugged.

A sense of urgency overtook me, a need to grab the moment, and I skidded up to the car, tugging at the handle of the passenger side. It was locked.

'Lois?' I tugged again. 'Lois? Open the door. Lois?' I slammed my hands on the window. '*Lois!*'

Moving woodenly, like someone with extreme arthritis, she lifted her hand and touched the window button. It unrolled and I put my head inside. I wanted to scream at her, *What have you done to Bamber? What, you bitch, what?* Instead, the training kicked in and I smiled. 'Hi,' I said, cautiously. 'Lois. You OK?'

'No, to be honest, I'm not very well, Alex, I'm afraid. It's not been a good day. I've been with Maryam and I had to leave. I just found her presence overwhelming. So now I'm just sitting here – looking at the lake. You know how it is. How are you?'

'I'm OK.'

'Do you want me to drive you home? I'd like the company.'

I hesitated. The car's interior smelled bad – of alcohol and something else. Now I could see Lois's face better I saw how bloodshot her eyes were, and that there was mascara streaking down her cheeks.

'Actually, no. That's kind, but I'd rather talk to you here.'

'Oh.' She pushed her wrist into her cheeks to stem the tears. 'Have I been caught out?'

'That depends on what you mean.'

'I mean, have you figured it all out? Because I thought you would eventually.'

'I have. And what I'd really like to know is why? None of the people you went after had done you any harm, Lois. Why did you put them – us – through all that?'

Lois dropped her forehead on to the steering wheel and began to weep. It was a small, mewling noise. Like a puppy whining. Instead of comforting her, while she cried I scanned the car, the dashboard, trying to work out what was happening here. The keys were in the ignition and the handbrake was on. I probably wouldn't reach the key and, even if I did manage to turn the engine off, the car was at such a steep angle that Lois would only have to disengage the brake and the Beetle would probably roll along the slip-way into the lake.

So that was the seriousness.

I took a deep breath. My pulse was thrumming in my skull. 'Lois,' I said carefully, deliberately. 'Can I get in the car?'

She didn't respond. I was about to repeat the question when she lifted her head, leaned across and unlocked the passenger door. I went round the back of the Beetle, hand on the metal body all the way, as if keeping contact with it might stop her from sliding it into the water. I opened the door and climbed in.

The interior was very warm. My clothing dripped all over the upholstery. I turned sideways in the seat and focused on Lois, really focused. I'd never before noticed her face properly. I'd never seen the yellow of her teeth. Or the greying roots of her hair. Everything about her was emerging from the foggy sameness I used to see in my friends' parents, and taking on sudden startling clarity in light of what she'd done. Where did I start to calm the situation down? How did I persuade her not to run the car into the lake?

'Lois. Mrs Hansel. Tell me about Sophie May.'

'What?'

'Sometimes I think I'm losing sight of her. I'm forgetting who she was. And I don't think it's a good thing, to forget. I think we should remember.'

Lois hitched in a breath. 'I don't know what you mean.'

'I think we should remember what she was like. Sophie May was so pretty. The prettiest thing I've ever seen. She loved Justin Bieber. That's what I remember. Loved Justin Bieber. What a beautiful couple they'd have made.'

'My God, yes.' Lois's face was broken. If I'd held out my arms, offered to hug her, she'd have accepted. 'So beautiful.'

'Did you ever send him a Facebook request from Sophie May's page?'

'I didn't think to.'

'You mean he never knew about her? She adored him.' I held Lois's eyes. 'There's that picture above your mantel-piece? She's in a pink T-shirt? Maybe you could send . . . '

I hesitated. The car had just jolted to the side. Confused I leaned back, tried to see what was happening. 'What was that?'

'I don't know.' Lois engaged and disengaged the gear. Pulled the handbrake up tighter and sniffed loudly. There were tears dropping from her chin. 'What were you saying?' She rubbed her face with the back of her hand and I noticed raw, bloody scratch marks on her hands. 'About Sophie May.'

'Yes,' I said hurriedly. 'And that picture. Maybe you could send it to Justin Bieber. What do you think?'

She wiped her nose. 'I'll end up in prison, I suppose . . . '

'That's a bit extreme. It's been difficult for you. Maybe a nice cup of tea and a chat, get ourselves cleaned up first?'

Maryam

It was raining outside – for the first time in what seemed like years – and about twenty yards away in the garden a fox, which had been making its way across the lawn, appeared to find the same surprise in the rain as Maryam did, because it stopped and turned to look at her across the expanse of grass, as if it suspected her of achieving this miracle. They were frozen, she and the animal, in a bubble of time. Then the fox flinched and turned tail, darting back the way it had come. She breathed again. She'd been released from the moment of suspension and forced to continue on her own timeline. The timeline in which the police were concerned for their safety, Lois had disappeared and Rhory was now unpicking a mystery envelope from Fenton and pulling out the contents.

'It's a note. And something else.'

He extracted a small bundle wrapped in tissue paper. He placed it on the table. It was about the size of a slab of bacon, but light. It sat there, drawing all the light into it.

Rhory unfolded the note. He read it, then flattened it out on the table for Maryam to read.

I found this in a safe that my wife owns. She doesn't know I have the combination. Make of it what you will. And understand why when I found it I decided I didn't want to go on living.

Maryam raised her eyes to Rhory, not breathing. 'What?' she said. 'What?'

'I don't know.' He was breathing hard.

They both stared in disbelief at the folded tissue paper.

'Lois?' Maryam said. 'What the hell is this to do with . . .?'

'Open it. She's your friend. You open it.'

She gulped down some air. Slowly, slowly, filled with apprehension, she unfolded the tissue paper and spread it out on the table between them.

It was a dog's collar. Red, leather and slightly scuffed. It was Tumble's.

Every now and then life had a habit of suddenly narrowing into a point. A place where time was as slow as in the black arches of outer space, where each heartbeat lasted a century and held the future and the past and all the memories of a lifetime.

It was Rhory who spoke first. Rhory who said, robotically, 'Where is Minty? Is she still asleep?'

'Of course she's still asleep,' Maryam said. Her mouth was like cotton wool, but she smiled. A wide, manic smile – confident, to kill any doubt. 'Why wouldn't she be?'

'She's in the workroom?'

'Yes,' Maryam said. 'Of course. Of course that's where she is. Where else could she be?'

Alex

Life makes perfect patterns sometimes. That the lake was here, I was here and so was Arran, just the way we had been two and a half years before.

All things come into a circle. Eventually.

The sound of sirens lifted from somewhere on the top of the escarpment. I was so relieved to hear them that I assumed they were coming for us, didn't stop to wonder how they knew so quickly. In front of us the lake was peppered with rain-drops. I knew all too well what happened under the water. I'd read from the accident report exactly what shape the lake-bed made. It was a very gentle slope for the first three yards. Then, abruptly, it dropped. To a depth of over thirty feet. Enough to submerge a coach, and quite enough to swallow a tiny little car like the Beetle.

Lois had been crying for a long time. At last she seemed to get a grip on herself. She pressed fingers into her eyes to stem the flow of tears. 'I'm sorry,' she gulped. 'I'm sorry – I don't know what to do with myself.'

'That's OK. Everyone feels like that from time to time. You're very normal, Lois.'

At that moment, just as the whole thing was beginning to wind itself down, turn into something sad and slow and calm, Arran appeared at the other side of the car, rain pouring down his face. He grabbed the door handle and shook it.

'No.' I leaned across Lois and shook my head at him. Waved him away. 'I told you no. Not now.'

But Arran was hyped-up and angry and he wasn't going to be talked down. He tugged at the driver door handle and slammed the flat of his hand on the window. 'Fucking bitch. Open the fucking door!'

I leaned across Lois and waved at him to get his attention. 'Seriously,' I yelled. 'Seriously – Arran. Me and Lois, we're OK. Go away. We're talking.'

But he wasn't listening. He put his foot on the door to give himself more leverage, his tongue between his teeth. Lois slammed her hands on the steering wheel, making me jump.

'So sweet, Alex. So sweet.'

'I'm sorry?'

'I said, so sweet. The way you look after him. Can you two be separated?'

'What?'

'Or are you the sexy loving couple? The ones who are going to go on to have ten perfect kids.' With her bloody, ragged fingers she pulled the corners of her mouth back into a hideous smile, baring all her yellow teeth and lolling her tongue out at me. 'Perfect, Alex. You're so perfect. I don't know why you ever bothered to come back and grace us with your presence. Don't you belong somewhere a little more stylish than Eastonbirt? Wouldn't you rather be in London with your snooty friends?'

'Don't do this, Lois.'

'Come on Alex – don't you think it's a bit of a step down for you? Actually, on reflection, you know what? You're right. You're ugly and you're not clever. So why the fuck are you still alive? Why, why, *why*? Your hair is like shit. Sophie May was blonde. She was so much more beautiful than you will ever be. And Arran loved her.' She turned her tearful eyes to Arran at the window. She put her finger on the button and the electric window lowered. 'You loved her, my Sophie May? Didn't you, darling? Didn't you?'

There was a long silence, only punctuated by sirens in the distance. Then Arran said simply. 'No. I didn't.'

On her lap Lois's phone rang She snatched it up, cancelled the call and turned the phone face-down. The car began that strange rocking again, as if it were on gimbals.

'What did you say, Arran?'

'You heard me. I said no. For me it was never going to be your daughter.'

There was a long-drawn-out silence. Then Lois jammed her foot on the clutch and slammed the car into first gear.

'Lois!' I reached for the handbrake. 'Stop it.'

Arran pushed his head into the window. 'What the hell are you doing?'

'What do you think I'm doing?' She revved the engine.

'Don't be crazy!'

I kept my hand hovering on the handbrake, ready to jerk it up higher. The keys in the ignition were not far; I could throw myself across her or Arran could reach them if he was quick enough. 'Lois, don't do this. Take your foot off the gas.'

'Very funny, Arran, very funny.' Lois gave a throaty laugh. 'You can be so innocent-acting, but when it comes to a girl – a proper and real girl, a genuine beauty – you have no idea. No idea. What sort of man are you? Go on, repeat after me: *I'm a shit excuse for a man and Sophie May was out of my league.*'

'Shut up,' he said clearly. 'Take the car out of gear and shut up.'

'Because she *was* out of your league? You know that, don't you? Say it.'

'Take the car out of gear. Do it now.'

In my jacket my phone was ringing. I couldn't reach it. I was thinking what one of the crash investigation manuals had claimed: that the accepted advice for people in sinking cars was all wrong. It was insane to keep the doors closed until the water reached the outside sills and the pressure equalised. The best chance anyone had was to get out of the car as quickly as possible; the moment you hit the water was the moment to fight for escape. I slithered my hands down to the door handle, checking I knew where it was.

'You know that,' Lois repeated to Arran. 'Don't you?'

'Fuck you, Lois. Fuck you and your idiot daughter. Fuck you both for everything you are and everything you've ever been.'

She hitched in a breath and reached for the handbrake. I grabbed her hand and she turned and spat at me. It hit me in the face. I didn't react in anger. I wiped it away and stayed calm.

'It's just for your safety, Lois. Just let me keep a hold on this while we finish talking about Sophie May.'

Arran was swift. The moment she'd turned to look at me he'd darted his hand in through the open window for the keys. But Lois was quicker. She sank her teeth into his arm. He yelled and pulled back and she followed up by throwing her door outwards. He didn't have time to react – the door hit him in the forehead and he dropped instantly, his injured arm slithering away from the window.

'Lois! Lois!' I yelled gripping her hand hard. 'No! This is worse. This is just making it worse for you.'

She elbowed me hard, grappling to release the handbrake. I flung myself sideways and used both hands to batter at her. I was scrabbling uselessly to find any leverage point, but she'd locked into the handbrake like a vice and already the car was limping in little stutters down the concrete ramp.

'Arran!' I screamed. 'Arran?'

I couldn't see him. I kept my hands on hers but straightened my legs and pushed myself up in the seat till my head hit the roof. I craned my neck over to see where he was. He was about three feet into the water, lying face down, motionless, his shoulders hunched awkwardly up.

'Arran! *Arran!*' Someone was shouting from the far end of the lake, waving their hands. I could vaguely sense a car further up the road reversing furiously and the sirens were getting louder. But it still didn't occur to me to wonder how they knew so quickly – nor why my phone was ringing so insistently. Just as it didn't occur to me, or to Arran, to really think about that rocking of the car shortly before it went into the water.

Sometimes in my darkest moments I have to take a breath and make a true account of what happened. Had I heard the faint, baffled noises from the boot of the car? Had I truly not noticed the plastic toy horse in the footwell under my feet when I'd jumped in? Or had I?

Honestly? I have to say – yes, maybe. I had noticed these clues. I had heard the noises in the back, I'd seen the plastic toy. But I was so scared, I didn't process the information. And when I chose to release my hold on the handbrake, so I could throw myself free of the car which was sliding towards the lake – when I saw the water cold and yellow pouring up through the engine block – had I ignored what I didn't want to know? As I ran round the back of the car and dropped myself on Arran, tugging him sideways so his face was out of the water – so I could lift him up and hold him, ramming my hands into his back until he spluttered and coughed – was I registering what sacrifice I had just made?

Arran was my kryptonite. Always has been, always will be. Still is.

He doesn't remember what happened. Maybe that's fitting, because he was the one who watched over me after the coach accident, protected my dreams and hallucinations. All he remembers is us clinging to each other on the edge of the lake, water swirling up the slipway over us, our teeth chattering, watching the car go in. Lois pinned back against the driver's seat by the force of the incoming water. The loud squeal of metal creaking the back end of the Beetle tilted upwards, revealing its exhaust pipe and axles. In the back window water swilling in creamy curlicues, and the stark, panicked white and pink blur of Lois, climbing back over the seats, crunched like a huge shrimp against the window, regretting what she'd done – fighting the water.

Now that there's a baby on her way for me and for Arran I can't help lying awake and thinking about her. Minty. How long was she conscious for, tied and gagged in the boot? How long? How scared was she? How much did she hear, how much did she cry? Did she hear me screaming, and did she sense the moment I made the decision to help Arran?

My baby turns and kicks. Next to me Arran murmurs something in his sleep. I fold my hands over my belly and whisper to her in there.

Araminta is your full name. Your grandmother asked for it – Grandma Maryam.

A-Ra-Min-Ta.

Or if that's too hard to say, we'll make it easy. We'll call you Minty for short.

Acknowledgements

With thanks to Phoebe Morgan, Kate Norman, Linda McQueen, Veronique Baxter, Lewis Csizmazia and all at Hodder & Stoughton and David Higham Associates.